3-2022

DATE DUE

		PRINTED IN U.S.A.

Hayner PLD/Large Print
Overdues .10/day. Max fine cost of
item. Lost or damaged item: additional
$5 service charge.

TO WRITE A WRONG

THE BLEEKER STREET
INQUIRY AGENCY, BOOK 2

TO WRITE A WRONG

JEN TURANO

THORNDIKE PRESS
A part of Gale, a Cengage Company

LIBRARY OF CONGRESS CIP DATA ON FILE.
CATALOGUING IN PUBLICATION FOR THIS BOOK
IS AVAILABLE FROM THE LIBRARY OF CONGRESS.

ISBN-13: 978-1-4328-9464-1 (hardcover alk. paper)

Published in 2022 by arrangement with Bethany House Publishers, a division of Baker Publishing Group

Printed in Mexico
Print Number: 01   Print Year: 2022

For Raela Schoenherr,
my extraordinary editor who has been
with me since my very first book.
Thank you for always being the calm
in whatever writing storm I find myself
in. It has been a delight working with
you all these many years.
Love you!
Jen

CHAPTER ONE

March 1887
New York City

There was not a shadow of a doubt left in Miss Daphne Beekman's mind that her days as a successful novelist were numbered.

Taking a sip of tea that had long gone cold, she grimaced and set aside the cup before she flexed her fingers. Placing them over the keys of her Remington typewriter, affectionately named Almira after her favorite aunt, she closed her eyes and fervently hoped that something of worth would spring to mind to write.

A moment later, her fingers pounded against the keys, the clacking of every key hit drowning out the sound of the wind that was howling around the Holbrooke boardinghouse. Reaching the last available line on the page, she pulled the paper from the cylinder and took a moment to read over what she'd typed.

Crumpling up the paper a blink of an eye later, she tossed it over her shoulder, where it joined the hundred or so other crumpled pieces of paper littering the room. Heaving a sigh, she was suddenly distracted from what could only be described as a dismal mood by the sound of ruffling feathers. Glancing around, she found Pretty Girl, a temperamental parrot that had a propensity for nicking sparkly items, waddling through the discarded balls of paper as she made her way for the crumpled ball Daphne had just tossed aside.

"If you think you're going to find a treasure in there, you're sadly mistaken," Daphne said, which didn't deter Pretty Girl in the least as she grabbed the paper with her beak and began shaking it from side to side, her shaking increasing when nothing sparkly fell from what she'd evidently thought was precious booty. Pretty Girl dropped the paper and stepped her way toward another crumpled ball.

"There's nothing of worth hidden in any of those, especially no words of worth — not that you'd be interested in that," Daphne said. "Every word typed out on those pages is complete rubbish. Frankly, I'm beginning to wonder what possessed me to think becoming a published author was a marvelous idea."

Pretty Girl's response to that was to fly from the floor and land on top of a lampshade beside Daphne's desk. "Tasty treats, tasty treats," she cackled.

"This is no time for treats. I'm facing a crisis right now, and I don't believe you're being very sympathetic to my plight. In case you haven't been listening, my writing career is undoubtedly doomed."

"Doomed, doomed," Pretty Girl screeched.

"That's hardly helpful." Daphne slouched down in the chair. "I never thought writing would turn so challenging, but with the pressures of deadlines and expectations of my readers, I'm turning more neurotic by the second. That is not benefiting my nerves, which are questionable at the best of times. I'm beginning to think I should simply abandon this ridiculous profession before it kills me."

"Kills me, kills me, awwk, kills me," Pretty Girl parroted before she launched into flight and flew out of the attic room Daphne rented from Eunice Holbrooke.

"So much for using you as inspiration for the pirate scene I'm not having any success completing. We'll see if I ever volunteer to watch you again when Nicholas and Gabriella go out of town."

Forcing herself to abandon her slouching, Daphne turned back to the typewriter. "This is not as difficult as you're imagining it is," she said firmly. "You write all the time. There has to be a way to get Mad-Eye Willy off the plank without him losing his life in the process."

Positioning her hands over the keys again, she closed her eyes, but instead of any reasonable solution to the Mad-Eye Willy dilemma springing to mind, a piece of chocolate cake drifted through her thoughts, the very idea of cake leaving her stomach rumbling. Opening her eyes, she shoved back the chair, rose to her feet, then flung herself directly on top of the crunched papers, flinging a hand over her forehead in a most dramatic fashion. Unfortunately, it didn't make her feel better in the least, and definitely did nothing to curb the hankering she now had for cake.

"You do *not* need cake," she told herself. "You're only thinking about it because Pretty Girl mentioned treats. Besides, you've already visited the kitchen twice today for cake, and at this rate, you'll be large as a house before you get close to meeting your deadline."

A yawn from underneath the settee drew

her attention, where she discovered Winston, a one-eyed dog that was sporting an eyepatch over his missing eye, watching her with what seemed to be annoyance on his brown furry face.

"Am I disturbing your nap?"

Winston blinked his one eye.

"If you'll recall," she began, sitting up, "I told you I have the habit of speaking to myself whenever I'm trying to compose a first draft. You certainly didn't appear bothered by my disclosure when you trailed after me earlier, especially when Precious, your lady love, tried to engage you in yet another game of tug-of-war with that stuffed rabbit Elsy knit for her."

Winston yawned again.

Daphne fought the inclination to yawn as well. "If you'll also recall, I told you that you could enjoy time away from your high-maintenance poodle with me, but only if you'd try your hardest to adopt the air of a true pirate dog. I was hoping that would lend me a substantial amount of motivation for at least two chapters, if not three."

Winston crawled out from underneath the settee, moseyed his way over to Daphne, and licked her cheek, leaving a great deal of slobber behind. He then headed for one of the narrow windows that flanked Daphne's favorite reading chair, edging behind the curtain and leaving only his backside in view.

"A view of your behind is hardly going to motivate me."

Winston burrowed another inch underneath the hem of the curtain.

Realizing she wasn't going to find much in the way of inspiration from Winston, Daphne gathered some crumpled balls of paper into her lap and spent the next few minutes lobbing them in the direction of her rubbish bin, not one of them hitting the mark. Abandoning that less-than-productive distraction when she noticed she now had paper balls scattered everywhere, she rose to her feet and began tidying up, abandoning that effort when she reached the trunk positioned at the foot of her bed.

Stored within the vast confines of the trunk were numerous disguises she'd begun collecting to aid with her second job — that being an inquiry agent for the Bleecker Street Inquiry Agency. As luck would have it, one of those disguises was a pirate outfit, rescued from the Cherry Lane Theater by Miss Lulah Wallace, a fellow Bleecker Street agent who also worked at the theater. That theater had recently performed a lackluster version of the *Pirates of Penzance,* and the reviews were so bad that the theater had been forced to close the show weeks earlier than expected. The owner of the theater had then demanded that all the costumes for that performance be tossed out, the poor man not wanting to have continued reminders hanging about of how dismally the show had been received.

Daphne flipped open the lid and dug out a pirate costume, hoping it would aid in her quest to finish at least one chapter that night. Five minutes later, she stood in front of her mirror, turning side to side as she admired her improved appearance.

Tan trousers cut off below the knee were certainly a departure from the skirts she normally wore. And even though the trousers were incredibly baggy on her slim frame, she thought they lent her a rakish air. She rolled up the billowing sleeves of the beige blouse that was missing a few buttons, then settled a battered tricorn hat over her perfectly ordinary brown hair. Returning to the trunk, she rummaged through it, disappointed when she couldn't locate the cutlass that would go far to complete her ensemble.

Pushing herself out of the trunk, she settled her attention on Winston's backside. "I think I left the cutlass at the agency. What say we go for a nice stroll and fetch it?"

Winston inched farther underneath the curtain.

Daphne began tapping her toe against the wooden floor. "Honestly, Winston, I have no idea why you're being so uncooperative tonight. Dogs are supposed to enjoy taking walks. Besides, I told Gabriella that I would be diligent in making certain you got enough exercise while she's away on a most difficult case. We've been closed up in the attic for hours. That means we're going for a walk, and I expect you to be happy about that."

It took a good few minutes to convince Winston he wanted to go for a walk, but after he eventually abandoned the curtain, making a big production of stretching, yawning, and sending Daphne injured looks, he finally began ambling for the door.

"Do know that I'll be informing Nicholas when he returns about your less-than-accommodating attitude of late," Daphne said as she and Winston left the room, earning a wag of a tail from Winston at the mention of his owner, Nicholas Quinn.

Unable to help but smile because Winston did have a certain charm about him, even when he was being difficult, they walked down the four flights of stairs that led to

14

the main floor and headed for the parlor, where she'd left the bag she never ventured from the boardinghouse without. Before she reached the parlor, though, Precious, the neurotic poodle Gabriella Quinn had come to own after a client decided she didn't want the dog anymore, came prancing down the hallway. With her sights set firmly on Winston, she began to yip up a storm around the stuffed rabbit she was carrying in her mouth.

A sappy-looking grin immediately settled on Winston's furry face, probably because Precious was already nuzzling him with her topknot.

"You're a complicated dog, Winston," Daphne said as he frolicked away with Precious. Following after them, she stepped into the parlor, finding Eunice Holbrooke, the owner of the boardinghouse, as well as the founding member of the Bleecker Street Inquiry Agency, sitting in a chair by the fire. Eunice was, as usual, dressed in stark black widow's weeds, although she'd abandoned her veils, probably because it was past ten and there was little chance anyone would show up unexpectedly at the door.

"Working late tonight?" Daphne asked.

Eunice dropped a file onto the stack of client files on the small table beside her, then blinked as her gaze traveled over Daphne. "Indeed, but you're evidently working late as well. Should I assume, given your appearance, that you're having difficulty with a particular scene?"

Daphne fetched her bag from where she'd left it earlier, then plopped down in a chair. "I'm in desperate need of motivation and am hoping this look will put me in a pirate frame of mind."

"I thought you were hoping Winston and Pretty Girl would do that for you."

"Well, quite, but they were less than co-operative. Winston's been snoozing all day, and Pretty Girl apparently got bored and flew out of the attic."

"Pretty Girl's on the loose?"

Daphne winced. "I'm afraid so, which means we'll be missing more silverware come morning, but not to fret. I found Pretty Girl's stash, so I'll retrieve the silver later. That will spare Alma a frustrating morning of trying to serve breakfast without utensils."

"I'm sure Alma will appreciate that, but returning to your pirate situation, I'm curious whether dressing like a pirate is actually getting you into a pirate frame of mind. You're not acting like I'd expect a pirate to act, nor are you speaking pirate right now."

"That's because I haven't assumed a full pirate identity yet. I think I left the cutlass that completes this outfit at the agency. I was just heading out to retrieve it."

"Why would the cutlass be at the agency?"

"I was considering hanging it on the wall of my office, because it seems like something an inquiry agent might have on a wall, but then I got distracted with some of our cases." Daphne settled into the chair. "I've been hoping a potential case will provide me with the spark I need to figure out this book I'm writing. Unfortunately, we don't seem to have any murder cases pending."

"We're not really the type of agency to take on murder cases. In fact, it's my humble opinion that murder is best left to the police department or the Pinkertons," Eunice said. "Murders do tend to come with murderers, who, I'm sure you'll agree, add a degree of danger I'm not certain we have the experience to handle quite yet."

"We've handled numerous dangerous cases — one, if you'll recall, that actually involved the death of a notorious villain."

"True, but since we completed that case, we've concentrated our efforts on tracking down missing people, missing fortunes, and delving into the backgrounds of unscrupulous types. While those cases involve a

17

measure of danger, tracking a murderer is on a completely different level."

"Agreed, but a murder investigation might provide me with wonderful fodder for my story." Daphne bit her lip. "Frankly, though, I'm not certain a murder case *would* help me because I'm beginning to conclude that I have nothing of worth left to write. My latest draft is filled with nonsense, which means my writing profession is destined for failure."

"You said that with the last book you wrote, the one your publisher is convinced is your best work to date."

"I might have bemoaned my fate as an author a time or two while writing that last book, but this time I *mean* it. I'm obviously an abysmal writer and all of my previous successes were merely flukes."

"You've become one of the most sought-after mystery writers in the country. I doubt you achieved that status because of numerous flukes."

"Perhaps not, but it's a distinct possibility that I've used up all of my writing talent," Daphne said. "I'm worried readers of Montague Moreland novels are going to be disappointed with this mess of a manuscript I'm attempting to plod through. That disappointment will certainly see my publisher parting ways with me and my readers abandoning me in droves."

"You know that's not going to happen, and even if it did, you could always reinvent yourself and write under your real name instead of your nom de plume once you pull yourself out of what is merely a writing slump."

"Readers don't want to read mysteries written by women, at least according to my publisher, hence the nom de plume *and* the reason I promised my editor I'd never let my true identity out."

"Every resident at the boardinghouse knows you're Montague Moreland."

"It would have been difficult to keep that from the ladies since I'm often typing away in my attic room at all hours, as well as wandering around the house, talking to the characters in my head. However, everyone here, including yourself, has sworn never to divulge my secret. I'm of the firm belief everyone is good for her word."

"We do have a most stellar group of ladies living here. But if your identity did leak — and not from us, of course — you could always write a different genre under your real name."

"But I adore writing mysteries."

"Then it's fortunate you're *not* an abysmal

writer and are certain to have a long and prolific career ahead of you."

"Did you miss the part where I said my current manuscript is a disaster?"

Eunice's lips twitched. "That would have been difficult to miss, given how dramatically you've stated the deplorable condition of your latest draft. Nevertheless, you must know that state is only temporary. It'll be a riveting read once you write the end and polish it up. It could be that you merely need to rethink the pirate scene you're determined to include."

"It's not merely a single scene. Mad-Eye Willy is the hero of the story and he is in every chapter. One particularly tricky scene has been giving me fits for the past two weeks. I simply cannot figure out how to get my hero pirate off the plank he's been forced to walk without sending him into the water. He'd certainly face a horrible demise if he toppled off the plank, given that I have an entire school of sharks swimming underneath him."

Eunice's brows drew together. "Not that I'm an expert on this, but a pirate seems like an unlikely hero."

"True, but as I was contemplating what type of man would make the perfect hero for my next book, I decided that my female readers might appreciate a pirate in that role. Many women long to meet men of adventure, as well as secretly long to be associated with dangerous men."

Eunice gave her nose a scratch. "Perhaps your difficulty with this book centers around the name you've chosen for your hero. Forgive me for pointing this out, but the name Mad-Eye Willy is a little off-putting. When I think of someone named Mad-Eye, I picture a dirty scoundrel who smells."

"My hero does *not* smell."

"And thank goodness for that." Eunice tilted her head. "I feel I also must point out that, at least in my case, when I think of the name Willy, my mind conjures up an image of a gentle, somewhat nervous man who is slight of build. The Willy I always associate with the name is not a man who'd ever be standing on a plank with sharks swimming underneath him."

The image of the man Eunice was describing immediately popped into Daphne's mind — a man named Willy who was not a pirate but a rail-thin, pipe-carrying, cardigan-wearing man, who was being attended to by someone because he was in frail health. She narrowed her eyes at Eunice. "You're going to have to have more care with any additional observations you

21

may want to toss my way."

"Why?"

"Because now, besides having to figure out how to get my pirate off the plank, I'm going to have to choose a different name for him because you've ruined Willy for me forever."

"Surely not?"

"I'm afraid so."

Eunice winced. "I beg your pardon for that, Daphne. I had no idea my observation would turn so concerning, but maybe you can change the pirate's name to Gentleman Jack. I've often seen that name used for pirates, and that would allow you to establish to your readers that even though he's a pirate, he's still a gentleman."

"And while that's an excellent suggestion, I have a brother named Jack. I've been remarkably unsuccessful using names of people I know in any of my books."

"You have a brother?"

"I have three of them. Jack's the oldest, followed by Arthur, then Frank."

"You've never mentioned any brothers. Truth be told, I thought you were alone in the world."

"I prefer to keep my life in New York and my family separate. My mother is not really supportive of my chosen occupation, nor is

22

she — or my father, for that matter — thrilled that I've gone off on my own and taken up residency here in the city. My brothers were skeptical at best when I decided to leave the family fold, and they still try to convince me to return to Boston any chance they get. As for my sister, Lydia, she's never been happy about anything I've done, but moving here has left her believing she's related to a woman who's taken leave of her senses."

"You have a sister too?"

Daphne smiled. "She's the baby of the family and is convinced my decision to move to New York has left a stain on the family name, which, in turn, has ruined her chances of securing an advantageous marriage."

"How could your decision do that?"

"Lydia's afraid that the most sought-after gentlemen won't want to chance courting her in case my oddness is something genetic."

"You're not odd."

"So says the woman who scares people by simply stepping into a room."

Eunice smoothed a hand down one of her black sleeves. "I do seem to frighten people whenever I go out and about, but returning to your family — here I've been of the belief that your greatest secret is your Montague Moreland books, but I might be wrong about that."

"My family isn't a secret. I merely don't discuss them often." Daphne got to her feet and slipped the strap of her bag over her shoulder. "But my family aside, I'm off to fetch that cutlass because the night isn't getting any younger and I have a chapter I need to finish."

"Would you care for me to come with you? I have five files of potential new clients to get through, but it's late."

"Thank you, but no. The agency is only a few houses away. Given the sound of the rain pounding on the window, it's clearly turning nasty outside. No sense in both of us getting soaked." She nodded to Winston. "Winston will do well as my guardian."

"He's a complete and utter coward more often than not."

"Winston's proven he can rise to an occasion if something concerning is transpiring." Daphne gave a snap of her fingers. "Come on, boy. Time for that walk."

It took more than a few minutes to convince Winston once again that he longed to go for a walk, especially after Precious, at the mere mention of a walk, plopped herself down beside Eunice and refused to budge.

By the time Daphne got Winston out of the room, shoved her feet into boots, and slipped into a traveling cloak, she was rethinking her decision to fetch the cutlass.

That rethinking was only reinforced when she stepped outside and rain mixed with sleet hit her squarely in the face. Tipping her tricorn hat lower, she hurried forward, thankful that the Bleecker Street Inquiry Agency was only five doors down, but with the wind howling around her, it seemed to be miles away.

Unlocking the front door of the agency, Daphne slipped into the hallway with Winston by her side, who immediately slouched toward the library, clearly in search of someplace drier.

Daphne turned on a small gas lamp in the receiving hallway before she shrugged out of her cloak, hung it up, then made her way to her personal office. Three minutes later, armed with the cutlass she'd found underneath her desk, she hurried down the hallway, shivering as she stepped into the library. Deciding it would be prudent to warm up before venturing into the storm again, she threw a few logs into the grate, smiling when Winston, who was stretched out in front of the fireplace, rolled onto his back and stuck his feet straight into the air as warmth spread throughout the room.

Sitting down on a divan close to the fire, Daphne settled back against the cushions, her gaze running over the numerous bookshelves filled with books on police procedures, city atlases, law books, and even a handful of the latest mysteries of the day.

Even though the Bleecker Street Inquiry Agency had only come into existence the previous fall after a resident at the Holbrooke boardinghouse, Miss Jennette Moore, now Mrs. Duncan Linwood, had been arrested and unjustly charged with theft, it had turned into a viable endeavor.

It had quickly become evident that many women in New York City were desperate for someone to give their problems the attention they deserved. These women had not found success using the tried-and-true avenues for justice, such as the police department or the Pinkerton Agency. Those agencies were run by men, and it was common knowledge that men didn't take women or their problems seriously.

The Bleecker Street Inquiry Agency believed every woman deserved to be heard, but more importantly, they *believed* them. That was why what had started out as the only way to clear Jennette's name had now turned into a lucrative business.

Cases were varied — from cheating husbands, to thefts, to missing people — and every resident at the boardinghouse was assigned to cases based on their different and varied skills.

Daphne's main job at the agency was to sift through their clients' disclosures, using the imagination that had allowed her to become one of the country's most popular mystery authors in order to create lists of possible suspects and motives. She enjoyed her role in the agency, especially because it generally kept her away from the action. The few times she'd been pressed into service had not exactly been pleasant experiences. Truthfully, they'd been downright horrifying, especially the night when she'd happened upon Mr. Nicholas Quinn for the first time and he'd pointed a pistol at her, which had resulted in her fainting dead away while in the middle of Jennette's case.

Granted, Nicolas hadn't been intending to shoot her, but she'd not known that at the time. All she'd known was that he was a threat, and she'd proven time and again that she wasn't a lady who dealt with threats in a calm and deliberate fashion, not with how she normally ended up unconscious on the floor every time she felt threatened.

"Hello? Anyone here?"

Daphne snapped out of her thoughts but found herself frozen on the spot because the voice that had just called out was certainly male and seemed to have come from within the agency, suggesting she might have forgotten to lock the door behind her — a mistake a seasoned inquiry agent would never have made.

"Go see who it is," she whispered to Winston.

It swiftly became evident that Winston was not going to embrace the attitude of a true pirate dog, or fierce guardian, for that matter, because he immediately crawled underneath the fainting couch.

That unfortunate state of affairs meant that she, Miss Daphne Beekman, a lady prone to swooning whenever her nerves got the better of her, was now on her own to deal with a mysterious gentleman who, hopefully, was not a criminal in search of his next victim.

CHAPTER TWO

Slipping out of her boots, Daphne crept across the library on bare feet and snagged up the cutlass, even though it was a flimsy excuse for a weapon because it was made out of pressed paperboard. She sent Winston a scowl, which he didn't see because he was now completely out of sight underneath the fainting couch. She then inched for the library door, lingering right inside it as she contemplated her options.

The most logical option would be to pretend she wasn't there and hope that whoever was in the agency would simply go away, leaving her in peace — or as much peace as she could possibly find after suffering such a dreadful fright.

The most *illogical* option would be to confront the man.

"Hello? I know there's someone here. I can see a trail of wet footprints moving down the hallway."

It was hardly a mark of a good inquiry agent that she'd not even considered the tracks her boots might have made. She cleared her throat.

"We're not open for business," she called.

"There's a light on and the door was unlocked."

"But if you'll look at the sign on the door, it states that our hours are from eight until five."

"There's no light on outside the agency, so I couldn't have seen the hours of operation posted."

Exasperation was immediate. "Then you'll have to trust my word on this and return on Monday when the agency opens again. We're closed on the weekends. If you're unaware, it's well past ten on a Friday night, which begs the question of why you would expect to find someone here in the first place."

"I assumed an inquiry agency was run like the police department, which is always open to investigate crimes."

"We're not the police department. We're also not currently open, nor will we be open again until Monday."

"It's imperative that I speak with someone tonight."

Edging into the hallway because, clearly,

the man was possessed of a persistent nature, and an annoying one at that, Daphne kept a firm grip on the cutlass as she tried to quiet nerves that were beginning to distract her. She made it all of two feet before she caught sight of the man, and that sight had her heart missing a beat because he was the largest man she'd ever seen.

She edged behind a coatrack, peering around it to get a better look at him. Well over six feet tall and with shoulders that suggested the man might earn a living as a boxer, he was her worst nightmare come to life. Large gentlemen were at the top of her long list of things that left her with a distinct urge to swoon — and not in a romantic, be-still-my-heart kind of way.

She swallowed past the lump that had formed in her throat. "As I mentioned, numerous times now, the agency is closed. Someone will be happy to speak with you on Monday morning."

"But I've made the effort to travel here tonight, and my patience is beginning to run thin over the notion you're unwilling to make an exception and speak with me merely because I didn't arrive during normal business hours."

"Hasn't anyone ever told you that impatience is *not* a virtue?"

Oddly enough, her question was met with silence until there was a rustling sound, one that almost suggested the man had withdrawn a notepad and was riffling through the pages.

Curiosity had her feet moving down the hallway. She stopped when she was five feet away from the man and realized he *had* pulled out a notepad and was now writing something down in it.

Ignoring that the palms of her hands had turned clammy, which was making it difficult to keep a firm hold on the cutlass, she lifted her chin. "What *are* you doing?"

The man continued writing before he finally lifted his head, revealing a face that had a marvelous bone structure, complete with a chiseled jaw and sharp cheekbones, highlighted by the hint of stubble. The stubble lent him a far too dangerous air, which had her brandishing the cutlass in his direction in what she hoped he'd take as a threatening fashion.

"I was writing that bit down about impatience not being a virtue. I've often heard the phrase patience *is* a virtue, but not the one you just mentioned."

"Why would you need to write that down?"

"I write down everything I find interesting because I never know when it may come in handy. But speaking of interesting . . ." His gaze traveled over her. "Why are you dressed like a pirate? And surely you don't believe that prop you're brandishing would do much harm if I were about to attack you, do you?"

She kept the cutlass aimed at him, even though her arm was beginning to shake because the cutlass was much heavier than she'd anticipated. "I'm sure my cutlass could at least slow you down if you *were* to attack, which I'm fervently praying you're not about to do."

"I'm certainly not here to attack you. I'm here to procure the services of the Bleecker Street Inquiry Agency. I've been told your agency, even though I understand you mostly cater to the feminine set, has seen great success with a variety of cases. I'm hoping you'll be able to enjoy success with the case I'm about to present to you, if you actually take up cases on behalf of gentlemen."

"Of course we take cases on behalf of gentlemen, although . . ." She wrinkled her nose. "Now that I think about it, we've not done that as of yet."

"Then I'm sure you'll want to take on my

case, because that will allow you to tell future male clients that you've had gentlemen clients in the past. With that said, but before I get into the particulars of my case, you've yet to explain why you're dressed like a pirate."

Daphne readjusted her tricorn hat. "I needed to get into a pirate frame of mind, which has nothing to do with this disturbing situation at hand."

"What disturbing situation? I already promised I wouldn't attack you."

"No, the troubling matter of you writing my words into that notepad. Why did you do that?"

"I'm a writer, which is why I'm curious about your attire because writers tend to be curious creatures. May I assume you needed to get into a pirate frame of mind because you're an actress?"

"Why would an actress be lingering about in an inquiry agency?"

"I'm sure I have no idea, but it was the only reasonable explanation I could come up with. Now that I consider the matter more thoroughly, are you, perhaps, working undercover?"

"No, but my appearance is not a matter for your concern. What *is* a matter of concern is what you intend to do with my statement regarding impatience not being a virtue."

"It's a witty line. I imagine I'll find a good use for it in one of my books someday."

His explanation went far to banish the fear that had pervaded her the moment she'd realized she wasn't alone in the agency. "You can't steal my words and use them as your own."

"There's no law saying I can't. As a writer, I often take liberties with conversations I've overheard and use them in my work."

"But what if I intend to use that line in something I may write someday?"

Skepticism immediately clouded eyes that Daphne only then noticed were a piercing shade of blue. "*You're* a writer?"

She couldn't claim to be surprised about the skepticism. Ever since she'd decided to become a writer when she was fifteen years old, skepticism had dogged her every step.

Her mother had not believed she'd find success with her writing and instead encouraged her to settle down with a nice local gentleman, or more specifically, Mr. Thomas Sibley, of Boston.

She didn't care for Thomas Sibley, which was why she'd decided five years ago, when she reached the ancient age of twenty, and after Thomas began pressuring her most assiduously to marry him, to leave her parents' comfortable house in Boston and move to New York to pursue her dream of becoming a published author.

Against the wishes of her mother and using money her aunt Almira gave her, thus the reason behind her typewriter's name, she'd procured her attic room at the Holbrooke boardinghouse. She'd then set about making appointments to share her three finished manuscripts with numerous publishing houses, appointments that had terrified her half to death.

That terror had only increased when she'd met with the publishers. To say they were dismissive of her work was an understatement. From the moment she explained she was submitting mysteries, not romances or fiction for ladies, they'd dismissed her out of hand, not bothering to read so much as a single page of her work.

It had been quite the eye-opening experience. However, because she certainly didn't want to suffer through hearing "I told you so" or through Thomas's determination to marry her, she'd taken the nom de plume of Montague Moreland from a character she'd written into a story in her youth, retitled her manuscripts, then sent them by post to publishing houses both in and outside of New York.

To her delight, she was offered contracts from numerous houses and, interestingly enough, the contract she decided to accept was not from a New York publishing house but a Boston one — Hammerstone, Lander & Company. The distance between New York and her previous hometown lent her a plausible excuse for why she couldn't meet with the publisher in person, especially after she developed some odd quirks for Montague to possess.

She'd explained to her new publishing house that she, or rather, Montague Moreland, preferred to avoid contact with people because he suffered from severe social anxiety, preferring to do all corresponding by post, and besides that, traveling on trains, which was the fastest way to get from New York City to Boston, resulted with him breaking out in rashes.

Those excuses worked like a charm until her first book, *Murder, Mayhem, and Misery,* released. It garnered attention right from the start, as well as rave reviews, which was why Mr. James Durnham, her editor at Hammerstone, Lander & Company, insisted on traveling to New York to meet her in person.

She'd been unable to come up with a

legitimate reason to refuse his request, and poor Mr. Durnham had been shocked to discover that Montague Moreland was not a man at all. In fact, he'd been rendered speechless a mere second after she disclosed her true identity. His speechless state had not lasted long, though, but after a lot of stammering and accusing her of questionable behavior, he'd finally settled down, likely because her book was selling off the shelves.

He decided there was nothing to be done but have Daphne continue on as Montague Moreland, although he insisted she sign a nondisclosure agreement stating she would keep her true identity a secret. And while that agreement allowed her the luxury of spending her time writing instead of promoting her work, it made it impossible for her to disclose the success she'd achieved. That meant any time she mentioned her fondness for writing, she was met with skepticism about her ability to write anything of worth.

"May I take your prolonged silence as an indication you're not comfortable speaking about your writing?"

Daphne snapped out of her thoughts. "It's not that I'm uncomfortable about my writing or unwilling to discuss it, but most people don't care to listen to me talk about my fondness for the written word. Besides, because you winced after I mentioned my writing, I got the distinct impression you're hesitant to actually hear whether or not I consider myself a writer."

The man smiled, revealing a dimple right beside the left corner of his mouth. "Forgive me if I winced, which was not well done of me, but you see, because I *am* a writer, and a published one at that, I frequently encounter aspiring writers who are eager to share samples of their writing with me. But more often than not, they seem to lack an above average proficiency with the English language. I'm afraid those writers then take issue with me when I suggest they spend additional time perfecting their craft." His smile turned rueful. "Truth be told, I've begun making a concerted effort to avoid placing myself in situations that have a tendency to turn somewhat . . . contentious."

Any lingering nervousness she'd been holding disappeared in a flash. "Ah, I'm beginning to understand the wince. You were obviously worried that if I admitted I'm a writer, that would then be followed by a request for you to peruse my work."

"That might have been at the back of my mind."

"I imagine it was, but no need to fret. I don't make a habit of sharing my work with random strangers who show up at the Bleecker Street Inquiry Agency."

The man's smile dimmed. "I've just realized we *are* complete strangers because we've yet to be introduced." He inclined his head. "Allow me to rectify that at once. I'm Mr. Herman Henderson."

For the briefest of seconds, Daphne felt a distinct urge to rush back to the library and fetch the smelling salts she always kept in her bag.

Not only was Herman Henderson one of her favorite mystery writers, but, more importantly, he was her biggest competitor.

He was known for penning mysteries set in exotic locations and filled with unusual plot twists and dire situations. He was also known as a recluse, a man who rarely left the confines of his mansion located on Irving Place in Gramercy Park, except to travel around the world in pursuit of adventures — or at least that's what the gossips in the city said.

Why he'd left Irving Place to travel to Bleecker Street, and on a night that was dismal and growing more miserable by the second, sent Daphne's imagination humming into high gear.

Realizing that she'd gone mute again, and that Mr. Herman Henderson was obviously waiting for her to tell him her name, Daphne dipped into a curtsy, which was an unusual thing for her to do considering she was wearing trousers. "It's a pleasure to make your acquaintance, Mr. Henderson. I'm Miss Daphne Beekman, an agent of the Bleecker Street Inquiry Agency, as well as a writer in my, ah, spare time. I'm also a devoted reader of your books."

She straightened and took a step closer to him. "You said you wanted to hire us to take on a case, but is there a chance that you're really visiting the agency at such a peculiar hour because you've found yourself stuck in a chapter and are in need of fresh inspiration, perhaps hoping to find that with one of our past cases?"

"It's a pleasure to meet you as well, Miss Beekman," Herman began, presenting her with a bow. "And no, I'm not here for inspiration, although that's an intriguing idea and one I'll contemplate further when I'm at my leisure. The reason I'm here is because I'm interested in hiring the Bleecker Street Inquiry Agency to investigate an unpleasant matter for me."

"That's too bad," Daphne began, earning a raised brow from Herman in the process. "I could have assisted you if you're in need of fodder for future story lines, but I'm afraid, as I mentioned already, the agency is not open for business. And before you point out that I'm here, let me tell you that I'm not the one who initially decides what cases we take on, which means speaking with me will be a certain waste of your time."

"But it's of the utmost importance I speak with someone tonight. I can't wait until Monday when the agency reopens."

"Why not?"

"I might be dead by then because someone is trying to murder me."

Daphne's eyes widened. "Murder you?"

"Indeed."

Her pulse kicked up a notch.

Here she'd just been complaining to Eunice about not having access to a murder investigation, and lo and behold, an attempted murder case seemed to have landed in her lap.

She cleared her throat and tried to assume a serious air instead of allowing herself to grin in pure delight. "How do you know someone wants to murder you?"

"Because someone tried to run me over when I was heading out to attend a literary

42

event held at Mr. Jay Storrow's residence on Madison Avenue, and —"

"You're acquainted with Mr. Jay Storrow?" Daphne interrupted, her pulse kicking up another notch because Mr. Storrow wrote glorious gothic novels that Daphne devoured, even if they did leave her cowering under her covers as she read them long into the night.

Herman raked a hand through dark brown hair that had been stylishly arranged — until he'd raked his hand through it, that was. "Jay and I are fellow mystery writers, so yes, I'm acquainted with him. But if we could return to the business of someone wanting to *murder* me?"

Daphne struggled to rein in thoughts that were scattering every which way. "Yes, quite right, forgive me. I fear my love of the written word is distracting me from your situation. But, speaking of the written word, and before I forget, I really enjoyed *Murder at Middleton Manor* and felt it was your best novel to date."

"You've read one of my novels?"

"As I mentioned, I'm a devoted reader of your work, which means I've read *all* your novels," she said. "I would love to hear how you come up with some of your plots, but since you're clearly not here to discuss your books, allow me to return to the someone-seems-to-want-to-murder-you business."

Herman's eyes twinkled. "Is it odd that I suddenly find myself not as desperate to discuss that particular nastiness and would rather discuss in more detail what you enjoy most about my books?"

She certainly couldn't blame him for wanting to continue with talk of how she enjoyed his books. She adored when anyone broached the topic of Montague Moreland books within earshot of her, even though she could hardly enjoy an honest conversation with readers of her work, given that only a select few knew her true identity.

"Perhaps we'll have time to further discuss your books after I take down your statement," she settled on saying.

"You're going to make an exception and listen to the details of my case even though the agency isn't currently open and you don't make decisions on which cases to take?"

"I fear the lure of an honest-to-goodness murder investigation is too tempting to ignore."

"I'm not dead yet."

"An excellent point, and if our agency takes on your case, hopefully you'll avoid that state altogether. If you'll follow me, we should repair to the library." Daphne turned and began padding down the hallway on bare feet that were becoming extremely chilled, not that she was going to mention that fact to Herman, since it was hardly appropriate to be missing her stockings when she was in the presence of a gentleman, or a potential client.

Stepping into the library, she hurried across the room, set aside the cutlass, then picked up her bag and sat on the fainting couch Winston was still underneath as Herman settled into a chair.

Opening her bag, she pulled out a knobby pair of brightly colored socks that Miss Elsy Evans, fellow agent and resident of Holbrooke boardinghouse, had made for her, and pulled them over feet that were now practically frozen. After giving her toes a wiggle, she retrieved her notepad and turned her attention to Herman. "Now then, you said someone tried to run you over. Have you considered that it was an accident caused by a distracted driver?"

"I did consider that, but after the second attempt, I began questioning the matter, and then, after the third and fourth attempts, I realized that I was experiencing something of much greater concern than distracted drivers."

"You've been almost run down four times?"

"I have, and then there's the troubling notion that I believe someone was sneaking around my house on Irving Place last night."

"Why do you believe that?"

"I heard noises coming from one of the secret passageways located behind my bedchamber wall."

Air suddenly became difficult to come by. "You have secret passageways in your house?"

"I do, as well as in my house on the Hudson."

"Those must have been some interesting meetings with your architect when you were having your houses built."

"I hope you won't be disappointed to learn that I had nothing to do with the creation of the secret passageways," Herman began. "My father, God rest his soul, is the one responsible for that. He always had a taste for the unusual and thought secret passageways lent our homes a mysterious air."

"I don't think he was wrong about that," Daphne said, refusing the desire to question Herman further about passageways that could definitely be used in one of her stories. She tapped her pencil against her notepad. "You said you heard noises coming from a passageway. What did you discover when you went to investigate?"

"Why would you assume I went off to investigate?"

"Because you write riveting murder mysteries, rife with danger on every other page. I would think, if nothing else, your curiosity would have gotten the better of you and prompted you to track down the source of the noise."

Herman's brows drew together. "I'm a fiction writer, Miss Beekman. And even though I write murder mysteries, those murders, as well as the heroes who vanquish the villains in the end, are merely a figment of my imagination. I'm far too responsible to go traipsing off to investigate an unknown noise because that could have gotten me murdered in my own house, or worse, seen the members of my staff put in harm's way."

Daphne blinked. "You merely ignored the situation?"

"Of course not. I did what any responsible homeowner would do. I roused the entire staff. That caused a huge ruckus, which apparently sent whoever was in the passageway fleeing from the house since I didn't hear so much as a creak through my bedchamber walls when I finally decided it might be safe to return inside."

It took a great deal of effort to refuse a sigh because, clearly, one of her favorite authors, whom she'd assumed patterned his dangerous heroes after himself, was not remotely close to the true-life hero she'd thought for certain he'd be.

CHAPTER THREE

When Miss Daphne Beekman sent him a look filled with what could only be described as deepest disappointment, Herman felt the oddest inclination to embellish the story of how he'd handled the mysterious noise the night before.

He would definitely come across more favorably if he mentioned that he'd insisted on reentering the house first to take a look around to make certain there were no villains lurking about before he allowed the members of his staff to return to their respective rooms.

Realizing that his thoughts were traveling in a very unlikely direction, because he'd never had the urge to embellish a story in order to make himself appear more favorable, Herman struggled to rein in his peculiar thoughts as he settled his attention on the woman dressed as a pirate and wearing a pair of spectacles with the thickest lenses he'd ever seen.

The second he caught her eye, though, he felt another unusual urge to tell the woman that although he did lead what many would consider a less-than-adventurous life, he wasn't a boring sort and was more than receptive to stepping out of the safe haven of the world he lived in if the right adventure presented itself. That particular urge left him feeling more than a little bewildered.

He'd never, or at least not since his parents had perished at sea when he'd been ten years old, felt a need to pursue an adventure-filled life. The loss of his parents, as well as the loss of his grandfather, who'd been with his parents at the time of the disaster, had convinced him that a life of adventure and danger was not the life for him.

"Perhaps it would be best for us to start with the carriage that tried to run you over," Daphne said briskly, interrupting his musings as she flipped open a notepad that looked remarkably similar to the one he always carried with him. She withdrew a stub of a pencil from her bag. "What can you tell me about that carriage?"

Herman shook his head, trying to banish thoughts that were doing their very best to distract him. "Ah, well, I believe it was black."

Daphne began rubbing her temple. "I'm going to need more than that because carriages are generally black. Were there any distinguishing markings on it, or better yet, do you believe the same carriage tried to run you down all four times?"

"I didn't stick around to notice if it was the same carriage or not. My most pressing priority was trying to escape being run over by rapidly moving carriage wheels. It would have been somewhat difficult to outrun a carriage and commit to memory any details about that carriage at the same time."

She stopped rubbing her temple. "How were you able to outrun a rapidly moving carriage?"

"I make it a habit to enjoy vigorous physical exertion every day, which allows me to sustain many exercises, such as running, for long periods of times."

Curiosity swirled in her green eyes. "What type of physical exertions besides running do you participate in?"

"Fencing, rowing, riding, swimming, boxing, hiking, and target practice, to name a few."

She frowned. "Fencing, as well as boxing, are considered dangerous activities and are activities that normally ensure that a person is possessed of strength, which could have come in handy if you'd investigated the incident last night and encountered the culprit lurking in the secret passageways."

"Unless that culprit had been in possession of a weapon. Bullets win against fists every time." He rubbed a hand over his face. "But in the spirit of full disclosure, I should tell you that I'm not actually a man who enjoys seeking out danger. In fact, because fencing and boxing are considered quite dangerous, I've taken steps to ascertain that specific safety measures are always in place whenever I participate in those activities. I use protective tips on my fencing weapons, and I wear special padding, along with protective headgear, whenever I box."

A clear dollop of disappointment flickered once again through Daphne's eyes, until she wrinkled her nose. "I doubt padding can spare you bruises while boxing if you're up against an opponent with a good arm."

"I always spar with my cousin, Mr. Sheldon Clarendon. Sheldon, while fast on his feet, is smaller than I am, which means the blows he lands barely leave a mark on me."

"And does Sheldon enjoy sparring with you, given the difference in your sizes?"

"We've never discussed the matter, but I assume he enjoys getting into the ring with me or he would have discontinued our weekly bouts years ago."

"Hmm . . ." was all Daphne said to that as she scribbled something down in her notepad. "Returning to the carriage situation, are you certain you don't remember anything else about the carriages, because noting they were black isn't exactly helpful."

"I'm afraid that's all I recall about them."

Daphne abandoned her notepad. "I don't believe you're putting enough effort into what you remember. In your book *The Curious Case of Mr. Stanley,* Detective Morris gave a detailed description of the scene where he was attacked by Mr. Stanley in a dark alley."

"You've read *The Curious Case of Mr. Stanley?*"

She waved that aside. "I already told you I've read all your books. But because your description of Detective Morris's attack was so vivid, I imagine you're a gentleman in possession of at least a semblance of observational skills."

"I'm sure some would consider me observant, but what you're apparently not grasping is the idea that I write *fiction.* I write that fiction in the comfort and safety of my *home*. There was nothing comfortable or safe about finding myself the target of some lunatic bent on running me down. That means any observational abilities I may possess weren't in play because I thought I was soon to meet a grisly end."

She gave another wave of her hand. "The best writers draw from real-life observations all the time to make their stories believable. And because you *are* one of the best writers of the day — and no need to turn all modest about that because there's no disputing your abilities — I believe you observed more than you realize when you were almost run over. We just need to pull that information out of you." She leaned forward. "What can you tell me about the driver of this carriage?"

The odd thought flashed to mind that being grilled by a slip of a woman dressed as a pirate was a very unusual experience, and frankly, not one he was enjoying, even with her throwing unexpected compliments his way.

"I always find that closing my eyes helps me recall details," she said, sending him a pointed look.

His first impulse was to ignore the look, until he remembered *he'd* sought her out, not the other way around, and *she'd* agreed to listen to his story even though the Bleecker Street Inquiry Agency was technically closed.

Sitting back in the chair, he closed his eyes and tried to recall anything Daphne might find worthy of writing in her notepad.

"Try to picture the scene unfolding in your mind," he heard her say. "What street were you on, how crowded was that street, and what was the driver wearing?"

To his surprise, a mere thirty seconds later, an image of the driver flashed to mind, which had him opening his eyes. "He was dressed in black and wore a black top hat, and he was concealing the lower half of his face with a kerchief. As for the streets, I was on Madison Avenue, heading to Jay Storrow's literary salon, when the first attempt occurred. Next was on Fifth Avenue after I left Hearn's Department Store. After that was Broadway, where I'd gone to see an opera at the Metropolitan Opera House. The carriage incident took place as I was crossing the street after the performance. The most recent incident happened on Forsyth Street this afternoon, which is why I'm here so late at night. I've decided I need professional assistance before someone succeeds in murdering me."

Daphne's gaze sharpened on him. "What were you doing on Forsyth Street, or better yet, what were you doing in the Lower East Side?"

"Research."

"But you've been giving me the distinct impression you're not a gentleman who seeks out danger."

"Riding through the Lower East Side in my carriage isn't what I'd consider a dangerous activity."

"It is when you depart from your carriage in one of the seediest parts of the city, something you obviously did at some point since someone tried to run you down."

Herman frowned. "A fair point, but I was armed and it was the middle of the afternoon, so it wasn't as if I was courting danger by stepping out of my carriage — not until that carriage tried to run me over, that is." He nodded to her notepad. "It might be best not to write down where I was this afternoon, though, since my grandmother would find that information troubling."

"I hardly believe I'll ever be in the position to share my notes with your grandmother."

"Which is probably true, but if the Bleecker Street Inquiry Agency does take on my case, I imagine someone from the agency will want to converse with my grandmother and could, unintentionally of course, mention something to her about my trip to the Lower East Side. My grandmother, Mrs. William Henderson, or Mildred, as she's known to her friends, suffers from a nervous condition. That condition requires her to keep smelling salts at hand, which is why I strive to withhold anything that's not imperative for her to know so that she doesn't suffer an unnecessary fit of the vapors."

"As a woman who suffers from nerves as well, I've found that my nervous condition only intensifies when people purposefully withhold information from me."

"I doubt you suffer nerves to the extent my grandmother does. As I just mentioned, she's never without her smelling salts, which she uses often."

Daphne reached for her bag, fished through it, then withdrew what was clearly a vial of smelling salts. "She sounds like a woman after my own heart."

Herman blinked. "But you're an inquiry agent. I would think every woman who works at your agency needs nerves of steel to successfully fulfill the requirements of the job."

"And the women who work in the field, most notably Gabriella Quinn, *do* have nerves of steel. I, on the other hand, have a limited role out in the field and am only required in the most desperate of circumstances."

"What constitutes a desperate circumstance?"

"I was once pressed into service because I was the only one who fit into a Cleopatra costume."

Herman's brows drew together, but Daphne waved him off before he could ask another question.

"That incident took place before we were officially an agency. I'm pleased to report that even though I swooned numerous times while dressed as Cleopatra, I'm becoming less swoony these days. Granted, when I encountered the Knickerbocker Bandit, I did faint, but in my defense, one of the Knickerbocker Bandit's men charged at me with a knife, and who wouldn't faint when facing certain death?"

Herman considered her for a long moment before he rose to his feet. "Forgive me, Miss Beekman, but I'm afraid the Bleecker Street Inquiry Agency may not have the, er, qualifications needed to do justice to an attempted murder investigation. I'll now beg your pardon for taking up your time and take my leave because it may be for the best if I were to seek out the services of the Pinkerton Agency."

Daphne's nose wrinkled. "I would have thought, given the seriousness of your case, you'd already sought out the Pinkerton Agency. Frankly, I believed you were here because they declined to take on your case, given the sketchy details you're able to recall."

"Would the Pinkertons really turn down my case because of sketchy details?"

"I have no idea. I'm not a Pinkerton, although we do have a Pinkerton by the name of Agent Cooper Clifton who works with us. He's been given permission to instruct us on basic investigative techniques, and he also gives us thrice weekly physical exertion classes, sometimes held on the weekends, depending on Cooper's schedule." She shuddered. "I've come to think of those lessons as cruel and unusual torture sessions, and I don't really understand why I even need to attend them since I don't venture out into the field all that often."

Herman retook his seat, curiosity making it all but impossible for him to leave. "Why would the Pinkerton Agency assist your agency? Aren't you in competition with them?"

"Hardly. They're the Pinkertons. We're merely a small agency that caters to people who can't convince the more established agencies their problems are worth investigating." She leaned forward. "As to why they're assisting us, I believe they're doing so because they've realized that including more women agents could be beneficial to solving some of their cases. By lending us the expertise of Agent Clifton, I believe the powers that be at the Pinkerton Agency hope we'll decide to close our doors and join their ranks. There's little chance any of our agents would abandon the Bleecker Street Inquiry Agency to become lady Pinkertons, though." She smiled. "None of us care to be at the beck and call of men."

Having no idea how to respond because any response from him, a man, might come off the wrong way, Herman elected to change the subject. "Tell me this, Miss Beekman, is it true that your agency was responsible for solving not only the Knickerbocker Bandit case but the Linwood jewel heist, as well?"

"We were."

Herman settled back into the seat. "Perhaps I was too hasty in dismissing the qualifications of your agency."

"And perhaps you weren't, because we haven't investigated a murder attempt yet, so it might be in your best interest to hire the Pinkertons instead."

"You suggested that the Pinkertons may not want to take on my case. Besides, I originally decided not to contact the Pinkertons first because I'm worried that if I involve that agency then my grandmother will take note of any Pinkerton agents assigned to my case and will worry needlessly."

"Someone apparently wants to murder you. Her worrying wouldn't be needless." Daphne glanced at her notes again. "However, since you're here now, we might as well continue. At the very least, I may be able to provide you with a few theories you could take to the Pinkertons, which could see them agreeing to take up your case. With that said, allow us to return to this coachman. You mentioned he was wearing a handkerchief. That suggests he's either a paid member of the criminal persuasion hired to kill you, or he's someone known to you and took care to conceal his identity in the event he was unsuccessful with doing you in."

"I can't think of a single person who'd

want me dead."

"Have you ever stolen the affections of a lady from one of your friends?"

"Absolutely not."

"How about stolen another author's idea for a plot line?"

"You can't be serious."

"Surely you've considered that you've annoyed someone, haven't you?"

"I make it a point to avoid annoying people in general, so no, I haven't considered that an acquaintance might want me dead."

"You've annoyed me numerous times and we've only just met."

Before he could think of a response to that, Daphne flipped to a fresh page in her notepad. "Tell me about your family."

"No one in my family wants me dead."

"So you think, but you've already admitted that you share boxing time with Mr. Sheldon Clarendon, your cousin. It could be that Sheldon doesn't enjoy your boxing sessions and has decided to end those sessions in a very definitive manner."

"Sheldon would be without the income he earns from me if I were to stop breathing. He chooses to work for me since his mother is very opinionated about how he spends the allowance he gets from the Clarendon family. He won't be free of his mother until he gets full access to his trust fund, something he won't get for three more years when he reaches the age of twenty-eight."

"What type of work does Sheldon do for you?"

"He does research, transcribes my notes, and then takes those notes to a typist before sending them off to my publishing house."

"Does he enjoy that type of work?"

"He's never lodged any complaints. However, he doesn't merely work for me to earn additional income. He's also hoping to learn more about the writing craft because he longs to become a published author."

"Does he have an above average proficiency with the English language?"

"Hard to say. He has yet to muster up the courage to let me read anything he's written."

"He could definitely be a suspect." Daphne wrote Sheldon's name at the top of the blank page.

"Sheldon doesn't want me dead."

"Perhaps not, but he can't be counted out as a suspect until he's investigated." She flipped to another blank page. "Now then, tell me about this grandmother of yours."

"My grandmother's mission in life, after

my parents and my grandfather's ship went down when they were off on one of their adventures, has been to keep me alive. She would be the last person we'd need to add to a list of suspects."

"What about your siblings?"

"I'm an only child."

"What about your aunts, uncles, and other cousins?"

"I can't think of any aunt, uncle, or cousin who'd want me dead."

Daphne set aside her notepad. "From the cases we've investigated, more often than not, the source of the conflict usually revolves around money and usually involves people known to one another. There's a good chance that the attempts on your life could be at the hand of a relative interested in inheriting whatever fortune you'd leave behind."

"While it's true I'm in possession of a respectable fortune that I inherited from my parents when they died, as well as the fortune I've begun to amass from the sales of my books, I don't believe any of my relatives would go to the extreme length of killing me off to secure a piece of it. Frankly, I'm beginning to find your questions disconcerting."

Daphne took off her tricorn hat, laid it

beside her, then ran a hand over brown hair that was pulled into a knot at the nape of her neck. "And I'm beginning to find your objections to my questions rather curious. You decided to seek out the services of an inquiry agency, and the word *inquiry* means an act of asking for information, which I thought you, being a wordsmith, would know."

Herman frowned. "I know the definition of inquiry."

"Why, then, are you balking at answering my questions?"

"Because no one in my family wants me dead."

She arched a brow. "No one in your family suffers from a gambling problem or living beyond their means?"

"I don't believe so."

"But you don't know for certain, do you?"

"I suppose I don't."

"Which is why the Bleccker Street Inquiry Agency may be the perfect agency to help you after all. We're incredibly efficient when it comes to delving into backgrounds. I assure you, if any of your relatives have financial troubles, we'll uncover exactly what those troubles are and to what extent."

"My grandmother will not appreciate

anyone looking into personal family business."

"Perhaps not, but I doubt she'd appreciate you ending up dead either. With that said, let us move on from talk of your family, which I've found less than helpful, to talk of your friends. Tell me about them, or better yet, tell me what you enjoy doing with them."

Herman leaned back in his chair. "Most of my friends are fellow writers, but I don't think any of them have a reason to murder me. Writers in general aren't known to be particularly bloodthirsty, even if a good many of us compose stories that might leave readers believing otherwise."

"I bet if we dig a little deeper into your friendships, you'll be surprised at how many of your writer friends have motives for wanting you dead, or at least maimed."

"And I bet you're wrong about that."

Daphne gave an airy wave of her hand. "Allow us to respectfully disagree about that. But, moving on, tell me a bit about what you talk about with your writerly friends when you get together. I'm sure you must discuss plotlines and ways to kill off the victims in your stories, but what other topics are broached?"

"We rarely discuss plotlines or murder

methods. Our discussions normally revolve around sentence structure or the overuse of common phrases."

"No talk of poison or unique ways to set up the perfect murder?"

Herman tilted his head. "I don't recall ever discussing those types of subjects with my writerly friends."

"That's too bad because it could have lent some insight into how your friends think, or better yet, lent clues as to which of your friends may want to murder you, especially if, for example, someone recently talked about poison and how best to administer it."

"I'm suddenly thankful there's been no talk of poison on the chance one of my writerly friends *does* wish me a speedy demise."

"I'm sure you are." Daphne began writing in her notepad. "Tell me, though, why do you and your friends prefer talk of sentence structure over poison? Poison would be far more interesting."

"True, but writers should never ignore the nuances of sentence structure or anything related to the writing process."

"Well, quite, but I imagine the literary salons you're visiting are attended by writers who already understand sentence structure. Talk of poison, on the other hand, might be more beneficial because it would undoubtedly spark some creative thinking."

"Which is a very interesting theory," Herman said before he frowned. "You seem unusually well versed with matters concerning writing, but you have yet to tell me what you write."

Daphne removed her spectacles and began cleaning the lenses with her sleeve. "Surely I mentioned it, didn't I?"

"No, you didn't."

She seemed to take an inordinately long time to return her spectacles to her face. "I hope you'll avoid wincing again after I disclose to you that I write . . . poetry."

In all honesty, Daphne's disclosure didn't surprise him in the least. There were many women of his acquaintance who dabbled in poetry. However, what did surprise him was the distinct trace of amusement in her eyes, although he didn't have the foggiest notion why disclosing she wrote poetry would amuse her.

He crossed his arms over his chest. "What are you currently working on?"

"I would think that's obvious. A poem, of course."

"What type of poem?"

The amusement lurking in her eyes intensified. "Didn't you say you're always hesitant to encourage writers to share what they're writing with you because you're afraid they might not be proficient with the English language?"

"You don't seem to have an issue with the English language."

"True, but I fear I might be a horrendous poetry writer, and if I share what I write with you, you'll then be forced to crush my tender, poetic feelings. By crushing my feelings, you might also leave me with the distinct urge to encourage Eunice Holbrooke to refuse to have the Bleecker Street Inquiry Agency take on your attempted murder case."

As an argument for not sharing more about her writing with him, Herman thought it was a sound one. Nevertheless, he found himself unwilling to abandon the topic. "I doubt your poetry is horrendous and I can be gentle with any critique if I set my mind to it. So, with that said, allow me to encourage you to share a few snippets from any verses you've recently completed."

The amusement in her eyes disappeared in a flash, replaced with what almost seemed to be incredulity. "You want me to recite, as in out loud, my poetry?"

He barely managed to swallow the laugh that had almost escaped him. "Indeed, and know that I'm waiting with bated breath to hear what you've composed thus far."

Chapter Four

For a few seconds, Herman didn't think Daphne was going to grant his request, but then she sent him the barest hint of a nod, folded her hands primly in her lap, and closed her eyes.

"Her skin was soft as a baby's behind," Daphne began, "her lips as rosy as wine, and while my love for her was not returned, I couldn't help but yearn for . . ." Daphne's eyes flashed open. "That's as far as I've gotten. I've been trying to fit in something more about the tragic hero, who's a pirate, but I'm having difficulty fitting any pirate talk into the stanzas."

Herman didn't know whether to rise to his feet and give her a standing ovation for what was the worst recital of poetry he'd ever heard, or give her that ovation for having what was undoubtedly an unusual mind, one so unusual that she was able to compose horrendous poetry on the spot.

Clearly, Miss Daphne Beekman was *not* a poet, although he had the sneaking suspicion, given her comments about what authors at literary salons should be discussing, that she *was* a writer. What she wrote, though, or better yet, why she didn't want to share that with him, was a mystery that begged to be solved.

"What did you think about what I've composed so far?" she asked.

He fought a grin as he pulled himself back to the odd situation at hand. "In my professional opinion, your poetry shows some, ah, interesting possibilities, although it does need a great deal of polishing. I definitely understand more clearly why you're dressed as a pirate, what with how a pirate is the hero in your latest poem. Looking for inspiration, are you?"

"I've been experiencing a lack of creativity of late and was forced to take drastic measures."

"And are you finding inspiration now that you're wearing pirate attire?"

"You just heard the first part of my poem. How inspiring would you say it's been for me?"

"Perhaps you might need to search for additional inspiration."

Daphne suddenly bent over, but not

before he caught sight of her grinning. She then, for some unknown reason, began talking to the space underneath the fainting couch she was sitting on. A second later, a paw materialized from underneath the couch, followed by a large beast of a dog that was wearing an eyepatch.

Daphne straightened and sent the dog a fond look. "I seem to be running out of options as pertains to my pirate situation. I spent the entire day with this darling, but his appearance did absolutely nothing to inspire me."

"It was brave of you to put that patch over the poor pooch's eye. I can't imagine he appreciated that, and it also seems, given the size of him, he has some very large teeth."

"Winston's wearing a patch because he's missing an eye, and I'm not responsible for the patch, his owner is. Plus, while his teeth are large, he's woefully lacking in courage. He stuffed himself under the fainting couch the moment I asked him to investigate your arrival."

Herman considered Winston. "I'm sorry to say that if a pirate dog doesn't provide you with an incentive to fix your pirate dilemma, I don't know what will, unless you could dig up a parrot."

"I've already found a parrot, one that goes

by the name of Pretty Girl, and have volunteered to watch her while her owners are away, even though I'm deathly afraid of birds."

"Has that helped?"

"I spent hours with Pretty Girl today as well, and since, again, you've heard my poem, I'm convinced she is not going to provide me with the breakthrough I need." She gave Winston a brisk pat. "And with all that out of the way, let us return to the pressing matter of someone wanting you dead, which has nothing to do with my fondness for poetry. I believe we were discussing your literary friends, but since you can't seem to accept the idea that any of them want to do you in, what about your friends who aren't literary types?"

"I can't think of a single friend who'd want me dead."

Exasperation flickered through her eyes. "Forgive me, Mr. Henderson, but I'm not getting the impression you're really using what I assume is an intellectual mind to its full capacity. Someone apparently wants to murder you. Murder, as I'm sure you realize from all the murders you've written about, is an act of passion, brought about because of an intense emotional state. That suggests the person behind the attempts on your life is probably someone known to you and could have murderous intentions toward you because of a perceived slight."

"I haven't slighted any of my friends."

"What about ladies?"

Herman frowned. "Ladies?"

"Quite right. I suppose I should have asked this before, but what about your wife? Could she want you dead?"

"I'm not married."

She jotted that down in her notepad. "So that's one suspect we don't need to worry about. What about any ladies you may be courting?"

"I don't make it a habit to court numerous ladies at the same time."

"Which is commendable of you, but I'm sure there must be a few ladies out there seeking your affection. From what you've disclosed, you're a wealthy gentleman, and, I must add, a handsome one, and I'm sure there is many a young lady who'd like to catch your eye."

Male satisfaction immediately coursed through him. "You find me handsome?"

"I'm not blind, Mr. Henderson, or at least not blind when I'm wearing my spectacles. Of course you're handsome. You're also reasonably intelligent, and there are many ladies who find that appealing."

"Reasonably?"

"Surely you don't expect me to proclaim you're unusually intelligent, do you, not with the way you haven't considered who might be behind your own demise? But returning to the ladies," she continued before he could respond to that first bit, "I'll need a list of every lady you've escorted to the opera or other events around the city, as well as any lady you might know who holds you in a semblance of fondness." She tucked the pencil behind her ear. "I'll also need a list of places you frequent often. I'm actually surprised to discover you attend places like the opera, given that the limited gossip I've heard about you over the years has painted you as a recluse who prefers to remain inside the confines of your mansion on Irving Place, except when you're traveling the world, searching for fodder for your stories."

"I don't travel the world, Miss Beekman. I prefer to live that type of adventurous life vicariously through my characters. With that said, though, I'm by no means a recluse."

Daphne frowned. "I've not heard any rumors that you mingle with the New York Four Hundred, an exclusive group that I imagine would enjoy having someone with your acclaim attending their events."

"My family was once firmly ensconced within New York high society. But when my parents and grandfather died, my grandmother stopped attending social events and withdrew from society. And while I've been invited to enter the hallowed circle of the New York Four Hundred, I've declined."

"Because you prefer spending your time with other writers, discussing riveting topics such as sentence structure?"

"Clearly you're a bit skeptical of the merits of that type of talk, but no. I've chosen to avoid society for the most part because if I were to spend time in that illustrious circle, people would begin to start paying calls on my grandmother again, something that could very well see her taking to her bed and never stirring from it."

"That's a very considerate attitude to embrace in regard to your grandmother," she said. "But society aside, tell me this — if you don't travel the world, how do you come up with such descriptive passages in your books, especially the ones set in exotic locations?"

"My late mother left behind numerous journals. She was a gifted writer, and she describes the exotic lands she and my father traveled to in wonderful detail."

Daphne's eyes began to sparkle. "May I

dare hope that you occasionally share some of the entries in these journals with others, and if so, do I also dare hope that your parents, at some point in time, encountered a pirate?"

"I'm afraid I've yet to run across anything pirate related."

Her face fell. "That's too bad, although I suppose it's not well done of me to question you about pirates in the first place. You are, after all, here to seek out the professional services of the Bleecker Street Inquiry Agency, not provide me with inspirational tidbits for my, uh, poetry. So, returning to your case, when do you think you'll be able to get me the list of all of your friends, acquaintances, and young ladies known to you?"

He retrieved his notepad from his pocket, flipped it open, then thumbed through the pages. "As luck would have it, I have a fairly extensive list available now because my grandmother has convinced me to host a house party at my residence on the Hudson at the end of next week." He began tearing out some pages. "Everyone who'll be in attendance is accounted for here."

He handed Daphne the pages, which she immediately began looking through, lifting her head a moment later.

"Why is Miss Finetta Shoenburger's name circled?"

"Sheldon wanted to make sure I remember to give Miss Shoenburger and her grandmother, Mrs. Shoenburger, some undivided attention during the house party."

"Why?"

"Because Mrs. Shoenburger is a close friend of my grandmother, and, ah, it's somewhat difficult to explain the reason behind the undivided attention. Or rather, ah, embarrassing."

Daphne examined the notes again and jotted something next to Finetta's name. "I'm sure you do find it embarrassing that your grandmother, along with Miss Shoenburger's grandmother, have decided to use your house party as a venue for their matchmaking."

Herman scratched his chin. "How did you come to that conclusion? It's not as if I gave you much to work with."

"It's my job at the agency to make reasonable deductions from statements our clients provide me with. I'm reasonably good at what I do. Besides, your grandmother's desire to delve into matchmaking was hardly difficult to figure out, since grandmothers often resort to matchmaking attempts when their grandchildren reach a certain age."

She peered at him through the thick lenses of her spectacles. "You have to be at least thirty, which means, given your unmarried state, there was every likelihood your grandmother would decide to help you on your way to wedded bliss. She's probably of the opinion you've been dragging your feet."

"For the record, I'm thirty-one, and, yes, Grandmother believes I've been negligent when it comes to the ladies. But in my defense, I've been occupied with daunting deadlines over the past few years." He smiled. "That preoccupation has now resulted with Grandmother deciding to lend me a helping hand. Finetta Shoenburger is the lady my grandmother wants to see me settle my affections on the most, although there are several other ladies she's been bringing into conversations of late. Those ladies have also been invited to the house party. Sheldon marked their names with asterisks in my notes so that I'll be certain to direct some special attention their way, which will keep Grandmother from becoming distressed."

"That was very thoughtful of Sheldon."

"Does that mean you no longer consider him a suspect?"

"Not at all. People can be thoughtful and shifty at the same time." She poised her pencil over the page with Finetta's name now written on it. "Is Miss Shoenburger a lady you hold in great affection, and if so, does she return that affection?"

"I'm not well acquainted with Miss Shoenburger, although we seem to attend many of the same events."

"No doubt due to the manipulations of your grandmothers."

"Indeed. With that said, though, we've not spoken more than a few words to each other."

"Hence the reason for the house party," Daphne said, writing something down.

He craned his neck to see what she'd written. "Did you make a notation questioning why Finetta and I have not spoken much?"

"I did. It's odd that you wouldn't engage in more active conversation with a young lady whom your grandmother wants you to court."

"Finetta's very shy, and when you add in the fact that I seem to make her nervous, there's nothing odd at all about our not conversing more."

"Your size is probably responsible for her nervousness," Daphne said as she began writing again. "You are unusually large, which lends you an intimidating air."

"I'm a writer. Writers aren't known to be

81

intimidating sorts."

She lifted her head. "That's not true. Many readers are intimidated by their favorite writers because they admire their work and believe writers are overly intellectual sorts, which apparently intimidates many people. Perhaps Miss Shoenburger, besides being intimidated by your size, is an admirer of your work, which results in her becoming tongue-tied in your presence." She tapped her pencil against the notepad. "Granted, there is the possibility she only tolerates your presence because of her grandmother. That right there could be reason enough to add her to the top of the list of credible suspects." She returned to her notes, but before Herman could compose a suitable argument about why Finetta was the last person who should be on a list of suspects, Daphne caught his eye. "I'm beginning to think your house party may give the Bleecker Street Inquiry Agency a prime opportunity to investigate those nearest and dearest to you. That is, if the agency decides to take up your case."

"How would you do that without being obvious? The majority of the guests attending the house party are known to each other. New faces would definitely stand out, as well as draw suspicion."

Daphne rose to her feet and began pacing around the room, not stopping until she'd circled the room seven times. "Someone from the agency will have to go undercover, perhaps as a servant, or . . ."

Her eyes went distant as she resumed her pacing, stopping after she made it another three times around the room. "Instead of a servant, perhaps it would be better to have an agent pose as your assistant. An assistant would be expected to be in your company often, which would allow one of our agents to observe your guests."

"Which is an intriguing idea, except that Sheldon might take issue with my bringing on another assistant."

"If Sheldon's responsible for the attempts on your life, bringing in a new assistant could very well lead to him escalating his attempts to murder you."

"But if Sheldon isn't responsible, bringing on a new assistant will offend him. I would not care to do that."

"Which is very considerate of you, and that means . . ." Daphne stopped talking as she began pacing again, making it four trips around the room before she stopped and arched a brow. "You said that Sheldon takes your work to a typist?"

"I did."

"Well, that's the solution, then. *I* know how to type, which gives you a very plausible reason for hiring me."

Herman rose to his feet. "You told me you rarely work in the field because of the questionable state of your nerves."

"My nerves seem to become less questionable when I'm in disguise."

"You said you fainted numerous times while disguised as Cleopatra."

"True, but I'm much less likely to swoon these days."

"*Much less likely* is not the same as never likely to swoon, especially if, in the course of investigating my guests, you happen upon the would-be murderer."

She winced. "I suppose that might be problematic."

"Or deadly, and you might be the person to end up dead." He caught her eye. "Perhaps it might be for the best if a non-swooning agent takes over my case."

"No one else knows how to type, and again, I'm sure my swooning won't be an issue since . . ." Daphne suddenly stopped talking as her eyes widened.

Concern was swift and had Herman taking a step closer to her. "Is something the matter?"

"Shh . . ." she whispered, her gaze fixed

on something behind him. "Someone's moving down the hallway. There's a shadow flickering."

To Herman's disbelief, she darted around him, dashed to where she'd left her cutlass, snagged it up, then took him completely aback when she stepped in front of him and brandished the cutlass in the direction of the doorway. "Stay behind me," she demanded.

"Don't be ridiculous. Get behind me."

"I'm the trained, or somewhat trained, professional here."

"No, you're not, but now's hardly the time to debate the matter, and —"

Whatever else Herman was about to say died on the tip of his tongue when a huge brute of a dog suddenly materialized in the doorway, followed by a second dog. They stopped in the doorway and settled their beady eyes on Daphne, who was now waving her cutlass back and forth, the dogs' heads moving from side to side as they considered her every wave.

"Put the cutlass down and get behind me," he said through lips that barely moved.

"I'm not allowing you to sacrifice yourself for me. You're the client."

"I won't be sacrificing myself because those are my dogs, Wolf and Hound."

"What in the world could have possessed you to acquire such terrifying creatures?"

"Four attempts on my life springs to mind, but the dogs won't attack me, although I can't say with any certainty that they won't go after you."

"Can't you just call them off?"

"I only acquired them this afternoon. I'm afraid their trainer hasn't completed our lessons yet. The only thing I know about them is that they'll protect me from harm at any cost."

"I'm not a threat to you."

"Your cutlass waving suggests otherwise, so please, stop being stubborn and lower your weapon."

Daphne shot a glance to the dogs and shuddered. "They're growling."

"A less-than-encouraging sign." Herman edged his way in front of Daphne, even though she tried to scoot around him again, right as Winston released a growl of his own, one that seemed to have a touch of a whine mixed in.

Chaos immediately erupted.

Wolf and Hound started howling as they surged into motion with Winston clearly in their sights. The poor pirate dog immediately turned tail and scampered across the room, launching himself over the fainting couch and disappearing from sight, the wolfhounds in hot pursuit. Their progress was interrupted when Daphne raced after them, waving her cutlass madly about.

Lunging forward, Herman tried to block Daphne from the dogs, who were now snarling at her, but before he could get to her, Wolf — or perhaps it was Hound, he couldn't really tell them apart — grabbed hold of her cutlass with his sharp teeth, shaking his head from side to side and ripping the cutlass from Daphne's grasp. A second after the cutlass clattered to the ground, Daphne spun on her heel and raced toward the fainting couch Winston had disappeared behind.

Unfortunately, before Herman could do more than grab Wolf, Hound sank its teeth into the hem of Daphne's trousers. In an instant, Daphne went from trying to scramble over the fainting couch to slumping against it, her nerves evidently not up for an attack from a wolfhound since, clearly, she'd succumbed to a fit of the vapors and was now in the throes of a most spectacular swoon.

CHAPTER FIVE

"I'm now regretting stating so emphatically to Mr. Herman Henderson last night that my swooning days were becoming less frequent," Daphne said, tossing the medicine ball Agent Cooper Clifton had chosen for one of their physical exertion sessions to Miss Ann Evans, who didn't flinch as she caught the heavy ball. "Because I fainted dead away when I thought I was about to be devoured by his massive dogs, I was definitely premature with making such a statement."

Ann tossed the ball to her sister, Miss Elsy Evans, who stumbled a few feet backward and sent her sister a scowl, one Ann ignored as she tucked a flyaway strand of red hair behind her ear and grinned at Daphne. "I imagine it was embarrassing for you, swooning like you did. But on a brighter note, you must have found it incredibly romantic that not only did Mr. Henderson get you out of your swoon by plying you with your smelling salts, he then carried you back here to the boardinghouse. Why, if a gentleman like Mr. Henderson ever carried me around, I'd be hard-pressed not to descend into a swoon as well."

"I wasn't feeling the least bit swoony when he was carrying me, Ann, more along the lines of mortified. Mr. Henderson was a potential client, not a suitor," Daphne argued. "Besides, he only insisted on carrying me because his dogs were responsible for my swoon in the first place. He felt he was to blame for that fiasco because he couldn't get them to abandon their pursuit of me and Winston." She shook her head. "Poor Winston is now refusing to leave the house. Last I saw of him, he was hiding underneath a table in the kitchen, looking pathetic."

"Be that as it may," Ann argued back, "Mr. Henderson is undoubtedly the most handsome potential client we've seen since we've opened our doors, as well as being the most chivalrous, no matter that you feel his actions were driven by a sense of guilt."

"He's the first male client we've seen, so of course he's the most handsome one, but I believe you're missing a key point here. His dogs almost ate me."

Ann gave a wave of a muddy hand. "From what Mr. Henderson said after he gently set you down on the sofa in the parlor, and then tucked a blanket around you, he was hopeful his dogs were merely trying to intimidate you, not eat you."

"I still don't understand how those dogs got out of the carriage and into the agency in the first place," Miss Judith Donovan said, catching the ball Elsy tossed to her before she heaved the medicine ball toward Ann, who didn't bother to catch it because she took that moment to move closer to Daphne. The ball whizzed past where she'd recently been standing, landing with a splat in a large puddle left over from the storm the night before, spraying everyone with mud in the process.

Daphne took off spectacles now dotted with brown specks, wiped them with the part of her sleeve not drenched with muddy water, then returned them to her face. "Mr. Henderson thinks he might not have latched the door to his carriage securely, which allowed the dogs to sneak out, evading the notice of Mr. Henderson's coachman. He also believes he might not have completely shut the agency door after he entered. It certainly doesn't speak well of my competency as an inquiry agent that I never

90

thought to double-check the door after I agreed to speak with Mr. Henderson about his case."

Ann settled a knowing look on Daphne. "It's telling, you agreeing to speak with him about his case when the agency was closed."

"The only thing telling about it is that I couldn't resist the lure of an attempted murder case, one that could very well cement our burgeoning reputation as a credible agency that can compete with all the other private investigation agencies in the city." Daphne blew out a breath. "With that said, it's highly unlikely we'll ever see Mr. Henderson again. No one in their right mind would want to hire an agency where one of the agents fainted over an unexpected circumstance, even if said agent had an excellent reason to do so."

"Ladies," Agent Clifton growled, striding up to join them, looking anything but pleased as his gaze settled on the medicine ball still lying in the puddle, "if you've neglected to remember, we're outside on this chilly March morning not to share snippets of gossip but to attempt to increase your strength. You're hardly going to do that if the only muscle any of you seem to be using is your mouth."

Ann frowned. "Is a mouth actually considered a muscle?"

Agent Clifton merely sent Ann a quirk of a brow before he retrieved the medicine ball and then, without a by-your-leave, threw it Daphne's way. It was sheer luck she managed to grab hold of the slippery thing, although the force of the ball whacking into her did have her wobbling around as she tried to maintain her hold on it.

"Allow me to remind you of the rules of this particular endeavor," Agent Clifton continued. "You're supposed to toss the ball as quickly as you can from one person to the next because this is meant to be a vigorous exercise. By overexerting yourself, you'll begin building up your upper-body and lower-body strength, but the vigor only occurs if the momentum is kept up."

"You do realize it's not yet eight in the morning, don't you, as well as being a Saturday — a day many young ladies take to sleep in?" Daphne asked before she hefted the ball in Agent Clifton's direction, refusing a sigh when it plummeted two feet in front of him, splattering everyone with mud once again. "I don't believe my ability to summon up any vigor begins until afternoon."

"I'm sure that'll change after another month or so of participating in my physical exertion regime," Agent Clifton returned.

"We've been at these sessions for over three months as it is," Daphne said, swiping a muddy hand over her face. "Surely you don't expect us to continue on with them for another month, do you?"

"Of course not. I expect you to continue enjoying vigorous exercise for as long as each of you continues to be an inquiry agent. You never know when you'll be in a situation where physical stamina is all that stands between you and certain death, which means all of you need to embrace more activity on a daily basis."

"But couldn't we do that embracing after lunch?" Daphne asked, which earned her a roll of the eyes from Agent Clifton before he retrieved the ball again and tucked it under his arm as if it weighed nothing at all. "Shall we move on to the rope station?"

A chorus of groans met that question because the rope station was the least favorite of every lady involved with the Bleecker Street Inquiry Agency, save Eunice, who flatly refused to participate in the exertion activities at all. Given that Eunice was a somewhat frightening lady, Agent Clifton hadn't argued with her, which had left Daphne considering adopting a frightening attitude of her own, if only to get out of an activity she abhorred.

As Ann, Elsy, and Judith trudged over to the rope station, which was actually just a long length of rope tied to a branch of the tallest tree in the back courtyard of the boardinghouse, Daphne fell into step beside Agent Clifton, who was watching her in a very considering fashion.

She swiped at some mud that was dribbling off her face. "I'm being unreasonably churlish with you this morning, aren't I?"

"You're definitely not being cheerful."

She released a sigh. "And I beg your pardon for that, Agent Clifton. I didn't sleep well last night, but my lack of sleep is not a good excuse for abusing you with my ill humor."

"Perhaps your mood would improve if you'd abandon the Agent Clifton business. Such formality is unnecessary since we spend so much time in each other's company. You must call me Cooper."

"I believe that *will* improve my mood, although . . ." She caught his eye. "You should consider that a lack of formality may result in many of us balking more vocally at some of your somewhat unreasonable demands, such as scaling a tree before the sun has fully risen."

"I wasn't going to offer the courtesy of

my given name to *all* the ladies."

Daphne stopped in her tracks. "Then I'll not be able to accept your offer because, if you've forgotten, all of the ladies are inquiry agents who look at everything with an eye for intrigue. As such, they'll see me using your given name as an indication that our relationship has changed."

Cooper's eyes widened. "Surely you're not suggesting that if we address each other informally that others will take that to mean we're, er, romantically involved?"

"That's exactly what they'll think."

"But romance has never entered my mind concerning you."

"And I now find my mood beginning to take a turn for the dismal again."

He winced. "Forgive me, Daphne. That didn't come out well, but . . . you're not romantically interested in me, are you?"

"Will you be disappointed to learn that I think of you as my fourth brother — and an often-irritating fourth brother at that?"

Cooper took off the cap he was wearing, ran a hand over his short blond hair, and grinned. "Thank goodness for that because, for a second there, I thought I'd insulted you. And I'm not disappointed in the least about your thinking of me as a brother. I think of you as my third sister, although you're not nearly as annoying as my actual sisters are."

"I didn't know you had sisters."

"I have two, and they're constantly drawing up lists of ladies they believe I should marry. Then they get annoyed with me when I don't give their lists what they believe is proper consideration."

"You don't care for the ladies on those lists?"

He shrugged. "I'm sure many of the ladies are lovely, but I'm perfectly capable of finding a lady on my own, although the demands of my job have left me with little time to devote to courting any lady." Cooper's gaze darted to where Ann, Elsy, and Judith were now standing by the rope station, regarding the rope dangling from the tree rather forlornly. His gaze lingered on Ann before he returned his attention to Daphne. "Perhaps you're right, though, and I should suggest that all the ladies at the agency address me by my given name. That would alleviate the chance of anyone concluding you and I share anything other than a friendly type of affection for each other."

Daphne glanced at Ann, who'd turned and was giving Cooper a thorough perusal, although Ann abruptly spun around and returned her attention to the rope when she caught Daphne watching her.

Daphne smiled. "We certainly shouldn't allow any of my fellow agents to think we're romantically involved, not when that might put a damper on potential possibilities I never considered."

"What in the world are you talking about?"

She gave his arm a bit of a swat. "Come now, Cooper, you can't tell me that a few of the ladies here haven't attracted your attention. And if that is the case, your dilemma of never having time to devote to ladies won't be an issue." She tilted her head. "Tell me this, though. Have you been torturing us with these physical exertion lessons because it's allowed you to spend your mornings in the company of ladies you may find . . . intriguing?"

Cooper raked a hand through his hair again. "Honestly, Daphne, maybe I *should* consider holding these lessons later in the day because clearly your mind is a scary place to visit first thing in the morning." He gestured to where Judith was now trying to scale the rope, the fabric of her skirt getting twisted around her legs before she made it three feet off the ground. "But to answer your question, no, intriguing ladies of the Bleecker Street Inquiry Agency are not why

I've been insisting on the physical exertion lessons."

"Then what is behind these lessons you know we loathe?"

Cooper smiled and nodded to where Judith had gotten her legs untangled and was once again hauling herself up the rope. "I meant what I said earlier. I don't want your lack of physical stamina to ever be responsible for any of you coming to a bad end. I've become fond of everyone at the agency — and not in a romantic fashion, before you ask. Seeing all of you make progress with becoming more physically fit is remarkably satisfying to me."

"And here I've been under the mistaken belief that you're a less-than-sentimental man, but underneath that gruff exterior, you have a heart that's soft as a . . . well, nothing springs to mind except a baby's behind." Daphne grinned. "That analogy, though, might only be because I recently used it when I was reciting poetry to Mr. Herman Henderson yesterday."

Cooper returned the grin. "Ah, yes, your poetry." He shook his head. "From what I've gathered through listening to your conversations with your fellow agents, you've been experiencing trouble with your writing of late. That had me wondering if

98

the reason behind your being so keen to take on Mr. Henderson's case — before you swooned in front of him, of course — was because you thought it would provide you with a much-needed spark to get your writing back on track."

"Will you think poorly of me if I admit you're spot-on about that?"

Cooper's grin dimmed. "Did it never cross your mind that you'd be placing yourself in direct danger by volunteering to go undercover in an attempted murder investigation? Danger that you, of all people, are ill-equipped to handle?"

"The danger involved didn't really cross my mind until I repaired to my room last night after Mr. Henderson took his leave. I believe it was after midnight when I decided I might have been a little rash to volunteer to take on an undercover position. However, around one in the morning, a different plan came to mind, one where the agency would send not only me but another agent or two to assist with collecting information at Mr. Henderson's house party. That plan, sadly, will never amount to anything because Mr. Henderson is probably paying a call on the Pinkertons to have your agency take on his case."

"I'm not planning to call on the Pinkertons, unless, of course, the Bleecker Street Inquiry Agency decides my case is not one the agency wants to represent."

Daphne turned around, her gaze settling on none other than Mr. Herman Henderson. To her concern, a mere five seconds after she caught sight of the man, her pulse began galloping madly through her veins.

It was quite unlike her pulse to gallop simply because a handsome gentleman was in her vicinity, even one who was incredibly well turned out in a suit of charcoal gray. However, there was no denying that there was something about Herman Henderson that, whether she cared to admit it or not, appealed to her. Whether that appeal was caused by his handsome face, or the fact that he had carried her all the way down Bleecker Street the night before, or that they shared a common interest in writing mysteries was definitely up for debate.

Realizing she was all but gawking at the man, Daphne summoned up a smile. "Mr. Henderson. I wasn't expecting to see you again today. Or, frankly, ever."

"I don't know why you wouldn't expect to see me again," Herman countered. "You and I never finished our discussion last night regarding my case. Since someone is still intent on seeking my demise, I would have thought you'd know I'd be back to see you bright and early this morning, even with it being a Saturday, and even with your agency not open on the weekends." He held out his hand to Cooper. "I don't believe we've met. I'm Mr. Herman Henderson."

Cooper stepped forward and shook Herman's hand. "Agent Cooper Clifton of the Pinkerton Agency."

"Ah yes. Miss Beekman told me last night that your agency and hers often collaborate together," Herman said. "May I assume she mentioned something to you about the concerns I brought to her last night?"

"She said you're worried someone wants to murder you."

"That does seem to be the case, although I didn't run into any difficulties last night after I saw Miss Beekman home."

"I don't know who would have dared approach you while you were in the company of your vicious guard dogs," Daphne muttered.

"An excellent point, although I have already returned them to the man I bought them from. I stopped by his place of business before I traveled here."

Daphne frowned. "Why would you do that?"

"They attacked you."

"Because they thought I was a threat."

"True, but it wasn't worth placing you in harm's way to keep them. And since they also tried to take a few bites out of Mr. Andrew Ware, the man who was acting as my coachman last night, I had no choice but to return the dogs." He patted one of his pockets. "If it eases your mind, I'm carrying my pistol with me, and yes, I do know how to shoot it."

"Your being armed does lend me a sense of relief, but putting that aside, you just stated that Mr. Ware was *acting* as your coachman." Daphne tapped a finger against her chin. "What happened to your normal coachman? Has he suddenly disappeared? We recently handled a case that involved a coachman, and that coachman turned out to have a rather interesting part in one of our most troubling cases to date."

"Nothing happened to him. He's still gainfully in my employ, but Andrew has a special talent with horses. He's far more capable of driving me out of a dangerous situation if the person wanting me dead escalates his attempts and moves from merely trying to run me down to something more concerning."

Daphne reached into her pocket, withdrawing her notepad and pencil. "You didn't mention an Andrew Ware last night. He's one of your employees?"

"He's my bookkeeper and is responsible for keeping all of my accounts. More importantly, though, he's one of my oldest friends. His father managed my father's stables, hence the reason behind Andrew's ability with horses. When I told him about the second carriage incident, he didn't hesitate to insist on driving for me." Herman smiled. "He does have other bookkeeping clients, though, which is why I know driving me around is an imposition for him, not that he'd ever complain. I'm sure Andrew would be only too happy to relinquish his driving to an agent of the Bleecker Street Inquiry Agency, if your agency has a competent driver who could take over for him."

Daphne winced. "Miss Elsy Evans is our most frequent driver, but I'm not sure her skills would be comparable to Mr. Ware's." She nodded to Elsy, who was in the process of climbing up the rope, pulling herself up a foot and then sliding back down six inches before pulling herself up another foot. "That's her over there."

Herman's eyes widened when Elsy began sliding rapidly down the rope, releasing it when she was about two feet from the ground. She landed in a heap of mud-splattered fabric. He turned back to Daphne. "How long has she been a driver?"

Daphne looked at Cooper. "What's it been now — five, six months?"

"That seems about right," Cooper said. "But even with Elsy getting driving lessons from Phillip Villard, she's probably never going to be anything but an adequate driver. She might be able to outrun a killer, but only because she still frequently loses control of the horses when she gets overly anxious. Being chased by a killer would definitely see her turning a little anxious."

"I think I'll continue on with Andrew as my driver," Herman said firmly.

"Or I could take over, if you'd agree to allow the Bleecker Street Inquiry Agency to collaborate with the Pinkerton Agency on your case," Cooper said.

"You'd be willing to do that?" Herman asked.

"If you're willing to pay our fees, certainly."

"I would be more than happy to pay any fee that would see whoever is behind the attempts on my life firmly behind bars."

Cooper glanced to Daphne. "What do you think? Are you agreeable to the idea of allowing me to work with you on this case?"

"Your assistance would be much appreciated, especially with Gabriella and Nicholas, who everyone knows are our most competent agents, out of town right now." Daphne nodded to Ann, who'd managed to climb to the top of the rope and was currently sitting on a branch, swinging her legs that were covered by the trousers all the ladies wore underneath their skirts during their exertion lessons. "In that plan I mentioned to you earlier, I was thinking it might be beneficial to have someone with me to help gather information at Mr. Henderson's house party. Ann told me earlier that the ladies she's paid to be a companion to are leaving the city to shop in Paris for the next month or so. Evidently those ladies have asked relatives to join them on their respective trips, so Ann's services aren't needed. I imagine she'd be able to join us and may even relish the opportunity of getting out of the city after deciding she and Gus are not well suited."

Cooper's gaze darted to Ann, then back to Daphne. "She's no longer enjoying company with Nicholas Quinn's coachman?"

"Ann has recently decided that Gus, while a charming man, is far too charming to every lady he encounters. In fact, Ann's of the opinion he's an incurable flirt, although

105

I have to admit that's a touch hypocritical because Ann frequently enjoys a spot of flirtation as well."

"She doesn't flirt with me," Cooper said.

Daphne's lips curved. "I've noticed the lack of flirting on Ann's part and have just recently, as in this morning, formed a few opinions about that circumstance — none of which I'm going to share with you, of course."

Cooper frowned. "Why not?"

"Because Ann is a friend. It would be a less-than-friendly gesture for me to share my opinions about her with you."

"But I thought we were friends."

"Which means I won't share my opinions about you to Ann either."

"I wouldn't have thought you'd have any opinions about me that you'd want to share with Ann" was all Cooper said to that as he shot another glance to Ann. "Your opinions aside, though, Ann has proven herself invaluable when it comes to gathering gossip. If she's agreeable to joining us, her abilities to snoop around could lend us an advantage. But what position would she be able to step into that wouldn't arouse suspicion from Mr. Henderson's guests?"

Herman cleared his throat. "We could always bring her in as a companion for my grandmother. I've been telling Grandmother she might enjoy a companion's company, so she won't be suspicious if Ann shows up to take that position."

"That would give her unfettered access to all your guests, especially your female ones," Daphne said.

"Then I'll tell my grandmother I've found her a companion," Herman said. "As for you, Miss Beekman, I had a few thoughts last night regarding how you might want to disguise yourself to blend in with my guests."

"I've had a few thoughts as well, although I have to be upfront and tell you that I've yet to broach your case with Eunice Holbrooke, even though I don't believe she'll balk at taking you on as a client," Daphne said. "With that said, and before we discuss matters further, I have to ask why you want to continue on with the Bleecker Street Inquiry Agency. I behaved in an unprofessional manner when I swooned, and that swoon happened after I assured you I wasn't prone to swooning as much as I used to be. That must have left you questioning the credentials of the rest of the agency."

"On the contrary, it did nothing of the sort. It wasn't as if your fit of the vapors came as much of a surprise, not after you made a point of confessing how your nerves occasionally get the better of you," Herman said. "Even still, that wouldn't have deterred me from wanting to hire your agency because you impressed me last night before you swooned."

"Impressed you how?"

"You didn't hesitate to question me in a relentless fashion, not backing down when I admittedly turned defensive about the questions you were asking. You're obviously more than competent when it comes to puzzling out plots, and that's what I need — someone to puzzle out the plot of who wants to kill me."

"Then I suppose there's nothing left to do now but speak with Eunice and then devise a plan of how we proceed from here," Daphne said. "You said you've had some thoughts about how I should disguise myself?"

"Well, first, in order to keep the peace with Sheldon, we'll tell everyone you're my new secretary, hired on because you know how to operate a typewriter. That will spare Sheldon the bother of having to travel all the way across the city to deliver my manuscripts to the establishment that usually types out my work," Herman said. "He shouldn't be upset about that because he was recently complaining about how long he had to wait for my last manuscript to be typed. Secondly, and because you'll be adopting the role of a secretary, I thought you should assume a wallflower disguise."

Daphne frowned. "I'm not certain you're understanding how disguises work."

"Of course I do. I often include them in my plots."

"Then you'll understand why I can't go undercover as a wallflower, considering I'm a wallflower by nature."

Herman's brows drew together. "Why would you think that?"

"Why wouldn't I think that?"

"Because you, Miss Beekman, are no wall-flower."

In the blink of an eye, Daphne's knees went all sorts of wobbly, and it took a great deal of effort to keep them from buckling and just as much effort to not grin from ear to ear. "Thank you for saying that, Mr. Henderson," she finally said. "And while not seeing me as a wallflower is one of the nicest things anyone has ever said about me, I assure you that there are more than a few people who would disagree with your assessment."

Amusement flickered through his eyes. "And I assure *you,* Miss Beekman, that anyone who believes you're a wallflower hasn't taken the time to see who you truly are. Wallflowers fade into the background. You're a lady who stands out in a crowd."

A prickle of something interesting began tickling her skin, followed by the thought that she was going to have to carry her smelling salts with her whenever she was in the vicinity of Mr. Herman Henderson, because . . .

"I think she's going to faint."

Blinking herself back to the situation at hand, Daphne found Cooper peering at her with clear concern in his eyes.

"I'm not going to faint. I'm merely feeling a touch warm, probably caused by the vigorous medicine ball activity."

"That was a good fifteen minutes ago," Cooper pointed out.

"I've, ah, always found the effects of vigorous activities linger with me for quite some time." She nodded to Herman. "But returning to the disguise business, while, again, it was very kind of you to proclaim you don't believe I'm a wallflower, I'm afraid that donning that particular disguise won't provide me with the inspiration needed to effectively ferret out a would-be murderer. I believe I'll be much more effective going undercover if I choose a disguise that's completely opposite of my normal personality. I'm much braver the deeper in disguise I am."

The amusement in Herman's eyes was immediately replaced with apprehension. "You're not about to suggest you don a pirate disguise, are you?"

"Certainly not. That would have your guests avoiding me. But dressing last night as a pirate did play a part in my deciding, as I pondered your case last night, what the perfect disguise would be for me to assume at your house party."

Cooper cleared his throat. "Forgive me for pointing this out, Daphne, but you swooned last night while dressed as a pirate."

"True, but not until I was set upon by fearsome dogs that longed to devour me. Before they arrived on the scene, my nerves were barely an issue, and that speaks volumes, given that I found myself alone at the agency with a stranger — and a large stranger, at that."

Cooper tilted his head. "What disguise could you possibly assume that will allow your nerves to not be an issue when you have to interact with Mr. Henderson's guests?"

"I'll need to attend the house party as a

111

lady of sophistication since I'm about the least sophisticated lady I know."

It should have come as no surprise when Herman and Cooper exchanged rather telling looks.

She crossed her arms over her chest. "Do neither of you believe I can pull off sophisticated?"

Cooper rubbed a finger against his nose. "Sophisticated is not a word that springs to mind when I think about you."

"I can do sophisticated."

Cooper shot a look of obvious desperation to Herman, who immediately began nodding. "I'm sure you *believe* you can assume the role of a sophisticated lady," Herman began, "but if you were to disguise yourself as a wallflower, you'll then be able to eavesdrop on all of my guests. Everyone knows that wallflowers are always overlooked."

"But eavesdropping will only take me so far," Daphne countered.

Herman frowned. "I fail to understand how adopting a sophisticated air will be more effective than a wallflower. The ladies my grandmother has invited to my house party are demure, retiring sorts, ones who would most assuredly give a sophisticated woman a wide berth."

"On the contrary," Daphne argued. "It'll be a moth-to-the-flame situation. Retiring young ladies are fascinated by sophisticated and worldly ladies. You mark my words, they'll be flocking around me from the time I arrive at your house."

"You're going to disguise yourself as a sophisticated *and* worldly lady?"

She gave a bob of her head. "It just came to me. A worldly lady would most assuredly attract a lot of attention. And, before either of you turn skeptical about that, you must also remember that I'm, ah, a poet. Everyone knows that most poets are worldly creatures. Why, I'm sure that once all the guests learn about my poetic abilities, they'll be scrambling to spend time in my company."

Daphne was not amused when Cooper suddenly spun around and strode away, his shoulders shaking in a very suspicious fashion.

"May I assume you've shared some of your poetry with Agent Clifton?" Herman asked, watching his retreating form.

"I might have mentioned the baby's bottom line to him today, but this really isn't the moment to discuss poetry. So, returning to my idea — a lady of sophistication is exactly the right identity for me to assume.

I'm well-versed in current events and politics, and after I read a few of the latest fashion magazines, I'll be capable of discussing that riveting topic as well. And because Monsieur Villard has been itching to take me in hand, this will give him the perfect reason to do that. I'll look exactly how everyone expects a lady of sophistication to appear."

"I don't know a single lady on my guest list who'll want to discuss politics or current events with you."

"I wasn't planning on talking to the ladies about those subjects. I'll reserve political talk for the men."

"I think you should leave the men to Agent Clifton."

"Because your gentlemen guests are going to be clamoring to spend time with a man who is going to be posing as your coachman?"

"You might have a point."

"Quite."

"But even so, you must realize that secretaries don't normally engage in conversations with their employer's guests. It might be hard to explain why my secretary is hobnobbing with everyone in attendance."

"I didn't consider that," Daphne conceded, tapping a finger against her chin before she brightened. "May I assume Sheldon attends events you host?"

"He does, but Sheldon's my cousin."

"And he's also your assistant. I'm going to pose as your secretary, and those positions should be equal in rank. You can use that as the reason behind including me in all the planned activities, saying something to the effect that you didn't want me to feel slighted, or you didn't want me to feel inferior to Sheldon, which might lead to animosity between the two of us."

Herman's brow furrowed. "I'm not certain that's a credible reason. It seems somewhat flimsy."

"It's not flimsy. It's brilliant, just as my disguise will be."

Herman opened his mouth, then closed it, as if he couldn't think up an argument to that. He frowned. "You just mentioned Monsieur Villard, as well as a Phillip Villard who is apparently giving one of your agents driving lessons. He's not the same Monsieur Villard who owns Villard's Dress Shop, is he?"

"One and the same. He's a good friend of mine who, besides being one of the most sought-after dressmakers in the city, helps the Bleecker Street Inquiry agents dress appropriately for whatever case we may be involved in."

"Why would Monsieur Villard involve himself with your agency?"

"We often suggest his dressmaking services to our clients." She smiled. "He's also smitten with Miss Elsy Evans, our coachwoman."

"I'm beginning to think your agency is far more complex than I realized."

"You have no idea." She gave a wave to Cooper, who was now standing with Ann, Judith, and Elsy, all three ladies dripping with mud.

"We're going to repair to the agency to discuss Mr. Henderson's case with Eunice," Daphne called.

Cooper nodded to the rope. "You haven't climbed this yet."

She bit back a grin. "True, but we shouldn't keep Mr. Henderson waiting while I complete my exercise regimen for the day."

"I don't mind waiting," Herman said.

Daphne wasn't certain, but she thought she saw Herman's lips twitch just the slightest bit. "That was not well done of you," she muttered before she squared her shoulders and marched her way toward Cooper, eyeing the rope. "I really see no reason for me to have to complete this particular task right now, Cooper. It's not as if I'm ever going to have to scale a tree."

"You were forced to escape from a costume ball out a second-story window," Cooper pointed out. "There's a chance you may need to do that again at some point."

"That's highly unlikely."

A quirk of a brow was Cooper's only response to that.

Realizing there was little chance Cooper was going to let her avoid the rope, Daphne reached out and grasped it in her hand. Giving it a tug to make certain it was still attached to the branch, she positioned herself in front of the tree trunk and then began pulling herself up. Her arms began shaking before she'd made it more than four feet up, and then a bee began buzzing right by her ear.

Unfortunately, swatting away a bothersome bee while climbing turned out to be a less-than-stellar idea because before she knew it, she was plummeting through the air.

A second later, she released an *oomph* as she hit the ground, the thought coming to her that she might have been a touch premature proclaiming she could embrace the role of sophisticated lady because there was absolutely nothing sophisticated about being sprawled in a mud puddle while under the watchful eye of a client — and an incredibly handsome client at that.

CHAPTER SIX

"I'm beginning to wonder if you were right and that the person trying to kill you might be a complete stranger to you after all."

Turning, Herman discovered Agent Cooper Clifton standing two feet away from him, the man's ability to steal up on a person incredibly unnerving, although given how many times the agent had stolen up on Herman over the week he'd been working undercover as Herman's coachman, one would have thought the man would have stopped taking him by surprise.

"Why do you wonder that?"

"Well, not only have there been no attempts on your life since we arrived at your Hudson estate two days ago, but everyone I've spoken with here has nothing but nice things to say about you."

"You sound disappointed about that. I, on the other hand, would hope most people *do* have nice things to say about me."

"I'm sure you do, but it makes the task of determining who wants you dead more difficult." Cooper ran a hand over his face. "Murders are usually committed by people known to the victim, but if that's not the case with you, it means we're dealing with an unknown. It could be anyone — even one of your readers who might have taken issue with the way you ended one of your books, or perhaps didn't care for how you killed someone off in a story."

"I haven't killed off anyone who didn't deserve an unfortunate end."

"What about animals?"

"Who wants to read about Fluffy the rabbit coming to an abrupt end?"

"I take it that means you avoid animal deaths, but . . . you've written about a Fluffy?"

"Since you're unfamiliar with Fluffy, I'm going to assume you're not a reader of my mysteries."

"I'll make sure to remedy that straightaway," Cooper said. "I have the newest Montague Moreland book to read, though, before I tackle one of yours."

"Montague Moreland does seem to be a reader favorite these days. He certainly has a way with writing dastardly plots into his stories."

"You read Montague Moreland's work?"

"Indeed. It's imperative for me to keep abreast of what other popular writers are writing, which allows me to plan accordingly for future projects."

"Daphne mentioned that exact notion to me not long ago. She enjoys barraging me with questions about my investigations and then discussing how she can use what I disclose in her writing."

Herman frowned. "She uses details from your Pinkerton cases in her poetry?"

"I'm not sure she's using those details in any poems because she hasn't shared any verses that center around missing people or bank robberies," Cooper said. "Truth be told, I'm somewhat hesitant to believe poetry is her genre of choice."

"And here I thought I was the only one who wasn't convinced Daphne's a poet. Any thoughts as to why she tells everyone she's a poet if she's not?"

"It's Daphne. Who knows what goes on in that complicated mind of hers?" Cooper shrugged. "But she might refuse to disclose what she really writes because women, and the talents they possess, are often deemed inconsequential by men."

"An interesting theory and might *exactly* explain why Daphne withholds the truth about her writing from everyone," Herman agreed. "I'm afraid the writing world most definitely holds women in disdain, unless they write books targeted toward a female audience. Even then, women writers don't receive the same level of respect men do."

"What I've come to realize during the time I've worked with the Bleecker Street Inquiry Agency," Cooper said, "is that women and their abilities should not be dismissed out of hand. The ladies involved with the agency are some of the brightest ladies I've ever met and have proven they have much to offer in the field of investigative work."

"It's still unusual that Daphne would use poetry as her genre of choice when she talks about her love for the written word."

"It's probably because there are very few people who enjoy listening to poetry. Most certainly don't enjoy listening to bad poetry, something Daphne seems to excel at composing."

"I'm surprised you haven't pressed her about what she really writes."

"And spoil the fun of her making up ridiculous verses on the spot? I think not."

"Speaking of Daphne . . ." Herman pulled out his pocket watch. "She should be arriving soon." He lifted a hand to shade his eyes from the sun, no trace of a carriage on the long drive that wove its way through a good portion of his six-hundred-acre estate. "I'm currently risking my grandmother's discontent by abandoning my guests to wait for Daphne, but I thought it would be wise to be immediately available to her once she arrives. Her nerves might be questionable since she's traveling on her own. I would hate to leave her swooning on the front vestibule before she's had a chance to convince everyone she's a sophisticated woman of the world."

"Maybe we should have brought Daphne along with us instead of having Ann and me arrive with you at your estate two days ago before your guests arrived."

Herman's lips curved. "Monsieur Villard was adamant that he needed additional time to finish up Daphne's wardrobe. He had a frantic look in his eyes when he made that declaration, something Daphne noticed as well because she was quick to assure everyone she'd be fine traveling on her own."

"Time will tell about that." Cooper's gaze settled on something behind Herman. "Someone just walked through the front door, so this is where I'll take my leave." With that, Cooper strode down the steps that led to the circular drive.

"I hope I didn't interrupt an important conversation with your coachman."

Turning, Herman found his grandmother, Mildred Henderson, heading his way, her attention settled on Cooper as he walked down the drive toward the coaching house that was out of sight of the main house, and past the Gentlemen's House, where any unmarried male guests stayed.

Mildred was looking well turned out in an ivory afternoon gown, her gray hair swept back from her face and secured in a knot at the nape of her neck. That she was almost seventy years old came as a surprise to many people because she could have easily passed for sixty. She, on the other hand, often claimed she would look even younger if she'd not suffered so much heartache in her life.

It was Herman's opinion that his grandmother's decision to step away from the hustle and bustle of life had been an unfortunate one, because the grandmother he had known from the time he'd been born until he'd turned ten had been full of fun and possessed an exuberance for life. Those qualities disappeared the moment she'd learned her husband, son, and daughter-in-law had been lost at sea.

Mildred had started to suffer horrible attacks of anxiety from that point on, those attacks increasing whenever she became worried about Herman. She'd eventually begun taking to her bed every time he came down with so much as a simple cold.

Herman's concern for her well-being had steadily grown over the years, which was why he hadn't balked when she'd taken a marked interest in matchmaking. Lately, that interest had seen her abandoning her preference to hide from the world, as she'd begun planning events such as the house party they were currently hosting. Herman took her willingness to host a house party as a step in the right direction, even though her matchmaking efforts were somewhat awkward for him since he'd been having a difficult time relating to any of the young ladies his grandmother wanted to become the future Mrs. Herman Henderson.

It wasn't that there was anything wrong with those ladies. Truthfully, they seemed delightful, except for the pesky feeling he had that none of them were the least bit enthusiastic about spending time in his company.

It was troubling, this lack of enthusiasm from the ladies, and left him in the unenviable position of spending an inordinate amount of time standing beside young ladies who seemed as if they wanted to be anywhere except standing next to him.

"Shall I assume that I *did* interrupt an important conversation with your coachman, one that might concern something troubling you're reluctant to disclose to me?" Mildred asked, stepping closer and pulling him from his thoughts.

He took hold of her arm and gave it a comforting squeeze. "Nothing troubling has occurred, Grandmother. Cooper and I were merely discussing horses. Nothing for you to fret about."

"But your new coachman *has* given me something to fret about," Mildred argued. "You've not told me anything about the man, nor what happened to Jenkins."

"Nothing happened to Jenkins. He merely took a few weeks off because he needed to visit his family."

Mildred's gaze sharpened on Herman. "Jenkins is an orphan. What family could he be visiting?"

Clearly, even though his grandmother had been hiding herself away for years, her mind was still sharp as a tack because Jenkins *was* an orphan, something Herman had forgotten. He summoned up a smile.

"On further consideration, I believe Jenkins may have mentioned he was off to visit an old friend who was like family. As for my new coachman, all you need to know is that Cooper came highly recommended. But speaking of new hires, how are you enjoying Miss Ann Evans?"

Mildred swatted away a fly that was buzzing by her head. "Ann is a charming young lady who is very solicitous of my nerves. She's even offered to read some books to the ladies to keep them entertained if they don't feel up to participating in some of our more vigorous activities planned, such as croquet."

"I never realized croquet was considered a vigorous activity."

"It entails walking about the lawn while swinging a mallet, so it's a very vigorous activity indeed. I'm certain many of the ladies gathered here will not want to participate in that type of activity, which is why it was lovely of Ann to volunteer to read to the ladies during the croquet match."

"Then I'm glad she was available to take up the post of paid companion to you."

"As am I. However, with that said, I'm concerned about all the new hires. You're not hiding something from me, are you?"

Before he could summon up an appropriate response to what was turning into a tricky conversation, the sound of hooves pounding against the cobblestone drive drew their attention.

The oddest inclination to laugh struck when a most unusual carriage raced into view. It was pure white except for the gold gilding that made up the trim and was drawn by four magnificent black horses that were wearing gilded harnesses and had gold feathers woven into their manes.

"Who in the world is that?" Mildred breathed. "Or better yet, why would anyone be agreeable to travel in a carriage moving at such a frightening rate of speed?"

He braced himself for what was certainly going to be another difficult conversation. "I believe that's my new secretary."

Mildred cocked a thin brow his way. "You've hired a secretary?"

"Did I neglect to mention that?"

"You did — and on purpose if I'm not mistaken, probably done so as to spare the state of my nerves."

"I do try to avoid upsetting you."

"You're failing miserably at that right now." Mildred lifted her chin. "Do not tell me that you've decided to get rid of poor Sheldon, have you? That would be difficult to explain to his mother."

"I'm not getting rid of Sheldon. Besides, he's my assistant, not my secretary, and the only reason I've hired a secretary is because I need someone who can type."

Mildred opened her mouth, additional questions clearly on the tip of her tongue, but before she could speak, the carriage pulled to a less-than-smooth stop beside the numerous steps that led to the front vestibule. Upon closer inspection, it turned out that there was not one but two coachmen sitting on the driver's seat. One of those coachmen Herman recognized as Monsieur Phillip Villard, whom he'd met not long after Daphne had taken her unfortunate tumble into the mud puddle during Cooper's physical exertion lessons.

Phillip was looking quite unlike his usual dapper self, although he had tucked what appeared to be a fashionable pocket square into the left breast pocket of his livery uniform, something a real coachman would have never worn, but something a stylish gentleman such as Phillip would have been hard-pressed to leave the house without.

Phillip took that moment to reach over and take the reins from his grinning counterpart, who turned out to be Miss Elsy Evans, who was wearing men's livery in an interesting shade of purple, her hair cleverly concealed underneath a top hat. Elsy straightened that hat before she leapt lightly to the ground and strode to the carriage door.

Anticipation began to build as Elsy opened the door. A second later, a lady's shoe came into view, and what a shoe it was. Made of an ivory-colored leather, it was a shoe one would expect to see in a fashion magazine — and a high fashion magazine at that.

A flutter of fabric drifted over the shoe as the lady wearing it stepped to the ground, and Herman felt his lips twitch when the lady wobbled in an obvious attempt to gain her balance.

Herman lifted his gaze and blinked, finding it almost impossible to fathom that the stylish, incredibly sophisticated, and yes, worldly lady standing outside the carriage was the same lady who'd been dressed as a pirate the first time he'd met her and dripping in mud the second.

He'd not believed Daphne when she'd claimed she could adopt a sophisticated look, but there was no question she'd done exactly that, or any question that the lady now adjusting spectacles that sparkled in the sunlight in no way resembled the Daphne Beekman he'd come to know.

Frankly, he didn't know what to make of her, nor did he know why he was suddenly finding it difficult to breathe in a normal capacity, but before he could dwell on any of that, his grandmother turned to him with a frown.

"On my word, but I don't believe I've ever seen a secretary who looks like that," Mildred said before she waved a gloved hand Daphne's way. "Honestly, Herman, what *could* you have been thinking? Surely you must realize that every lady here who might be interested in securing your affections will most assuredly see your new secretary as a distinct threat." Mildred squinted in Daphne's direction. "Is it my imagination or does she have the look of an adventuress about her?"

"She's not an adventuress, nor is she here to win my affections. She's simply here to type up my latest manuscript, and —"

"Herman," Daphne suddenly called, drawing their attention. "Be a darling and help me get Almira up the steps. She's heavier than she looks, and I wouldn't want any harm to befall her."

Mildred raised a hand to her throat. "Dare I hope you're not about to tell me Almira is yet another person you neglected to inform me you hired?"

"Almira is Miss Beekman's typewriter."

"How very odd," Mildred muttered before she squared her shoulders. "But Almira the typewriter aside, surely I misheard Miss Beekman and she did not just address you by your given name — or worse yet, call you darling."

He'd been hoping his grandmother hadn't heard that, but evidently, her hearing was just as sharp as her mind. "I believe she asked if I'd *be* a darling and help her with her typewriter, which is a great deal different than calling me darling."

"But she did call you Herman."

His mind whirled with numerous explanations, not one of them seeming very credible, probably because he had no idea why Daphne had decided to use his given name instead of maintaining the formal manner of address most secretaries kept with their employers. He forced a smile. "Miss Beekman enjoys adopting a level of informality with everyone she spends a lot of time with, and, in fact, prefers for me to address her as . . . Daphne."

Mildred's eyes widened. "Does she now?" She glanced Daphne's way, considered her for a few seconds, then returned her attention to Herman. "And you indulge Miss Beekman's preference for informality?"

His collar began to feel incredibly snug. "I might have used her given name upon occasion, but there really isn't any harm in that."

Mildred went from looking like a kindly grandmother to a formidable matron in a split second as she seemed to swell on the spot. "Of course there's harm in it." She moved closer to him. "I've spent the last twenty-odd years protecting you, and yet I'm getting the distinct impression that Miss Beekman is going to pose more of a danger to you than anything I could have ever anticipated." She shot another look to Daphne. "Do know that I'll be keeping a close eye on her, and if I'm proven right about that danger, I will not hesitate to see her removed from your vicinity, even if that means I have to toss her on the first available boat sailing down the Hudson myself."

CHAPTER SEVEN

Daphne hefted Almira from the carriage and set her down on the cobblestone drive, giving a swat to Phillip Villard, who was in the process of fiddling with her bustle, which would certainly come across as peculiar if any of Herman's guests were to take note of it since Phillip was currently dressed for the role of coachman, not dress designer.

"Really, Phillip, stop that," she said when her swatting had no effect on the man as he continued his fiddling.

"I'm not sending you off to meet Herman's guests with your bustle askew," Phillip shot back. "You're wearing an original Monsieur Villard traveling gown. It deserves to be seen in pristine condition. Bustles that are askew hardly lend a gown a pristine air, although how your bustle got in such a deplorable state is beyond me. It was perfectly in place when you got into the carriage before we left the city."

"We left the city what feels like days ago. I'd like to see you keep a bustle in place after enjoying a long and, need I add, bumpy carriage ride. Why you decided to dress me in a traveling gown that requires the largest bustle anyone has ever been unfortunate enough to wear is beyond me. I was forced to perch on the very edge of my seat for the entire ride."

"Large bustles are what any stylish lady is wearing this year. Because you're determined to pass yourself off as sophisticated, I suggest you stop complaining and readjust your attitude."

"It's hard to readjust an attitude when you're wearing what amounts to half a barrel on your backside. If you ask me, ladies of sophistication might want to consider balking at the ridiculous garments that male designers are always forcing them to wear. There's nothing sophisticated about being bottom heavy, which begs the question why ladies haven't risen up in revolt against such fashions years ago."

Phillip's brows drew together. "I've never heard the words *fashion* and *revolt* in the same sentence before. Ladies know that, on occasion, one must forgo comfort in order to present the world with a certain appearance."

"Wonderful advice coming from a gentleman," Daphne retorted. "But while forgoing comfort to embrace a certain style has certainly been the accepted rule for centuries, if we women would abandon fashions that leave us barely able to breathe, perhaps we could then begin to move forward in a truly progressive way, one where our clothing wouldn't limit what we can actually accomplish. We then wouldn't be subjected to wearing bustles or that most dreadful of inventions, the corset — an invention *I've* recently been considering abandoning."

"I hope you've set aside your determination to abandon your unmentionables, because I don't think my grandmother will look kindly on that. I would also caution you to avoid bringing up unmentionables in any conversations you may share with her. Unfortunately, she's already suspicious of you, and that's without the two of you exchanging so much as a single word."

Turning, Daphne found Herman striding down the steps to join her, looking dapper in a tailored blue suit and wearing a pocket square that Phillip was eyeing in approval. Elsy suddenly took hold of Phillip's arm and began pulling him toward the back of the carriage, muttering a reminder to Phillip that a coachman really shouldn't be giving Herman such a marked perusal.

Returning her attention to Herman, Daphne felt a most unexpected flutter set up residence in her stomach, until the words he'd recently spoken settled in.

"Do not say that your grandmother has already figured out that you've hired inquiry agents, because that will hardly bode well for the investigation that needs to be done at your house party."

"The suspicions my grandmother has formed have nothing to do with the investigation, but everything to do with you."

"But I only just arrived."

"And what an arrival it was," he said, nodding to the carriage. "I'm afraid your choice of vehicle only aided my grandmother's conviction regarding what type of lady you are." He winced. "After taking one look at you, she believes that you're an adventuress who is certain to dash the hopes of every young lady in attendance who is interested in me."

She drew in a sharp breath. "I've never *been* mistaken for an adventuress before and must admit I find that idea delightful."

"Delight is not a reaction I expected from my disclosure, but you must have a care with how you deal with my grandmother from this point forward. She, even with her questionable nerves, is not a lady to trifle with. Quite honestly, after she heard you address me by my given name, I wouldn't be surprised if she's even now devising a plan to see you quickly removed from my estate."

"Surely not."

Herman turned and waved to an older woman standing at the top of the steps. That woman, apparently Mildred Henderson, gave Herman a half-hearted wave in return before she turned on her heel, disappearing into the house. "Was there a reason you decided to adopt an air of informality between us?"

"Madame Sophia Calve suggested I adopt an informal air with everyone."

"I'm afraid you're going to have to explain that further."

"She's an opera singer."

Herman blinked. "You're talking about *the* Madame Calve?"

"One and the same." Daphne adjusted the brim of her hat. "I became acquainted with her a mere day and a half ago after she paid a visit to the agency, not that I can expand on that because it's a confidential matter. However, while she was waiting to speak to

Eunice, she happened to see Phillip."

Daphne gave a wave toward Phillip, who was now grunting as he tried to wrestle one of her large trunks from the top of the carriage, Elsy offering suggestions to him, which Phillip ignored.

"Madame Calve adores Phillip, as well as his designs, and insisted on accompanying him to the boardinghouse, where I was waiting for Phillip to alter my new worldly and sophisticated wardrobe." She smiled. "I knew within seconds of meeting Madame Calve that she was exactly the type of lady I wanted to portray myself as during your house party. Fortunately for me, she didn't hesitate to give me pointers so that I would be successful pulling off the daunting feat of adopting an attitude like hers."

"I have no idea how it came to be that Madame Calve convinced you to abandon formality between us," Herman said. "Secretaries are expected to address their employers as Mr. So-and-So. They're certainly not expected to call out to their employer in a manner that suggests there's more than a working relationship between them — something my grandmother, unfortunately, might believe."

Daphne's eyes widened. "Why would she believe that?"

"You asked me to be a darling and help you with your typewriter."

"Hmm . . . perhaps that was a bit much, but I was encouraged by Madame Calve to use endearments such as *darling, sugar plum, dearest,* and . . . well, I'll have to check my list for the other suggestions she gave me. I now find myself wondering if the use of *darling* was only supposed to be brought out under specific circumstances."

"I think you may want to abandon your use of endearments, especially since my grandmother will not react well to your calling me sugar plum. That would certainly leave her convinced you managed to entice me into hiring you by using your feminine allure, something I'm relatively sure she's already convinced you've done."

"She thinks I have feminine allure?"

"Why do I get the distinct impression, given the way your eyes have suddenly begun to sparkle, that you find that to be another delightful notion?"

"You'd find it delightful as well if no one had ever suggested you possess any allure. I may have to pen a letter to my mother straightaway and inform her of this unlikely happenstance. She'll find your grandmother's opinion about me very encouraging."

"Oh, this is going to be a disaster," Herman muttered.

"Now, don't be like that, sugar plum." Daphne reached into the carriage and withdrew her large bag, slinging the strap over her shoulder. "It's not going to be a disaster because what I observed the most about Madame Calve is that her appeal rests directly with her charm."

"My grandmother is hardly going to be charmed if you take to calling me sugar plum," Herman reiterated.

"I needed to see if it would roll off my tongue with ease, and I do believe it did, although *poppet* comes easier, as does *precious*. However, I can't very well call you precious because of Precious the poodle. If I start seeing that Precious in my mind, I may very well start laughing, which would completely ruin the façade."

"Do not, under any circumstances, address Herman as poppet."

Herman gave a bit of a start before he leaned forward and peered into the dark confines of the carriage. "I didn't see you there, Mrs. Holbrooke, but allow me to say that it's quite impressive how you're able to blend into the shadows so well, even though you do take a few years off a person's life when you finally decide to reveal yourself."

"I'm sure I only startled you because you're on edge these days, thinking an assailant could be lurking in every shadow, something we at the Bleecker Street Inquiry Agency are hoping to get rectified for you soon," Eunice said, sitting forward, not a hint of her face to be seen since she'd pulled her many veils into place. "But in the spirit of Daphne's embrace of informality, please, call me Eunice. Under no circumstance, though, should you call me sugar plum or, heaven forbid, poppet."

Herman's lips twitched. "I can't think of a circumstance where I'd feel inclined to call you sugar plum. Any suggestions on how I'm supposed to explain *you* to my grandmother? I was unaware you were joining us."

"No need to fret because I'm not joining you," Eunice returned. "I decided it would be prudent to keep Daphne company on the long ride here to help keep her nerves in check."

"How *is* the state of her nerves?"

"Didn't see a trace of them on our journey, so I believe she's fine."

Daphne crossed her arms over her chest. "You told me you were accompanying me because you needed to provide Elsy and Phillip with a chaperone, and because you wanted an opportunity to enjoy the luxurious carriage Madame Calve so generously loaned to us for the trip."

"Who wouldn't want to ride in a carriage like this?" Eunice asked, giving the cushy seat a pat. "And I did want to provide Elsy and Phillip with my services as a chaperone. It would have been irresponsible to leave them alone together on the long ride back to the city. That could have caused all sorts of talk, even with Elsy dressed as a man."

Herman scratched his chin. "I never considered that Bleecker Street agents needed to worry about chaperones."

"It's a matter we certainly can't neglect," Eunice said briskly. "The reputations of our agents must be protected at all costs because there are many men in the city who are already doing their best to see our little agency close its doors forever. That means we can't chance any hint of impropriety. Those men would swoop on that in a heartbeat, even with our now having the blessing of Reverend Patrick Danford, vicar at St. Luke's Chapel. Reverend Danford has recently begun aiding us with cases that involve unethical landlords. However, even with his participation, we still face challenges from men in the city who don't believe women have any business operating an inquiry agency."

Herman shoved a hand in his pocket, retrieving his ever-handy notepad. "I know this is hardly the time to linger about asking questions, but I can't resist asking how Reverend Danford is assisting you with unethical landlords, or better yet, how he became involved with the agency in the first place."

Eunice scooted forward on the seat. "One of our agents, Miss Betsy Adler, works during the day as Reverend Danford's assistant at St. Luke's. She told him about a landlord we were investigating who takes money from single women, then claims they never paid him rent and evicts them without notice. Reverend Danford was troubled by that and insisted on traveling with Betsy to have a chat with this man."

"We were pleased to discover that the inclusion of a man of the cloth had this landlord miraculously remembering that he collected rent from these women," Daphne added. "Reverend Danford offered to step in if we were presented with other cases involving unscrupulous landlords. Sadly, we've been presented with numerous cases of that, which has kept Reverend Danford and Betsy busy." She smiled. "They've discovered a great deal of success when Reverend Danford begins reciting verses from Proverbs, his favorite one being 'Bread of deceit is sweet to a man; but afterwards his mouth shall be filled with gravel.' "

It really came as no surprise when Herman began scribbling away.

"It appears your entrance has drawn attention, what with all the people who are now streaming out of Herman's house," Eunice suddenly said, interrupting Herman's writing. "I believe this is where Elsy, Phillip, and I should take our leave."

Daphne glanced up and discovered at least twenty people mingling in the vestibule, the sight of them causing the breath to catch in her throat.

"You'll be fine," Phillip said, moving to stand beside her. "Just remember, you're a lady of sophistication. Everyone will be clamoring to seek your favor, as well as discover who created your delightfully stylish wardrobe."

Her breathing immediately returned to normal as she grinned. "And I'll be certain to tell them that every article of clothing I possess came from Villard's Dress Shop."

Phillip rubbed his hands together. "I can already envision the sales. But do take care, and remember, if you feel you're getting in over your head, Ann is here to help you, as well as Agent Clifton." He turned to Herman before he gestured to the pile of trunks now stacked on the drive. "Shall I take those inside, or shall I leave them for one of your footmen?"

Herman stuck his notepad back in his pocket and turned his attention to the trunks, his eyes widening. "My footmen will take care of that. But surely not all four of those trunks are for Daphne, are they?"

Phillip smiled. "A sophisticated woman requires an extensive wardrobe." He brushed a piece of lint from his sleeve. "We're fortunate I've been designing my own line of late, which is how I was able to provide Daphne with enough clothes to see her through a week's stay here."

"It looks like she's intending to stay a month."

"Be thankful this is spring and not winter. Had it been winter, she would have needed at least eight trunks." Phillip sent Daphne a wink, then went to join Elsy, who'd already climbed up on the driver's seat and was smiling as she held the reins in a somewhat practiced hand. Her smile dimmed when Phillip held out his hand, and with a dramatic sigh, Elsy turned the reins over to him.

"I'll see you next week," Eunice said when Daphne stuck her head back into the carriage to bid her friend good-bye. "If you have any difficulties, send a telegram, but I'm sure you'll be fine. Remember, you're braver than you think, which reminds me." Eunice began rummaging around in her reticule. "Reverend Danford wanted me to give you this."

Daphne unfolded the paper and read over the words written on the page. *Be strong and of good courage; be not afraid, neither be thou dismayed: for the Lord thy God is with thee whithersoever thou goest.* She tucked the paper into her bag. "It's an encouraging verse, although I'm not sure God expects me to be courageous. I began asking Him for courage years ago, but sadly, that request has never been granted."

After bidding Eunice another good-bye, Daphne stepped away from the carriage, watching as Phillip steered it expertly around the circular drive and began heading down the lane. Drawing in a steadying breath, she squared her shoulders and faced Herman's house, taking a second to appreciate the magnificence of his country home.

Three-and-a-half stories high, the exterior was a moody shade of pewter and appeared to be stucco overlaid on stone. *Dignified* was the word that sprang to mind to describe the air surrounding the house, likely brought about because of the four pillars that reached to the second level and flanked a door that was stained a deep mahogany. At least twenty steps led from the drive to the vestibule, and as Daphne's gaze returned to the front door, she discovered Herman's guests still assembled there, their attention turned her way.

She readjusted the spectacles Phillip had insisted she purchase to complete her masquerade, ones that sported glittering cut-glass stones marching along the frame that tended to blind her if the sun hit them just right, and took a closer look at Herman's guests. Half of them were ladies, all of whom seemed to be whispering behind gloved hands, their attention settled on her.

That attention recalled her to the role she was supposed to be playing.

Refusing to acknowledge nerves that were attempting to make themselves known, Daphne raised a hand and sent the crowd what she hoped would come across as a languid yet oh-so-sophisticated wave.

It took a great deal of effort to swallow a laugh when every guest waved back at her.

Herman picked Almira up before he offered her his arm. "Are you ready for this?" he asked.

"As ready as I'll ever be." She linked her arm with his and then they began to climb the steps, finding herself praying that the heels she was unaccustomed to wearing wouldn't trip her up. Reaching the landing, she breathed a sigh of relief, the relief short-lived, though, when she realized that Mildred Henderson had reappeared and was currently in the process of shooing all the guests into the house.

Herman pulled Daphne to a stop and winced, a telling gesture if there ever was one. "Now, no need for alarm, but it appears that Grandmother wants to be introduced to you without an audience."

"I'd be less alarmed if you hadn't just winced," Daphne muttered right as the last of the guests disappeared through the front door and Mildred turned her attention on Daphne.

Daphne felt a distinct inclination to turn and flee down the long drive when Mildred began looking her up and down, quite as if she were taking her measure. Given the way Mildred's brows were now drawn together, it was not much of a stretch to conclude the lady found her lacking.

"Grandmother," Herman began as he gave Daphne's arm a reassuring squeeze, which did have the inclination to flee fading the slightest bit, "it is my pleasure to introduce you to Miss Daphne Beekman. Daphne, this is my grandmother, Mrs. William Henderson."

Summoning what she hoped was a charming smile, Daphne dipped into a curtsy and straightened, not taking it as an encouraging sign when Mildred narrowed blue eyes on her. "I'm delighted to meet you, Mrs. Henderson."

For the briefest of moments, Mildred didn't respond, her gaze settled on Herman's arm, one that Daphne was now gripping rather tightly with her gloved hand. The impulse to flee returned in a flash.

Mildred lifted her chin and directed a smile at Daphne that held not a smidgen of warmth. "And *of course* it's delightful to meet you as well, Miss Beekman. I hope you'll enjoy your stay here on the Hudson, however brief it may turn out to be."

CHAPTER EIGHT

To Herman's astonishment, Daphne's decision to adopt the role of sophisticated and charming lady of the world seemed to be working.

From the moment she made her appearance on the back veranda, after freshening up in the attic room she was to share with Ann, Daphne had garnered attention from every guest in attendance. Most keen to make her acquaintance had been the gentlemen, who clamored for an introduction to her, then proclaimed themselves completely charmed when she insisted they address her as Daphne.

The ladies seemed to be charmed by Daphne, as well, flocking around her as they *ooh*ed over her afternoon gown that had a bustle even larger than the one she'd been wearing when she'd arrived at his estate. Daphne took the attention in stride, even as she peppered her conversations with his guests with the most unusual of endearments.

So far, he'd heard her call Jay Storrow *buttercup,* Martin Corrigan *dearie,* Charles Bonner *ma puce,* which was rather odd because Herman was relatively certain that translated to *my flea,* and Albert Gallatin, who'd never been comfortable speaking with the lady set, *sweet pea.*

She'd not reserved her endearments only for the gentlemen, though. Miss Finetta Shoenburger had become *mopsy,* Miss Alida Armstrong *doll,* Miss Vanetta Cornbury *mon chou,* which he thought meant *my cabbage,* and then Miss Martha Mulvey *mon lapin,* roughly translated into *my rabbit.*

He hadn't been able to resist scribbling all those names down in his notepad because given the enthusiastic reaction to her endearments, he was considering having a future character in one of his books embrace a fondness for pet names.

As Daphne mingled with his guests, dispensing sweet nothings at will, Herman hadn't neglected to notice her teetering more than a few times on the heels he was relatively sure she was unused to wearing. To give her credit, she'd recovered nicely after every wobble, her recovery aided time and again by gentlemen who couldn't offer her the use of their steadying hands fast enough.

Their solicitous behavior toward Daphne was leaving him feeling disgruntled, as well as annoyed, which was decidedly out of character for him, especially since he didn't want Daphne to suffer a tumble. He knew full well he couldn't monopolize her time, nor neglect his other guests by sticking to her side in case she stumbled again, especially when he was aware that Daphne was doing exactly what he'd hired her to do — ingratiating herself with his guests in order to ferret out a would-be murderer.

To give her credit, she was certainly succeeding with the whole ingratiating business, even though the tactic she was using — blatant flirtation — was causing his grandmother to look as if she were actually contemplating her earlier threat of personally escorting Daphne to the ferry station and buying her a one-way ticket back to New York City.

Thankfully, Ann Evans had apparently realized how irritated Mildred was becoming and had stepped in and gotten his guests settled around the veranda, telling them she was about to begin reading the first chapter from her favorite Montague Moreland book.

He wasn't surprised when Daphne chose

to sit directly next to Miss Finetta Shoenburger, instead of sitting beside any of the gentlemen who'd extended invitations for her to sit beside them during the reading. Miss Shoenburger was, after all, at the top of Daphne's list of possible suspects.

Mildred had not cared for Daphne's desire to make an acquaintance with Finetta in the least, making her way across the veranda for an intervention, one that never occurred because Ann took that moment to begin chapter one of *Murder, Mayhem, and Mischief.* That had Mildred stopping in her tracks, then taking the nearest available seat, obviously unwilling to interrupt an activity she'd assured their guests they were going to adore, even though she settled a frown on Daphne.

When Ann finished chapter one and continued to chapter two, Herman noticed Daphne perusing the crowd, peeping over one of the brightly colored fans his grandmother had provided to stave off the heat, even though it was a mild spring day. As she gazed around, she kept swaying back and forth, as if she were having a hard time maintaining her balance on the chair, the monstrous bustle she was wearing taking up most of the seat.

"As difficult as this is for me to admit,

I'm enjoying this reading of Montague Moreland's book."

Pulling his attention from Daphne, who was now smiling at Finetta, who'd just gasped at what even Herman had to admit was a riveting passage in Moreland's book, he found Mr. Jay Storrow, one of a half-dozen writers he'd invited to the house party, strolling up to join him.

Herman smiled. "Moreland does craft an exceptional mystery."

"Have you ever met him?"

"No, but I had the pleasure of meeting Mr. James Durnham, Moreland's editor, at a literary luncheon last year. When I inquired about his reclusive client, all Mr. Durnham would say about the man was that Moreland treasures his privacy."

"Treasuring privacy or not, I find it curious that a writer of Moreland's acclaim is rarely seen. In fact, I don't know any other writers who've met the man," Jay said.

"It is curious, and I'm surprised Mr. Durnham hasn't insisted Moreland make at least a few public appearances. There's nothing that sells more books than allowing readers an opportunity to meet their favorite author in person."

Jay nodded to Ann, who was now gesturing wildly with one hand while holding

Moreland's book in the other. "He might have made at least one public appearance, because that copy Miss Evans is reading from is signed and includes a personal note to Miss Evans from Moreland."

Before Herman could respond to that, Ann closed the book and smiled. "That's the end of chapter three. I'll stop there for the day and pick up again tomorrow." She directed her smile at Mildred. "If I'm not mistaken, your grandson has arranged for a rousing game of croquet next, hasn't he?"

"I believe he has," Mildred began, "although I know many a young lady might not care for such a strenuous activity, so do continue with the story, Miss Evans."

To Herman's surprise, Finetta suddenly raised her hand. "Forgive me, Mrs. Henderson, but if Miss Evans continues, the guests interested in playing croquet may be reluctant to do so now because the mystery is really beginning to heat up." She nodded to Miss Martha Mulvey, who was the paid companion to Finetta's grandmother. "Miss Mulvey has remarked several times about how much she's looking forward to the croquet match, but I can see that she's clearly as swept up in this enthralling story as everyone else is. She'll be forced to miss what I'm convinced are going to be thrilling chapters, as well as miss clues as to who the dastardly culprit is behind trying to murder the hero."

"Everyone should have already surmised that the culprit is, of course, the butler."

Directing his gaze to the gentleman who'd just possibly ruined the book for many guests, if he'd been correct with his conclusion, Herman was unsurprised to discover the man behind the statement was Mr. Charles Bonner, a writer himself, who should have known better than to divulge anything about a plot twist to a rapt audience. He was also the man Daphne had called *ma puce,* and amusingly enough, given that the man had just made an incredibly rude declaration, the endearment that meant *my flea* seemed rather fitting.

Before he could summon a response to Charles's rudeness, though, Daphne was rising to her feet.

"Begging your pardon, Mr. Bonner," she began, "but I fear you're completely off the mark. I assure you, the butler is not to blame."

An indulgent smile played around the corners of Charles's mouth, one Herman had seen often, especially when Charles felt he was speaking with a person not possessed of the lofty intellect he often claimed to possess. "While it is true that I've not read this particular book, butlers are often to blame for the skullduggery at hand."

Daphne readjusted her spectacles. "Not in any Montague Moreland book I've read. Nor do I believe you'll find that somewhat trite trope in any of Herman's books or Mr. Jay Storrow's work, for that matter."

Jay stood up a little straighter. "She's read my books?"

"All of them," Herman said as Charles began turning red in the face.

"What did you mean by trite trope?" Charles demanded.

Daphne tilted her head. "Come now, *ma poule,*" she began, causing Herman to swallow a laugh because he knew for a fact that *poule* was French for chicken, not that he was certain Daphne knew that. "From what I've heard about you, you're an author who has sold an impressive number of books. With that type of success, I would assume you know exactly what a trite trope is. Writing a butler into the story as the dastardly villain who is disclosed, of course, at the very end of the tale is a trite trope if there ever was one and should be avoided at all costs."

As Charles's face began to turn from red to purple, Daphne directed her attention to

Perkins, Herman's butler, who'd been standing off to the side of the room. "I'm certain you would agree with that, wouldn't you, Mr. Perkins?"

Perkins blinked, blinked again, then began looking decidedly uncomfortable, probably because of all the attention now being directed his way.

Perkins was not a man who liked attention, preferring to maintain a stoic demeanor at all times, something he'd claimed to have learned at his former place of employment, where he'd been the under-butler to a butler who'd once worked for a member of the British aristocracy.

Oddly enough, even though he'd been trained by such an illustrious butler, and even though Perkins was always dressed to perfection in a formal dark suit, with nary a hair out of place, he was merely adequate at his duties. Truthfully, the main reason Herman had hired the man five years ago was because Perkins was distantly related to Mr. Conkling, who'd been the Henderson butler when Herman's father had been alive. Mr. Conkling had, tragically, perished in the same boating accident as Herman's parents.

"I'm sure it's not my position to comment one way or the other," Perkins said, drawing Herman from his thoughts. "But please, you may address me as simply Perkins, Miss Beekman. There's no need for the mister."

Daphne beamed a bright smile at the man. "And aren't you just *adorable*? How kind of you to insist I adopt an informal attitude with you, which means you must call me Daphne in return."

Perkins's mouth gaped open the slightest bit as Mildred rose to her feet, her color high and her eyes flashing in a most un-Mildred-like manner. Before Perkins or his grandmother could get a word out of their mouths, though, such as the fact that he hadn't exactly been offering Daphne leave to abandon formality with him because everyone addressed Perkins as Perkins, Daphne was walking Perkins's way, wobbling a bit on her heels. She stopped directly in front of him.

"As for it not being your place to give your opinion, Perkins, I fear I must disagree with that. Who better to add some valuable insight on this matter than a real butler?" She gestured around the room. "There are many mystery writers in attendance right now. You'd be doing them a great service by disclosing your thoughts."

Perkins gave a bit of a shudder. "I really *don't* have an opinion on the matter because I've never dwelled on it before."

Daphne tilted her head. "Dwelled on the idea of butlers being used as villains, or dwelled on murderous intentions in regard to your employer?"

In the blink of an eye, Herman understood exactly why Daphne had the reputation at the Bleecker Street Inquiry Agency of being a master at figuring out plots. What had started as an innocent questioning of the butler seemed to have turned into something so much more.

"I have *never* had murderous intentions toward Mr. Henderson," Perkins said firmly. "Logically, it makes no sense for a butler to murder anyone in the family he serves because that would inevitably deny him his livelihood."

Instead of responding to that, Daphne flipped open her notepad and began jotting something down, drawing more than a few curious looks from the guests in the process and causing Charles Bonner to move to join her.

"What could you possibly be writing?"

Daphne lifted her head and smiled. "I couldn't resist jotting down what Perkins just said, because that was a brilliant explanation for why a butler wouldn't want to follow through with a dastardly deed even if he did have murderous intentions toward his employer." She gestured to the group of writers standing on the veranda. "Frankly, I'm surprised none of you saw fit to write that down, as well. It was very insightful and certainly allowed us a glimpse into the mind of a butler, which I don't believe any of us have the privilege to do often."

Charles's lips quirked into yet another indulgent smile. "I believe I'm finally beginning to understand what motivated you to make your absurd declaration about trite tropes. You long to become a writer, don't you?"

Daphne tucked her notepad into a pocket. "I'm already a writer. A, ah, poet, to be exact."

Charles's smile turned more indulgent than ever. "And you think you'll have a need for a butler in a piece of your poetry?"

"One never knows what may capture a writer's interest, turn into a muse for them, and result in a brilliant piece of work. I'm currently writing a poem that has a pirate in it, but I could possibly decide to include a butler, as well. The possibilities for conflict are endless since butlers and pirates don't normally share time on a page with each other."

Whatever Charles said in response to that, Herman didn't hear because Mildred suddenly materialized by his side, her cheeks a noticeable shade of pink.

"You've hired a woman who fancies herself a writer? Honestly, Herman, did you not consider that there could be a distinct possibility she only wants to work as your secretary because she's interested in stealing your words and passing them off as her own?"

"She writes poetry. The words I write are hardly conducive to poetry."

"Perhaps she's not content with simply penning poems. She might have grander plans in mind — those plans assisted by a touch of plagiarism."

"And perhaps it wasn't a good idea to have Ann read from a Montague Moreland novel because your imagination has obviously gone into high alert."

"I'm not simply imagining that Miss Beekman could very well be up to something. I've always been intuitive about such matters, and my intuition is humming madly away."

Since Daphne was definitely up to something, but not anything he wanted to disclose to his grandmother, Herman was thankful when Miss Martha Mulvey walked up to join them.

"Shall we gather the guests who want to

play croquet before that" — she turned and nodded to where Daphne and Charles now seemed to be engaged in a heated debate — "turns more concerning than it already is?"

"A wonderful idea," Herman said, stepping forward and gesturing to the crowd milling about the veranda. "If the guests interested in playing croquet will follow me, the staff has set up the croquet field on the side lawn, which offers a lovely view of the Hudson."

Thankfully, Daphne abandoned her debate with Charles and joined a group of young ladies, moseying with them toward the side lawn.

Mildred took hold of Herman's arm before he could move to join his guests. "I'm finding myself very confused as to why Miss Beekman is being included in the festivities. Are you not worried that her inclusion is going to be a source for gossip at some point since it's rather unusual for a secretary to enjoy all the amusements offered at a house party?"

"I couldn't very well have excluded her, not when Sheldon's always invited to join in with any festivities we host."

"Sheldon's your cousin. Family can be expected to be included."

He summoned up a smile. "True, but

Sheldon's also my assistant. I certainly wouldn't want to injure Daphne's feelings by excluding her since assistants and secretaries are remarkably similar positions."

"That type of logic suggests you should also consider inviting the butler and the housekeeper to join the croquet match because their positions are considered the highest in the household."

Clearly, he'd been spot-on when he'd told Daphne her explanation for mingling with his guests was a flimsy one and really should have convinced her to think up something better.

Taking a second to try to figure out where to take the conversation from there, Herman was spared a response when Mildred sent him a look of exasperation and marched away at a very fast clip, straight in Daphne's direction.

Knowing there was nothing to do but try and distract his grandmother before she reached Daphne, Herman strode into motion, making it all of three feet before he was intercepted by Charles Bonner, who was looking incredibly put out.

"You might want to speak with your new secretary about the inadvisability of insulting your guests, Herman," Charles began. "I'd hate to see anyone feel compelled to vacate this charming house party over the inappropriate insults your secretary may level at them, such as the one she leveled against me."

Herman began walking toward the croquet field again, Charles falling into step beside him. "I don't know how Daphne insulted you."

"She called the butler business a trite trope."

"And how was that an insult to you?"

"The butlers in both of my novels, as you should well remember, turn out to be the villains. Not only was I insulted by Daphne suggesting that specific plot point is trite, but I was also insulted because even though it appears she's well-read, she's evidently never bothered to pick up one of my books, which have been very well received."

Since no good could possibly come from telling Charles he'd never been able to finish either of the man's books, which was why he hadn't known Charles had written butlers as the murderer in both works, Herman struggled for a reply that wouldn't further injure the man's wounded pride.

"I'm sure Daphne meant no personal offense. Since she's seemingly not read your books, you shouldn't be too put out with her, not when the butler trope is known to be somewhat overused at times — not, of course, by a writer of your caliber but by other, less-accomplished writers."

"I don't write trite."

"Then there's nothing for you to take issue with, is there?"

Charles looked as if he wanted to argue that point but was interrupted from doing so when they reached the group of guests gathered on the side lawn. Miss Martha Mulvey immediately handed Herman a mallet, but Charles shook his head.

"No need to find me a mallet because I don't enjoy croquet," he said.

"Of course you don't" was all Miss Mulvey said in reply before she smiled at Herman. "Sheldon told me you prefer using the red mallet. I took it upon myself to get the red mallet for you so you wouldn't have to miss playing with your favorite color."

Herman returned the smile. He'd only recently become acquainted with Martha after she took up the position of paid companion to Finetta's grandmother and began attending the same gatherings that he and Finetta did. She was a pleasant young lady, who was very considerate, and it hadn't escaped his notice that she and Sheldon were beginning to spend an inordinate amount of time together.

"That was kind of you," he said. "But tell me, where *is* Sheldon? I saw him this morning, but I haven't seen him since. It's not like him to miss the festivities we've planned."

"I believe he's still on a research mission, trying to track down some historical articles for you. He was hopeful the local bookshop might have additional insight on books he could order to help him find whatever it is he needs to uncover for you."

"What research is that?" Daphne asked, coming to stand beside him, her eyes bright with curiosity behind the lenses of her stylish new spectacles.

"I've been considering taking my characters in my latest draft on a quest to locate El Dorado," Herman answered.

The curiosity in her eyes increased. "Fascinating. Are you intending on having them discover the lost city of gold?"

"I haven't plotted that far out yet."

"A quest like that would certainly allow you to thrust your characters into some interesting scenes, and it's unfortunate I didn't know of your interest in El Dorado earlier. I'm an avid collector of research books, which I read to benefit my, ah, poems. I've encountered passages in some of those books that deal with El Dorado and would have been happy to share those books with you."

"You use research books to aid your poetry?" Charles asked as he joined them, evidently having been eavesdropping on their conversation.

Daphne's eyes narrowed for the briefest of seconds before she smiled. "I'm a writer of epic poems, my dear pumpkin. As such, I need to be well versed in history to do justice to my work. With that said, though, I won't bore everyone here with more details regarding my poetry because that hardly makes for riveting conversations."

"I think I speak for all of us when I say no one could possibly be bored by you, Daphne," Martha said, stepping forward and taking hold of Daphne's arm. "But enough with the writing business. We've a game of croquet to play."

"I'm afraid all the mallets are spoken for, so I'll be sitting this match out."

Realizing it could be a disaster in the making if Daphne was left out of the game when Charles wasn't playing either, Herman handed her his mallet. "You must take my place."

It didn't escape his notice that Daphne took the mallet rather reluctantly. "You have played croquet before, haven't you?"

She winced. "Played may be a bit of a stretch since I've never been what anyone could call an overly athletic sort. I normally muddle my way through games such as croquet." She glanced over her shoulder, her gaze settling on her enormous bustle. "I've also never played while dressed in this particular state of fashion, which could turn problematic."

"I'm sure you'll play well," Martha said, sending Daphne a commiserating smile even as she gave her arm a pat. "It is difficult for we ladies to embrace an athletic attitude while dressed in the first state of fashion, but I have a feeling you'll rise magnificently to the occasion." With that, Martha tugged Daphne into motion, and together, the two ladies strolled away arm in arm, chatting as if they'd been close friends for years.

"I can certainly see why you hired her," Charles said, drawing his attention. "She possesses a great deal of feminine allure, but have a care, Herman. Ladies like Daphne are trouble."

The thought immediately sprang to mind that he might need to limit the time he spent in Charles's company for the foreseeable future. "I didn't hire Daphne because of her allure. I hired her because she knows how to type."

Charles's attention immediately settled on Daphne's retreating form as interest flickered through his eyes. "You don't say. Is she any good at typing?"

"She is."

Charles rubbed a hand over his chin. "I've been looking for a good typist."

"And you should probably continue looking because I doubt Daphne will be interested in typing for you after you made it a point to annoy her."

"Perhaps I should try to make amends for that," Charles said even as he hurried away, leaving Herman behind.

Herman made it all of three steps after Charles before he was pulled to a stop by Ann, who'd taken a very firm grip on his arm.

"If you're considering interceding between Charles and Daphne, I'm going to recommend you reconsider that," she said. "Your grandmother believes Daphnc has nefarious intentions. If Mildred sees you paying Daphne marked attention, we might very well have a situation on our hands that involves Daphne being yanked off the case and sent back to the city."

"I know my grandmother has her suspicions, but it's not really fair to leave Daphne to deal with Charles Bonner on her own."

"Daphne's perfectly capable of taking on a pompous man, but your grandmother might be a different story, unless you're willing to disclose to Mildred what we're actually doing here."

"Admitting to Grandmother that someone is out to murder me would certainly bring on a fit of the vapors, which would then see her repairing to her bed, which would then ruin her enjoyment of the house party."

"Then let Daphne get on with what she does best and keep your distance. If you're concerned about your grandmother enjoying the house party, you should make an attempt to spend more time with the young ladies Mildred has taken such pains to invite here." Ann nodded across the lawn. "Finetta is currently standing by herself. Your grandmother will be pleased if she sees you chatting it up with a lady she's decided would make a wonderful Mrs. Herman Henderson."

"I'm not convinced Finetta actually wants to become Mrs. Henderson."

"You'll never know the answer to that unless you spend more time with her, so go."

"I didn't realize the ladies of Bleecker Street were quite so tenacious."

Ann grinned. "Tenacity is exactly why

we've seen so much success, so go and let me get back to my job, as well."

Knowing it *would* please his grandmother if he sought Finetta out, he began making his way across the lawn, stopping every now and again to speak to different guests.

After thanking Mr. Irwin Rosenward, a gentleman who was a family friend of Finetta and her grandmother, for his kind words about Herman's latest book, he moved to stand beside Finetta.

It did not escape his notice that Finetta immediately began inching away from him, her slight movements coming to an abrupt end when she was given a less-than-subtle shove by her grandmother, which had any space she'd been able to put between her and Herman disappearing in a flash. After sending her grandmother a grimace, she turned to him, a strained smile on her face.

"I thought you were going to play croquet with your guests," she began.

"We were short on mallets, but is that why you aren't playing as well?"

"No, I'm just not very good at croquet." Finetta's lips curved as she settled her attention on Daphne, who was laughing because she'd completely missed her ball after taking her first swing. "Daphne doesn't seem to be very good at it either, but she doesn't seem bothered by that."

"That's because she's an overly confident lady," Mrs. Shoenburger said, stepping forward. "It's been my experience, though, that gentlemen don't appreciate overconfidence in a lady and much prefer a more demure and reserved nature." She arched a brow Herman's way. "Isn't that right, Mr. Henderson?"

"Demure is certainly an attribute most gentlemen appreciate" was all he could think to respond right as Daphne released another peal of laughter when her ball went rolling in the wrong direction and down a slope that left it woefully far from her intended target.

"You're going to have to hit that hard to get it back on the lawn," Jay called to Daphne, who sent him a cheeky grin before she sauntered off in the direction of her ball, swinging her mallet back and forth as she went.

The next few minutes passed in casual chitchat with Finetta and her grandmother, with Herman finding it increasingly difficult to concentrate on their talk of the weather as Daphne kept circling her ball, checking out different angles as she waited her turn again.

"Alright, Daphne, you're up. Remember,

hit it hard," Jay called, which had Daphne readjusting her spectacles before she nodded, drew back, and with a resounding *whack,* sent the ball airborne, which was quite the feat given the heaviness of the ball.

Unfortunately, it remained airborne for quite a long time, and concerningly enough, it was sailing directly for his grandmother.

CHAPTER NINE

"All things considered, that turned out far better than I expected. It could have been a catastrophe of epic proportions," Daphne said, tugging off the high-heeled shoe that had caused her foot to go numb as Herman joined her beside the fallen tree trunk she'd plopped down on.

"I suppose that's one way of looking at the matter," Herman began, raking a hand through hair that was standing on end. "Frankly, I think we should be thanking our lucky stars that my grandmother turned out to be far fleeter on her feet than I ever imagined. With that said, even though she managed to duck out of the way of a flying croquet ball, she's now convinced you've got dastardly intentions toward her. I'm sure her overly active imagination is stewing about those intentions right now, even though she's supposed to be resting up before dinner, along with the other guests.

That means we're *still* facing a catastrophe because she wants you gone by morning, when the first ferry departs for the city."

Daphne began rubbing her foot in earnest, hoping the feeling would return before she had to put her shoe back on following the impromptu meeting she was having with Herman in a secluded stretch of forest on his grand estate, their absence from the house hopefully going unnoticed due to the planned respite before dinner. "She can't honestly believe I deliberately aimed for her, can she? Frankly, the only explanation I have for hitting that ball so hard is that Cooper's physical exertion lessons must be having more of an impact than I thought."

"And I'm sure Cooper will be delighted to hear that. My grandmother, on the other hand, would take that theory as further proof you deliberately set your sights on her," Herman said as Daphne leaned over to begin unlacing her other shoe, using the buttonhook she'd stashed in her bag. "Allow me," Herman surprised her by saying, kneeling down and taking the buttonhook from her.

After making short shrift of the many buttons and laces, he straightened and frowned as she eased off her shoe. "I realize Phillip provided you with a wardrobe that would

177

do the most sophisticated of ladies proud, but you might want to abandon the heels for a day or two. You limped all the way here."

"Because I have a blister or three that have been plaguing me for the last hour," Daphne said, reaching back into her bag to retrieve a small wad of cotton. "Turn around."

"Why?"

"Because I need to remove my stockings to attend to the blisters."

Herman spun around, presenting her with his back.

"Thank you," she said, easing a stocking down her leg and wincing when she got a look at a blister that was red and puffy. Taking a second to wrap it in cotton, she rolled her stocking back up her leg, secured it with her garter, then moved to the other leg, wincing again when she found not one but two blisters on that foot. "I might have to become more active with the suffrage movement, because it's becoming clear that if we women were to rise up against the restrictive and, need I add, painful fashions we're expected to embrace, we'd be far happier."

"You're going to add suffragist to your résumé now, along with inquiry agent and poet?"

Daphne began wrapping cotton around

her foot. "I've always had an interest in the suffrage movement, which only increased after becoming involved with the Bleecker Street Inquiry Agency. Being an inquiry agent has shown me to a greater extent how unjust the world is for women. We have extremely limited rights, even with our making up half the world's population. Those limited rights have made it nearly impossible for us to procure positions that provide us with an income that would allow us to sustain anything but the bare minimal existence. That restricts our options for our futures and leaves marriage as the most viable option. With that said, for those of us who have chosen not to marry, we're often painted with a very unkind brush. Everyone assumes we're miserable women, bereft of the privilege of having a man look after our best interests."

"You've elected to never marry?"

She slid her stocking over her foot. "I don't know if I ever consciously made that decision, but I am twenty-five, well past the first blush of youth. The odds are not in my favor for settling into wedded bliss at this point in my life."

"Twenty-five is hardly ancient."

"It is if you're a woman. Besides, it's common knowledge that gentlemen prefer young ladies fresh out of the schoolroom. There's a general belief that younger ladies are more manageable than older ones, who are far more opinionated." She leaned forward and began the tedious process of buttoning herself back into her shoes, relieved to discover that the cotton was making her blisters less painful. A few minutes later, she smoothed the skirt of her afternoon gown back into place. "You may turn around again."

"Not all gentlemen are opposed to spending time with opinionated women," Herman said as he settled himself on the tree trunk beside her.

"I'm sure that's true, but we've seen cases at the agency where husbands react in very unacceptable ways simply because their wives have the audacity to voice their opinions about one disturbing situation or another. One woman we represented was facing a stay in an asylum simply because she'd questioned her husband about the amount of time he'd been spending with an actress. He didn't appreciate the questioning and was looking into having her committed, using female hysteria as the reason to see her locked away for however long he felt it necessary."

Herman immediately retrieved his notepad from his pocket. "What happened to that client?"

"Eunice and Ivan Chernoff, who has worked for Eunice for years and is now, rather reluctantly I have to admit, involved with the agency, did some digging and discovered that this lady's husband was involved in some shady business dealings. Those dealings would not have been looked upon favorably by the board of directors he serves with on a very profitable railroad venture. After Eunice disclosed what they'd discovered, the man decided it might be best to abandon his efforts to see his wife locked away."

"Why is Ivan reluctantly involved with the agency?"

"He believes it puts Eunice in danger."

Herman frowned. "Do Eunice and Ivan enjoy more than a working relationship?"

Daphne returned the frown. "I've never gotten that impression, but Ivan is remarkably protective of her. Truth be told, I've often wondered if they share some type of family relationship, such as siblings or cousins."

"You haven't asked her?"

"It's Eunice. She's very stingy with details concerning her life, and because she's a rather frightening woman, no one presses

181

her on the matter."

Herman smiled. "She is terrifying, especially with how she's able to sneak up on a person." His smile dimmed. "But tell me this, is it a frequent occurrence, men having women committed to asylums even if those women are not mentally unstable?"

"Sadly, yes. I can personally attest to the truth of that since there was talk in my past because of my frequent fits of anxiety and swooning that I would benefit from a stay in an institution. I was not in accord with that talk and refused to consider an asylum as an option to cure me of my nerves."

"Someone wanted to have you committed?"

"Indeed. A gentleman by the name of Mr. Thomas Sibley." She blew out a breath. "Thomas is a friend of my family, specifically my brother Jack. Thomas didn't appreciate it when I turned down what certainly wasn't a marriage proposal but a demand. Frankly, he seemed flummoxed by the idea that a wallflower would reject him, which was apparently behind his conclusion that I was suffering from female hysteria. He then concluded I was in desperate need of a stint in the local asylum. He broached the subject with my mother, and when I realized she was actually taking his suggestion under consideration, I began making plans to leave Boston."

"That must have been a difficult decision for you to make."

The concern in Herman's eyes left Daphne feeling a little fluttery, a feeling that was certainly unexpected, as well as providing her with a distraction that was hardly professional.

She cleared her throat. "It was difficult to leave everything I knew behind, but I don't regret it. However, we're getting decidedly off topic." She retrieved her notepad and pencil from her bag. "I'd like to go over just a few of my observations with you, beginning with what I've observed about Finetta. She was inching away from you earlier, lending me the distinct impression she really *doesn't* care to be in your company."

"I told you I make her nervous, but I don't think she needs to be on your list of suspects. I find it difficult to believe a shy and demure young lady like Finetta would want to murder me."

"You should never underestimate young ladies, nor should you — not that it's really my place to mention this — subject young ladies to your company when they obviously aren't keen to spend time with you."

Herman gave a very un-Herman-like roll

183

of his eyes. "I'm well aware of that, and I don't normally foist my attention on ladies who aren't interested in it. However, Ann told me it would soothe my grandmother's nerves to see me speaking with Finetta, which is actually why I continued conversing with her."

"Perhaps it's time for you to discontinue being so solicitous of your grandmother's tender sensibilities, especially when it doesn't seem to me as if her nerves are nearly as troublesome as you made them out to be."

"She repairs to her room at the slightest provocation."

"She didn't repair to her room today after I almost took her head off."

"True," Herman admitted. "Odder still is that I saw her wave off the attention Dr. James Gibbons was attempting to give her after the croquet disaster. It's quite unlike my grandmother to ignore her physician, which I believe speaks to the state of her temper after she realized you were the one behind the unfortunate incident."

"Does your grandmother's physician frequently attend events your grandmother hosts?"

"Dr. Gibbons is often in my grandmother's company and has been so since my parents perished almost twenty years ago."

Daphne flipped to a blank page and added Dr. Gibbons's name to it.

"Surely you don't believe Dr. Gibbons has anything to do with the attempts on my life?"

"He can't be ruled out until I learn more about him, especially if he has more than a professional interest in your grandmother. If that is the case, he could benefit from your demise if he were to, say, become more than Mildred's physician."

"The thought of my grandmother being romantically involved with anyone is not one I want to contemplate."

It took a great deal of effort for Daphne to refrain from rolling *her* eyes. "Your grandmother is a very attractive lady. I'm sure Dr. Gibbons has taken note of that over the years. And while I understand it's difficult for a grandson to think about his grandmother being romantically involved with anyone, there is the possibility that Mildred keeps Dr. Gibbons readily available for reasons other than his medical assistance."

"I don't believe I'm enjoying the direction this conversation is traveling."

"Which is why it's fortunate you've hired

me to look into matters you're uncomfortable with, and I can assure you I'll be looking into Dr. Gibbons. I'll also be looking into whether or not his solicitous behavior toward your grandmother has actually benefited the state of her nerves or harmed them."

"What do you mean by that?"

Daphne added a note beside Dr. Gibbons's name and looked up. "You said Mildred often repairs to her bed when she's anxious. Her physician could very well have ulterior motives for encouraging her to retreat from the world when her nerves come into play." She frowned. "Out of curiosity, has your grandmother always suffered from nerves?"

"Her bouts of anxiety began after the loss of my grandfather, father, and mother. Before their deaths, she didn't suffer from nervous bouts."

Daphne wrote that down. "Interesting. That supports the conclusion I've been coming to that anxiety is usually a direct result of a traumatic event — a trigger, if you will, that then turns into a chronic condition."

"Is a traumatic event responsible for the state of your nerves?"

Daphne tilted her head. "I can't say with

any certainty because I don't quite remember when I began suffering anxiety attacks, although I believe they started when I was about thirteen." She pressed a hand to a stomach that had begun to churn, a frequent occurrence whenever she turned her thoughts to the origin of her anxiety. She forced a smile. "But we're getting woefully off topic again and our time is limited, so returning to Finetta."

"I can't imagine there's much left to discuss about Finetta. She's one of the shyest ladies I've ever met, and I highly doubt she has what it takes to murder me."

"She didn't hesitate to stand up to your grandmother earlier when she didn't want Ann to continue on with the Montague Moreland book."

"Her voice was shaking when she voiced her concern," Herman countered. "That implies that Finetta Shoenburger is about as likely to want me dead as Perkins does."

"Your butler has not been ruled out as a suspect."

"You yourself made a fairly sound argument about why the butler is rarely the villain, as did Perkins."

"Just because he vehemently denied having murderous intentions toward you does not mean he wasn't lying about the matter.

187

Murderers, I'm sure you'll agree, are very proficient with lying."

"I've never actually met a murderer."

"Something you should remedy at some point to benefit your writing career, and —" Daphne suddenly stopped talking when, from out of the corner of her eye, she saw something moving through the trees. For the briefest of seconds, she thought it might be a deer, but then she realized it was a man, and one who seemed to be holding what appeared to be a lethal-looking axe in his hand.

"We have to go," she said, grabbing hold of Herman's arm. She tugged him forward and broke into a trot.

"What's wrong?" Herman demanded.

"Don't panic, but there's an armed man in the forest."

"Armed with a pistol?"

"No, an axe." Daphne slowed her pace when Cooper suddenly burst into view, dashing past them a second later, his pistol drawn.

"Keep moving," she said when Herman began to drag his feet.

"I can't let Cooper deal with this on his own."

"He's a Pinkerton. It's what you've hired him to do, so let him do it," she said, ignoring what was clearly a stitch in her side as she tugged Herman onward, gritting her teeth when he stopped moving, causing her to stop as well.

Giving his arm a yank, not that it budged him a single inch, which suggested she'd not garnered as much strength as she'd thought from Cooper's exertion lessons, she abandoned the effort of prodding Herman forward when another man burst on the scene, running at them from a different direction.

Realizing time was of the essence, she dropped her bag to the ground, fumbling around in it until she found her derringer. With a hand that had begun shaking more than slightly, she turned the pistol on the rapidly approaching man right as Cooper dove through the air and brought the axe-wielding man to the ground.

CHAPTER TEN

If someone had told Herman a month ago that he'd find himself being protected from his best friend, Mr. Andrew Ware, by a small wisp of a woman holding a tiny derringer, he would have told that someone they'd taken leave of their senses.

Nevertheless, here he was, in the midst of a most unusual situation, one that held a touch of melodrama, and one that was certainly going to provide him with fodder for a future story at some point.

"I could use a little assistance, Herman. If you've neglected to notice, there's a man sitting on top of me."

Shaking aside all thoughts of potential story lines, Herman turned and found his cousin, Mr. Sheldon Clarendon, lying flat on his back, Cooper sprawled on top of him.

He glanced at the abandoned axe lying three feet away from Sheldon and frowned. "I'm sure Cooper will be happy to let you up after you explain what you were trying to do with that axe."

"I would think that needs no explanation," Sheldon returned, peering up at Herman through brown hair that was decidedly rumpled and almost obscuring his view.

"He was trying to murder you," Daphne said with a definitive nod as she kept her pistol directed at poor Andrew, whose forehead was now beaded with sweat, probably because he'd noticed that Daphne's hand was shaking.

Andrew dashed a hand over his brow. "Sheldon wasn't trying to murder Herman."

"So says the man who was obviously Sheldon's co-conspirator."

Taking pity on poor Andrew, who was white as a ghost and seemed about ready to take a page out of Daphne's book and suffer a fit of the vapors, Herman stepped closer to Daphne and relieved her of the pistol.

"Daphne, this is Andrew Ware, my best friend," he began, lowering his voice. "He was the man who was acting as my coachman before Cooper took over, and I've told him about hiring your agency. Since he knows I have professionals on my case, it's highly unlikely that he's here right now with murderous intentions on his mind."

Daphne shot a look to Sheldon, who was now in the process of arguing with Cooper about letting him up, and gestured to Herman and Andrew to follow her, moving a good twenty feet away from Sheldon before stopping. She arched a brow Herman's way when he joined her. "Have you considered that Andrew might have volunteered as your coachman to confuse the issue of who wants you dead?"

Andrew pulled out a handkerchief and began dabbing it across his forehead. "Am I to understand that I'm now a potential suspect?"

"Given what I just witnessed, you're now a prime suspect," Daphne said.

Andrew stopped dabbing. "I don't want Herman dead. I certainly wasn't trying to attack him a few minutes ago, and I definitely didn't try to run him over with a carriage. If you've forgotten, I began driving his carriage after the first two incidents. It would have been impossible for me to do that driving while trying to run him over with a different carriage the last two times his life was threatened."

"True, but there's no saying you're not in cahoots with Sheldon."

"I'm not in cahoots with anyone, but is it

normal for an inquiry agent to let a suspect know they're under investigation?" Andrew asked.

"Shh, keep your voice down," Daphne whispered. "The last thing we need is for Sheldon to become aware that an inquiry agent is on the scene." She blew out a breath. "As for your question, no, it's not normal, but this is an unusual situation because Herman told you he'd hired my agency to investigate his case. With that said, don't think for a minute, if you are behind the attempts on his life, that you'll be getting away with it because I intend to keep a very close eye on you."

As Andrew immediately began sputtering protests, Herman realized the situation was only going to go downhill from there, unless, of course, Sheldon had a reasonable explanation about the axe. Leaving Daphne's side, he strode back to Sheldon, who was red in the face as he tried to wrestle his way from underneath Cooper. "I don't think Cooper will release you until you explain the axe."

Sheldon stilled before he sent Herman a scowl. "I'm sure if you actually stop and think about the situation, you'll realize exactly what I was attempting to do. But since you've yet to do that and this Cooper gent is remarkably heavy, allow me to set the matter straight. I noticed you walking into the forest a while ago and thought I'd take the opportunity of your being away from your guests to prove to you that you're completely wrong about that scene you're trying to include in your latest draft. It's not working, and the reason it's not is because you've given your villain a ridiculous axe to use against the hero. And even though trying to sneak up on a person with an axe is not something I make a point of doing, I knew drastic measures were needed to get you to rethink that scene."

"It's not ridiculous. I've never used an axe as a weapon before, which means it's a fresh twist for my latest book."

"It would only be fresh if the axe scene worked, which it doesn't," Sheldon argued. "I had quite the time of it trying to steal up on you because an axe is unwieldy, as well as cumbersome. Your hero would have to be completely oblivious to his surroundings to miss an assailant trying to take him down with an axe attack. I don't believe oblivious is a characteristic you want for your hero."

"I didn't hear you stealing up on me, which suggests it *is* possible."

"I imagine the only reason you didn't hear me was because you were preoccupied with that lady I saw you speaking with, which I don't blame you for in the least considering she is" — Sheldon glanced Daphne's way — "lovely."

Sheldon's gaze shifted from Daphne a second later, a scowl settling on his face as his attention sharpened on Andrew. "What are you doing here, Andrew?" he called. "When we parted ways at the house after sharing a carriage back from town, you mentioned you were off to clean up for dinner."

Andrew stopped speaking midsentence with Daphne and immediately strode over to join them, seemingly not upset in the least to discontinue what had obviously been a bit of an argument with Daphne.

"I'm here because I thought it might be prudent to warn Herman what you were planning."

Sheldon blinked. "Why would you want to warn him? It's not as if it was likely I was going to take him by surprise, although I wasn't counting on him being preoccupied with a lady, which might explain how my little experiment has now turned into a complete fiasco."

"It could have very well turned into an even larger fiasco if you *had* taken him by surprise," Andrew shot back. "Usually when

195

a person is confronted from out of the blue with an axe, there's every reason to believe that person is going to react. Someone could have ended up losing a limb, and wouldn't that have put a damper on the house party?"

"He does make a good point," Herman said. "Grandmother would be beside herself if one of us was permanently maimed. She'd probably take to her bed for a month."

"Which is why you should have a talk with . . ." Andrew nodded at Daphne, who was strolling up to join them. "Clearly, I was intent on a noble mission, one that has now spared your grandmother's nerves because I took it upon myself to intervene. Because of that, I definitely don't belong on any list."

"I'm not taking you off the list, nor should you even be talking about the list be-cause . . ." Daphne shot a look to Sheldon, who was now looking beyond bewildered.

Andrew threw his hands up. "Fine, I won't talk about it." He nodded to Herman. "I'll leave you to sort all of this out. I'm going to head back to the house because your grand-mother might also feel compelled to take to her bed if all of us show up late for dinner." With that, Andrew sent a glare to Daphne before he stalked away.

Refusing a sigh over the unexpected state of his afternoon, Herman turned back to Sheldon, who, unfortunately, was still lying on the ground, Cooper apparently less than willing to let the man loose just yet.

"You can get off him, Cooper. He wasn't trying to harm me."

Cooper tilted his head. "You're really trying to write a scene where the villain is going to attack someone with an axe?"

"Why do I detect a trace of skepticism in your voice?"

"Because an axe is an unlikely weapon if there ever was one," Cooper said as he pushed himself off Sheldon, earning a grunt from Sheldon in return. "However, I suppose the story your cousin told is genuine, which is unfortunate because —" Cooper abruptly stopped talking, winced, then strode over to the axe and picked it up.

"Why would it be unfortunate that my story is believable?" Sheldon asked. "Or better yet, who *are* these people?"

"Ah . . ." Herman began.

"I'm Miss Daphne Beekman, Herman's new secretary," Daphne said, stepping forward when Herman continued to struggle for a reply. "The man who was recently sitting on you is Cooper, the new coachman."

Sheldon pushed himself off the ground and settled a frown not on Daphne but on Herman. "Did she just say she's your new secretary? Given the way I saw you speaking with her before, I was under the impression that she was a guest."

The unexpected thought suddenly came to mind that springing Daphne on everyone with no warning was probably not one of his brightest decisions.

Herman cleared his throat. "Daphne *is* my new secretary and is not a guest, although she's certainly included in all of the events we've planned for the guests this week."

"And the reason behind hiring a secretary?"

"Ah . . ." was all Herman had readily available to reply to that, his mind unusually devoid of words or reasonable explanations at the moment.

"I can type," Daphne said, evidently realizing he was floundering. "And since Herman told me you've been complaining about how long your usual typing service takes, I'm sure you'll appreciate my joining Herman's team."

Sheldon didn't bother responding to that, instead cocking a brow Herman's way. "Why didn't you discuss it with me before hiring her?"

Unfortunately, instead of his mind providing him with a quick and logical response, all he had at his disposal was a "Hmm."

Daphne tipped her spectacles, sent him a look that clearly stated she thought he was being less than helpful, and then returned her spectacles to their proper position and settled a smile on Sheldon. "Herman didn't have time to discuss it with you because it was a spur of the moment decision on his part, done so because I'm in high demand and had numerous offers of employment I was considering when I made Herman's acquaintance."

Sheldon's brow furrowed. "You keep addressing Herman by his given name."

"You're right." She turned to Herman. "I believe it might be best if I give you a moment alone with Sheldon to explain the particulars of my employment. I'm getting the distinct impression your cousin isn't going to be amiable to anything I may have to say about the matter. If you need me, I'll be over on that tree stump, writing down a few notes."

Sheldon waited until Daphne took a seat on the stump before he narrowed his eyes on Herman.

"Care to explain to me why you've hired a

secretary who looks as if she should be spending her days shopping in Paris? Or better yet, why there seems to be a distinct lack of formality between the two of you?"

"We, well, ah, decided to abandon formality because you and I, er, embrace an informal attitude."

"What could I possibly have to do with how you and your secretary address each other?"

Herman forced a shrug. "You're my assistant, which is on the same level as a secretary. I thought it was only fair to adopt an air of informality with Daphne so that she wouldn't feel slighted. That's also why I've invited her to attend all the festivities planned over the next week, because you'll be attending those festivities as well."

"I'm your *cousin.* It would be curious if you called me anything other than Sheldon. And *I'd* definitely feel slighted, as your *cousin,* if I wasn't invited to enjoy the festivities at your house party."

"Which is why I'd thought you'd understand my reasoning behind including Daphne. Feeling slighted is hardly something anyone enjoys."

Cooper took that moment to cough behind his hand before he jerked his head Sheldon's way. "If you'd excuse us for just a moment, I forgot something of extreme importance I need to tell Mr. Henderson about his . . . horses."

Before Sheldon could voice a protest, Cooper took hold of Herman's arm and hurried him away, not coming to a stop until they were out of Sheldon's earshot.

"You're making a muddle of this" were the first words out of Cooper's mouth.

Herman raked a hand through his hair. "Too right I am, but if you'll recall, I tried to tell Daphne that her explanation regarding why she was mingling with my guests was rather flimsy. She then sprung the whole abandoning of formality business at me as soon as she arrived. I'm afraid I've not been exactly eloquent with explaining that business to anyone, my grandmother included."

"Perhaps it would have been wiser if Daphne would have assumed the role of a journalist who had come to your estate to write up a piece on you. That would have been far easier to explain."

Herman frowned. "Why didn't you mention that idea earlier? That would have been a brilliant disguise for her."

"It just came to me."

"Which is too bad because it's not as if we can change course now and tell everyone she's a journalist."

"Too right we can't, but you're going to have to try harder with sounding credible when you answer all these questions about Daphne. Just speak in a forceful tone and then try to change the subject as quickly as possible."

"That's your advice?"

"It's the best I've got, and since I'm hardly going to benefit the situation by sticking around as your cousin badgers you with more questions, I'm going to take my leave. I won't be far away, just out of sight behind some trees." Sending Sheldon an inclination of his head, which Sheldon acknowledged with a frown, Cooper settled the axe he was still carrying over his shoulder and strode away, stopping to whisper something to Daphne before he disappeared into the forest.

"A new secretary *and* a new coachman?" was the first question Sheldon asked after Herman rejoined him. "What happened to Jenkins?"

"He's taking some time off to visit friends."

"Jenkins doesn't have any friends, a direct result of his surly nature."

Herman ran a hand over his face again, feeling quite as if he'd landed smack-dab into one of his more complicated plots, and one he had no idea how to get out of successfully.

"Why does your coachman carry a pistol?" Sheldon shot at him next.

"Ah, well . . ." Herman smiled when a perfectly reasonable explanation came to him from out of the blue. "Because I'm often traveling to Five Points on research outings these days, I needed someone qualified to protect the carriage while I'm visiting some of the more unsavory spots on the Lower East Side. Cooper is very proficient with a pistol, as well as with driving carriages."

"Why does your secretary carry a pistol?"

"Ah . . ."

"I carry a pistol because I'm often a woman alone, and women can't be too careful these days," Daphne said, strolling up to join them. She began fiddling with her stylish glove, revealing the face of a delicate watch through a discreet slit that Phillip had included with the design. "I thought I should point out to both of you that the afternoon is quickly getting away from us. That means we need to make haste back to the main house because there are more activities planned, mainly the dinner party Mildred has been looking forward to all day." She settled a smile on Sheldon, which faded in a trice after her gaze traveled the length of him . . . twice. She turned to Herman. "I thought you said Sheldon's smaller than you."

"He is smaller than me. Half an inch shorter to be exact."

Sheldon crossed his arms over his chest. "Why would you and your new secretary be discussing my size?"

Not a single explanation sprang to mind. He smiled at Daphne. "Why don't you tell Sheldon the story of how we were discussing the disparities between our sizes."

She sent him a wrinkle of a nose, as if she expected better of him, before she turned to Sheldon. "There's nothing unusual about my discussing your size with Herman. Your cousin made a point of telling me about the state of Mildred's nerves before he hired me so that I could be mindful of those nerves during the time we're here on the Hudson. I believe I then asked him how *he's* mindful of her nerves, and he went on to explain to me the many measures he puts into place when he's participating in what his grandmother would see as dangerous activities, such as boxing. When I pointed out that even safety measures enacted while boxing can fail, he told me he always spars with you, which minimizes the danger level, given that you're smaller than he is."

She looked Sheldon up and down again. "Having seen you up close, though, I'm not so certain Herman's sparring with you can be considered safe. Frankly, I think the two of you are the exact same height, and I believe that you, Sheldon, are broader than Herman."

Sheldon took to standing a little straighter and, if Herman wasn't mistaken, puffed out his rather impressive chest. "I've thought for some time now that I'm more muscular than my cousin."

"Which makes me wonder why Mildred accepts Herman's explanation as to why it's safe to box with you," Daphne said.

"That would be on account of the time Herman broke my nose and the damage I didn't do to him after he did that breaking." Sheldon shook his head. "I mean, I did punch him back, but unfortunately my aim was off, because I was distracted by all the blood pouring from my nose. I only managed to give his ear what amounted to nothing more than an aggressive tap, something his grandmother took as my inability to land good punches, which then seemingly convinced her once and for all that I'm a safe boxing companion for Herman."

Something interesting flashed through Daphne's eyes. "I imagine it must have annoyed you that you didn't cause Herman any harm after he broke your nose."

"Broken noses happen all the time in boxing. I'm certainly not holding a grudge about it, nor am I holding a grudge that there's now a bump on it." Sheldon smiled. "I've been told the ladies find it dashing."

Daphne leaned closer to Sheldon, her attention on his nose. "There is a bump — one you must notice every time you look in the mirror."

Sheldon shot a look to Herman. "Why does it seem as if your secretary is far too interested in the state of my nose?"

"She's odd that way?" was all Herman could think to respond.

"I'm not odd," Daphne said firmly. "Merely curious about how a gentleman really feels when he gets his nose broken by another gentleman, especially when that gentleman is one's employer."

"Herman's my cousin first, and cousins don't let something as trifling as a broken nose damage their relationship," Sheldon said, pulling out a pocket watch and taking note of the time. "But it looks as if the afternoon really is getting away from us, which means we should get back to the house."

Daphne nodded. "We should indeed, although I'm afraid I'm not finished speaking with Herman about the, ah, details of my work schedule. You won't mind if we don't walk back to the house with you, will you?"

"What details do you need to work out with him about your schedule?" Sheldon asked.

"Just the particulars about when you'll be working with him." She smiled. "I do my best typing in the afternoon because I'm not much of a morning person. That's why I've suggested to him that you work with him in the mornings."

Sheldon's eyes narrowed as he crossed his arms over his chest. "Don't you think it's rather presumptuous of you to tell me, the man who has been Herman's assistant for years, what schedule I'm going to adhere to now? Perhaps *I* prefer working with Herman in the afternoon, which means you're going to have to adjust your schedule, whether you're a morning person or not."

Daphne considered Sheldon for a long moment before she shook her head. "That's nonnegotiable. I don't work in the morning."

Sheldon shifted his attention to Herman. "I have no idea why you'd hire a secretary who doesn't work in the mornings, but I hope you'll have a chat with her once I take my leave of you, to explain how seniority works. I have seniority; she doesn't." He narrowed his eyes on Daphne, considered her for all of a second, then spun around and strode away.

He made it all of a few feet before he called over his shoulder to Herman. "Would you do me a favor and make certain that Miss Beekman isn't seated next to me at dinner tonight? I fear I'm not feeling particularly charitable toward her right now. I would hate to have a delicious meal ruined simply because I'm seated next to a woman I'm apparently going to have to work with, even though I wasn't given the courtesy of my opinion about that before you hired her."

"I'm not planning on attending the dinner, so you won't need to worry about sitting beside me," Daphne said before Herman could answer.

"Wonderful," Sheldon said before he strode into motion again.

"Why do I get the distinct feeling you were deliberately baiting Sheldon — quite as if you wanted to set him against you?" Herman asked after his cousin disappeared from sight. "That kind of antagonistic attitude is quite out of character for you."

"How clever of you to pick up on that," Daphne began, "and yes, I was trying to set him against me. It seemed to me that he may have a touch of a temper, given how quickly he reacted to the schedule I mentioned. Because of that, I decided to change strategies with him. I was, at first, thinking a collaboration might work well to get information out of him, but he's far too inquisitive for his own good, which could mean trouble for the investigation. Now, with him at odds with me, he'll stay out of my way, and if he is responsible for the attacks on you, his animosity may have him escalating whatever plans he has in motion."

"I really don't believe Sheldon is behind the attempts on my life."

"And if that's true, I'll be sure to beg his pardon for my blatant rudeness once we solve this mystery."

"An apology he may very well refuse." Herman offered Daphne his arm, and after they fetched her bag, they began strolling through the forest in the direction of the house.

"Why did you tell Sheldon you weren't attending the dinner tonight?" Herman asked.

"I thought your grandmother would appreciate a respite from me, which will also allow her to enjoy a dinner party she obviously went to great lengths to plan."

"That's very considerate of you, but how will that help the investigation?"

The corners of her lips curved. "Ann can be chatty enough for both of us. Besides, I'll still be moving forward with the investigation. I'll just need you to show me how to access those secret passageways you mentioned."

The mere thought of Daphne traipsing alone through the secret passageways sent apprehension coursing through him. "Perhaps you should wait until we can explore those passageways together. I'd hate for you to become disoriented and get lost in one of them while I'm entertaining my guests and unlikely to find you for hours."

"I'm not going to get lost, and no, I'm not waiting. Stealing behind walls will allow me a marvelous way to eavesdrop. But there's no need for you to worry. I'm sure I'll be perfectly fine."

Even with Daphne having reassured him again, after he'd shown her how to access the secret passageways and given her a brief tour, that there was nothing to worry about,

Herman couldn't seem to help himself.

Taking a sip of wine, he glanced around the table, nodding to Martha Mulvey, who was sitting beside Sheldon, smiling widely as she sent Herman a nod in return before she replied to whatever it was Sheldon had been saying to her.

Sheldon was still looking a touch sulky, but there was nothing Herman could do about that, even though he was relatively certain Sheldon wasn't behind the attempts on his life.

His grandmother, on the other hand, was in rare form this evening, chatting it up with Mrs. Shoenburger, her eyes sparkling as she kept turning her attention to Finetta, then back to Finetta's grandmother, leaning her head closer to Mrs. Shoenburger as she whispered furiously behind a fan she'd taken to waving enthusiastically about.

A quick glance to Finetta showed that young lady doing her best to ignore her grandmother and Mildred, keeping her attention fixed squarely on Andrew. Andrew often sat beside Finetta at events because Mildred didn't want to make it too obvious about whom she specifically had in mind to become Mrs. Herman Henderson, not wanting to incur the disappointment of other young ladies she had in her sights for

Herman.

"Someone mentioned that we might enjoy a spot of archery tomorrow," Jay Storrow said, drawing Herman's attention from across the table.

Herman smiled. "I thought that might be amusing for many of the guests, although . . ." Whatever else he'd been about to say got stuck on the tip of his tongue when a large painting hanging over one of the buffet tables suddenly swung open.

A second after that, Daphne plunged through the large opening that was behind the painting and tumbled head over heels through the air, landing right on top of the buffet table, sending china crashing to the floor as she released a less-thansophisticated shriek.

CHAPTER ELEVEN

"I must admit, it took me by complete surprise when Mildred didn't see you tossed on the first ferry leaving for the city this morning, Daphne. Granted, Herman did come up with a brilliant explanation about why you were skulking about in the secret passageways, but I'm not convinced Mildred actually believed him."

Daphne abandoned her typing and settled her attention on Ann, who was sitting underneath a large maple tree where Daphne had set up a makeshift desk. Ann was currently feigning interest in a passage she was intending to share later from her Montague Moreland book, doing so to distract from the fact she was actively engaged in a conversation with a woman who'd caused quite the ruckus the night before.

"I'm surprised I'm still here, as well, since I completely disrupted Mildred's dinner party," Daphne said, releasing a sigh. "I really should have rethought removing my shoes and prowling about in my stockings. I didn't take into consideration that stockings can turn slippery on wooden floors. If only I hadn't leaned forward to peer through that peephole, I wouldn't have slipped, nor would I have caught myself by grabbing hold of what turned out to be the latch that opened the concealed door."

"You're fortunate you didn't kill yourself by falling from such a height."

"I'm fortunate Phillip insisted on dressing me in enormous bustles. I credit the bustle I was wearing yesterday with saving my life because it cushioned my fall. It also saved me from getting cut with all that china I shattered." Daphne glanced down at the pages of Herman's handwritten manuscript that she was currently typing out, tipping her spectacles down as she tried to decipher a word. "I'm fairly certain this is not the word Herman intended to use, if it is, indeed, *incapacitated.* Doesn't seem like the right choice because it's not allowing the sentence to flow. *Rendered senseless* might work better."

"Are secretaries supposed to change the words of their employers?"

"Doubtful, but I'm not actually a secretary, and Herman will probably appreciate my editing skills, not that he's aware I have those."

"I suspect there are relatively few people who believe you're a great editor considering your fondness for sharing snippets of your poetry."

Daphne typed *rendered senseless* onto the page. "I do seem to have a knack for composing awful poetry."

"On purpose."

"I can't deny that, although I've never really had an aptitude for composing credible poetry. But we're getting distracted. You've been so busy of late that we've not had much time to exchange notes. I'm dying to hear if you've learned anything that will benefit our case."

"Being busy is an understatement, and I couldn't very well have exchanged notes with you last night, not after Mildred asked me to keep her company while she calmed down after you literally crashed her dinner party. By the time she finally went to bed, it was after midnight, and you were already fast asleep when I repaired to our room."

"Which speaks to how much excitement I experienced yesterday. I rarely fall asleep until the wee hours of the morning." Daphne typed out another sentence. "Did

Mildred have to resort to using her smelling salts after my unexpected fall through the painting?"

"No, even though her physician kept suggesting she do so to help alleviate the anxiety he was convinced she was experiencing. Frankly, I don't believe she was anxious in the least — more along the lines of infuriated."

Daphne abandoned the typewriter and reached for her notepad. Flipping through the pages, she found the one reserved for Dr. Gibbons and jotted down his insistence on the use of smelling salts.

"You think there's something odd about Dr. Gibbons?" Ann asked.

"I think it's odd he'd insist Mildred make use of smelling salts she obviously didn't believe she needed."

"Perhaps he was merely being cautious. He has been attending Mildred for years and must know what's needed in regard to her nerves."

"Or he's been coddling her throughout the years, which has resulted in her taking to her bed perhaps more than necessary."

"For what purpose?"

"No idea, but I'm going to have to make a point to speak with Dr. Gibbons to see if I can discover why he indulges Mildred and her nerves." She flipped to the back of the notepad where she'd written suggestions Madame Sophia Calve had so graciously given her. "I believe I'll use what Madame Calve called her flattery technique on Dr. Gibbons. Apparently, flattery is the best way to get a gentleman to answer questions he might otherwise be reluctant to answer."

"That sounds more like flirting than flattery."

Daphne gave a bit of a shudder. "Flirting makes me nervous. Flattery I can manage."

"From what I've observed, flirting with the guests seems to be second nature for you."

"If that's true, it's only because it's not really me flirting. It's the persona I've adopted. But speaking of that persona, perhaps it's time for me to give one of those languid waves Madame Calve suggested I do every so often."

Glancing around, Daphne noticed Finetta Shoenburger and Martha Mulvey watching her, their heads bent closely together. She'd asked Herman to set her table away from where his guests were enjoying an early afternoon respite, hoping the distance would discourage any of them from interrupting her work, while also allowing those guests to see that she could, indeed, type,

217

something she'd overheard Mildred questioning.

Sending Finetta and Martha a languid wave of her hand, she smiled when Finetta returned the wave, her smile dimming when Martha stuck her nose in the air and turned her head, a clear dismissal if there ever was one.

"Why do I get the distinct impression Martha is no longer keen to cozy up to me?"

"I'm surprised you're only now picking up on what I've noticed is an intentional coolness toward you on Martha's part," Ann said. "Did you not see her get up from where she was sitting next to Irwin Rosenward when you joined their table at breakfast this morning to go sit next to Charles Bonner?"

"I'm afraid I didn't because I was barely awake," Daphne said before she frowned. "She must be exceptionally put out with me, though, if she removed herself from Irwin to join Charles. He is one of the most disagreeable men I've ever had the misfortune to meet. Irwin, on the other hand, seems to be a pleasant sort, and he went out of his way to inquire about my poetry this morning."

"I'm surprised Irwin didn't take leave of your presence, as well, if you actually recited some of your poetry to him."

Daphne smiled. "It was much too early for me to compose a single horrendous verse, so Irwin was spared a reason to make a speedy departure."

Ann returned the smile. "He has no idea how fortunate it is that you take forever to wake up in the morning. But, returning to Martha being put out with you, I believe it has something to do with how Herman raced to your rescue last night. Not only did he take special care getting you down from the buffet table, and then making certain you'd not been cut by broken china, he also rushed to defend you when Mildred accused you of being up to no good. I was watching Martha throughout Herman's earnest explanation, and the longer Herman spoke, the more unpleasant her facial expressions turned."

Ann tapped a finger against her chin. "At first, I thought she might have been so annoyed because she's sweet on Herman and didn't like the attention he was settling on you. But then she hurried off to join Sheldon. And when she began whispering furiously in his ear, I knew I was wrong to think she was sweet on Herman."

When Ann stopped talking and sent Daphne an expectant look, Daphne wrinkled her nose. "I have no idea where you're going with any of that."

"Honestly, Daphne, have you still not woken up yet? You need to keep up with me. You see, when Herman told everyone he asked you to explore the passageways because he wanted you to see if his inclusion of such passageways could be beneficial to his latest draft, Martha clearly took that as a sign Herman was considering replacing Sheldon with you because normally Sheldon does that type of research for him."

Daphne blinked. "Ah, I see where you're going with this now. Martha is clearly put out with me because she and Sheldon evidently believe Sheldon's position is in jeopardy, hence Martha's outrage on his behalf."

"Exactly, although before you decide to add that to Sheldon's page for why he's a prime suspect, I have to admit I'm not certain he's our man. There are so many better potential suspects in attendance — Andrew Ware now being at the top of my list."

"Andrew's at the top of your list?"

"He is, especially since I've come to the conclusion that he and Finetta, after watching them throughout the dinner last night, appear to be smitten with each other."

Daphne reached for her notepad and flipped to Andrew's page. "Jealousy would be great motivation for attempted murder, although Herman's convinced Andrew's not a viable suspect."

"That's because Andrew is Herman's friend, and Herman doesn't seem to be the type who'd expect betrayal from a friend. With that said, Andrew's not the only man I believe deserves further investigation. All the other authors here seem to watch one another in a most suspicious manner. I caught Jay Storrow with clear temper in his eyes when someone mentioned that Herman's latest novel is currently on its fifth printing."

"Herman's book has gone into a fifth printing?"

"I think you're allowing yourself to become distracted with unimportant details while missing the general point. Jealousy seems to be rampant with many of the people who are currently surrounding Herman." Ann rubbed her temple. "I don't know about you, but there are so many possible suspects that I keep getting everyone confused."

"It's the same for me as well," Daphne admitted. "Keeping Andrew and Sheldon straight at first was difficult, until I began associating Sheldon with the bump on his nose and Andrew with that unruly curl he has right above his left ear."

"I haven't noticed that curl."

"You will now. As for all the other authors, it's difficult to keep them straight because besides Jay Storrow and Charles Bonner, they tend to keep to themselves and don't speak much." She flipped through her notepad. "How about we try to make this easier on ourselves? I'll concentrate on the authors and you concentrate on the young ladies in attendance, especially Finetta. We'll need to put some effort into discovering whether you're right about a budding romance between her and Andrew."

"I'll make sure to sit next to Finetta at afternoon tea today."

"And since Mildred told Herman I'm not welcome to join her and the ladies at that tea, perhaps I'll join the gentlemen doing a bit of target practice and see if I can draw out any of the authors who've yet to say much." Daphne glanced back at Herman's manuscript and frowned. "Does this look like *palpable* to you, or is it *panicky*?"

Ann got to her feet and peered at the word Daphne was pointing out. "Hard to say."

"Would you care for my opinion?"

Looking up, Daphne found Sheldon

standing a foot away from her, a frown on his face. She summoned up a smile. "I would. I'm sure you're used to deciphering Herman's handwriting."

Sheldon stepped closer and glanced at the page. "It's *palpable,* which you might have been able to figure out if you'd read the sentence more thoroughly. Or perhaps you did read the sentence but didn't comprehend it because you were more concerned with chatting it up with Miss Evans instead of concentrating on Herman's manuscript."

Even though Daphne understood why Sheldon was put out with her, his suggestion rankled. "Or perhaps I'm merely unaccustomed to Herman's handwriting."

"A reasonable explanation — something you seem to have at your disposal often." Sheldon glanced at the piece of paper rolled into the typewriter. "And while most of the guests are enthralled with how rapidly you're able to type, I'm curious as to whether you've actually typed anything of worth or if your fingers are merely flying across the keys for show."

Annoyance was swift. "If you'll allow me a moment to finish this page, I'll show you exactly how worthy my typing is."

Bending over, she began typing away, thankful that Herman hadn't listened to her when she'd suggested he give her something besides his manuscript to type. It wasn't that she hadn't wanted to help him out by typing his latest chapters, but because she and Herman were in direct competition with each other, she felt it unfair to see his latest work in progress when he wasn't being offered the same courtesy with her latest draft.

When she'd pointed out the pesky notion that she could very well get inspired by something she read in his manuscript and then use that in her poetry, he had waved that right aside and left her feeling all sorts of odd emotions.

It was a quandary, the emotions Herman caused her to feel, especially when she was determined to prove her worth to the agency. She was relatively certain that feeling all warm and fuzzy about a client wasn't what anyone would consider proper feelings for a true inquiry agent to have.

Blinking herself out of her thoughts when she realized she'd reached the last line on the page, she ripped the paper from the cylinder, handing it to Sheldon.

"And isn't this an unexpected sight, seeing you and my cousin collaborating together. Dare I hope the two of you have set aside your differences and are intending to move forward in an amicable fashion?"

Glancing around Sheldon, Daphne discovered Herman smiling back at her, clearly pleased at what he thought was an improved state between her and his cousin.

Unfortunately, there was no way to allow him to continue thinking that, not since Sheldon was now scowling up a storm as he read the page she'd just typed.

"Sheldon's concerned my typing outside in view of your guests has simply been for show," Daphne said.

Herman's smile dimmed as he looked to Sheldon, who wasn't paying him any mind, then back to Daphne. "Given the pile of typed pages on your desk, I'm sure Sheldon's soon to apologize for what was an uncalled-for accusation."

Sheldon handed the typed page to Herman. "I wouldn't hold your breath for that apology, Herman. Take a look at this. I don't remember you using the phrase *rendered senseless* before."

"Probably because it's not a phrase I've ever used."

"How curious, then, that it's typed on the page you're holding." Sheldon leaned forward and pointed to a line. "It's right there, which indicates your new secretary is taking liberties with your story."

A bit of what seemed to be amusement flickered through Herman's eyes as he settled his attention on Daphne. "Didn't care for the way I constructed that sentence, did you?"

"I thought *rendered senseless* would describe the result of the conflict better than *incapacitated.*"

Herman tilted his head. "Hmm . . . you might be right about that." He nodded. "We'll keep *rendered senseless,* and I thank you for improving my sentence."

Sheldon settled a glare on Daphne for the briefest of moments before he threw up his hands, muttered something to the tune of "Unbelievable," then stalked away without another word.

"And here I just said I didn't believe Sheldon could be a prime suspect," Ann said as she watched Sheldon make a beeline for Martha Mulvey, the two of them bending their heads together a second later. "He might need to go back to the top of the list, but" — she craned her neck — "there's Mildred. I told her I'd help get the guests organized for the next round of thrilling entertainment, which is a bout of archery. If you'll excuse me?"

As Ann strolled away, Daphne caught Herman's eye. "I should beg your pardon for changing your work, Herman, or I at least should have asked you about it first."

He smiled. "I'm not overly concerned about that, Daphne. As I said, you improved the sentence, so it's fine. Besides, if there's something you change or have already changed that I don't agree with, I'll make corrections when I get to my final edit."

"Sheldon seemed put out that you didn't take me to task for the change I made."

"That's because Sheldon and I are constantly at odds over changes he believes I should make, but ones I don't agree with. He's still relatively new to the writing process and will try to insert words I've deliberately avoided because I've used them in earlier chapters. I know for a fact I've never used *rendered senseless,* so in this particular case, overuse is not an issue."

"I once overused the word *snort.*"

His smile turned into a grin. "You wrote a poem that included snorting?"

For the briefest of seconds, Daphne felt the strongest impulse to disclose what she really wrote to Herman.

It was an impulse brought about by the sheer notion that, even though she'd clearly overstepped her role as his secretary, Herman hadn't gotten angry with her, but had instead considered her suggestion and then decided to keep it.

She had the sneaking suspicion he would be a writer she'd enjoy discussing matters of craft with or working together with to figure out how to fix a plot that wasn't working, quite like her pirate plot at the moment.

She was a solitary writer by choice. However, at times she longed to share her love of the written word with someone who loved words as well, someone who wouldn't mock her for choosing a profession that wasn't considered acceptable for women and who would understand her need to write down the stories in her head and share them with the world.

Someone exactly like Herman.

Shoving aside the urge to disclose all when she finally remembered she was under contract to keep her identity a secret, Daphne forced a smile as she struggled to think of some credible response to make about snorting and poetry.

Thankfully, she was spared a response when Mildred called out to Herman, gesturing to catch his attention. "We're about to begin the archery, Herman. Do come join us."

Herman sent Mildred a nod before he held his hand out to Daphne. "Care to try your skill with a bow and arrow?"

She glanced to where Herman's staff had set up targets made out of hay bales and shuddered. "While I'm sure Cooper would love to see me doing some manner of physical exertion, I've never been very good with a bow and arrow. And after my croquet experience, I'm not willing to risk another debacle. I don't think Mildred will allow me to stay if I unintentionally hit anything other than the target."

"I'm sure you're not that horrible with a bow and arrow. You seem to know your way around a pistol."

"I'm only adequate with a pistol, and that's because Cooper has all the inquiry agents practice daily — well, except for Eunice, of course. She doesn't need any practice."

"Why not?"

"She can hit a bull's-eye from a distance most people can't even imagine."

Herman's notepad was out of his pocket in a blink of an eye. "Where'd she learn to shoot?"

"No idea. Eunice isn't exactly forthcoming with personal anecdotes."

"Herman," Mildred called again, a distinct hint of impatience marking her tone.

Herman tucked his notepad away. "Duty calls."

"So it does," Daphne said, returning to her typing as Herman walked away to join his guests.

She made a point to lift her head every other sentence to keep an eye on the archery contest, even though Ann was doing the same, as was Cooper, who was brushing a horse beside the cliff that led down to the Hudson.

Finishing the chapter ten minutes later, Daphne rose to her feet, taking a second to stretch muscles that had been still for too long. Her attention was suddenly captured by the sight of Andrew Ware standing beside Finetta Shoenburger, showing her the proper way to hold a bow.

Andrew was standing a little too close to Finetta than was strictly proper, but Finetta didn't seem to mind. In fact, Daphne saw her inch ever so closer to Andrew, her cheeks a delicate shade of pink as she smiled at him and fluttered her lashes.

Wandering as nonchalantly as she could over to join the guests, Daphne kept an eye on Finetta and Andrew, wanting to get a better look at what was clearly a budding romance, and one that might be the reason behind the attempts on Herman's life.

Sending a smile to Jay Storrow, who was speaking with Mr. Martin Corrigan, an author who wrote incredibly detailed and complex murder mysteries, Daphne edged her way around the crowd, hoping no one noticed the blatant interest she was directing Andrew's way.

"On to something?"

Daphne raised a hand to her throat when Herman materialized by her side. "Don't do that. You scared me half to death. I'll hardly be able to convince anyone I'm a sophisticated woman of the world if I suddenly faint dead away simply because you approached me."

He grinned, a sight that made her lose her train of thought for a second, until Mildred called out to Herman again, obviously not caring for the fact that her grandson was grinning at his secretary.

"I think your grandmother's annoyed with me again," Daphne muttered.

"Why would she be annoyed with you? You've been behaving yourself all afternoon."

"I just made you grin."

"Ah, well, now there's a reason for annoyance. I'd better go speak with her before she gets herself riled up."

As Herman walked away, Daphne returned her attention to Finetta, who was now surrounded by numerous gentlemen, all of whom seemed to be giving her pointers about archery. Finetta sent Andrew what could only be described as a flirty smile before she drew back her arrow, turned toward the target, but then, for some inexplicable reason, turned again, no longer aiming for the target but toward Herman.

"Herman, look out!" Daphne called, bolting after him.

Herman stopped walking, but any further warnings she wanted to voice came to a rapid end when she felt something hit her backside. Twisting around, she blinked, and then blinked again when she realized there was an arrow sticking out of her dress. Before she could process that sight, Herman was by her side, scooping her up into his strong arms right as a feminine shriek rent the air.

Craning her neck from the safe confines of Herman's embrace, Daphne peered in the direction of the shriek just in time to see Finetta Shoenburger fall to the ground in one of the most spectacular swoons Daphne had ever seen, complete with billowing fabric and even a poof of dust.

CHAPTER TWELVE

"Are you keener to believe me now about ladies not being counted out as possible suspects?"

Herman stopped readying his boat and squinted at Daphne, who was looking quite stylish today for their rowing excursion in an ivory walking gown with little pink flowers dotting the fabric. The wide-brimmed pink hat she was wearing exactly matched the flowers, as did the pink gloves that sported fashionable pink buttons.

"I'm still not convinced Finetta deliberately tried to shoot me," Herman countered. "She's retreated to her bedchamber for over a day now, and even Dr. Gibbons is becoming concerned over her continued state of hysterics."

"States of hysteria can be feigned."

"True, but I don't believe Finetta's swoon was feigned. It took five passes of smelling salts under her nose before she stirred.

From what I understand, they usually work after one or two whiffs."

Daphne began inspecting the oar she'd be responsible for plying, one that was attached to the side of the boat directly behind the seat he would sit on. "The use of smelling salts is not a pleasant experience, so perhaps you're right about Finetta not feigning her swoon. It once took over five passes of a smelling salt vial under my nose for me to come to after I'd suffered a most dreadful fright. The scent that lingered in my nose was not one I would intentionally want to smell again, even if I needed to feign a swoon."

Herman straightened. "What could have possibly frightened you that much?"

"I've never discovered the answer to that," Daphne said, trailing a gloved finger along the smooth surface of the oar. "It was years ago, before I moved to New York. I'd gone with my brothers and a few of their friends to watch a firework display to celebrate the Fourth of July. All I really remember about that night was deciding to repair to the carriage to fix some pins that had been blown out of place by the wind. On my way to the carriage, something jumped out at me."

"Something?"

Daphne shrugged. "I don't know what it

was. All I recall seeing was a flickering shadow before I felt something touch my arm. Then I fainted. Luckily, my coachman thought he heard something and came to investigate, finding me lying on the ground. He called for my brother Jack, who knew where to find my smelling salts."

"No one discovered what frightened you?"

"The general consensus was that it was a stray dog that jumped up on me, but . . ." She frowned. "It didn't seem like a dog."

"Did it seem more like a person?"

"That's what I suggested to my brothers. But after my brothers, along with Thomas Sibley, George Potter, and Anthony West, went to look around, they didn't find any strangers lurking about, which is when they decided I'd been set upon by a stray dog."

Herman frowned. "Wasn't Thomas Sibley the man who asked you to marry him?"

"He was, but he didn't *ask* me to marry him. He *told* me I was going to marry him, which is not the same thing at all. However, I don't enjoy talking about Thomas. So, to return to the pressing business at hand, we were speaking of Finetta and the likelihood that she's the one behind the attempts on your life."

"Andrew's convinced she's not," Herman argued. "He was with Finetta when she lost her balance right before she let the arrow fly. He's certain it was an accident."

"No one shoots a person with an arrow by accident." She fiddled with a button on her glove. "Perhaps I should question the other men who were surrounding Finetta at the time of the accident to get their take on the matter."

"You don't believe Andrew's account is accurate?"

Daphne abandoned her fiddling and laid a hand on his arm. "I'm afraid I don't."

Finding it somewhat difficult to concentrate on the conversation because her touch was sending a very peculiar sensation through him, Herman shook his head, trying to clear it. "Why not? Andrew was close to Finetta at the time of the accident. He, of anyone, should know exactly what happened."

"Have you considered that the two of them might be collaborating together?"

He arched a brow. "Why would Andrew be collaborating with Finetta?"

"Have you not noticed that Andrew seems to be unusually fond of Finetta?"

"Andrew's fond of many ladies."

"Did you miss the part where I said *unusually fond* of Finetta?" She gave his arm a pat. "If it's escaped your notice, they spend a lot of time in each other's company. They also seem to enjoy easy conversations between them, something you certainly don't enjoy with Finetta."

Herman's thoughts, which he'd still been having a hard time gathering together after Daphne patted his arm, immediately snapped back into place. "You think Andrew is romantically interested in Finetta?"

"Regrettably, I do, and I think that interest is reciprocated, which gives both of them ample reason to want you out of the picture."

It took all of five seconds for Herman to think that through. "No, I'm sorry but Andrew isn't capable of plotting my demise. He's a good man, and his friendship with me is true. He would never want me dead, whether there's a lady involved or not."

"And while I find your loyalty to your friend commendable, Andrew is attracted to a lady you've been considering marrying. If you're dead, he would be free to pursue her without complications."

"Which is true, but Andrew knows I'll never marry Finetta, even though he and I have never discussed the matter."

"How could he know that?"

"Because it's obvious that Finetta would be miserable married to me. The last thing I would ever entertain is marriage to a woman I'll make miserable."

"But you agreed to host a house party that your grandmother filled with eligible young ladies, all of whom are remarkably similar in disposition to Finetta, and all of whom seem to go out of their way to avoid you."

"Don't tell my grandmother this, but I'm not considering marrying any of the young ladies she's assembled here for the explicit reason you just stated — they go out of their way to avoid me."

"The last person I'd tell that to would be your grandmother. She dislikes me enough as it is. But you should consider telling her that yourself. She seems to have put a lot of effort into this house party, as well as a lot of effort into selecting young ladies for you."

"An effort that has seen her rejoining the living."

Daphne's brows drew together. "You're tolerating being paraded in front of young ladies because it's gotten your grandmother reengaged with life?"

"I'm sure you'd do the same."

"If you'd met my grandmothers, you wouldn't have made that statement."

Herman grinned. "Why do I now feel a distinct need to meet them?"

Daphne returned the grin. "No idea.

238

They're both rather quarrelsome ladies who spend their time pointing out my many and varied faults. But we're once again getting woefully off topic. We were speaking about Andrew and how it could be a possibility he and Finetta are conspiring to kill you."

"They're not — at least Andrew's not. He was by my side when I learned my parents died, and he's never left it since. With that said, though, it was negligent on my part to not realize he's attracted to Finetta. I'll need to speak with him about the matter straight-away and tell him that I would harbor no ill feelings toward him if he's got courtship on his mind." He frowned. "I can only hope, though, that Finetta's grandmother will be agreeable to Andrew courting Finetta, something that may be behind Andrew's reluctance to publicly declare his affec-tions."

Daphne tilted her head. "Should I assume Mrs. Shoenburger might take issue with the fact Andrew earns a living as a bookkeeper?"

"Indeed. Not that this is well-known, but Finetta is an heiress to an impressive fortune she inherited from her parents when they died. That's why her grandmother wants to see a union between me and Finetta, as I have no interest in her fortune. However, from what my grandmother said, there have been a few gentlemen who've pursued Finetta because they want to get their hands on her bank account."

Daphne pulled her notepad from her bag, flipping it to a blank page. "I've not heard anything about Finetta being an heiress."

"She's not a lady who travels in high society, so there's not much gossip bandied around about her."

"High society or not, I should have spent more time digging into Finetta's circumstances. Her being an heiress could change all the theories I've constructed so far."

"Because there might be someone out there interested in her money who wants me out of the picture?"

Daphne sent him a smile that did unusual things to his pulse. "See, I knew you had it in you to puzzle out clues regarding your own case."

Herman wasn't certain if it was Daphne's smile or her compliment that was sending his thoughts scattering again, making a retort next to impossible. Thankfully, though, he was spared a response when his grandmother strolled into view, holding Sheldon's arm as they headed along the river path toward them.

"Herman, there you are," Mildred called. "I've been looking all over for you."

Daphne released a sigh. "I was hoping to avoid another confrontation with your grandmother until at least dinner. It's barely past noon and I'm not at my best for witty repartee until at least three."

"There's no saying my grandmother has sought us out because she wants to confront you. If you'll recall, she was very appreciative of your saving me from being shot by an arrow yesterday."

"Today is a different day. I'm sure she's thought of some new complaint to lodge against me," Daphne muttered right before Mildred and Sheldon reached them.

It was not a reassuring sign when Mildred took to looking Daphne up and down. She then released her hold on Sheldon's arm and stepped closer to the boat, peering from one end of the boat to the other.

"What are you doing?" Herman asked.

"Looking for Miss Beekman's typewriter." She nodded to Sheldon. "Sheldon told me that he had to get up at the crack of dawn in order to go over some research with you because" — she smiled a less-than-pleasant smile in Daphne's direction — "your secretary doesn't care to work early in the morning and insists on working with you in the afternoon, right when your guests are repairing to their respective rooms to get ready for the late-afternoon entertainments."

She arched a brow Herman's way. "When I saw the two of you heading toward the river, I was of the belief that Miss Beekman had decided to work outside again. However, since there's no sign of her typewriter, I'm now left with nothing to conclude but that the two of you are taking your boat out for purely entertainment purposes. I don't believe that's a good idea."

"I told you she'd be lodging a new complaint against me," Herman heard Daphne mumble before she squared her shoulders and settled her attention on Mildred.

"While I understand you believe I'm some sort of adventuress out to use my feminine allure to capture the attention of your grandson and thus steal attention away from ladies you've hand-picked for your grandson, I'm doing nothing of the sort. Frankly, taking a boat out to row on the Hudson seems a bit like torture to me and isn't something I'd choose to do for entertainment purposes."

Mildred's smile turned more unpleasant than ever. "And yet it must be a torture you're willing to suffer through in order to stay in Herman's good graces."

Herman rubbed his hand over his face

before he forced himself to step between the two ladies, even though doing so could be detrimental to his health.

"Daphne is not the one who suggested the rowing, Grandmother," he began, which had Mildred snapping her attention to him, her eyes narrowed. "I was the one who suggested it because Daphne has some concerns with a chapter she's recently typed. I'm more likely to listen to her concerns with an open mind if I'm out on the water rowing, an activity you know always settles me."

Sheldon glanced at Daphne. "What chapter concerns you?"

Daphne readjusted her spectacles. "The one with the axe scene."

Sheldon blinked. "You have concerns about that, as well?"

"It doesn't flow easily. I've been telling Herman you've been right about the scene all along, but he's remaining annoyingly stubborn about it." She shook her head. "An axe, as you pointed out in your notes, is not the best choice of weapons for this villain, whereas the rapier you suggested would change the tone of the scene for the better."

Sheldon's eyes crinkled at the corners. "I thought the rapier would lend a more dangerous air."

"I'm in full agreement with you," Daphne said. "Unfortunately, your cousin is still not convinced, which is why I agreed to go rowing with him. To put it bluntly, Mrs. Henderson, I'm not a lady who appreciates physical exertion this early in the day, but I'll do it if it results in Herman making some necessary changes to his draft."

"It's after twelve, which is hardly early in the day," Mildred said shortly.

"That's debatable."

Mildred lifted her chin. "My grandson prefers to row when the sun is barely up. As his secretary, you should be the one to make concessions. You should have dragged yourself from your bed this morning to join him on the water if, as you claim, you're convinced one of his chapters is sorely lacking."

"I didn't say it was sorely lacking. I merely said I have concerns." Daphne frowned. "But speaking of rising when the sun is barely up, dare I hope that Finetta has abandoned her bedchamber and returned to the house party festivities? I didn't see her when I ventured downstairs for my coffee. And while I understand she suffered quite the upset yesterday after she shot me, I hate to think the poor dear is still so distraught about the matter that she's lingering in bed."

To Herman's surprise, Mildred gave a very unexpected roll of her eyes.

"I'm afraid Finetta has still not ventured out of her room, requesting a tray be delivered to her this morning. As a woman who suffers from a nervous condition, I am sympathetic to her distress — to a certain extent. However, the archery fiasco was sheer carelessness on her part. If she was that inept with a bow and arrow, I would have expected her to sit out the event. She could have done extensive damage to Herman if you and your bustle had not been a much-needed barrier between him and a deadly weapon."

Daphne's lips twitched. "On my word, Mrs. Henderson, if I didn't know better, I would think you actually approved of my actions yesterday."

"I already told you I appreciated your intervention," Mildred returned. "But appreciation is not the same as approval. If not for the size of your bustle, you could have been gravely injured. It was a rash decision on your part to rush toward Herman, and I'm not a lady who approves of rash behavior. With that said, I also don't approve of carelessness, which means" —

she caught Herman's eye — "I've decided Finetta is not a lady I care to see you court. In fact, I've suggested to Mrs. Shoenburger that she might want to consider departing the house party early, taking her irresponsible granddaughter with her."

"That's certain to make matters more interesting," Daphne said under her breath before she directed a bit of a tight smile Mildred's way. "While I certainly understand why you're annoyed with Finetta, I would hate for the poor lady, along with her grandmother, to miss the remainder of the festivities. Besides, you and Mrs. Shoenburger seem to be friends, and friendships don't often survive when one friend demands another take leave of their presence."

As his grandmother retreated into silence, apparently needing a few moments to think that through, Daphne turned to Sheldon. "If we could return to Herman's latest manuscript, I read through the pages of notes you've compiled regarding El Dorado and the lost city of gold angle he's planning to include. I'm not sure he's committed to that angle just yet, but I believe you're on to something, especially the part about having him use a house's secret passageways to further the suspense of where an El Dorado map could be hidden. I was intending to discuss that with him as we row down the Hudson and wondered if you had any other thoughts on the matter."

Sheldon's lips curved the slightest bit. "I have a few, but they're not well-formed yet, which is why I was considering venturing into the passageways this afternoon to see if anything inspires me, like a nice hidey-hole where someone could stash a map. I think a discovery like that written into Herman's book would open up all sorts of possibilities."

Mildred cleared her throat, drawing Herman's attention. "You've not said a thing to me about writing a story set in El Dorado."

"True, but I discuss my settings and plots with you after I've made a firm decision." He smiled. "There's little point in telling you about a story that could very well change a day later." He nodded toward Sheldon. "We ran across a notation Mother jotted down about her and Father having an interest in El Dorado, but we've yet to find any additional mentions. That's why Sheldon's been making so many trips to bookshops, trying to find additional research material we might find useful. He hasn't found much, which means I'll probably need to change my setting soon."

"I don't think readers would be very

interested in a place like El Dorado," Mildred said. "Everyone knows the lost city of gold is merely a fairy tale, and you're not known to write fairy tales, dear."

Something about the way Mildred was avoiding his eyes had Herman reaching out to take hold of her hand. "Why am I getting the distinct impression there's another reason behind your reluctance to see me write about El Dorado?"

Mildred winced. "Was it that obvious?"

"I'm afraid so, just as I'm afraid, now that I think about it, that your reluctance might have something to do with my parents."

She gave his hand a squeeze. "Evan and Sarah discussed trying to discover El Dorado at one point and were incredibly excited about the possibilities. However, they were unable to locate proof of the lost city of gold because of their untimely deaths."

"And it would bother you to have me write about a quest my parents were never able to pursue?"

"Will it disappoint you if it would?"

Herman pulled his grandmother close, gave her a hug, and smiled. "It's only a book, Grandmother, just as El Dorado was only a thought. I'll choose another setting for my book." He caught Sheldon's eye.

"I'm going to need you to delve back into Mother's journals because we're going to need a new setting, unless you've already run across another location I can use."

"I did find a most informative book about the West Indies the other day," Sheldon said, his eyes turning distant. "You could always have your hero uncover a diary in a secret passageway, one that, hmm . . . maybe gives clues about a past murder, and clues that lead the hero to the West Indies."

"Oh, I like the sound of that," Daphne said, but instead of expanding on the idea, she suddenly peered at something across the river. Without saying a word, she hurried to where she'd left her bag on the ground and began rummaging through it. In the blink of an eye, she was pulling out a pair of opera glasses, training them across the water.

"We need to get on the river, and the sooner the better," Daphne said, catching Herman's eye. "I just caught a glimpse of the most beautiful, ah, heron, and I need to get a closer look at it. I'm sure it's exactly the bird I need to finish my latest poem."

"You're going to include a heron in a poem about a pirate?" Sheldon asked.

"If I can make it work, certainly," Daphne said before she shoved the opera glasses back into her bag and sent a subtle jerk of her head toward the river.

Knowing there was little chance Daphne had actually spotted a heron, while also knowing that, if what she'd seen had something to do with his case, she'd hardly be able to explain anything to him until they got on the water, Herman took a second to tell Mildred he'd meet her back at the house, then moved to the bow of the boat, dragging it into the water.

He spent a good few minutes explaining to Daphne how the oar she was going to use worked, an explanation he was convinced she'd not actually listened to, since she'd grabbed hold of her oar the second he'd stopped his explanation and began applying herself vigorously to pulling it back and forth at a furious rate, which only resulted in them moving about in circles. Ten minutes later, they were finally making their way from shore.

Conversation was nonexistent while he steered them out into the current, Daphne emitting some rather telling grunts as she tried to keep her oar in synch with his.

"I thought you always took your rowboat out by yourself," she said, releasing another grunt as water splashed over him, a direct result of her overly vigorous handling of her oar.

"I do."

"How do you manage the oars, then, since they're positioned for two people?"

"I don't have them positioned as they are now when I go out on my own."

"So why, pray tell, did you have to position them for two people today? We could have been across the river by now if I weren't responsible for one of the oars."

"Cooper asked me to include you in the rowing. He believes any progress you've made increasing your physical stamina has suffered since you're no longer participating in his thrice-weekly regime."

"I'll be having a word with Cooper at my earliest convenience."

Herman glanced over his shoulder and grinned when he caught sight of Cooper rowing another boat about fifty feet away from them. That Cooper was probably vastly amused at the difficulty Daphne was experiencing was not in question, especially when the Pinkerton man sent Herman a flash of a smile before he returned to his rowing, his oars cleaving through the water with what seemed to be little effort on Cooper's part.

Herman turned back to Daphne, who was

no longer rowing because she'd pulled out her opera glasses and was scanning what seemed to be an incredibly distant shore — one that shouldn't be so distant given the time they'd already spent on the water.

"Care to finally tell me what we're really about to chase down? I know it's not a heron."

"I caught sight of a lady striding into the forest. I think it's Finetta."

"Grandmother said Finetta is still in her bedchamber."

"She must have snuck out," Daphne said, lowering her opera glasses. "I don't see her anymore, but we'll pick up the chase after we get the boat to shore."

"We'll get to shore faster if you row with me instead of against me. Would it help if I say 'row' every time you're supposed to pull back on the oar?"

"Couldn't hurt."

To Herman's surprise, after he began chanting "row," the boat began to skim over the river, getting them closer and closer to shore until Daphne suddenly stopped rowing, which sent the boat veering to the right.

"What's wrong?" he asked.

"We appear to be taking on a bit of water."

A gurgling sound had Herman spinning around, and given the water that was now gushing up from what seemed to be numerous holes in the bottom of the boat, they were taking on more than a bit of water.

"Please tell me you can swim," he said.

Before Daphne could respond to what was a very important question, the boat began sinking at a rapid rate — so rapid, in fact, that he barely had time to grab hold of Daphne's arm before they were in the water and being pulled downstream by a very strong current.

CHAPTER THIRTEEN

"I'm going to have to rethink my stance on bustles, because who would have thought that the monstrosity Phillip insisted I wear with this lovely walking gown would actually serve as a flotation device?" Daphne asked as Herman towed her closer to shore, keeping one of his strong arms wrapped securely around her torso while using his other arm to cleave through the choppy water.

A rather waterlogged snort was Herman's first response to that. "While I admit I'm also surprised your bustle seems to have captured a large air bubble, what say we leave further talk of bustles in general until we reach shore?"

"But then I might focus on our concerning situation. I don't believe it'll help you if I descend into a swoon, which will turn me into a dead weight."

"Then by all means, tell me whatever else

you want to about bustles."

Daphne peered through lenses that were dripping with water, trying to see if the trace of amusement she'd heard in Herman's voice was causing him to smile, because it was quite the man who could smile while lugging a woman through a river that was swollen because of recent spring storms.

When all she could make out was a blurry blob that was probably Herman's face, she abandoned her scrutiny and settled for blinking water out of her eyes instead. "You have to admit the bustles I've been wearing have been far more versatile than anyone could have expected them to be. Why, the general consensus about bustles is that they merely allow a lady a pleasantly shaped backside. However, my bustles have now saved me after a nasty fall and cuts from broken china, blocked an arrow that could have killed me, and have now spared me from a horrible drowning."

"We're not to shore yet. There's still a chance we'll drown."

"You seem to have us well in hand, Herman, so I don't believe that's true. But would you care for me to try to swim a little on my own?"

"I saw firsthand the extent of your arm strength when you tried to climb that rope.

And even if I didn't question your ability to swim very far, I have no intention of letting go of you."

"Aren't you getting tired?"

"Not tired enough to where you need to start swimming."

Even though she was presently in the Hudson River and being swept along on a current that Herman was valiantly fighting through, Daphne felt a most unexpected sense of security.

Yes, they were in a dangerous situation, but she had every confidence that Herman would see her safely to shore because he was exactly what one expected of a man who possessed a chivalrous nature. He would do whatever it took to see after her well-being, no matter the cost to himself.

"You're almost there, Herman," Daphne heard Cooper yell. "I'm coming in to help you."

"That would be —" Herman began, the rest of his words lost when they hit a patch of white water and the bubble that had been helping Daphne keep afloat disappeared as her gown seemed to soak up every bit of the Hudson it could. She felt the current begin to tug her under, but then Herman's arm tightened around her as he pulled her back to the surface. A moment later, another set of hands took hold of her, and a few seconds after that, she felt welcome rocks beneath her feet as Herman, with Cooper's assistance, tugged her into shallow water.

Stumbling through water that seemed determined to drag her back into the depths of the river, Daphne drew in a breath of much-needed air right as Herman swept her into his arms, striding with her through the swirling water until he reached the river-bank. He didn't stop when he reached the shore and instead carried her up the bank and set her on her feet beneath a large willow tree.

"Are you all right?" he asked.

She couldn't help but smile. "I'm alive, so yes, I'm fine. You?"

He returned the smile. "Alive as well, so very fine indeed, although . . ." His smile faded. "You must be freezing."

"She can wear my coat," Cooper said, shrugging out of his coat and holding it out to Daphne.

She took a step forward, then faltered, the weight of her wet gown, not to mention all the unmentionables she was wearing, making it difficult to maintain her balance. "I'm afraid I might be too water-heavy to move."

"I can carry you," Herman didn't hesitate to offer.

She arched a brow. "Through the forest and after Finetta, if she's the one I saw from across the river?"

"I think we should return home. You're soaking wet. There's a bridge not far from here, one Finetta must have taken because it's relatively close to my house."

"I'm sure there are many inquiry agents who suffer soakings every now and again while working a case. I'm certainly not returning to the house simply because I'm drenched." She began wringing water from her skirt, then abandoned that less-than-helpful solution when she realized it would take her all day to get the water out. "I'm going to need both of you to turn around."

"Why would you need us to do that?" Cooper asked.

"Because I need to remove my bustle and other, ah, articles of clothing before we can get on our way."

"What?" Cooper and Herman asked together.

"I'm fairly certain you heard me the first time, so if you'd be so kind as to turn around, I'd appreciate it."

Cooper spun around, whereas Herman didn't move, cocking his head to the side.

"How do you intend to remove your bustle on your own? You can hardly move.

I'm relatively certain bustles are difficult to get off in the best of circumstances, and this is hardly the best of circumstances."

"I'll manage."

"Or I can assist you."

Heat immediately settled on her face. "You've apparently forgotten that I'm not actually a sophisticated woman of the world, Herman. Someone like Madame Calve wouldn't bat a lash at your offer, whereas I, Miss Daphne Beekman, a confirmed spinster if you've forgotten, am not exactly comfortable with the idea."

"I won't look."

"How would you be able to accomplish that?"

Herman shrugged. "I can assemble and disassemble a pistol in pitch darkness. I'm sure your bustle will be far easier to manage than that, so I won't need to look. Turn around."

She swiped what felt like a piece of seaweed from her face. "Why would you need to know how to take apart a pistol?"

"Research for my book *Death Comes to Baxter Hall.* The hero needed to assemble a pistol when he was hiding in a cave. I figured I should learn how to do that so my scene would be believable. I also thought that while I was at it, I might as well see if I could learn how to disassemble a pistol without light as well."

"That's some dedication to your craft."

"I'm sure you're just as dedicated with your poetry."

The urge hit her yet again to disclose the truth of her writing to him, brought about, no doubt, because the man had surely just saved her life, which made it seem less than principled for her to continually withhold the truth from him.

Pushing aside the urge because she had, after all, signed a nondisclosure agreement, Daphne turned around, realizing she had no choice but to accept Herman's assistance since there was little likelihood she'd be able to get out of the bustle on her own.

"What do you think Finetta's doing, if that was who you saw earlier?" Herman asked as Daphne felt his hand settle on her hip, his touch causing the heat that had already settled in her cheeks to intensify.

She cleared her throat. "Since she's supposed to be languishing in bed, her nerves still questionable, I imagine she's up to no good."

"Or she could have decided that fresh air might steady her nerves."

"There's plenty of fresh air to be had on your back veranda. That she chose to cross the Hudson and disappear into a grove of trees seems remarkably suspicious."

"I suppose it does at that," Herman said right before Daphne felt her bustle fall to the ground,

Herman tugged her skirt into place a second before he stepped away from her. Turning, she found him with his eyes shut and a smile on his face.

"I told you I wouldn't need to look."

"And I'm quite impressed." She took a step forward, but the excessive amount of fabric now dragging on the ground due to the lack of her bustle made walking all but impossible. "I'm not sure this is much better. Keep your eyes shut and, Cooper, don't turn around yet."

Three minutes later, devoid of her petticoats, pantaloons, and stockings, Daphne slipped the strap of the bag she'd had the presence of mind to throw over her head before the boat sank from her shoulder and opened it, pulling out a wicked-looking knife she'd gotten for a steal at a local market.

"What are you doing?" Herman asked.

Glancing to him, she found his eyes still closed. "I'm going to cut away part of my walking gown. There's no way I'll be able to make it far with what amounts to a mountain of soggy fabric dragging behind me."

Herman's eyes flashed open before he strode to her side, his eyes widening when he caught sight of the blade. He held out his hand. "What say you let me handle the removal of excess fabric for you?" he offered. "Seems like that might alleviate the chance of your losing a finger."

"That sounds more than disturbing," Cooper said. "Can I turn around yet?"

"Yes, you can turn around," Daphne said as she handed Herman the knife. "And I wasn't in danger of losing a finger."

Cooper spun around, his gaze settling on the knife before he narrowed his eyes on Daphne. "We haven't had a single lesson on knives yet, which means that's the last weapon you should be carrying around with you. You're barely proficient with a pistol, and a knife, well, you're liable to poke your eye out with it, or cut off a finger, like Herman said."

"What a lovely image poking my eye out with a knife brings to mind," Daphne said. "But before you descend into a more detailed lecture about knives, I believe our time would be better spent discussing Herman's boat and why it sank. Clearly, something troubling is afoot."

Cooper stilled. "You believe it was intentional?"

"Yes, which means someone at the house party really is trying to kill Herman."

"How was the boat tampered with?" Cooper pressed.

Herman looked up from where he'd been cutting through a ruffle. "I think someone drilled holes in it, then packed those holes with sawdust — a trick I used in my latest book."

"And doesn't that lend the situation a curious twist," Daphne said. "I'd be interested to learn if Finetta has read your latest book."

"But even if she has, and even if it was Finetta you saw disappearing into the forest," Cooper said, "I'm perfectly capable of investigating this on my own, leaving you to repair to the house to change out of your wet clothing."

Daphne raised her chin as Herman made his final cut with the knife. "Absolutely not. I don't need to be pampered, which means I'm not going back to the house." She shrugged into Cooper's jacket, then picked up her bag.

"I'll carry that for you, and no, I'm not trying to pamper you," Herman said, taking the bag from her and then offering her his arm, amusement twinkling in his eyes. Together, they headed for the forest with Cooper in the lead, walking into the trees where she'd last seen Finetta disappear what seemed like hours before.

"There's a clearing not far from here," Herman said five minutes later. "It might be the perfect spot to hold a clandestine meeting, if —" Herman stopped walking as Ann suddenly materialized through the trees, walking their way.

"What do you suppose Ann's doing out here?" Daphne asked.

"Perhaps something concerning really is transpiring," Cooper said, striding to meet Ann, who immediately flashed Cooper a smile, then took hold of his arm and pulled him closer to Daphne and Herman.

"Thank goodness all of you are here," Ann began, her voice no louder than a whisper. "I saw Finetta slip out the back door earlier, so I decided to follow her because she's supposed to be recovering from 'the incident,' as Mildred keeps referring to the archery fiasco yesterday. I then saw Mr. Andrew Ware following her as well, so I hung back a discreet distance, thinking I should still follow them if only to prove our theory about their fondness for each other. I almost lost them because I had to make sure Andrew was out of sight before I crossed the bridge. But then, unfortunately, when I caught up with them, I was not prepared for what is currently happening just past the tree line. I was returning to the house to get help, so thank goodness all of you are here. There's no time to explain further, though, because the situation is turning dangerous."

"Dangerous how?" Cooper asked.

"A pistol is involved."

"We shouldn't tarry," Cooper said, withdrawing his pistol and moving with Ann through the trees, Daphne and Herman following them. Stopping behind an enormous maple, Cooper nodded to Herman. "I'm going to investigate. You'll stay with the ladies?"

"Of course."

"We're inquiry agents," Daphne said firmly. "As such, we're not being left behind, and I'll thank you to discontinue that nonsense."

Exasperation clouded Cooper's eyes. "You do recall that your strength is contemplating plots and Ann's is collecting gossip, don't you?"

"I'm hardly likely to forget that, but since you're the one who keeps insisting we participate in physical exertion lessons, as well as other lessons on how to handle dangerous situations in the field, it seems somewhat counterproductive to now insist Ann and I stay behind instead of getting experience out in the field."

"She does make a most compelling argument," Ann said.

Cooper rolled his eyes before he muttered something about Daphne being obstinate, although he didn't mention anything about Ann being obstinate, then strode forward and out of the trees.

Daphne snagged hold of Ann's hand and hurried after Cooper, making their way into a small meadow, Daphne stopping in her tracks at the sight that met her eyes.

Mr. Andrew Ware was standing in the middle of the clearing, a pistol in his hand, while Mr. Irwin Rosenward was standing a good twenty feet away from him, holding fast to Finetta's arm, who seemed to be struggling to get free from him.

Before Daphne could do more than take in the scene in front of her, Herman strode into the clearing, his gaze settled on Andrew.

"What are you doing?" he demanded.

Andrew gave a jerk of his head in Irwin's direction. "That's a question you should ask Mr. Rosenward."

"He's a madman," Irwin hollered. "He wants to shoot me."

Herman switched his attention to Irwin. "Madman or not, Irwin, you need to release Miss Shoenburger. She should have no part in whatever quarrel you currently have with Andrew."

"I don't have a quarrel with Andrew," Irwin shot back. "Or at least I didn't have a quarrel with him until he pulled a pistol on me."

Herman arched a brow Andrew's way. "And you pulled a pistol on him because . . . ?"

"He was threatening Finetta," Andrew said. "I saw her leaving the house and thought she looked distressed, so I followed her. I certainly never imagined the source of her distress was Irwin, a man I'd been under the assumption was a friend to her family. When I happened upon them, he was shaking her."

"I was only shaking her to calm her down because she was becoming hysterical," Irwin said.

"I've never heard that shaking a lady in the midst of hysteria is a recommended solution," Andrew shot back. "One would think a gentle embrace would be far more effective, or even a nice pat on the back."

"Considering Finetta punched me when I tried to embrace her, taking hold of her shoulders and giving her a shake was the only course of action left to me since I didn't want her to punch me again."

"If Finetta resorted to punching you, you must have been threatening her." Andrew drew off one of his gloves and threw it in Irwin's direction. "I demand satisfaction."

"Did Andrew Ware just challenge Irwin Rosenward to a duel?" Ann breathed, her eyes wide as her gaze shifted to Andrew, then to Irwin, then to Finetta, then back to Andrew again.

"I believe he did," Daphne said.

"There's no reason for you to demand satisfaction," Irwin said, dashing a hand over a forehead that was now perspiring. "Finetta and I have merely suffered a small misunderstanding, one we've yet to resolve because you took it upon yourself to stick your nose into business that doesn't concern you."

"It was not a small misunderstanding," Finetta said as she tried to shrug out of Irwin's hold. "And I'll thank you to release me."

"I can't do that because Andrew will shoot me the second you step away from me."

"It's nothing less than you deserve," Finetta retorted right before she stomped on Irwin's foot, earning a howl of pain from him before he dropped her arm. Finetta didn't hesitate to bolt across the meadow, not stopping until she reached Andrew. Andrew immediately thrust his pistol into Herman's hands right before he opened his arms and gathered Finetta close to him.

"Considering Finetta doesn't appear to be suffering from hysteria any longer," Daphne whispered to Ann, "I believe the case can certainly be made that an embrace is a far more effective cure for a bout of hysterics than shaking is."

"Too right it is," Ann whispered back. "And it seems we were right about the affection Andrew and Finetta share for each other." She wrinkled her nose. "But what in the world do you think Irwin Rosenward is up to?"

"I think it's time to find out," Daphne said, nodding to Cooper, who returned the nod before he moved into motion.

Stopping in front of Irwin, who was bent over rubbing his foot, Cooper cleared his throat. "Mr. Rosenward, I believe I have a few questions for you, ones I'm going to insist you answer."

Irwin straightened. "Why would a coachman have any questions for me, or better yet, why would you think I'd answer a coachman's questions?"

"Unfortunately for you, I'm not a coachman. I'm Agent Cooper Clifton of the Pinkerton Agency."

"What's a Pinkerton doing posing as a coachman at a house party?"

"That's really none of your concern, but what is of concern to me is what you were doing with Miss Shoenburger."

"He was trying to blackmail me," Finetta called from the safe confines of Andrew's embrace.

"I didn't see that one coming," Ann muttered.

"Blackmail you?" Cooper pressed. "For what?"

"There's no need for us to discuss this now, Finetta," Irwin said, taking a step toward her, but stopping when Cooper blocked his way. Irwin was forced to crane his neck and peer at her over Cooper's shoulder. "It's a personal matter between us, and it will not serve you well to disclose anything."

Finetta stepped out of Andrew's embrace, scowled at Irwin, then directed her attention to Cooper. "What I'm about to disclose does not speak well of my character, but I simply cannot live with the foolish decisions I recently made.

"I've been distraught of late over the pressure I've been feeling from my grandmother, as well as Mildred, to further my acquaintance with Herman." She turned to Herman. "I know full well that you're not interested in furthering our acquaintance either but are too much of a gentleman to let that be publicly known. You're also reputed to be incredibly solicitous of your grandmother, and because Mildred seemed determined to see a match between us, I'm afraid I, well, took it upon myself to ascertain that wouldn't happen."

"You decided to murder him," Daphne said, stepping forward and drawing Finetta's attention.

"I most certainly did not decide to murder him," Finetta all but sputtered. "But I did seek out Irwin's counsel on the matter, something I'm now regretting."

"My counsel was sound," Irwin argued.

Finetta ignored him and turned her attention back to Cooper. "After remarking to Irwin right before the reading of the Montague Moreland book how impressed I was with Daphne and how displeased Mildred seemed to be about the arrival of an outspoken, sophisticated lady of the world, Irwin suggested that I take a page out of Daphne's book and become more vocal at the house party, perhaps even daring to go so far as to argue with Mildred in front of everyone. He believed that might have her becoming annoyed with me and abandoning her desire to see me married to her grandson." Finetta's lips curved. "The perfect opportunity for that, of course, occurred when Mildred wanted Miss Evans to continue reading while the croquet match played out. And even though my knees were knocking, I voiced my objections, drawing Mildred's displeasure in the process."

"But it wasn't enough to have Mildred abandoning her plan, was it?" Ann asked, coming to stand beside Daphne.

"Miss Evans," Finetta said with a frown. "I didn't notice you there. What are you doing out here?"

Ann gave a breezy wave of her hand. "Mildred asked me to check on you to see if you were feeling better. I noticed you leaving the house and was concerned that you might still be lacking the, er, proper amount of stamina needed to walk about the grounds. I felt it prudent to follow you in case you began feeling faint again."

"I was hoping no one else took note of my leaving the house," Finetta said.

"Mr. Andrew Ware certainly did since he followed you here," Irwin said. "Clearly I've been played for a fool because I was under the impression you and I shared an understanding."

"We've never had any type of understanding between us," Finetta argued.

"We never had a verbal understanding," Irwin countered, "but we had an understanding all the same. Young ladies do not seek out a gentleman's counsel unless they hold that gentleman in very high regard."

"I did at one time hold you in high regard, but not regard I ever thought you'd misconstrue to be of the romantic type."

"Is that a result of your apparently holding foolish romantic notions about Andrew Ware?" Irwin asked.

"My feelings for Andrew are not foolish."

"On the contrary. Andrew is a bookkeeper who does not have the wherewithal to keep you in style. Besides that, your grandmother will never approve of him."

Finetta's eyes flashed. "I don't need to marry a gentleman who has the wherewithal to keep me in style, because, if you've forgotten, I'm an heiress. Frankly, a bookkeeper would be the perfect man for me because he would know how to manage that large fortune I possess. As for my grandmother's approval, while I certainly hope she'll give it to me, it's not going to deter me in the least if she doesn't." She turned and sent Andrew a lovely smile. "Andrew is the love of my life and I intend on marrying him — that is, if he wants to marry me."

"This just keeps getting more and more interesting," Ann whispered, giving Daphne's hand a bit of a squeeze.

As Andrew began beaming at Finetta, Irwin's face turned red. "How romantic, Finetta, but just how likely do you think it'll be that Andrew will want to marry you after he discovers that you deliberately tried to shoot Herman with an arrow yesterday?"

CHAPTER FOURTEEN

"I believe we're finally getting around to what is behind that blackmail business," Daphne said, coming to stand beside Herman, her brown hair straggling around her shoulders, her pins and hat evidently lost in the Hudson.

The urge to laugh struck him from out of nowhere.

Yes, they were currently witnessing a scene that could have come directly out of one of his novels. But nevertheless, the sight of Daphne looking bedraggled and completely dwarfed by Cooper's coat, which still revealed the lower half of a dress that certainly looked as if it had been hacked at with a knife, amused him. The sight also left him feeling somewhat off-kilter because, in all honesty, he'd never seen a lady look more appealing, even with the lenses of her spectacles smeared with mud.

"Here, allow me to help you with those,"

he said, reaching out to take the spectacles from her face, leaving her blinking at him in return as he used the least soiled part of his shirt to wipe the mud away. He handed them back and watched as she returned them to her face, blinking a time or two before she smiled.

"Thank you, Herman. I was wondering why everything seemed somewhat spotty. I've also been wondering why no one, not even Ann, has remarked on our sodden state."

He swallowed the distinct urge to laugh again.

It was a testament to the unusualness of Daphne's mind that she'd be wondering such a thing, especially after the disclosure Irwin had just made.

"I believe our woebegone condition has gone unnoticed because there's something much more interesting occurring," he said, waving in the direction of Finetta and Irwin, who were currently glaring at each other.

Daphne wrinkled her nose. "I suppose you have a point, but I know I would have noticed, even if I'd been involved with something else, if two people arrived in my midst looking as if they'd fallen into the Hudson. It's not as if it's swimming season yet." She glanced to Irwin and Finetta.

"But, returning to the situation at hand, I'm not sure what to make of any of this just yet, although I'm coming to a few conclusions regarding Irwin, the most important of which centers around the notion that he is not the quiet and unassuming gentleman he presents to the world. In fact, I'm beginning to believe he's a bit of a rogue."

"I can't argue with that, nor can I argue that I might not have taken your warning about young ladies and their talent for duplicity seriously enough. Obviously, Finetta is far more cunning than I gave her credit for. I definitely wasn't expecting to hear she'd deliberately tried to shoot me."

Daphne frowned, but before she could say anything, Finetta stepped forward, her eyes blazing as she began marching Irwin's way.

"You know I never intended to shoot Herman," Finetta began. "I've never been able to hit so much as the side of a barn with a bow and arrow. You're well aware of that, which is why you suggested I try to stage an accident when I was shooting my arrow in order to convince Mildred that I'm far too accident-prone to be a good candidate to marry her grandson." She inclined her head to Herman. "Everyone knows your grandmother is militant about keeping you safe."

"I wasn't aware that was such public knowledge" was all Herman could think to respond.

Finetta waved that aside. "Well, it is but . . ." She returned her attention to Irwin. "After I reflected on our plan, I decided I couldn't go through with it. I certainly wasn't expecting you to take matters into your own hands — literally. I was shocked when you stepped close to me as I was getting ready to shoot my arrow, and that shock only intensified when you had the audacity to take hold of my, ah, hip and turn me around. The sheer surprise of your touch took me so aback that I panicked and let the arrow fly, my heart missing a beat when it burrowed into poor Daphne's backside."

"That was unexpected, but it's not as if Daphne was injured," Irwin said. "And I would think you'd be more appreciative about my stepping in. Mildred has decided you're too accident-prone for her liking and thus not an appropriate candidate to become Mrs. Herman Henderson."

"I'm hardly appreciative of your giving Daphne a dreadful fright and almost killing her," Finetta shot back.

"And here I was under the mistaken belief that your descension into hysterics was a way to distract everyone from what really happened — that being that the situation was no accident."

"It *was* an accident because, again, I decided I couldn't go through with your plan. You, however, proceeded forward with no warning to me."

Cooper cleared his throat. "I'd like to know why you *took* matters into your own hands, Mr. Rosenward."

Irwin let out a huff. "You said you were a Pinkerton. One would think you'd be more astute."

"Given the precarious position you're in," Cooper said, "I don't believe it's in your best interest to insult me."

Irwin shrugged. "Perhaps not, but I would think with what I've disclosed that you would have already concluded that I was under the mistaken belief that Finetta was romantically interested in me. Because of that, I felt compelled to intercede in her affairs on her behalf. Obviously, she does not return the affection I carry for her, which leaves me feeling quite the fool for having involved myself with her in the first place."

"You've never given me a reason to believe you hold me in any affection other than friendship," Finetta said, taking another step closer to Irwin. "Truth be told, you're more a friend to my grandmother than you are to me, and you have to be at least twenty years older than I am."

"Most women prefer older gentlemen because we're well established in life. That means we're more adept with lending young ladies our invaluable guidance."

Daphne released a snort. "May I assume, Irwin, that you, believing that nonsense you just spouted about guidance, decided it would be in Finetta's best interest to marry you? And when she obviously refused marriage, you tried your hand at blackmail?"

Irwin's brow furrowed. "What an imagination you have, although I'm not certain why you've decided to interfere in all this. You're merely Herman's secretary. You should remember that."

"I don't heed advice from men who try to blackmail women."

"I didn't try to blackmail Finetta," Irwin argued. "I mean, yes, I might have told her she was not rationally thinking through my offer of marriage, but I don't consider that blackmail."

"You didn't offer to marry me," Finetta said, her color high. "You told me I was going to marry you."

Daphne gave a bit of a shudder, rubbing

her arms, which had Herman moving closer to her.

"Are you cold?"

"More a case of remembering how I felt when Thomas told me I was going to marry him instead of him asking me," Daphne said. "But I'm fine, thank you."

Herman opened his mouth, but before he could point out that Daphne didn't exactly look fine because her cheeks were a shade paler than they'd been just seconds before, Finetta blew out a breath of clear disgust.

"And not only did you tell me I was going to marry you, Irwin, you then told me I should be thankful you were still willing to make such an offer after I shot Daphne. When I refused, you threatened to spill my secret unless I changed my mind, which is, in fact, blackmail."

"I disagree," Irwin countered. "I was merely pointing out that having such a troubling secret would burden you for the rest of your life. If you married me, there would be no need for that secret to ever come to light."

"It has come to light," Finetta pointed out. She nodded to Daphne. "You seem to have a level head on your shoulders. Tell me this, if you were in my position now, how would you proceed?"

Daphne readjusted her spectacles. "I'd tell Irwin that he's to have nothing further to do with you. I'd also demand he tell you if he might have, perhaps, gone out on his own — on your behalf, of course — to discourage Herman from courting you."

Right there, in the middle of a meadow, of all places, Herman found himself completely enthralled with the unique lady looking as if she'd recently almost suffered a drowning, which she had.

That Daphne, even under the most unusual of circumstances, was able to sort through pieces of the puzzle that made up his case and present it in a way that seemed effortless as she tried to get answers concerning his situation left him beyond impressed, as well as a bit awed over what was undoubtedly a very intellectual mind.

"I'm not sure I understand what you're suggesting," Finetta said, drawing Herman from his thoughts.

"I'm suggesting that Irwin could be responsible for the four near-accidents that Herman suffered not that long ago, when he was in his carriage," Daphne returned.

Finetta raised a hand to her throat as everyone turned their attention to Irwin, who was rather red in the face.

"Please tell me Daphne's wrong," Finetta

whispered.

"It wasn't an attack by carriage. I was merely hoping to scare him, which I then hoped would have his grandmother insisting on canceling the house party, which would then allow you to avoid Herman's attention." Irwin pulled a handkerchief out of his pocket and dashed it over his forehead. "I was only looking after your best interests, and since no one was injured, I don't believe there's any need to make a fuss over what was just a bit of mischief on my part."

"Were you responsible for sneaking through the hidden passageways at Herman's New York residence?" Daphne shot at him next.

"Why would I do something like that?" Irwin demanded. "That's trespassing, which is against the law."

"So is trying to run a man over with a carriage," Daphne pointed out.

"But I didn't run him over, so no harm was done."

"I'm sure Herman feels differently," Cooper said before he turned to Herman. "It may be best if I take Irwin in for further questioning. He's admitted to being behind the carriage attacks, which is, as Daphne mentioned, against the law. I can use the police building in Hyde Park, which isn't far from here. We often assist the police with different cases, so it won't be an issue if I ask to use one of their interrogation rooms."

Irwin began backing away from everyone. "I'm not going to be treated like a common criminal, and I certainly won't agree to visit an interrogation room. I've already admitted what I've done."

"I'm not certain you *have* admitted everything you've done," Cooper countered. "We've yet to discuss the matter of the boat."

"What boat?" Irwin demanded.

"The boat that just sank with Herman and Daphne in it."

Irwin's gaze swept over Daphne, then moved to sweep over Herman. "Now that you mention it, they do seem unusually wet. But I had nothing to do with that."

"That remains to be seen," Cooper said.

"No, no it doesn't," Irwin argued before he jerked his head in Andrew's direction. "If you ask me, Mr. Ware is the one you should be questioning because he would have the most to gain from Herman's demise. With Herman dead, he could pursue Finetta freely, not bothered by the guilt he must be feeling over mooning over a lady everyone knows Herman was supposed to marry."

"I would never even consider murdering Herman," Andrew said, catching Herman's eye. "You know that, don't you?"

"Of course I do," Herman said. "Although you probably should have mentioned your affection for Finetta to me. Might have spared us a bit of drama."

Andrew blew out a breath. "I was intending to tell you but thought it would be best to wait until after the house party. Proclaiming that I'm in love with Finetta would have created all sorts of drama, especially with your grandmother and Finetta's grandmother."

"You're in love with me?" Finetta breathed, raising a hand to her throat.

Andrew was by her side in an instant, taking her other hand in his before they both began gazing soulfully into each other's eyes, quite as if they didn't have an audience watching them.

"This is definitely going to have to go into one of my, ah, poems someday," Daphne muttered.

Herman grinned, but before he could respond to that, a loud thud drew his attention — a thud that was a direct result of Irwin hitting Cooper over the head with a large limb before bolting into the forest.

CHAPTER FIFTEEN

"I don't know about you, but I'm beginning to think we're not going to be able to claim complete success with Herman's case, no matter that we discovered Irwin was behind the carriage attacks."

Daphne stopped typing the notes pertaining to Herman's case and sent a nod to Ann, who was standing on the other side of the small table Daphne was using underneath a shade tree. "Since Irwin did elude capture by jumping on the horse he'd taken from Herman's stables, I'm afraid I have to agree with you. But with local police and the Pinkertons actively searching for him because he attacked Cooper and technically stole one of Herman's horses, he'll eventually be found. He seems unusually good at hiding, though, given that he's not been seen since he attacked Cooper two days ago. That means we have no idea if he was telling the truth about the boating incident or sneaking around Herman's secret passageways."

"I'm hoping Miss Martha Mulvey was right when she mentioned the rumors she'd heard regarding Irwin — that he's a gambler who may be in debt to some questionable characters," Ann said. "If proven true, it's understandable why he involved himself in Finetta's affairs. He's evidently in desperate need of her fortune, which explains why he resorted to blackmail."

"It does suggest the man is capable of doing more than merely chasing Herman with a carriage. Still, until he's found, we can't let our guard down, nor can we discontinue our investigation in case there's someone else out there determined to lay Herman low."

"It didn't help our investigation when Finetta blurted out to the guests everything that happened after we finally managed to get back to the house."

Daphne wrinkled her nose. "That was unfortunate, but I imagine the poor lady simply couldn't help herself since her nerves were frazzled. However, Finetta confessing what part she'd played in everything, along with Irwin's duplicity, and then telling everyone Cooper was a Pinkerton definitely didn't help the investigation." Daphne blew out a breath. "I suppose the only positive we can take away from Finetta's disclosure was that she didn't know we were hired by Herman as well. That, at least, has allowed us to continue at the house party as if I'm merely Herman's secretary and you're Mildred's paid companion."

Ann shot a glance to Mildred, who was sitting with Dr. Gibbons, waiting to watch some of the gentlemen enjoy a few bouts of fencing, Herman being one of those gentlemen.

Mildred, surprisingly enough, had not said much regarding the fact that Herman hadn't told her about the attempts on his life, nor that he'd withheld Cooper's true identity.

Instead, after Finetta finished spilling the beans regarding her involvement with Irwin and her scheme to avoid a continued association with Herman, Mildred had merely sent Herman a considering look before she'd become distracted by Mrs. Shoenburger's descent into hysterics. Those hysterics had been a direct result of Finetta, after she'd confessed about her involvement with Irwin, declaring that she was in love with Andrew Ware.

Complete chaos had descended over Herman's house, so much so that Mrs. Shoenburger needed to borrow Mildred's smelling salts before she'd called for their carriage and insisted they return with all due haste to the city. She was so distraught that Finetta had agreed, reluctantly of course, to depart to New York, telling Andrew they'd sort everything out after she got her grandmother settled down.

As Finetta and Mrs. Shoenburger whisked away in their carriage, the other guests gathered around Herman, clamoring to learn every last detail about the attempts on his life.

That clamoring had gone far to put a wrench in the investigation because everyone was now aware that a Pinkerton had been hired, one who, even though still recovering from a nasty gash on his head, remained in residence at Herman's estate.

"Mildred's continuing to give poor Andrew the evil eye," Ann said, turning back to Daphne. "She told me she blames him for all the young ladies and their mothers departing from the house party not long after Finetta and her grandmother left. According to Mildred, the mothers were worried their impressionable daughters might be unduly influenced by Finetta's unlikely romance with Andrew. If you ask me, though, that was complete nonsense because Andrew, and perhaps Sheldon, are the only gentlemen in attendance who aren't well-established or dripping in funds. And because Sheldon has obviously set his eye on Martha Mulvey, I'm not sure what all the fuss was about."

"I believe some of the mothers were concerned their daughters would set an interested eye on Cooper, especially since he has been looking rather roguish after Irwin's attack. There does seem to be something about a dangerous and handsome rogue that many ladies can't ignore."

Ann drew herself up. "I never considered that the young ladies might settle an interested eye on Cooper. Although, hearing that, I don't believe I'm upset in the least that the mothers and their daughters made hasty departures."

"I thought you weren't interested in Cooper."

"Not that I'm admitting I'm interested in the man, but it's not difficult to see how adorable Cooper is, as well as not notice how remarkably competent he is at his profession. Competent men have always held a special place in my heart, as have adorable men — not that I'm saying Cooper has a special place in my heart, mind you," Ann hurried to add.

Daphne glanced to where Cooper was

currently lounging in a chair, pulled close to where the men were getting ready to fence. "I'm not sure *adorable* is how I would currently describe Cooper. He does have a large swathe of bandages wrapped around his head and his eyes are ringed with bruises."

Ann directed her attention to Cooper as well, her cheeks turning pink when Cooper sent her a wave. She spun around and began fanning her face with the Montague Moreland book she was holding. "There really is something compelling about a gentleman who has the look of a rogue about him."

"And that right there is why you should stop insisting he hasn't stolen at least a piece of your heart."

"I'll be sure to do that, just as soon as you stop denying you only view Herman as a client."

"He is a client."

Ann rolled her eyes. "You're being deliberately obtuse, but since you evidently don't care to discuss your feelings for Herman, and I don't care to spend the next few minutes trying to drag confessions out of you, shall we return to talk of our case?"

"Since our case is why we're still on the Hudson, that would be for the best. However, just so you know, I have nothing to confess, which means end of story in regard to Herman and me."

Ann's only response to that was another rather telling roll of the eyes.

Electing to ignore that because anything she might add would only have Ann more convinced that there *was* something besides a working relationship between herself and Herman — not that Daphne was completely opposed to that idea, if only she thought Herman would be receptive to it, which she was certain he wasn't — Daphne returned to her notes.

"Did I mention that Herman's now including me in the literary chats he's been holding with his fellow authors?"

"You did, and not that I want to gloat, but there was a distinct twinkle in your eye when you mentioned you'd been included, a twinkle I believe was there because being a part of the literary chats allows you to spend more time in Herman's company."

Daphne's lips curved. "You certainly are relentless when you get a bee in your bonnet. I'm sure, though, that the twinkle you saw was simply a result of my looking forward to the literary chats. My inclusion will allow me to get to know the authors better, as well as give me an opportunity to charm them so they'll begin letting their guards down around me and hopefully disclosing something useful in the process."

"It would be helpful if one of them would disclose they harbor resentment toward Herman, perhaps because he's more successful, or a better storyteller, or . . ." Ann's voice trailed off, the reason behind that evident when Jay Storrow strolled up to join them.

He stopped beside Ann and nodded to the Montague Moreland book she was still holding. "Thinking about continuing on with Moreland's story?"

"Seems somewhat pointless now that the captive audience I was reading to is no longer here."

Jay looked to where Miss Martha Mulvey was helping Sheldon arrange the protective padding that was needed for the fencing bout. "Miss Mulvey is still here. She was enjoying the story."

"True," Ann said. "But she's the only young lady still in attendance, an unusual circumstance to be sure. It was shocking when Mrs. Shoenburger terminated her employment because she believed that Martha must have known about Finetta's affections for Andrew and never disclosed what she knew to Mrs. Shoenburger."

"If you ask me," Daphne said, "it was

quite unfair of Mrs. Shoenburger to terminate Martha's employment, not to mention
unfair that she refused to allow Martha to
travel with them back to the city. Martha
hasn't given any indication she knew about
Finetta's love for Andrew, and leaving the
poor lady behind was not well done of Finetta's grandmother."

"I wouldn't fret about that, Daphne," Jay
said. "Martha has not made it a secret she's
fond of Sheldon, nor has she seemed overly
distressed about being left behind. She also
seems to be lending a great deal of comfort
to Mildred, who cannot be pleased about
how her house party has turned out.
Frankly, I've been expecting Mildred to
repair to her bedchamber with her smelling
salts in hand, given that all the ladies she
was hoping might become Mrs. Herman
Henderson have now fled from the estate."

"One would think that would be the case,
but I've not seen Mildred take even a whiff
of her salts," Daphne said.

"That's because she's too busy keeping an
eye on Herman — and you," Ann muttered
under her breath right as Charles Bonner
walked up to join them.

It was rather telling when Ann immediately slipped away without another word as
Charles stepped up to Daphne's makeshift

desk and began peering at one of the pages Daphne had typed earlier for Herman. Picking up the notepad where she'd jotted down notes concerning her pirate scene, she placed it on top of the pages she'd typed for Herman.

"What a completely unnecessary move to keep me from getting a glimpse at Herman's work," Charles said with a sniff.

Daphne forced a smile. "Forgive me if I offended you, Charles, but Herman doesn't allow anyone to see his work in progress."

"He's clearly allowing you to see his latest work."

"I'm his secretary. It would be difficult for me to type up his chapters if I didn't actually get to see them."

"Hmmm. . . . I imagine that would be problematic."

Wondering how in the world a man who seemed to be less than quick-witted was capable of penning novels that sold remarkably well, Daphne pulled the paper filled with the notes she'd been typing about Herman's case from her typewriter, slipped the paper as discreetly as she could into a folder, then slid the folder underneath her notepad.

To her annoyance, Charles leaned over the table to peer at the notes in her notepad.

"That doesn't look like Herman's hand-writing," he said.

"That's because it's mine."

Charles sent her a hint of a smile before he picked up her notepad and had the audacity to begin reading through her notes. "Interesting. It appears as if you weren't fibbing about that pirate nonsense."

"Why would you have thought I was lying about my pirate?"

Charles shrugged. "It seemed like an unlikely hero to me for a poem, how-ever . . ." He set the notepad down on the table, reached for Daphne's pencil, then began adding notes of his own to her page.

"What are you doing?" she asked.

"I just had a few thoughts that should make your pirate idea plausible. I'm listing some character attributes you'll find useful, and I think it'll be helpful if you include a romance thread. You should also give your pirate a sensitive nature, which will go far in impressing your heroine." He stopped writ-ing and lifted his head. "I'm not actually partial to poetry, finding it . . . what is that word you seem to enjoy using? Oh yes, *trite*. But I understand how to create the perfect hero, and you might be on to something with using a pirate in that role, even if that is quite unconventional."

"I respectfully disagree with that, Charles," Jay said, looking over Charles's shoulder to read over the notes Daphne had made, as well as the ones Charles had just written. "Readers, in my opinion, won't be receptive to a pirate, much less a sensitive one. They much prefer a pirate to be the villain in a piece, but . . ." He stepped next to Charles and leaned forward, pointing to one of the notes Daphne had made. "What's this about falling into the ocean amidst a frenzy of sharks?"

Charles began scratching through some of Daphne's notes. "The sharks will have to go, but with them gone, your poem might show some potential. In fact, I could see someone writing a novel and including such an unlikely hero. A pirate-themed novel would, you mark my words, be a best seller."

In the blink of an eye, clarity struck from out of nowhere.

Quite like Herman had come to the conclusion he'd been wrong about the axe, she knew without a shadow of a doubt that she'd been wrong about her pirate, and all because Mr. Charles Bonner, one of the most questionable authors she knew, thought she was on to something.

She'd somehow convinced herself that a pirate would be a marvelous hero, a man of adventure who both male and female readers would enjoy rooting for, but clearly, she was off the mark about that, which meant . . .

She was going to have to scrap her latest draft and start from scratch, while also figuring out exactly who the perfect hero would be for her to write about and all while being under a rather daunting deadline.

"How goes the typing?"

Shaking herself from the epiphany she'd just had that was going to demand a lot of work on her part, Daphne realized that Herman had now joined them.

"Daphne seems to believe I'm trying to sneak peeks at your latest work," Charles said before Daphne had a chance to respond.

"I don't *seem* to believe that," Daphne began. "I *do* believe that because it's exactly what you were trying to do."

Charles's lips thinned before he shrugged. "We authors are always curious as to what our competition is writing, but it's not as if I need to steal Herman's work. I've found incredible success with the two novels I've published and have no doubt that the one I'm currently working on will see the same success, if not surpass it."

Daphne tilted her head. "Didn't you say

yesterday that you've only just started your third novel and were still contemplating whether or not it was going to be a murder mystery or an adventure story? If you were to change genres, your book might not be as well received as the others because your mystery audience might not care for an adventure story."

"My readers are so loyal to me that they'll buy any book with my name on it, no matter the genre. Besides, I've been growing bored with murder, which is why I'm contemplating venturing into the thrilling world of exotic locations."

"Aren't you a little hesitant to venture into that world, since Herman has seen so much success with using exotic locations?" Daphne asked. "You said only yesterday that you're a competitive man, but going up against Herman in what is certainly a competitive publishing market may not sit well with you in the end if your sales don't compete with his."

Charles seemed to swell on the spot. "Of course my sales will be comparable to his, and I'll thank you to keep those types of insulting remarks to yourself." With that, Charles spun on his heel and stalked away.

"I'm not sure that was wise of you, Daphne," Jay said, frowning at Charles's retreating back. "He may seem like a fool at times, but he's got a vindictive streak a mile wide. He won't take kindly to your suggesting he won't be as successful as Herman if he includes exotic locations into his books."

"Then he really wouldn't have taken it kindly if I'd asked him what I really wanted to ask him — if he'd been trying to sneak a peek at Herman's latest draft because he needed some ideas," Daphne said.

"No, he wouldn't have taken kindly to that at all, so I suppose it's a good thing you showed some restraint," Jay said, his lips curving. "However, even if Charles had gotten more than a glimpse at Herman's draft, Herman wouldn't have anything to worry about. Charles is not the writer Herman is and would not be able to do justice to the quest for El Dorado."

"I don't remember telling you I was considering an El Dorado theme in my latest book," Herman said.

Jay shrugged. "I heard it from Martin Corrigan yesterday at our literary chat. You must have already left the room, but we were all in agreement that the lost city of gold is an excellent idea. Truth be told, I'll be waiting with bated breath to learn the particulars of how you're going to handle the plot."

"And while I have no idea where Martin heard about El Dorado, I'm afraid you're going to be holding that bated breath for some time, because I've decided to move on to another location."

Jay immediately perked up. "That's too bad, but if you're not going to use it . . ." He muttered an excuse under his breath and hurried away, grabbing up a jacket that was slung over a chair and retrieving a note-pad from it, which he immediately flipped open and began scribbling into.

"Jay's definitely staying on the list," Daphne said, earning a laugh from Herman.

"Just because Jay has clearly absconded with one of my abandoned ideas does not mean he's a murderer. In all honesty, I would think he just proved he's not the culprit because there was nothing subtle about his actions just now."

"He stays on the list."

Herman laughed again before he extended his hand to Daphne. "Since you're obviously firm on that, allow me to artfully change the subject. How do you feel about rapiers?"

"I don't have much of an opinion about them because I've never held one. Cooper has yet to introduce rapiers into our lessons."

"We should rectify that straightaway."

Daphne blinked. "You want me to join in with a bout of fencing?"

"That might be a little too ambitious, but you can at least look over my rapier collection and get a feel for one." He nodded to the stack of papers on the desk. "Allow me to take those into my library so you won't worry someone may try to sneak a peek at my current draft before we repair to the fencing field, known to true fencers as a *piste* or strip."

"Should I take it there aren't many true fencers at this party?"

"Indeed, hence the reason for calling it a fencing field, which will spare me some lengthy conversations with curious authors."

Exchanging smiles, Daphne watched Herman stride for the house with the pages she'd typed out before she turned back to the guests, taking a moment to look each one of them over as they mingled about on the lawn.

Sheldon and Martha were speaking with Mildred and Dr. Gibbons, while Jay Storrow had abandoned his notepad and was now looking over Herman's rapier collection with Martin Corrigan, who was pointing to the protective tips Herman insisted were a must for their fencing matches.

Cooper was chatting and exchanging smiles with Ann, his smile disappearing when Charles Bonner joined them. Charles didn't stay with them long, though, not after he apparently asked Ann if he could borrow her Montague Moreland book, which he took with him to a shady tree, sat down, and began reading.

Normally, Daphne was delighted to witness anyone reading her work, but because it was Charles, she couldn't help but wonder if some of her scenes might soon find their way into Charles's new novel.

"Collecting more thoughts on the guests?" Herman asked, returning to her side.

"That is what you're paying me to do."

"And you're doing a wonderful job of sorting through all the suspects." He smiled. "I was quite impressed with how you uncovered all that nastiness about Irwin, especially when I wasn't certain it was wise to pursue Finetta after our unexpected dip in the Hudson. If you hadn't insisted on pressing on, we might never have known it was he who tried to run me over."

"If only I was convinced he was responsible for all your mishaps."

"If he's not, I've every confidence you'll figure out the culprit."

Butterflies immediately began fluttering in

her stomach, but since butterflies were not what a true inquiry agent should experience simply because she'd just been given one of the nicest compliments of her life, Daphne settled for sending Herman a smile as they strolled over to where everyone was now gathered for fencing. They joined Jay and Martin, whom Daphne had not spoken to often because Martin was a quiet gentleman, which was too bad because she longed to learn more about his writing process.

Martin handed Jay the rapier he was holding before he turned to Herman. "Jay was just telling me he wants to fence with you because he feels that will help improve his fencing abilities, so he's going to take my place. I'll wait and fence with Sheldon, who was going to spar with Cooper, until Dr. Gibbons voiced his concern that fencing may reinjure Cooper's head."

Daphne glanced back at Cooper, who seemed to be fine, but who also seemed completely content to chat with Ann. That suggested the Pinkerton wasn't too worried about his head, but adhering to the doctor's concerns had now lent him the perfect opportunity to indulge in a bit of flirting.

"Martin was showing me all the extra precautions that have been taken with the equipment," Jay said, holding up the rapier and showing Daphne where a protective sleeve had been attached to the tip of it. "I was wondering why Mildred wasn't putting up a fuss with this activity, and now I know."

Herman looked to Mildred and grinned. "Considering Grandmother has parked herself close to the fencing field, I'm not sure she's going to avoid fussing at some point."

"Perhaps now isn't a good time for me to inspect the rapiers," Daphne said. "If she sees me near them, I imagine she might demand an end to the activity."

"You're not going to be engaged in an actual match," Herman countered. "Which means Grandmother will have no reason to fuss."

"If you're certain it won't cause problems with your grandmother," Daphne began, accepting the rapier Jay offered her. She smiled and gave it a few experimental swings. "It's far lighter than I expected."

"Rapiers are light, but they're not meant to be swung around like a bat," Herman said, his eyes twinkling. "Come on, I'll show you how to wield it properly."

Unable to resist the lure of learning how to wield a rapier, especially when that unforeseen skill might come in handy with a future story, Daphne walked with Herman to the middle of the fencing field, nodding to Sheldon, who was holding up a protective chest pad. "I think Sheldon's trying to get your attention. He seems to want you to put some protective gear on before we begin, which isn't a bad idea, given how athletically challenged I am. I would hate to accidentally stab you and leave you bleeding all over the place."

"You could intentionally stab me with your rapier, and it wouldn't pierce my skin because of the protective sleeve over the blade." He nodded to the rapier. "Go ahead. Give it a try."

"You want me to stab you?"

"It might give you some great inspiration, because how often are you encouraged to stab a person? Besides, as I mentioned, it won't leave a scratch."

Exchanging a smile with Herman, because they both knew she'd be incapable of turning down his offer to stab him, Daphne gave the foil a few tentative thrusts, then turned to Herman, sent him a cheeky grin, and stabbed the foil at him, making contact with his arm.

To her absolute horror, a second after she felt the tip meet its mark, blood began to seep through the white sleeve of Herman's shirt. A second after that, black dots began obscuring her vision, and even though she tried to fight against the blackness, she felt the rapier slip from her hand before she crumpled to the ground.

CHAPTER SIXTEEN

A mere blink of an eye after Herman realized he'd actually been stabbed, he realized Daphne was in trouble.

Grabbing hold of her just before she hit the ground, he swept her into his arms, ignoring that his right arm was beginning to burn where the rapier had pierced his skin.

"Herman, have you taken leave of your senses? This is no time for chivalry. Set Miss Beekman down this instant so Dr. Gibbons can attend to you," Mildred said, hurrying toward him, her face white as she held fast to Dr. Gibbons's arm.

"I'm fine, Grandmother," he reassured her. "It's probably just a scratch. If you'll excuse me, though, I need to get Daphne inside."

"You'll do no such thing." Mildred gestured to Jay. "You can take Miss Beekman inside."

Having absolutely no reason to trust any

of his guests because, obviously, someone had tampered with the protective sleeve he'd attached to every rapier, nor would he have relinquished Daphne even if all of his guests weren't now suspects, Herman shook his head at Jay, who was already holding out his arms. He then turned and found Ann standing beside Cooper, who was picking up the rapier Daphne had dropped. "Ann, will you get Daphne's bag? We're going to need her smelling salts."

As Ann spun on her heel and raced away, Herman headed for the house, holding Daphne close.

Perkins was already holding the back door open, stepping aside as Herman strode through it. "Is the young lady all right, sir?" Perkins asked.

"She's suffered a fit of the vapors."

"How regrettable. Did she injure herself? There appears to be blood dripping on the marble."

"The blood's mine, not hers, and we'll worry about the mess later. If you could bring me a basin of cold water and some cloths, I'll be in the music room."

Striding past Perkins, who was now looking at him in horror, Herman made his way down the back hallway and into the music room. He headed for the divan that was placed beside the piano, laying Daphne on it, concern flowing freely when he noticed the paleness of her face.

Placing his hand on her forehead, his concern increased when his touch met skin that was decidedly clammy.

"I found her bag. Give me a minute to find her smelling salts," Ann said, rushing into the room. She dropped Daphne's bag on the floor and began tossing out item after item as she searched for the smelling salts. "How does she fit all this in here, and why wouldn't she keep her smelling salts on top of this mess? It seems like they'd be far more important than this book on poisonous plants."

"Why would Miss Beekman need a book on poisonous plants in the first place?" Mildred asked, coming up behind Herman to peer over his shoulder. "Seems somewhat suspect. And why would she keep smelling salts in her bag? Most women of the world, as I've heard her proclaim to be numerous times, aren't prone to swooning."

"There's nothing suspect about Daphne's book because she's an avid reader with diverse tastes. As for her swooning, I imagine even a woman of the world would be expected to swoon after what Daphne just experienced."

"Her swooning could have been avoided if she hadn't stabbed you."

"I told her to stab me, never believing the precautions I'd taken would fail in such a spectacular fashion." Herman glanced to the door as Perkins hurried through it, water sloshing on the floor from the basin he was carrying, not that Perkins seemed to notice, which was a testament to the dire situation at hand.

He set the basin beside Herman and handed him some cloths. "I brought enough so you'll have some to mop up that arm of yours, as well."

"Herman's going to need more than a mopping up," Dr. Gibbons said, moving to Herman's side. "Allow me to attend to Daphne while you repair to your room. Given the amount of blood soaking your sleeve, stitches are going to be in order."

"I'm not leaving her," Herman said, earning a grumble from Mildred even as she handed her vial of smelling salts to Ann, who'd almost emptied Daphne's entire bag on the floor and not found any success with locating Daphne's salts.

"While I would expect nothing less than you taking it upon yourself to see after your secretary, you're dripping blood on the Aubusson carpet. You're not going to be any use to Miss Beekman if you lose so much blood that you faint," Mildred said.

Even though there was nothing that would have him leaving Daphne's side, his grandmother did have a point. He dipped one of the cloths into the basin, wrung it out, then placed it on Daphne's forehead before directing his attention to Dr. Gibbons. "Can you stitch up my arm in here?"

"I can, but you're going to have to sit down for me to do that. Daphne's merely fainted. She'll be fine while I see after you." Dr. Gibbons glanced to Mildred. "You and Miss Evans will need to leave the room. Stitches aren't pleasant to receive, and there's certain to be a great deal of discomfort on Herman's part. Frankly, one groan from your grandson might be enough to send you, as well as Miss Evans, into the same state Daphne's in."

"Don't be ridiculous," Mildred countered, lifting her chin. "I'm not going to swoon, nor will Miss Evans, who is certainly a no-nonsense type of lady." She moved beside Ann, took hold of the vial Ann was struggling to open, gave the top a twist, then moved closer to Daphne, waving the vial under Daphne's nose.

Herman's concern increased when Daphne didn't so much as twitch, but

312

before he could suggest he take over for his grandmother, Dr. Gibbons began cutting away his sleeve.

"It's going to take at least ten, if not twenty, stitches," Dr. Gibbons said after he considered the wound. He snatched up one of the cloths Perkins had provided, dipped it in the water, then began cleaning Herman's arm. "The blade made a mess of your arm, probably because the young lady was very enthusiastic about the way she thrust it into you."

"Which I encouraged her to do," Herman said when Mildred began muttering something about questionable behavior under her breath. He caught Dr. Gibbons's eye. "You might as well get on with it, and don't worry that I'll be a difficult patient. I've had stitches before, and while they're not pleasant, I assure you, they're not something I won't be able to tolerate."

Mildred raised a hand to her throat. "When have you had stitches?"

"I don't believe now is exactly the moment for me to recount all the times I've needed them, Grandmother. I'll simply leave it that I've had stitches before and clearly didn't suffer any lasting repercussions because of them."

Mildred narrowed her eyes on him.

"You've had stitches numerous times in the past?"

Dr. Gibbons cleared his throat and sent Herman a telling look. "Perhaps it would be best if Ann sees after Daphne. Mildred, while not distressed, certainly seems agitated."

Mildred released a snort, sent Dr. Gibbons a scowl, then returned to waving smelling salts under Daphne's nose, which, once again, did nothing to restore Daphne to consciousness.

"Since your grandmother is now occupied, as well as obviously determined to prove she's not overly agitated," Dr. Gibbons said quietly, gesturing to a chair that sat on the other side of the piano, "shall we begin?"

The next twenty minutes were not what Herman would consider enjoyable, although he barely noticed the last few stitches Dr. Gibbons made because Mildred had abandoned the smelling salts and begun to dribble water over Daphne's face. Leaning forward, which earned him a rebuke from the doctor, Herman stilled as Daphne's lashes began to flutter.

"We should put her glasses on," Ann said, snatching up Daphne's glasses that someone had placed on a small table. She slid them into place right as Daphne's eyes opened, closed, then opened again, her gaze darting around the room before it settled on him.

Her lips curved into a smile. "Herman. Oh, thank goodness, you're alive. I had the most unusual dream where you were covered in blood and looking quite as if you were at your last prayers."

He returned the smile. "As you can see, I'm fit as a fiddle."

"She seems confused," Mildred said as Daphne's eyes closed again and her forehead puckered, as if she'd taken to thinking about something troubling.

"I'm sure she is confused. She's been unconscious for over thirty minutes," Herman said.

Daphne's eyes flashed open. "I was unconscious?"

Ann took hold of Daphne's hand. "We were beginning to worry because you were out for so long."

"That was hardly professional of me, especially after I've made such an effort to convince Herman I'm no longer prone to swooning."

Mildred's eyes immediately narrowed on Daphne. "Why would you make an effort to convince Herman of such a thing?"

Daphne shifted her attention from Ann to

Mildred, blinking a few times, as if she were still having difficulty focusing. "Ah, Mrs. Henderson. I didn't realize you were here, but . . . what are you doing here?"

"Herman insisted I see after you while Dr. Gibbons patched him up."

Daphne blinked again. "That was very nice of you."

"I didn't have a choice in the matter because, again, Herman insisted. But returning to the swooning business? Can it be that I've been right about you all along and that you *are* up to some manner of subterfuge?"

Daphne raised a slightly shaky hand to her forehead and began to rub it. "I'm not sure I'm quite up to answering so many questions right now, Mrs. Henderson."

"And I have to agree with that," Herman said. "You've suffered a traumatic incident, so I'm certain my grandmother will concur that this is hardly the moment for questions."

"But Miss Beekman might actually answer my questions truthfully since her guard is down," Mildred countered. "I mean, yes, you did encourage her to stab you, but how was it possible that she was able to draw blood? I think it's only right that I should expect an answer to that very important question."

Daphne's eyes widened before she caught Herman's eye. "Goodness, I did stab you, didn't I?" Her gaze drifted to his arm, her eyes widening to the size of saucers. "Are those stitches?"

Mildred nodded. "Seventeen of them. You sliced him up rather dreadfully."

"Honestly, Grandmother, you're not helping the situation," Herman said before he moved next to Ann, who scooted out of the way to give him room to kneel next to Daphne. "You mustn't fret about my stitches because it wasn't your fault."

"I don't know how you figure that. I stabbed you, which means the fault definitely rests with me."

"Indeed it does," Mildred said, nodding more vigorously than ever. "And when you pair that stabbing with what I can only describe as shady activities on your part, such as when you almost took off my head with a croquet ball, I'm convinced it's now time for you to pack your bags and return to wherever it is you're from."

Herman ran a hand through his hair, wincing when the motion left his arm burning more than ever. "Forgive me, Grandmother. You know I appreciate how protective you've been over the years, but there's no need for you to protect me from Daphne. I assure you, she's not out to harm me."

"She stabbed you, so she's already harmed you. And, she has a book about poisonous plants stashed in her bag. I certainly won't stand by and remain silent, not when she might decide to poison you next."

Daphne's brows drew together. "I wouldn't poison Herman. Besides, I've yet to find time to read that book, so I have no idea how to go about poisoning anyone."

"And that type of thinking is exactly why I want you gone from this house with all due speed," Mildred shot back.

Daphne opened her mouth, but before she could respond, Andrew strode into the room.

"We've got a bit of a situation happening in the library, Herman," he began. "Agent Clifton has gathered all the remaining guests there and has begun questioning them about the recent incident. I'm afraid your writer friends are not pleased to discover they're now considered suspects of foul play."

"Why would any of Herman's writer friends be considered suspects?" Mildred asked. "Miss Beekman is the one who stabbed him, so I would think Agent Clifton's time would be better spent questioning her."

"They're considered suspects," Andrew began, "because after inspecting the rapier Daphne was wielding, Agent Clifton discovered the protective sleeve had been cut. If you'll recall, Daphne was typing most of the afternoon and wasn't expected to participate in any of the fencing activities. That means she wouldn't have had an opportunity to tamper with the weapons."

Mildred's eyes widened. "Did you say the rapier was *tampered* with?"

"I don't think now is the time to continue this conversation," Herman said, his eyes darting to his grandmother, which earned him a grunt from Andrew.

"You need to stop coddling your grandmother," Andrew said. "Clearly, something troubling is afoot. It's not fair to her to continue to shield her from the unpleasant fact that someone besides Irwin is obviously out to murder you."

Mildred immediately took a seat on the divan, evidently not noticing that she was now sitting on Daphne's legs. "Murder?"

"Indeed," Andrew said.

For the span of what felt like hours, a myriad of expressions crossed Mildred's face, expressions that went from disbelief to disappointment and then to temper. "How long have you suspected that more than one person might want you dead?" she finally asked.

Herman rose to his feet, deciding now was the time to disclose all, as well as answer his grandmother's question, because Andrew was right. He was doing a disservice to Mildred by leaving her in the dark.

"I've suspected it ever since Irwin didn't know anything about the boat and was also taken aback when he was pressed about prowling around the secret passageways in my house in the city."

The temper in Mildred's eyes increased. "You never mentioned anything about any prowling."

"Because I knew you would worry needlessly."

"My worry wouldn't be needless, because someone seems determined to kill you."

"I said almost exactly those same words to him not too long ago," Daphne said, retreating back into silence when Mildred shot her a look before she settled a glare on Herman.

"So, if I'm understanding correctly," she snapped, "Agent Cooper Clifton has remained on-site not because he's recovering from a blow to his head, but because you're still facing some unknown threat?"

Herman rubbed a hand over his face. "I'm afraid so."

Mildred drew herself up. "I see. And while I'm sure you thought you were being considerate of my nerves by withholding from me the dire situation you're facing, I find I'm in full agreement with Andrew's suggestion." She lifted her chin. "Madness has obviously descended upon our house, which means I'm now going to insist you discontinue coddling me. I'd like to hear the truth — all of it."

"I don't believe now is really the time to hear a full disclosure, Mildred," Dr. Gibbons said, looking up from where he'd been returning his needle and thread to his medical bag. "Your nerves have already suffered from witnessing Herman being stabbed. I was just about to recommend you repair to your room and take a nap. Perhaps this evening you'll be up for hearing all of Herman's truths."

Mildred's eyes flashed. "This is hardly the moment to suggest a nap. In fact, I'm now going to expect you to discontinue coddling me as well." She gave a bob of her head to Herman. "With all that nonsense out of the way, tell me everything. We'll be far more capable of dealing with whatever trouble is currently stalking you if we present a united front, something that will be impossible to do if I'm kept out of the loop."

Before Herman could disclose a single thing, though, a knock on the door drew everyone's attention. A second later, Martha Mulvey entered the room.

"Forgive me for interrupting," Martha began, "but I'm afraid the situation in the library is escalating. The writers are now hurling accusations at one another, and I'm afraid those accusations may soon be followed by fists. Sheldon's trying to aid Agent Clifton with calming the situation down, but I believe they'd appreciate some help. Agent Clifton mentioned something about needing more muscle."

"Oh for heaven's sake. Muscle isn't what's needed; some common sense is," Mildred said, pushing herself up from the divan and marching out of the room.

"We should definitely repair to the library," Daphne said, swinging her legs over the side of the divan and getting to her feet, wobbling just a bit.

Herman was by her side a second later, lending her a steadying hand. "You should stay here and rest. You're clearly unsteady on your feet. I'll help Cooper."

"My legs are simply asleep because Mildred was sitting on them. They'll wake up in a moment. Besides, staying behind is not an option since it's my job to —"

"Your job to what?" Martha pressed when Daphne simply stopped talking, evidently realizing that Martha was still in the room.

"Ah, well, take notes," Daphne said, taking hold of the arm Herman offered her. "One never knows when the need for thorough notes will come in handy." She stomped one foot against the floor, then the other. "I think I can make it to the library now, where I'll immediately begin taking some, um, notes."

Herman's lips twitched as he headed for the door with Daphne still stomping beside him, Ann, Andrew, and Martha following close behind. As they reached the library door, the sound of raised voices was impossible to miss.

"This is going to be interesting," Daphne muttered.

Unable to argue with that, Herman walked through the door, taking a moment to take in the chaos unfolding before his eyes.

Cooper was standing in the middle of the room, trying to quiet everyone down by waving his hands in the air, not that anyone was paying him the least little attention. Most of the authors gathered in the library were shouting at one another, the din so loud it was difficult to make out exactly what anyone was saying.

"Seems to me you'd be the one most likely to want Herman dead," Herman heard Martin Corrigan shout at Jay. "You've mentioned more than a few times how Herman's last book has gone into its fifth printing. None of your books have enjoyed that many prints."

Jay drew himself up. "That's ridiculous. I'm not going to kill a man simply because he outsells me."

"Murders have happened for lesser reasons," Martin threw back at him.

"*You're* the one who was supposed to fence with him," Jay shot back. "If you ask me, that's telling in and of itself, especially after you ceded your time with Herman to me. Seems to me that suggests you were looking for a scapegoat."

Martin's face began to mottle. "I have no reason to murder Herman. I'll never sell as many books as he sells, but unlike you, I'm content with my sales. I have no need to measure my success against any other author."

"I don't know a single author who is content with their sales," Charles called from where he, curiously enough, was sitting in a chair, far removed from the fray, the Montague Moreland book he'd borrowed from Ann open in his lap. "I mean, granted, I sell more books than most of you assembled here, but I'm always looking to increase my sales."

James and Frederick Basil, brothers who wrote humorous mysteries together and who'd remained in the background for most of the house party, exchanged glances before Frederick stepped forward. "You only sell more books because your family goes out and buys all of them."

Charles shut the Montague Moreland book with a snap. "That is blatantly untrue."

James shook his head. "It's not and you know it. Frederick and I have seen members of your family descending on bookshops and then leaving with every book of yours that shop had for sale."

Charles rose to his feet. "Are you suggesting I'm a cheat?"

"There's no suggesting about it," James said.

Instead of responding to that, Charles headed for the door, his way blocked by Cooper, who was now looking rather harried, as if his time as a Pinkerton had never prepared him for dealing with a room filled with temperamental writers. Spinning on his heel, Charles stalked his way over to a

window that flanked Herman's desk, presenting everyone with his back.

A loud whistle from Daphne had the
room, surprisingly enough, falling silent.

"If I could have your undivided attention,
my darling, darling writers," she began,
sending the room at large a lovely smile
when all the gentlemen turned her way. She
then gave a languid wave of her hand, quite
as if she'd suddenly remembered some of
the suggestions Madame Calve had given
her about how to attract and hold attention.
"While I understand that the unfortunate
incident that recently happened between
myself and Herman has set everyone's
nerves on edge, if I may make a suggestion?"

"Of course you may," Jay called, returning
the smile Daphne was now sending him.

"And aren't you just a sugar plum to be
so accommodating?" she asked, which had
Herman swallowing a laugh.

"To continue," Daphne said, as Herman
tried to get his amusement in check, "what
I believe all of you are forgetting is that you
write mysteries for a living. Clearly, the
rapier I stabbed Herman with was tampered
with and could have been tampered with by
someone in this very room. I would think
all of you, at least the innocent ones, would

be putting your talent for writing mysteries into action."

"You think we authors should try to figure out who did it?" Jay asked slowly.

Daphne beamed at him. "Too right you should. You can sift through clues, discuss everyone's whereabouts at the time of the incident, then discuss who might benefit the most if Herman would have suffered a mortal wound instead of the one I gave him."

"Herman's wound was not insignificant, if that's what you're suggesting," Mildred said from where she'd taken up a spot beside Valentine Hageboom and Albert Gallatin, two writers who'd obviously felt uncomfortable with all the shouting and had taken refuge behind a large fainting couch that was placed in front of a bookshelf.

"I wasn't suggesting it was," Daphne returned. "Nevertheless, it wasn't a mortal wound, but it could have been if the rapier had been wielded by a more experienced fencer." She nodded to Cooper. "Perhaps we should begin by having you tell us what you've discovered so far."

Cooper raked a hand through his hair. "I've not discovered much, other than that the protective shield was split on purpose."

"A concerning discovery, and one that

should be written down. If there are no objections, then I, as Herman's secretary, will act as the notetaker as we strive to puzzle this mystery out."

No one objected to Daphne's offer, and after sending the room at large a smile, she nodded to Charles, who'd moved from the window and was standing beside Herman's desk. "Would you be a dear, Charles, and bring me my notepad? It's on top of the pile there. It's the same one you so helpfully wrote down some suggestions in about my pirate."

Charles picked up the notepad, but instead of walking to Daphne's side to hand it over, he began reading over the notes on the page, his brow furrowing the longer he read.

"Have you thought of something more regarding my pirate?" Daphne asked, which earned her a wave of a hand from Charles in return but not a response.

"Daphne can't begin to take notes, Charles," Jay began, "until she has her notepad. If you've decided you don't care to help us puzzle out this mystery, just say so, but you're being somewhat rude by withholding her notepad and delaying our discussion."

Charles lifted his head. "Since my integrity

has been unjustly questioned, I *was* prepared to sit this out and allow all of you to blunder about playing detective. However" — he smiled — "I believe *I've* just figured out who the culprit is, and I assure you, it's not a person anyone here has even thought about."

"Do not say that you're about to try to convince everyone Perkins is to blame," Martha Mulvey said, stepping forward as Perkins, who'd been standing still as a statue by the door, began edging up against a bookcase, almost as if he were hoping to avoid becoming the object of everyone's attention again. "In this particular case, I'm fairly sure the butler didn't do it since I was helping Sheldon lay out protective gear, and I can vouch for Perkins in that he never got anywhere near the equipment."

Charles's eyes narrowed. "If I hadn't already figured out who the culprit was, Martha, you might have just implicated yourself and Sheldon. But to address your statement, no, Perkins didn't do it. Although, again, it is *not* a trite plot twist when the butler is responsible. Furthermore, to avoid additional accusations being tossed around amongst us, which will most assuredly cause hard feelings that will then see our literary group disbanding, allow me to present my conclusion." Charles set aside Daphne's notepad, not bothering to say another word as he gazed around the room, evidently enjoying the suspense his statement had caused.

Daphne stepped forward. "I think I speak for all of us in saying enough of the drama, Charles. Clearly, we're now waiting with bated breath to hear your conclusion, so . . . ?"

Charles's smile widened as he stepped around the desk, made his way to the very center of the room, then brandished the book he was still holding. "It's Montague Moreland."

Daphne slid her spectacles down her nose and peered at Charles over the rim of them. "I believe I again speak for all of us, Charles, in saying that's an unlikely conclusion because Montague Moreland, as everyone knows, is not present at this gathering."

"Isn't he?" Charles countered.

"Stop playing games, Charles," Jay said, stepping forward. "While you may find this situation amusing, someone seems determined to harm Herman. This is no time for ridiculous antics on your part."

"But I'm not playing a game," Charles said as he flipped open the book, brandishing the page where Montague Moreland had scrawled out an inscription to Ann. "You see, this is Montague Moreland's signature, and curiously enough, it just happens to match" — he strode back to Herman's desk and snatched up Daphne's notepad — "this handwriting, which means Montague Moreland is definitely in our midst. However, Moreland is not a he but a she and, to be more exact, is none other than Miss Daphne Beekman."

CHAPTER SEVENTEEN

As everyone in the room took to gaping Daphne's way, she found herself in the unusual position of not being able to come up with a single word to say in response to Charles's claim, which was rather concerning considering she was a wordsmith, after all.

Quite honestly, the only thing that kept whirling through her mind was that the very last person she would have ever imagined figuring out her secret had to be, without a doubt, Mr. Charles Bonner.

Drawing in a deep breath, she struggled to gather wits that could only be described as scattered as she tried to compose a plausible response to Charles's claim. Unfortunately, nothing sprang to mind.

Chancing a glance at Herman, she found him considering her closely, smiling ever so slightly, although why he was smiling, she truly had no idea.

"I *knew* it," Mildred proclaimed, abandoning her spot by Valentine and Albert, who were both looking keener to be in the library than they'd been only moments before. "I *knew* there was something suspicious about you, and there we go. You're here under false pretenses."

"Ah . . ." Daphne began, unable to finish her sentence because Mildred began advancing on her, the outrage stamped on her face having any thoughts Daphne had been able to gather scattering to the wind again.

"I said from the moment I caught my first glimpse of you that you were an adventuress. Turns out I'm right. Using your feminine allure, you convinced my Herman you were merely a secretary, and yet you're no secretary at all, are you, Miss Beekman? Although I doubt that's your real name."

"Daphne Beekman *is* my name," Daphne said, resisting the urge to fidget when Mildred stopped a mere foot away from her, the temper brewing in her eyes not an encouraging sign.

"But you're not a secretary, even though you can type. I imagine you honed that skill while typing out your own novels, but tell me this — did you ingratiate yourself with my grandson because you've run out of fresh material and thought to steal his work?"

"Ah . . ."

Ann stepped up beside Daphne, taking hold of her hand as she nodded to the room at large. "Have none of you considered that Daphne might have signed my book as an amusing joke, done so after I commented to her that I was disappointed I'd not been able to secure the real Montague Moreland's signature, even after writing to his publishing house with my request?"

As far as reasonable explanations went, that one certainly had merit and had Daphne longing to give Ann a round of applause over her brilliant thinking under what could certainly be considered a great deal of pressure.

"I don't know anyone who'd want a false signature written in an expensive book," Charles argued as he held up the book. "This is a first edition, and it's bound in leather. One would think, if you're truly a Montague Moreland reader, that you would hold out for the real signature, which, again, I believe you *have* written in your book." He gave a shake of his head. "I find it interesting, though, Miss Evans, how you apparently feel compelled to rush to Daphne's defense."

Ann lifted her chin. "I rushed to her defense because you're off the mark about her. As I said, I had her pen a false signature in my book as a bit of a lark, nothing more."

Jay Storrow stepped forward. "But you were in possession of that book before Daphne arrived at Herman's estate. I know for a fact that it was signed before she got here because I saw that signature with my own eyes. If what you're saying is true, that suggests the two of you knew each other before the house party, although I don't believe either of you allowed any of us to know you were previously acquainted with each other, which raises a few red flags."

Mildred settled a sharp eye on Ann. "Do not say that you and Miss Beekman are in league together, Miss Evans."

"I don't believe I should say another word," Ann muttered as Charles began ambling across the room, clearly delighted with himself for believing he'd solved the mystery.

"An interesting plot twist," he mused, looking all around to authors who, every one of them except Herman, were nodding in agreement. "Seems as if there's a conspiracy afoot, one that involves not only attempted murder but the theft of Herman's latest work. With most of us in this room familiar with mysteries, I would have to say that it's not a stretch to think that Daphne, alias Montague Moreland, is out of fresh material and decided to help herself to Herman's latest manuscript. She was then intending on murdering him so she could pass his words off as her own without anyone the wiser."

Charles's attention settled on Daphne. "You did say that Herman never allows anyone to read his current work in progress, although I have to assume you were wrong about that since Sheldon obviously reads drafts, so no one except you and Sheldon know anything about the story he's writing. And," he continued when she opened her mouth, "I'm sure I don't need to tell you that theft is often used as the motive for murders in many a mystery."

Daphne waved that aside. "There's no conspiracy afoot, Charles, at least not in regard to Ann and me because we're not the ones responsible for attempting to secure Herman's demise."

Charles ignored that as he turned to Cooper, who was once again raking a hand through his hair and looking as if he had no idea how to proceed with what was quickly turning into a peculiar predicament.

"I think you'll agree, Agent Clifton, that

I've uncovered the culprit — or perhaps culprits, if it turns out Miss Evans is working with Daphne — behind the attempts on Herman's life. If you'll recall, Daphne fell out of one of the secret passageways, which I felt was suspect even with Herman telling everyone he'd encouraged her to explore them." Charles sent Herman a commiserating look. "Not that I don't understand why you were quick to provide Daphne with an excuse for sneaking about your house. She is a *most* intriguing lady, even with the possibility she's a would-be murderess, and we gentlemen are known to lose our heads when it comes to intriguing ladies."

Herman's eyes darkened. "I think that's quite enough, Charles."

Charles sent Herman an even more commiserating look. "Come now, Herman. I realize you're embarrassed to be presented with proof of Daphne's duplicity, given that everyone has remarked on how taken you seem to be with her. However, you must look at the evidence. Besides the secret passageway incident, she was also with you when the boat sank, and she recently stabbed you. And," he continued, cutting Herman off when Herman tried to say something to that, "I noticed a book on poisonous plants in her bag earlier. If that isn't a telling sign, I don't know what is."

Unwilling to allow Charles's suggestion that Herman had been hoodwinked by her to go unchecked, while also knowing Herman wouldn't disclose the truth about her being an inquiry agent simply to refute Charles's declaration, Daphne cleared her throat, drawing everyone's attention. "First, I'd like to adamantly deny once again that I'm contemplating Herman's demise."

"Of course you're going to deny that because I doubt you'd enjoy finding yourself behind bars," Mildred said, gesturing to Daphne's gown. "Your fancy wardrobe wouldn't be allowed in jail, and now that I think about it, your wardrobe is far too expensive for a secretary to afford."

"An excellent observation, Mildred," Charles said. "It's also further proof that she *is* Montague Moreland, because Moreland books bring in quite the profit, at least according to rumor. I imagine the rumor mill is going to have a field day when this bit of gossip gets out."

Herman stepped forward. "That really is enough, Charles. I'm afraid everyone's imagination is running away with them, but heed me well — Daphne is not a would-be murderess."

"And while *I* understand why you would

338

not want to believe that a lady you obviously hold in affection wants you dead," Charles argued, "she is Montague Moreland, and thus she has a great deal to gain if you're no longer alive. You're her biggest competitor. With you out of the way, she'll be the premier mystery writer in the country."

"I'm known as a popular mystery writer," Jay said to no one in particular.

"Not as popular as Herman and Moreland," Charles countered. "Although I'm sure I speak for all of us when I say that learning Montague Moreland is a lady is troubling."

Daphne stiffened. "Why would that be troubling?"

"Because women have no business writing for the mystery market, and your sales have infringed on the sales of men who write mysteries," Charles returned as he began advancing Daphne's way, his advance coming to a rapid end when Cooper stepped in front of him.

"There's no evidence Daphne is actually Montague Moreland," Cooper began, "and no evidence she had anything to do with the incidents that have occurred here on the Hudson. I believe, as Herman stated, your imagination is getting the best of you,

Mr. Bonner. I suggest you discontinue with your wild conspiracy theories and allow me to get on with what I do best — investigate crimes in a methodical and precise manner."

"I'm not sure how good you are at your job, Agent Clifton, because I guarantee you this — Daphne Beekman *is* Montague Moreland. As a Pinkerton, you should be able to see the truth of that," Charles argued. "She's been attending our writing gatherings, and I, along with quite a few others, have remarked on how knowledgeable she is about the writing craft. We've also spoken about how curious it is that Daphne hasn't impressed any of us with her poetry samples. But knowing now that she writes under the nom de plume of Montague Moreland, everything makes sense.

"I would feel much relieved if you, Agent Clifton," Charles continued, "would take Daphne into custody. If she *has* taken up the position of Herman's secretary in order to steal his work, there's no saying she doesn't have her eye on stealing work from all of us or that she isn't intending on plotting out our demises as well."

Temper had Daphne waving that nonsense aside. "Those are the most absurd accusations I've ever heard, Charles. And while, yes, I am a woman, and yes, I am a writer, and fine, yes, I am in fact Montague Moreland, I'm not a thief or a would-be murderer. I have enough fodder for story, gained through my extensive research for every book I write, to last me for decades."

Charles blinked. "You're admitting you're Montague Moreland?"

"Only to put an end to this absurdity. I'm risking my entire career by disclosing the truth to all of you because I'm under contract to keep my real name, as well as my gender, a secret. Unfortunately, given the circumstances, I don't believe I can adhere to the strict nondisclosure I signed because my nom de plume is distracting everyone from the real issue at hand — that being who actually *does* want to murder Herman."

"Or you can be distracting us from your guilt by justifying your decision to hoodwink the entire reading world by allowing them to believe Montague Moreland is a man when you're nothing of the sort," Charles said.

"And that's some convoluted thinking there," Daphne shot back. "But before you begin insisting Agent Clifton haul me off to jail, something he's most assuredly not going to do, allow me to explain."

Mildred planted her hands on her hips. "Do you honestly believe that any of us are going to believe whatever story you weave next?" She released a huff. "I've read Montague Moreland books, and there's no doubt you're a gifted storyteller — so gifted, in fact, that you were able to convince my Herman you're a secretary."

"Daphne did not go to any extreme methods to convince me she's a secretary," Herman countered, moving to stand directly beside her and catching her eye. "I think now may be the moment when we disclose the full truth about you. I also believe it'll be best, or rather, more believable, if that truth comes from me."

She glanced around the room, refusing a wince when she noticed that all the authors were staring at her in a less-than-pleasant fashion. "By all means, disclose away."

Herman gave her arm a pat before he settled his attention on Charles. "I'm sure you'll be delighted to learn that you were right. Daphne is no secretary."

Charles puffed out his chest. "I'm often right about matters like this."

"Well, yes, and no," Herman said. "Because while she's no secretary, she's not here to steal my work or to murder me. She's here because, besides being a writer, she's an inquiry agent for the Bleecker Street Inquiry Agency, hired by me to solve the case of who wants to murder me."

Dead silence settled over the library as everyone turned their attention to Daphne.

Not wanting to let an avid audience go to waste, she inclined her head. "Everything Herman has just stated is the honest truth. So, with that now out of the way, and thank you, Herman, for disclosing that for me since I doubt anyone *would* have believed that coming from me, I believe it's time for me, as well as Ann, who is also an agent from the Bleecker Street Inquiry Agency, to do what we came here to do. We are going to uncover who wants to murder Herman and then see that someone placed firmly behind bars."

CHAPTER EIGHTEEN

"I don't believe there can be any doubt that the first case you and I were responsible for on our own has to be classified as an unmitigated disaster," Daphne said, tossing aside the pencil she'd been using to jot down additional notes on all the guests she'd interviewed the day before, none of whom stood out as a clear suspect.

Ann slouched down in her chair. "I'm afraid you're right, especially when all of our suspects snuck out of Herman's house last night, apparently unwilling to linger around until we figured out who the prime suspect is."

"That unfortunate circumstance has certainly waylaid our investigation since we have no idea who was responsible for the fencing incident," Daphne said. "And since we've received no word that Irwin's been caught, we've failed in a most magnificent fashion. We'll be lucky if we're ever sent out on another case again."

"No one at the agency will fault us for our disaster, given the daunting conditions we've faced. Besides, you're a partner in the agency, along with Eunice and Gabriella. I hardly think they'll chuck you out simply because of this."

"I might have to relinquish my partnership. It certainly won't aid our reputation if word gets out about the less-than-competent job I've done on Herman's case." She picked up her pencil again, twirling it around. "I suppose we can always hope that Gabriella and Nicholas will return soon. She'll know exactly how to fix this."

"We'll fix it before she gets back," Ann said firmly.

"How do you suggest we do that? Our suspects have bolted, and according to Cooper, they had every right to do so because we didn't have firm evidence against anyone."

"We may not have any firm evidence, but if you ask me, Charles Bonner was acting rather peculiar during the interviewing process. He seemed to be going out of his way to be charming to everyone."

"I think he was using charm to convince everyone to keep mum about the notion he may use underhanded methods to plump up the sales of his books. Since he's not normally a charming man, it was peculiar, but I don't believe his peculiarity in this particular instance is proof he belongs at the top of our suspect list."

"That's too bad, because Charles is an unlikeable man, and if we could prove him guilty, well, we wouldn't be feeling like such abject failures at the moment."

Exchanging commiserating looks, Daphne returned to her notes as Ann began wandering around Herman's office, Herman having graciously offered up his space to Daphne, Ann, and Cooper so that they could work on his case without interruption.

Not that there were many people left to interrupt them, save Sheldon, Martha, Andrew, and Mildred.

Sheldon, interestingly enough, after he'd learned Daphne's true purpose at Herman's estate, had become downright friendly to her, offering to take notes as she questioned the guests and not being annoyed when she'd told him she preferred to take her own notes.

He'd then, when she'd insisted he sit for questions, been more than accommodating. After she was finished, and after she'd come to the conclusion he really wasn't a viable suspect because he didn't have a plausible reason to want Herman dead, Sheldon had then turned the conversation to writing, or more specifically, his writing.

He'd asked her all about her editor and what was required of an author after signing a contract and had then, much to Daphne's surprise, excused himself for a few minutes, returning with his manuscript in hand, which he asked her to read.

She'd been worried Herman would take offense at that. But Herman had merely smiled and congratulated his cousin for finally having the courage to allow someone to read his work, even if that someone hadn't been him.

Herman was considerate that way, a trait she found all too appealing.

Truth be told, there was much that appealed to her about Herman, but given that she'd withheld the truth about her writing from him and had failed spectacularly with solving his case, she was firmly convinced there wasn't much he could find appealing about her.

It was a depressing thought, but frankly, she knew she wasn't a woman a gentleman like Herman would find appealing anyway. She was much too quiet, when she wasn't adopting a sophisticated woman of the world persona, and much too dowdy, when she wasn't styled by Phillip, and quiet and dowdy weren't characteristics a gentleman like Herman would find attractive in a woman.

He'd not been attracted to any of the young ladies his grandmother had selected for him — ladies who were exactly like Daphne, when she wasn't pretending to be someone else, that was.

Granted, she did think he enjoyed her company at times, but that wasn't enough to . . .

"What if the culprit really is Perkins?" Ann suddenly asked, drawing Daphne from her depressing thoughts.

"Why would Perkins want to kill Herman?"

Ann grinned. "I don't actually think he does, but that would be amusing if he turned out to be the guilty party, what with him being the butler and all." She bit her lip. "I do wonder if Jay Storrow might be to blame. He was a little too enthusiastic with proclaiming his innocence. He kept mentioning how many times Herman's books have gone into print, then following that up with how he doesn't envy Herman his success."

"I don't think Jay's guilty of plotting Herman's demise," Daphne said. "Frankly, the problem with all the guests we interviewed is that none of them seems to have a compelling reason to want Herman dead, including Jay. Yes, he's envious of Herman, but I get the distinct impression that at heart, he's a good man. He also genuinely appears to like Herman, as do all of the other guests — save perhaps Charles, but I'm not sure Charles likes anyone other than himself."

Daphne leaned back in the chair and tucked a stray strand of hair behind her ear, the elaborate hairstyle she'd been wearing since she arrived on Herman's estate now abandoned because there was little reason to continue on as a fashionable woman of the world. "I've been thinking we probably shouldn't have taken on Herman's case. I'm evidently not up for running a case without the expertise of Gabriella, and my lack of experience is exactly why I should have encouraged Herman to go with the Pinkerton Agency instead. It's his life we're talking about, something I seem to have taken far too lightly in my quest to secure a murder investigation for the agency."

"Herman *does* have the services of the Pinkertons because Cooper's on the case as well," Ann reminded her. "His involvement should lend you a bit of comfort because even with Cooper's experience, he's not been able to crack this case either. You're being far too hard on yourself, and besides, Herman doesn't appear to have any second thoughts about hiring us."

"That's just because he's too polite."

"He *is* very polite, but I believe he's impressed with us."

"How could he be impressed with us? We've failed to uncover anything of worth, completely disrupted his house party, and I stabbed him, for crying out loud. How can a man be impressed when the inquiry agent he hired took off a good bit of his arm?" She blew out a breath. "I've made a complete muddle of everything."

"But if you hadn't taken on this case, you would have never gotten to know Herman."

"Something I'm sure he wouldn't have minded in the least. If he wasn't acquainted with me, he wouldn't now have seventeen stitches marching up his arm."

"I haven't heard him voice a single complaint about his injury. If you ask me, that's telling."

Daphne rolled her eyes. "Oh, here you go again, seeing romance where none exists."

"And here you go again being evasive about the romance business."

"There's nothing to be evasive about. Herman and I enjoy a professional relationship, one that's destined to remain that way because I'm not exactly the type of lady Herman would hold in anything other than professional esteem." She held up her hand when Ann opened her mouth. "There's nothing more to say on the subject, so if we could return to the pressing matter at hand, that being our case, I'd appreciate it."

"I think a more pressing matter is convincing you that Herman holds you in more than professional esteem."

"Your stubbornness about the matter isn't going to convince me you're right."

"It was worth a try," Ann said as a knock sounded on the office door, and then, a second later, the subject of their discussion appeared, pausing inside the doorway.

"I hope I'm not intruding," Herman said.

"Not at all," Daphne said, gesturing him forward and hoping he wouldn't notice the heat that was creeping up her neck. "Ann and I were just discussing, ah, our progress with your case."

"Cooper and I were doing the same," Herman said, pulling a chair close to where Daphne was sitting. "He's currently finishing up a report to send to the Pinkerton headquarters, but he's not got much to report."

"We don't have much to report either," Daphne said, rubbing a hand over the back of her neck where tension had firmly settled.

"I'm sure that'll change at some point," Herman said. "I've consulted with detectives and the like while doing research for my stories, and they've frequently told me that it takes months to solve some of their cases."

"You could be dead by then."

"That's a cheery thought."

"Speaking of cheery thoughts," Ann began, moving for the door, "if you'll excuse me, I'm going to go see what Cooper is including in that report he's working on."

As Ann quit the room, Daphne squared her shoulders and caught Herman's eye. "Since we're now alone, this is the perfect moment to discuss something of a more personal nature with you." She blew out a breath. "I owe you an apology, and please forgive me for not apologizing sooner. I've been trying to get you alone ever since Charles figured out I'm Montague Moreland." Her lips curved. "Your grandmother seems to be making it a point to materialize whenever we find ourselves without company. So, before she shows up in here, allow me to simply say that I should have told you I'm Montague Moreland. I'm sure you're disappointed with me for withholding that information from you, especially after you entrusted me with your manuscript, not knowing that you were giving your work to one of your biggest competitors."

"There's no need for you to apologize, Daphne, nor is there a reason to fear I'm upset with you because you've seen parts of my latest manuscript. You're far too talented an author to need to steal anyone's work or ideas, so if you've been fretting about that, don't."

"I still should have told you."

"You're under contract to keep your identity a secret, and don't forget that I know all about contracts. And if you'll recall, you tried to discourage me from giving you my manuscript to type. I was the one who insisted on that, and that was with me knowing you're no poet."

"You didn't believe I was a poet?"

"Not after you recited that bit of nonsense about something being soft as a baby's bottom."

"That was remarkably awful," she admitted with a small smile.

"Especially coming from a lady who possesses more than her fair share of intellect."

Heat immediately settled on her cheeks. "Thank you."

"You're welcome." He rubbed a hand over his face. "I really can't believe I didn't figure out your real identity on my own. I've read every Montague Moreland book you've written, and now, after considering your writing, there is a distinct bit of you in all of your stories. If I'm not mistaken, one of your characters, Miss Dorothy Weathermill, bears a remarkable resemblance to you."

"I might have put a little dash of me into her character."

"Or a large dash, given the enormous bag she carries and the smelling salts she's never without." Herman shook his head. "It's very unfair you've been forced to write under a man's name. You've got an incredible talent for the written word, and it's unfortunate you're unable to allow the world to know you, not Montague Moreland, possesses that talent."

Daphne suddenly found it rather difficult to breathe.

No one had ever really appreciated her talent for writing before. Her mother had always encouraged her to keep her fondness for the written word under wraps when she was younger, believing Daphne would never secure a husband if word got out she was a bluestocking. And while her brothers had humored her and read many of the stories she'd penned in her youth, they'd never encouraged her to pursue writing as a serious endeavor, apparently under the belief, as so many people were, that a woman could not possibly have what it takes to find success in the publishing world.

"Thank you for that, Herman," Daphne finally managed to get past a throat that had turned constricted. "It's rare for me to be able to discuss my writing with anyone. But once again, we're becoming distracted from what you're actually paying me to do. We should return to the particulars of your case."

"If it's all the same to you, I'd rather talk writing. We'll have plenty of time to discuss my case later."

"You really want to discuss writing with me?"

"I've been dying to do exactly that ever since I learned you're Montague Moreland."

She fought a grin of pure delight. "And do you want to talk about sentence structure, like you do with your other author friends, or would you prefer to delve into something a little more . . . meaty?"

Herman laughed. "Since you've made your opinion well known for writers talking sentence structure, I think we should delve into plot points, or better yet, tell me about that pirate of yours that seems to be giving you difficulty."

Trying to focus on the words coming out of Herman's mouth, something that was rather tricky to do because his laugh had left her feeling overly warm and a bit flustered, Daphne struggled to regain her composure as she cleared her throat. "There's not much to say about my pirate except that, quite like your axe scene, I've decided he's wrong for my story."

"You're going to get rid of him?"

"I'm afraid I must because I've written the hero wrong. He shouldn't be a pirate, although what he should be is beyond me right now." She tapped a finger against her chin. "I imagine I'll eventually figure it out once I get back to the city. For right now, though, I'm more focused on your case, not a looming deadline."

"I'm not sure you'll have to worry about looming deadlines, especially after you see what's been written about you in all the papers."

Glancing to the door, apprehension was swift as Mildred strode into the room, her arms laden with newspapers, all of which she immediately set on the table in front of Daphne.

"We've just gotten the morning and afternoon papers delivered, a bit delayed since the recently hired newsboy couldn't find our estate. You're the news of the day and have made each and every one of the papers." She nodded to the pile on the table. "These are just a sample of the papers you've been written about in — the *New York Times,* the *New York Tribune,* and the *New York World.*"

"I've made the *New York Times?*"

"Indeed. It's a very detailed article, written by none other than Mr. Charles Bonner. He evidently sold it to every publication he could, and to give that man credit, it does make a riveting read."

Herman snatched up the copy of the *New York Times,* snapped it open, and disappeared behind it. The longer he read, the more apprehensive Daphne became.

"What does it say?" she finally asked.

"There are other papers," Mildred pointed out. "You could read the story for yourself, although I doubt you're going to be pleased with what's included in the tale. Charles discloses your identity as the author behind the Montague Moreland books and delves into your position as an inquiry agent. He does not seem overly impressed with your abilities there. In fact, he goes on for at least four paragraphs about how you were unable to solve Herman's case."

"Why would he have done that?"

Herman looked over the edge of the paper. "Because Charles has a vindictive streak a mile long, as I believe Jay mentioned to you. From the tone of his piece, I think he's still disgruntled about your being Montague Moreland, as well as enjoying far greater success than he could ever achieve. I believe his purpose in disclosing all is to damage your reputation as an author, subtly suggesting that a great writer of mysteries would have been able to solve the case of who wants to murder me."

"And isn't that going to complicate the case," Cooper said from the doorway, striding into the room with Ann by his side, both of them clutching newspapers. "By disclosing Herman's situation to the public, Charles has all but ruined our case. There's little likelihood that the responsible person won't lay low now, which means solving this case is going to be more difficult than ever."

"It's also going to ruin your chances of finding a bride, dear," Mildred said, sending Herman a look filled with disappointment. "What lady, pray tell, will risk attaching herself to you?"

The oddest desire to raise her hand in answer to Mildred's question struck from out of nowhere, a desire she, thankfully, resisted because there was little chance Mildred would take kindly to the idea that Daphne wouldn't mind attaching herself to Herman.

Before Herman had an opportunity to respond to his grandmother's question, though, a bit of a ruckus sounded from the hallway and Perkins all but stumbled into the office. The reason for the stumbling quickly became evident when Eunice glided into the room behind him, holding a pistol in her hand. She stopped for the briefest of seconds and glanced around, although how she could see through what looked to be at least five layers of veils was anyone's guess.

"Ah, Daphne, there you are," she said, striding in Daphne's direction. She then surprised Daphne when she gave her a quick hug before she stepped back and inclined her head at Herman. "Forgive me for making such a dramatic entrance into your home, Herman." She gave a wave of her pistol in Perkins's direction. "Your butler was reluctant to let me into the house, even after I told him I'm with the

Bleecker Street Inquiry Agency and needed to speak with Daphne immediately."

Perkins tugged down a waistcoat that had hiked up, probably due to all the stumbling. "Begging your pardon, ma'am, but one doesn't expect to open a door and discover someone like you lurking on the other side. I had no notice that you were expected, and the manner in which you're currently dressed is not one that gives a person confidence that you're not, well, in disguise."

"I'm in mourning," Eunice pointed out. "And you didn't receive notice of my arrival because I wasn't expected. With that said, though, I would have expected you to confer with Daphne about the matter before telling me I wasn't going to be permitted entrance. If you'd done that, you would have spared yourself a meeting with my pistol." She tucked her pistol into her reticule before she turned back to Daphne. "I'm sure you're wondering what I'm doing here."

"I imagine it has something to do with the articles in the newspaper, and I can't imagine you have pleasant news."

"Troubling news would explain my presence more accurately."

"How troubling?"

"Troubling enough," Eunice said, reaching into her pocket to withdraw a telegram. "This is from your publishing house. I took the liberty of opening it when it arrived and —" she lifted up one of the veils that was obscuring her face, giving Daphne just a hint of her features — "I'm sorry to say that your publisher is insisting on speaking with you in person to discuss the Montague Moreland situation."

Daphne forced herself to take the telegram from Eunice. "I'm sure they're curious to learn how my secret ended up in the papers. Are they traveling to New York to speak to me?"

"I'm afraid not," Eunice said. "They've demanded a meeting in Boston with you within the week, a request that, unfortunately, will give them the upper hand in this situation."

Daphne read over the telegram and frowned. "Demanding to see me within a week seems rather high-handed."

"I thought that as well," Eunice said. "That is why I'll be traveling with you to lend you what will certainly be much-needed support. I've already secured us train tickets to Boston, and there's a rented carriage waiting outside to get us on our way."

"Would you care for me to accompany you to Boston too?" Herman surprised Daphne by asking, his offer leaving her feeling overly warm again, as well as smiling, until Mildred stepped forward.

"That is completely out of the question," Mildred said, moving to take hold of Herman's arm. "Your life, if you've forgotten, is still in jeopardy. That means you need to stay close to home where Agent Clifton can keep an eye on you." She nodded to Ann. "You may stay as well and continue on with Herman's case." She settled narrowed eyes on Daphne. "Forgive me if this hurts your feelings, but it's because of you that everyone knows about the attempts on his life, which Agent Clifton has already admitted will see progress in the case stalling. I feel confident that Herman and his case will be far better off without you, which means you might want to consider taking yourself off his case once and for all."

CHAPTER NINETEEN

"I believe I found that passage we've been searching for, Herman, the one your mother wrote in regard to their plans to venture to the West Indies to explore the possibility of purchasing a plantation there."

Herman abandoned the journal he'd been reading as Sheldon turned his journal around, pointing to a page written in his mother's lovely script.

"See? Right there," Sheldon said. "Her research about the West Indies covers at least ten pages, and her description of sugar plantations is exceptional. It should be enough, when paired with the research books I've found, to give you the visual you need to write a credible setting now that you've decided to abandon the El Dorado idea."

Taking the journal from Sheldon, Herman skimmed through the first page. "Mother did take extensive notes about everything, and I think we're right about the West Indies being a good setting for my latest book. Discarding the few chapters devoted to El Dorado will require a few rewrites, but thankfully, most of the chapters I've written so far are setting up the adventure. It would have been more problematic if I'd reached the end of the book and decided to change the location after Grandmother made her concerns known."

Sheldon sat back in his chair. "Your consideration for your grandmother is, once again, commendable, although it's a little confusing why she was concerned about the El Dorado idea. Your parents obviously never made it to the West Indies, even though we discovered through your mother's writings that they planned to go there, and yet Mildred didn't bat an eye when we broached that location."

"It's difficult to understand Grandmother's reasoning at times, but I don't want her to become distressed about something that's within my power to control. It's of little consequence where I set my next story. My readers are more concerned with the plot than any location I may choose."

"Have you ever wondered what you're going to do when we deplete your mother's journals, and you don't have those as a resource?"

Herman rubbed a kink that had formed at the base of his neck from sitting so long. "Considering Mother left me numerous journals, I don't think I need to worry about that for a while."

"But you have thought about that, haven't you?"

"It may have crossed my mind."

"And has it also crossed your mind that you may need to personally travel around the world to discover new inspiration at some point in time?"

"Grandmother would take to her bed for months if I ever boarded a ship to explore a location for research purposes."

"You're probably right, but . . ." Sheldon glanced at the journal for a long moment before he caught Herman's eye. "Returning to your grandmother and her opposition to El Dorado, you don't think your parents were off to try and find El Dorado on their last trip, do you?"

"I suppose that's a possibility and would explain Grandmother's unexpected re-action." Herman frowned. "As you know, Grandmother never disclosed where my parents were heading on their ill-fated trip. And even though you and I have combed through all forty-seven of Mother's journals, we've never discovered so much as a hint of their final destination."

"You could always ask your grandmother about that. I guarantee she knows where they were heading."

"Grandmother's nervous condition always takes a turn for the worse whenever I question her about that final trip, which is why I quit asking about it. She takes to her bed enough as it is just trying to negotiate through normal days. She doesn't need me contributing to the frequency of her anxiety attacks."

"Perhaps not, but I don't think you're doing either yourself or your grandmother any favors by avoiding the issue of your parents' deaths. A great deal of time has passed since they died, time that should have softened the pain your grandmother experienced over their passing, and time that should have her realizing that it's your right to know what happened to your parents, besides the fact their ship went down in a storm."

"And those are valid points, and maybe someday I'll broach the matter with her, but not right now. As you know, she's taken to her bed again with her smelling salts nearby, stating that the house party, and the results of that party, were too much for her problematic constitution to handle."

Sheldon raked a hand through his hair. "Well, here's hoping she leaves her bed soon because I left numerous research books back in the city. It doesn't appear we'll be traveling there until Mildred recovers from her latest bout of nerves."

"You know you can always return to the city without me," Herman said before he smiled. "That would, of course, mean that you'd be there and Miss Martha Mulvey would be here, now that she's taken up the position of paid companion to Grandmother."

"Hmm . . ." was all Sheldon said to that, which was an interesting response. But before he could expand on it, the lady Herman had just introduced into the conversation suddenly wandered into the library, making a beeline for Sheldon the moment she caught sight of him.

"There you are. Mildred's decided to take another nap. She's apparently reluctant to have me sit with her while she rests, saying something about how it gives her the willies to think anyone is peering at her as she sleeps." Martha took hold of Sheldon's arm when he rose to his feet, Herman rising to his feet as well. "I thought it might be nice to take a stroll along the Hudson or perhaps take a tour of the Gentlemen's House now that there aren't any guests staying there. I've yet to see the inside of that building and am curious how it's decorated."

"It looks much the same as the main house," Sheldon said. "Except that there's a billiards table in the library, along with a dartboard."

"I love a good game of darts," Martha said before she frowned. "However, if I'm interrupting something, I can always go exploring on my own."

Sheldon settled a smile on Martha that, in Herman's opinion, almost seemed forced. "Herman and I just finished for the afternoon, but I'm afraid we won't be able to explore the Gentlemen's House today. Agent Bernie Shaw has recently arrived from the city and is currently staying there."

Martha's frown deepened. "Who?"

"Agent Shaw. He's one of the numerous Pinkertons who Cooper requested to help with Herman's case," Sheldon said. "What with Daphne leaving three days ago, and then Ann leaving yesterday to see if she could uncover anything yet unknown about the potential suspects who returned to the city, Cooper's been burning the candle at both ends watching over Herman."

Martha turned to Herman. "Don't you find it at all curious that the Pinkertons believe you still need to be guarded all the time? I would have thought with all the suspects having returned to the city that the danger to your life would have decreased."

"I'm apparently what the Pinkertons consider a high-profile client, and as such, they believe their reputation will suffer if I'm murdered on their watch." Herman nodded to Sheldon. "I'm off to check on Mildred before I settle down to write."

"And I'm off to take a stroll with Martha after I put the journals away."

Leaving Sheldon and Martha tidying up his office, Herman headed out of the room, finding Cooper sitting in a chair outside the door.

"Anything exciting to report?" Herman asked, earning a grunt from Cooper in response.

"I don't expect to encounter any excitement until we repair to the city," Cooper said, rising to his feet and pulling out his pocket watch. "Agent Shaw is due to take over for me in ten minutes, but be warned — he'll be in a surly mood because he's used to cases where danger is dogging our every step. Clearly, the danger has diminished significantly here on the Hudson these days."

"Something I'm quite content with since I

don't actually care for experiencing numerous attempts on my life."

Cooper grinned. "Don't blame you for that. In fact, I bet you're enjoying the peace and quiet that's settled over your house now that mostly everyone is gone."

"I was thinking the house seemed too quiet, especially after Daphne left so abruptly."

Cooper arched a brow. "Missing the chaos that surrounds Daphne all the time, are you?"

"Oddly enough, I am, which is strange in and of itself because I've not known her long."

"Daphne has a way of worming into a person's heart from the moment one becomes acquainted with her. I believe it's because she's so charmingly unique."

Herman came to an abrupt stop. "She's wormed her way into your heart?"

Cooper's first response to that was a snort. "There's no need to glare at me, Herman. Daphne and I are friends, nothing more, but that doesn't mean she can't own a piece of my heart." His lips curved. "Given the scowl on your face and given what I've observed whenever you and Daphne are together, I don't think I'm being presumptuous by stating that you're interested in pursuing more than a friendship with her."

"You've been observing me?"

"I'm a Pinkerton. I observe everyone, and some of the more interesting aspects I've observed about you are these — you take the chaos that surrounds Daphne in stride, you enjoy her company, and . . . you find her very appealing. It's written all over your face whenever you're in her company."

Herman blinked. "Is it really, or more importantly, do you think Daphne's observed that on my face as well?"

"Daphne is oblivious to her appeal, so no, I doubt she's noticed. Or if she has, she probably thinks you're looking at her so oddly because you've eaten something bad for lunch."

"That's how I look when I'm with Daphne? As if I've eaten something bad?"

"No, I was merely explaining what Daphne probably thinks. Surely you've realized that she doesn't look at the world as most people do, and because we've now brought Daphne into the conversation, I would like to know what your intentions are toward her."

"Isn't that a question usually reserved for a lady's father?"

"Since her father isn't here to share this rather telling conversation with you, I'm going to take the liberty of acting on his behalf."

Herman gave his nose a scratch. "Daphne and I barely know each other. That means it may be far too soon to be talking about my intentions toward her with you or with anyone else, for that matter."

"You haven't known each other long, that's true, but I wouldn't agree that the two of you barely know each other. Even though I've been told, mostly by my two sisters, that I'm woefully inept when it comes to understanding women in general, what I have learned in life is this — a certain amount of time is not required for us to know what our hearts want. Some people begin as friends and that friendship grows into something more as time marches on. Others, however, realize from almost a first glance or a first laugh that there's something special about a person, something that draws us to that person and makes us long to spend every moment from that point forward in their company."

"I wouldn't take you for a man who believes in love at first sight."

"I don't know if it's love at first sight," Cooper countered. "Perhaps more along the lines of the possibility of love *after* a first sight. That's what I think you've experienced with Daphne."

"The possibility of love after first sight?"

"Indeed. I also believe Daphne's experienced that with you."

Something that felt very much like satisfaction settled deep in his soul. "You really think so?"

Cooper smiled. "From what I've observed, she's very comfortable in your company, even though large men make her nervous. It's telling that she's not nervous around you."

"That could merely be because I'm a client."

"Or she finds you appealing, perhaps even intriguing. However, that's all I'm going to say about the matter. Daphne told me in no uncertain terms that friends are supposed to keep matters like that between friends. Since Daphne is my friend and you're my client, you're going to have to discover anything else about Daphne's feelings on your own."

"I thought we were on our way to becoming friends."

Cooper grinned. "And we will be friends, but not until I solve your case, at which time we will revisit the matter of Daphne and your intentions toward her at greater length. I'm hopeful that discussion will be sooner rather than later. But in order for us to do that, I need to put your case to bed, which means you need to convince your grandmother it's time to return to the city."

"How do you think I could go about that?"

Cooper tilted his head. "That's a tricky question, but I suppose you could suggest that we're allowing the suspect to plan a more thorough campaign to get rid of you the longer we languish in the country."

"That might convince her."

"She does seem to want to keep you alive."

"It's a very grandmotherly thing to do, and on that note, I'll go see if she's still awake."

"Let me know how it goes," Cooper said before he nodded down the hallway. "There's Agent Shaw. I'll fill him in on all the excitement that hasn't happened, then I'm off to take a nap."

As Cooper strode away, Herman headed for the upper hallway and walked to his grandmother's suite of rooms, knocking quietly on the door. When there was no response, he turned the knob and stuck his head into the room, catching a flash of something out of the corner of his eye.

That something turned out to be Mildred, who was racing across the room right before she leapt through the air in a very impressive maneuver, landing on her bed with a bounce. She promptly folded her hands demurely over her chest and closed her eyes.

"For a woman who is supposed to be napping, and also suffering from a horrible case of nerves, that was some remarkable agility on your part," Herman said, stepping into the room.

Mildred's eyes flashed open. "I wasn't expecting anyone to walk in on me."

"Clearly, but why are you feigning a case of the nerves? And don't try to deny it. I just saw proof that you're hardly so overcome with anxiety that you can barely make it out of your bed."

"I have my reasons."

Herman settled into a chair next to Mildred's bed and considered her for a long moment. "Would one of those reasons have anything to do with trying to keep me far removed from Daphne?"

Mildred sat up and stuffed a pillow behind her back. "You do know me well. But I only have your best interests at heart, dear, and I would hate to see you follow in Andrew Ware's footsteps and hie off after a woman you barely know, as Andrew did with Finetta."

"I'm fairly certain Andrew has known Finetta far longer than I've known Daphne."

"Unfortunately, I believe you're right. What he was thinking, though, making off with a lady you've had your eye on, is beyond me. It's also beyond me why you don't seem put out with him, even though he's probably left you in the lurch by returning to the city, where's there's little doubt he's neglecting your accounting books as he settles matters with Finetta."

"I'm the one who encouraged him to return to the city so he and Finetta can settle the unfinished business between them. My accounts aren't going to suffer if Andrew takes a week or so away from them."

Mildred waved that aside. "Your encouragement to Andrew to return to New York was very considerate and speaks well of your amiable nature. I, on the other hand, would not have been as considerate. He stole Finetta from you. And while you haven't said much about the matter, I'm convinced your friendship suffered a direct blow over his actions."

"Andrew didn't steal Finetta from me. She was never mine to begin with."

"But Andrew knew you'd set your sights on her."

"*You* set your sights on Finetta, Grandmother. And not that I want to upset you, given your nerves — although I'm convinced there's not much wrong with them at the moment — but neither Finetta nor any of the young ladies you decided would suit me would have been appropriate matches. Every young lady you invited to the house party had no interest in me."

"They had interest in you," Mildred argued. "They were merely too shy and nervous to let you know of it. Young ladies are often anxious in the company of gentlemen. Your grandfather made me downright queasy when I first met him, but three months later, after we married, that queasiness went away — or almost went away."

"I don't want to marry a woman I've ever made queasy. Seems rather disheartening. I'd much rather spend time in the company of a lady who isn't rendered nauseous by the mere sight of me."

"A lady like Daphne Beekman?"

Seeing no reason to deny it, Herman inclined his head. "Perhaps."

Mildred sat up a little straighter. "You must realize she's not an appropriate match for you. She's been lying to you all along. That, my dear boy, is hardly a mark in her favor."

"She didn't lie to me. She merely withheld the full truth about her identity, done

377

so because of a nondisclosure agreement."

"She attracts trouble like a flower attracts bees."

Herman's lips curved. "That's part of her charm."

"I would say it's a recipe for disaster, disaster you'll find yourself in the thick of if you don't come to your senses and admit she's wrong for you."

He reached for his grandmother's hand, giving it a squeeze. "After the discussion I just had with Cooper, I'm beginning to realize she's exactly right for me."

"You barely know her."

"Odd as this may sound, I feel as if I've known her for years, not simply a few weeks."

"I'm going to need my smelling salts."

He arched a brow. "You don't look like you're about to faint. In fact, your cheeks are flushed, and your eyes seem to be holding what almost appears to be temper."

Mildred withdrew her hand from his. "I don't get in tempers when it comes to you."

"I'm fairly sure the expression on your face right now says differently."

She narrowed her eyes. "My face wouldn't be saying anything at all if you would have only settled your affections on one of the many darling and, need I add, adventure-less young ladies I invited *for you* to our house party. Instead, you seem to have settled your affection on the one woman who seems to land herself in the midst of danger at the drop of a hat."

"It's not as if she does so intentionally. However, since I'm not going to deny that I hold Daphne in a great deal of esteem, along with affection, you're going to have to reconcile yourself with that. And if she returns my affections, you're going to have to learn how to get along with her since she'll become a part of both of our lives."

Mildred immediately snatched up the fan she always kept on her bedside table and began waving it furiously back and forth in front of her face. "I definitely need my smelling salts now. I feel an anxiety attack coming on."

Herman reached out and stopped the fan mid-wave, catching his grandmother's eye. "You don't need your smelling salts. You're merely using an anxiety attack as a way to avoid a conversation that's not to your liking."

"You've never questioned my anxiety attacks before," Mildred said, tossing aside her fan.

"I've never questioned your attacks before because I've always known you use your nerves as a way to ascertain I'll stay out of harm's way. Up until now, I've never taken issue with your tactics, but that's because the circumstances you've taken issue with over the years are normally centered around activities you consider dangerous, such as traveling. Traveling is relatively inconsequential to my life. Daphne, on the other hand, is anything but inconsequential."

Mildred scooted to the edge of the bed, swung her legs over it, then got to her feet, moving to look out the window. "I didn't realize you knew I've been using my nerves to manipulate you."

"I wouldn't say you've manipulated me." Herman smiled. "You've acted like the overly protective grandmother you are, and for good reason. Both of us suffered tremendously after the ship accident, and I've never begrudged you for wanting to keep me safe."

Mildred turned from the window, her eyes suspiciously bright. "You're far too considerate for your own good, Herman. You should begrudge me because I've taken great pains to stifle the adventurous spirit I know you possess."

"You haven't stifled my spirit," Herman countered. "It's not as if you locked me up in my room and threw away the key." He moved to stand beside his grandmother. "You've never made a big fuss over most of the questionable activities I enjoy, such as boxing. If you'd truly wanted to stifle my spirit, you'd have put your foot down over those activities."

"I never made a fuss because you went to such lengths to assure me you'd put protective measures in place with all those activities, those lengths making it impossible for me to protest because I would have ended up looking completely unreasonable." She gave a roll of her eyes. "You've tried to convince me boxing with Sheldon is perfectly safe because he's smaller than you. I do have eyes, Herman. Sherman's not been smaller than you in quite some time."

"Which proves without a doubt that you've not stifled me as much as you evidently believe you have. I do have to wonder *why* you never said anything, especially when you must know I would have discontinued some of my more questionable activities if I'd known you were aware of the danger they present me."

She released a sigh. "As I said, protesting would have made me look unreasonable. But, besides that, it wasn't worth the risk of having you realize how much of a burden I can be to you at times, or worth the risk that you would become annoyed with me and decide to embrace your adventurous spirit instead of curtail it in order to spare my nervous condition."

"You've never been a burden to me."

"Of course I have, and I've been unfair to you by taking to my bed whenever I felt you were considering venturing farther into the world."

"It's my choice to keep close to you, Grandmother, and I do so because you're the most important person in the world to me. You're the one who read books with me as we tried to manage our grief all those years ago, which allowed me to develop a love for reading, which then led to a love of writing, which then eventually led to my becoming a novelist. I never would have discovered the profession I love if not for you."

"But you might have discovered real adventures if I'd given you space to spread your wings."

"My wings are hardly fettered, and I don't long to experience adventures like my parents did. As I told someone recently, I'm perfectly content to live those types of adventures vicariously through my books." He took hold of her hand. "Yes, there are times I dream of taking a few trips here and there, but everyone dreams, Grandmother. You obviously believe that I've forgone trips because you forced me to stay close to you, but that's not true. I *choose* to stay near you. I enjoy your company. I love you more than life itself, and if not for you, I don't know how I would have survived losing my parents."

Mildred swiped away a tear that was trailing down her cheek. "I don't know how I would have survived losing them, and William, without you either." She blew out a breath. "Right after they died, I found myself questioning what I had done to deserve such a punishment from God, and truth be told, I was furious with God for taking them away. I felt as if He'd taken the light from my life and deprived you of parents who would never get to see you grow into a man. I began blaming myself for the accident, and I believe that blame is what led to the first of my anxiety attacks."

"Why would you have blamed yourself for a ship going down in a storm?"

"I blamed myself for not stopping them from getting on that ship in the first place," Mildred said. "Your grandfather was always a man with wanderlust, traveling about on his own when your father was young, and then taking Evan with him once your father was old enough to travel. He encouraged Evan to explore the world and encouraged him to embrace a life of adventure. I didn't like it, but I never stepped in and asked either of them to temper those adventures."

She dashed another tear from her cheek. "I was hopeful when Evan married your mother that he would settle down, embrace a life of domesticity, but Sarah enjoyed adventures as well, a characteristic that drew Evan to her in the first place. Even when you came along, their taste for adventure didn't abate. They frequently left you with me to travel the world, until finally, their travels resulted in death. I thought I should have done more, perhaps used guilt to persuade them to stay close to you, to raise you as parents are supposed to do. I became incredibly angry that your parents and William had been so careless with the lives God had given them, seeking out adventures instead of living normal lives. It was while I was so angry that I decided I was going to do everything in my power to suppress what I knew was an adventurous spirit in you, using your considerate nature as a way to keep you safe."

"I don't possess the same adventurous spirit my parents did."

"Adventure is in your blood, my boy.

That's why you're attracted to Daphne Beekman. She's an adventure in and of itself."

Herman smiled. "She's really not, Grandmother. As I've tried to explain to you numerous times, she was merely adopting the persona of a sophisticated woman of the world. She truly does keep smelling salts at the ready because she suffers from nerves as well."

"I find it difficult to believe that an inquiry agent possesses a nervous constitution."

"One of the things I admire most about Daphne is the fact that she seems to want to overcome her nerves and has done so by placing herself in uncomfortable situations. If nothing else, you should also admire her for that."

"Or perhaps use her as an example to overcome my own nerves?"

"I don't think you need to use anyone as an example of how to do that, Grandmother. Your nerves didn't come into play at all during the house party, even when you were presented with unexpected and difficult situations. If you ask me, that suggests you're far stronger than you think."

Mildred began blinking rapidly, probably to keep the tears that were shining in her eyes at bay. "You are far too good to me,

Herman. You should be angry with me and yet, here you are, being considerate and encouraging." She patted his hand. "I told you I was furious with God for taking your parents away from me, but what I didn't tell you was that my fury faded after I realized He'd left you to me. You've always been a great source of comfort, a light shining into my world even during my darkest days." She drew in a ragged breath. "I think it's past time, though, that you stop coddling me. Maybe I am stronger than I know, but I'll never know that for certain if I don't learn how to deal with the nuances and, yes, dangers of everyday life."

"Does that mean you're ready to abandon your bed and return to the city, as well as abandon your preconceived notions about Daphne and give her a chance to show you who she really is?"

"I suppose, because Daphne is apparently important to you, I can try my best to give her a chance. But if she stabs you again, all bets are off."

"I'll make certain to keep all rapiers out of sight when I'm in her company."

"A prudent decision," Mildred said before she sent him a rather sheepish smile. "I wasn't actually keeping to my bed because of Daphne this time, though. That decision revolved more around Dr. Gibbons — or more around the idea that he's disappeared on me."

Herman settled back in his chair. "Is this where you're about to disclose that there's something more between you and the good doctor besides a doctor-patient relationship?"

"Of course there's something between us. We've known each other for over twenty years."

"I may need to borrow your smelling salts before you expound on that."

Mildred stared at him for a long moment before she suddenly laughed, her laughter increasing so much that she had to pluck a handkerchief from her bedside table and dash it over eyes that were now watering.

A full thirty seconds passed before she gave a last hiccup of amusement and grinned. "Good heavens, that something isn't a romantic relationship, Herman. James is merely one of my best friends, but one who is being incredibly neglectful right now. He's gone back to the city and hasn't bothered to return to check on me, even though he must believe my nerves are suffering because of the attempts on your life. He's never neglected my nerves before."

Herman returned the grin. "You have no

387

idea how relieved that makes me."

"You're relieved I'm being neglected by my best friend?"

"I'm relieved you're not romantically involved with Dr. Gibbons."

She waved that aside. "I'm sure it would be disconcerting to think about me, your grandmother, in a romantic relationship. However, just so you know, I'm only seventy, dear. There are many gentlemen out there who've made it known they'd be more than happy to spend time in my company. Maybe now if I'm not keeping such a close eye on you, I'll have more opportunities to spend with them."

"I think this is where we return the conversation to Dr. Gibbons."

"Don't be squeamish, dear. It doesn't become you. As for Dr. Gibbons, I don't know what else to say about that matter. I have no idea why he's abandoned me."

"You did snap at him to stop coddling you."

"I didn't think that would have him fleeing to the city, never to return."

"Have you considered that you might have hurt his feelings?"

"I snap at him all the time. I would have thought he'd be used to it by now."

"I doubt you've ever told him to stop coddling you before. That was rather harsh."

Mildred released a sigh. "I suppose it was at that, which means I'm going to have to muster up a sincere apology, as well as beg his forgiveness." She caught his eye. "Would you mind terribly if we would return to the city soon so that I can make amends? Good friends are difficult to come by, and I wouldn't want to lose his friendship after all these years."

"Cooper has been champing at the bit to return to the city, so I won't mind at all. But while we're on the subject of Dr. Gibbons, you don't think there's an ulterior motive behind why he's always coddled you so much, is there?"

Mildred blinked before her lips twitched. "Do not say he's on Daphne's list of suspects."

"I'm afraid so."

"Oh, he'll enjoy hearing that. But you can tell Daphne, when you see her next, that I can personally vouch for James. He coddles me because of his mother. She died when he was a young man, and he pursued a degree in medicine because he felt she died a needless death." She leaned closer. "She suffered from nerves as well, you see, and became a victim of a questionable tonic that was given to her by a disreputable doctor."

"I'm sure Daphne will take him straight off the suspect list after learning that."

"I would think so, and with that settled, we should begin making preparations to return to the city so I can set matters right with my friend."

"I'm sure we'll be able to manage those preparations within a few hours, but will you be all right if after I get you back to the city and settled, I travel on to Boston to check on Daphne? I'll have Cooper call for a Pinkerton to watch over you until whoever is out to harm me is caught, even though no one seems to have you in their sights."

"I'll be fine. I'm not sure I'd enjoy having a Pinkerton trailing around after me."

"But you'll agree to that or else I won't feel comfortable leaving you."

"Of course I'll agree to it because I can see you're anxious to check on Daphne."

"I must admit that I am, because her secret would never have come to light if she'd not agreed to take on my case. I can't help but think the summons from her publishing house isn't going to bode well for her."

Mildred smiled. "And here's where I feel compelled to point out that you do indeed possess an adventurous spirt, because racing after a woman is an adventure if there ever was one — and one I'm not going to deny you this time."

"And here's where I point out to you that even if I do hie off on an adventure every now and again, and even if I learn Daphne might hold me in at least a smidgen of affection, I'll always come back to you, and you know I'm always good for my word."

After exchanging smiles with his grandmother, and after Mildred shooed him out of her room, saying she needed to pack, Herman headed for the Gentlemen's House, where he knew Cooper was going to be delighted to learn they were leaving the Hudson estate, even if leaving could possibly set him in the crosshairs of a would-be-murderer once again.

CHAPTER TWENTY

"After going over all the notes you compiled on possible suspects, I'm confident with saying that the most likely of perpetrators has to be one of Herman's author friends."

Daphne looked over her shoulder as Mary, her mother's lady's maid, wrestled another enormous bustle on her behind, smiling at the sight of Eunice sitting by the window, her veils shoved away from her face in a haphazard fashion.

"You know you could abandon your veils while you're in my old bedchamber, don't you? It's an unusually warm day, and it can't be comfortable having all those layers covering your head."

Eunice waved that aside. "I've grown accustomed to the veils, and there's no saying that those brothers of yours won't show up at the house today to see you, now that your mother has gotten the word out that you're home again." Her forehead wrinkled. "I'm still not certain why she waited three days to inform your brothers about that, though."

"She wanted to spend some 'quality time' with me, which roughly translates into her wanting a few days to interrogate me over what she's taken to calling my 'unfortunate circumstances.' My brothers can usually be counted on to take my side when Mother and I are at odds." Daphne winced. "She is certainly at odds with me right now because of all those articles Charles sold to every newspaper outlet he could find."

"He does seem to have been diligent in getting his story spread." Eunice took a second to write something in the notepad she'd commandeered from Daphne. "Seems to me his obvious animosity toward you and your success as an author makes him a lead suspect in Herman's case because Herman is a successful author as well, whereas Charles's sales are more questionable." She tapped the pencil against the notepad. "But if we may return to your mother for a brief moment. I know you're at odds with her, but from what I've observed, she seems genuinely concerned about your situation and is merely trying to convince you to move back to Boston because she wants to make certain no further harm is done to you or your reputation."

"I'm not that concerned about my reputation, given my advanced age of twenty-five. Besides, it's not as if I actually did anything to tarnish it. Writing is not a tawdry occupation, nor is being an inquiry agent."

Eunice laid aside the notebook. "But those are both occupations that could discourage gentlemen from courting you, something your mother is definitely worried about."

"I'm fine not being courted by a gentleman, and I'm reconciled to the idea that I'll probably end up a spinster."

Eunice rose to her feet and nodded to the lady's maid. "Would you mind excusing us for a moment, Mary?"

"And here the conversation was just getting good," Mary said with a grin before she dipped into a curtsy and hurried out of the room.

"I imagine she's off to give your mother a full accounting of every snippet of conversation she's been privy to as she's helped you get ready for the meeting with your publisher."

"Mary's been in cahoots with Mother for years," Daphne said, moving to her wardrobe and withdrawing one of the gorgeous walking gowns Phillip had made for her. "They're probably even now devising a plan to attract some Bostonian gentleman who wouldn't mind being married to a woman who all of Boston, at least according to my sister, Lydia, considers notorious."

Eunice stepped closer, took the gown from Daphne, and began wrestling it over Daphne's head, yanking it into place a moment later. "I don't often give my personal opinions about personal situations, but I have to tell you that you're fortunate you have a mother who wants to be involved in your life. Better yet, I'm truly convinced she only wants to see you live a happy life."

"Her idea of what constitutes a happy life is opposed to what I believe a happy life is. She's always dreamed I'd miraculously turn into a lady everyone clamors to be around, and because that's not who I am, I've always been a disappointment to her."

Eunice began fussing with Daphne's gown, tugging the fabric in place over the bustle. "I doubt you're a disappointment to your mother. I imagine she's incredibly proud of you, even if she doesn't understand the life you've chosen." She took a step back and eyed the fabric now cascading over the bustle. "Mothers can be complicated creatures, Daphne. I should know, because my mother is more complicated than you can imagine. She's incredibly dramatic, and her own father — my grandfather — called her a temperamental charmer with a flighty nature. Unlike your mother, when I disappointed mine by not wanting to travel the world with her on an extended tour when I turned seventeen, she left me to go on that tour on her own. I've not seen her since."

"You haven't seen your mother in over ten years?"

"I'm afraid not. And because I no longer live where I grew up, there's relatively little chance she'll ever be able to find me."

Daphne frowned. "You're an inquiry agent. I'm sure you could find her if you were to use the services of our agency to look into the matter."

"Now is not the time for me to try and locate her."

"Why not?"

"It's complicated."

"I see," Daphne said, not really seeing at all. "Perhaps your mother will try to locate you, then."

"She'd have a difficult time finding me because my name changed."

"She doesn't know about Mr. Holbrooke?"

"The Holbrooke situation didn't happen until three years after she left."

"That's an interesting way to speak about your marriage," Daphne said, but before she could press Eunice further, there was a knock on the door and then Clara, Daphne's mother, stepped into the room.

Clara shot a look to Eunice, who was already pulling her veils over her face, and gave a bit of a shudder, then turned her full attention to Daphne. Her eyes widened. "Goodness. Mary told me you were intending on wearing a lovely gown, but that's more than lovely." She stepped closer. "You look beautiful, darling, and I love how Mary styled your hair. How feminine those curls are, but . . ." Her attention settled on Daphne's face. "Have you considered abandoning your spectacles when you go off to meet your publisher today? They do give you the look of a bluestocking and don't complement your overall appearance."

Daphne slid her spectacles firmly into place. "I'm fairly convinced the bluestocking ship has already sailed with me on it, Mother. It has, if you've forgotten, been disclosed that I'm Montague Moreland, and a lady who writes books can't get much more bluestocking than that."

"I suppose you're right, but . . . still."

"There's no *still* about it. Besides, I can't see without my spectacles. I'm relatively sure my publisher is going to need me to sign a few forms, what with how I've broken my disclosure agreement, and it'll be difficult for me to do that if I can't see where I'm supposed to sign."

"You could always, ah . . . wear a monocle. One of those would be easy to tuck out of sight when you didn't need to see."

"And lend the impression I'm over ninety and at my last prayers? I don't know any young lady who sports a monocle these days."

"I suppose that is true," Clara said before she began walking around Daphne, taking in every aspect of her appearance. She stopped and tapped a finger against her chin, an ominous sign if there ever was one. "I was thinking we could, perhaps, use your almost-fatal drowning in the Hudson, which everyone read about in the papers, as a way to solicit sympathy from our friends when we attend the Devonshire ball tomorrow evening."

Daphne swallowed a sigh. "I am sorry, Mother, but as I already mentioned to you, Eunice and I are returning to New York City tomorrow morning because we need to continue with Herman Henderson's case. Our agency has already suffered a blow to its reputation after Charles wrote that dreadful bit about my being an incompetent agent. The only way I can prove him wrong is to solve the case, which means I won't be in Boston to attend the Devonshire ball with you."

Clara began waving a hand in front of her face. "The very idea of you working as an inquiry agent out in the field gives me heart palpitations." She caught Daphne's eye. "You don't want to be responsible for leading to my demise, do you?"

"If that's your way of convincing me to stay in Boston, or to attend that ball, you're going to have to try harder. I know you've never suffered a heart palpitation in your life."

"There's always a first for everything."

Thankfully, Daphne was spared a response to that nonsense when Mary stuck her head in the room. "Begging your pardon, but your sons have arrived, Mrs. Beekman."

"Maybe they'll be able to talk some sense into you," Clara said, tugging Daphne toward the doorway. She nodded to Eunice. "Would you care to join us, Mrs. Holbrooke?"

"How very kind of you, Mrs. Beekman, but I have some agency work to catch up on. Besides, I hardly believe Daphne's reunion with her brothers will be free of drama if I happen to skulk into view." Eunice let out what almost sounded like a laugh. "I tend to cast a slightly ominous presence whenever I enter a room."

Clara's lips twitched. "I do think you may be right about that." She took hold of Daphne's arm and walked with her out of the bedchamber as Eunice returned to looking through her notes.

"She's an interesting woman," Clara remarked. "But she seems to be a considerate woman, as well, because she definitely would have drawn attention away from your reunion with your brothers, something that might disappoint them because I know they're very anxious to talk to you."

"How anxious?"

Clara grinned. "Incredibly so."

"I was afraid of that," Daphne said, reaching the bottom of the stairs and turning right. And even though it was highly likely her three brothers were going to have a time of it at her expense because of her apparent notoriety, Daphne increased her pace as anticipation began to build. Her brothers were incredibly annoying at times, but she loved them to death and missed seeing them on a frequent basis. Walking into the library a moment later, she stopped just inside the door as her brother Jack caught sight of her.

"Ah, there she is," Jack proclaimed. "The prodigal daughter come home at last."

"She was home for a quick visit two months ago," Clara said as Jack, who was two years older than Daphne, strode across the library and swept Daphne into a bear hug.

"Was she really?" Jack asked, giving Daphne a squeeze before he stepped back. "It seems like it's been longer."

"It always seems like a person's been gone longer when their absence makes you miss them," Clara said. "Daphne's absence from this very house, however, is going to continue because she's refusing to listen to reason and move home."

"You don't honestly believe she'll ever move home, do you?" Jack asked, which earned him a sigh from their mother. He sent Clara a smile before he returned his attention to Daphne, giving her a thorough look over and grinning. "You're looking uncharacteristically well turned out today, brat. Perhaps New York City does agree with you after all, even though I've heard you haven't exactly been keeping yourself out of trouble there. Tracking down a would-be murderer and writing bestselling novels keeping you busy these days?"

"And aren't you just a *peach* for bringing up what you know is going to annoy Mother. She's been trying to avoid the particulars of my situation since I got here."

"And you find that surprising?" Jack asked, his lips twitching. "Honestly, Daphne, what could you have been thinking? Besides getting yourself involved in a murder mystery, Montague Moreland, I ask you? Couldn't you have come up with a more dignified pen name?"

"I kept thinking the name Montague Moreland sounded familiar," said Arthur, who was a year younger than she was. Jostling Jack aside, he pulled Daphne into a hug, gave her a kiss on the forehead, then released her. "For the life of me, though, I can't think where I've heard the name before."

"Montague Moreland was that ridiculous villain I created for the play I wrote when I was twelve, the one I made all of you act out for our neighbors that summer we stayed in the Hamptons." Daphne frowned at Jack. "I would have thought you'd have pieced that together by now since you were the one to play the role of Montague."

"How in the world could you have expected me to piece that together? It's not as if you ever gave me a single hint that you'd actually gotten published."

"How could you not have figured that out? I've been in New York for five years. How would I have been able to survive on my own all this time if I hadn't?"

"I thought Aunt Almira was still supporting you."

"Having Aunt Almira support me for five years would have been quite the imposition on her finances."

"True, but it's not as if I ever thought that my younger sister was perpetuating what has got to be one of the cleverest secrets the publishing world has ever hidden." Jack gave her nose a bit of a tweak. "You could have told me what you were up to."

She tweaked his nose right back. "I signed a nondisclosure agreement. You're an attorney, as are Arthur and Frank, which means you should understand the legality of nondisclosure agreements because you probably learned about them in your first year of law school."

"We're your family, brat. As such, you should have told us about your contract — or better yet, you should have had us go over that contract before you signed it." Jack caught her eye. "I would have encouraged you to refuse to sign a nondisclosure agreement, which would have allowed everyone to know who the author really was behind the brilliant Moreland mysteries."

A lovely warmth began flowing through

her. "You think my work is brilliant?"

Jack rubbed his chin. "Don't know why you'd find that surprising. I always told you that you could write, although I might not have encouraged you to pursue it, which was not well-done of me. I'd just hoped to spare you a large dollop of disappointment." He smiled. "I had no idea you, being a girl and all, would be able to find such success. But you've certainly done that, and I couldn't be prouder of you."

"I believe we are all proud of her," said Frank, their youngest brother, shoving Arthur and Jack aside to take their place. He promptly picked Daphne up, swung her around, then set her back on her feet and ruffled her hair.

"Do have a care with swinging Daphne around," Clara said, amusement marking her tone. "If you'll recall, you did that when she was fifteen and she tossed up her accounts all over you."

Frank grinned and took two very large steps away from Daphne. "I forgot about that."

"I'm not going to toss up my accounts."

"Good to know," a voice said from the doorway.

Daphne smiled as her father, known throughout Boston as the Honorable Burton Beekman, strolled into the library, dressed in his customary dark suit and carrying a walking stick that he set aside as he opened up his arms.

Daphne didn't hesitate to hurry into them, breathing in the scent of sandalwood as her father wrapped his arms around her and squeezed her tight.

Burton had not approved of her decision to move to New York City, but he hadn't stood in her way, even though her mother asked him to do exactly that. He'd then proceeded to write to her every week, including in every letter what he called "pin money," which was far more than a normal allowance and which he refused to take back from her, even when she told him she was perfectly capable of earning a living on her own.

Stepping back after her father placed a kiss on her forehead, Daphne smiled. "I wasn't expecting to see you home from work so early in the day."

"Your mother called a family meeting."

It was impossible to stifle a groan. "Oh . . . not a family meeting."

"What did you expect?" Clara asked, stepping up to them and accepting the kiss Burton placed on her cheek before she caught her husband's eye. "She's still refusing to move home, Burton. It'll be up to you and the boys to convince her otherwise."

A clearing of a throat from the doorway had everyone turning that way as Lydia, Daphne's baby sister, stomped her way into the room, her color high and her eyes flashing. "I, for one, don't think we should convince Daphne to stay, not after all the dreadful gossip I had to field about her while I was paying calls."

"Seems a little early for you to be done with calls, Lydia," Jack said, which had Lydia's stomping coming to an abrupt end as she settled a scowl on him.

"Mother called for a family meeting. But even if she hadn't, I would have cut my calls short today because" — she shuddered — "Daphne is the talk of Boston." Additional color stained her cheeks. "She's sufficiently ruined any chance I may have had of securing an advantageous match this year. What man wants to court a lady who has a notorious older sister?"

"Daphne's not notorious," Jack said, moving to stand beside Lydia, where he promptly kissed her forehead and sent her an indulgent smile, as if she were still five years old and being unreasonable, something Lydia had excelled at in her youth, and was still rather proficient in. "You're once again being overly dramatic, because you've never been in danger of not securing an advantageous match. There are many gentlemen interested in securing your affections, some of whom are friends of mine. The only reason you've yet to marry is because you're hoping your very own Prince Charming will descend on Boston and whisk you away to his castle."

"I'm not holding out for a Prince Charming," Lydia argued. "I'm merely holding out for a gentleman who makes my heart flutter." She turned to Daphne. "Thomas Sibley has been very attentive to me of late, and he is making a name for himself as a well-respected attorney. I was actually considering him — up until you went and brought such scrutiny on our family. I doubt he'll continue to flatter me now that the Beekman name is associated with scandals of epic proportion, and . . ."

Whatever else Lydia said, Daphne didn't hear because a mere second after her sister mentioned Thomas Sibley, her blood began to boil.

"You will not even consider allowing Thomas Sibley to flatter you, nor will you ever spend time in his company again," she said, interrupting Lydia's tirade and causing the room to fall silent.

"Why would you say that?" Lydia finally asked, raising a hand to her throat. "Thomas is a wonderful gentleman and has been fast friends with Jack for years." She narrowed her eyes. "Could it be that you have regrets for refusing his suit all those years ago and now long to have him turn an interested eye your way again?"

"The last thing I want is for Thomas to turn an interested eye my way. He's a disagreeable man who had the audacity to suggest to me, as well as to Mother, that I spend some time in an asylum after I turned down his suit."

Her father shot a look to Clara. "I never heard a whisper about sending Daphne to an asylum."

"Nor did I," Jack said, a flash of anger flickering through his eyes. "And one would have thought, what with Thomas being one of my good friends, that he would have mentioned something about that at some point over the past few years."

"It was only an idea," Clara said. "And it's not as if I expected Daphne to spend a long time there. I merely thought that having professionals look after her in an institution might very well cure her of her horrible bouts of anxiety, something Thomas was concerned about as well."

"My anxiety has been improving of late, likely due to my being preoccupied with other matters." Daphne returned her attention to Lydia. "But hear me well, Lydia. You will not have anything else to do with Thomas Sibley. I've met more than enough women through my work at the Bleecker Street Inquiry Agency who've found themselves threatened with time in asylums by their own husbands. Husbands, if you're unaware, have the right to have their wives committed and don't need a legitimate reason to do so. That Thomas Sibley tried to convince Mother to have me committed merely because I wouldn't marry him is a definitive sign that he's not a man any woman should marry, especially my sister."

Lydia narrowed her eyes. "But if Thomas is the only man still willing to pay me attention after this debacle of yours, you mark my words, I *will* accept his suit. I have no intention of turning into you — a confirmed spinster who'll never enjoy the attention of a gentleman, nor will you ever be able to claim that you've ever been kissed."

Even though Daphne was quite used to her sister's disagreeable disposition, Lydia's words sent temper flowing through her. Before she could respond, though, Garrison, the Beekman family butler, suddenly ap-

409

peared in the doorway, two gentlemen a few steps behind him.

To Daphne's surprise and delight, the gentlemen turned out to be none other than Herman and Cooper, although what they were doing in Boston was a bit concerning, as well as confusing.

"This isn't a bad time, is it, Daphne?" Herman asked as he stopped and glanced around the room, his use of her given name leaving her entire family gaping at him, especially Lydia, who was looking between him and Cooper, her forehead puckered, the expression on her face suggesting she couldn't comprehend why two such hand-some gentlemen had come to call on Daphne.

That expression had Daphne throwing caution to the wind. She sent Herman a waggle of fingers, which earned her an arch of a brow from him, before she directed the waggle at Cooper, who sent her a grin in return.

"Poppet, sugar plum," she exclaimed. "How marvelous to see you in Boston. Whatever are you doing here?"

"I think she's channeling Madame Calve again," Cooper murmured to Herman before he spun on his heel and headed out of the library, his shoulders already shaking.

As Cooper disappeared through the door, Herman turned a smile on Daphne. "Cooper and I thought you might need a bit of support. We didn't want to leave you on your own to deal with the repercussions from your publisher because of your work on my case. Charles Bonner was, after all, one of my guests, and I should have realized how put out he was with you and acted accordingly."

"How would you have done that?" Daphne asked.

Herman shrugged. "I should have told him before he and the rest of the authors fled my house on the Hudson that if he didn't behave himself in regard to you, I would let his little secret out about how he achieves such stellar sales."

"You would have threatened him with exposure?"

"I'm not normally so Machiavellian, but if it would have spared you all the trouble I'm sure you've been experiencing since we parted ways, yes, I would have threatened him."

Daphne suddenly found herself in dire danger of suffering a few heart palpitations of her own, quite like her mother had claimed to suffer from earlier.

"I believe that's the nicest thing anyone

has ever offered to do for me, Herman," she whispered right as her feet, seemingly of their own accord, began moving in Herman's direction. A blink of an eye later, she found herself standing directly in front of him.

"Did anyone else just catch that she called this gentleman by his given name or that when he first entered the room she called him either *poppet* or *sugar plum*?" she heard Jack ask no one in particular.

"It's wonderful to see you, Daphne. You're looking lovely today," Herman said quietly, his eyes warm and filled with something that had the breath catching in her throat.

"You're looking very well turned out as well."

"Who in the world is this gentleman?" Lydia demanded, the disgruntled tone of her voice reminding Daphne of the argument she'd not been enjoying with her sister before Herman had made his unexpected appearance.

Glancing over her shoulder, she found Lydia watching her with disbelief stamped on her face, that disbelief sending a flicker of annoyance through Daphne before she turned back to Herman.

"I'm really sorry about this, Herman," she whispered.

412

He blinked, just once. "Sorry about what?"

"Sorry about what I'm going to do next." With that, she threw caution to the wind yet again, stepped closer to him, took hold of the lapels of his jacket, reached up on tiptoe, and without allowing herself a second to rethink what she was about to do, kissed him.

CHAPTER TWENTY-ONE

"I really cannot beg your pardon enough, Herman," Daphne said, standing in a dimly lit hallway, though he could still see that her cheeks were decidedly flushed. "The only excuse I have for kissing you in front of my entire family is that I obviously took leave of my senses for a moment. Nevertheless, it was inexcusable for me to do such a thing and has now left you in a most unenviable quandary."

Herman took hold of Daphne's gloved hand. "I don't think you took leave of your senses, Daphne. I think your sister goaded you into reacting in such an unexpected but, need I add, delightful fashion. If I'm not mistaken, I believe I heard her say right before I entered the room that you were always going to be a confirmed spinster who would never enjoy so much as a kiss with a gentleman."

The blush lingering on her cheeks deep-

414

ened. "You found it delightful?"

"As delightful as can be expected when one is being kissed by a beautiful woman while an entire roomful of her close relatives looks on."

Daphne fumbled with the bag she'd slung over her shoulder.

"What are you looking for?" Eunice asked, gliding out of the shadows and scaring Herman half to death, a fright she didn't notice because her attention — or so he imagined, not that he could tell for certain since she was wearing at least four layers of veils — was on Daphne.

"Smelling salts," Daphne said briskly. "I fear recent events have left me with a distinct need of a few whiffs."

Eunice stepped next to Daphne, pulling Daphne's hand out of her reticule and giving it a firm pat. "You don't need smelling salts, even though your shared intimate moment with Herman certainly must have left you rattled. Just not smelling-salt worthy."

"I think it was definitely smelling-salt worthy," Daphne muttered even as she closed her bag and turned to Herman. "However, smelling salt–inducing event aside, I should not have kissed you merely to make a point to my sister, and for that I am sorry. My family is now, of course, expecting you to declare your intentions toward me, but know that there's no need for you to do that because, well, there's just not." Her shoulders drooped. "I'm afraid, though, that you're in for a rough time of it from my brothers."

Cooper stopped trying to shrug into his overcoat and grinned. "Your brothers have already begun trying to intimidate Herman while you were off fetching your bag before we go to your publishing house."

"Intimidate how?" Daphne asked, her eyes narrowing behind the thick lenses of her spectacles.

Cooper's grin widened. "Jack kindly offered to get in a boxing ring with him, Arthur offered to take him rowing, and Frank, well, Frank was the least subtle of the three and suggested they go out for a . . . how was that he put it? A spot of target practice?"

Herman returned Cooper's grin. "With me as the target, no doubt."

"Honestly, what *could* they be thinking?" Daphne asked, releasing a huff. "I'll have a word with them."

"There's no need for that," Herman said. "I'm perfectly capable of dealing with your brothers without your interference. Besides, I can't blame them for wanting to extract a pound of flesh from me. I did, after all, arrive in Boston unannounced, where I proceeded to address you by your given name, and then did absolutely nothing to stop you from kissing me."

"Why *didn't* you stop her?" Eunice asked.

It was a question that deserved some contemplation.

To say he'd been surprised when Daphne had grabbed hold of his lapels was an understatement, but he could have stopped her when he realized what she was intending. Yet . . . he hadn't *wanted* to stop her.

The kiss she'd given him had been fleeting at best, a mere touch of her lips against his. But he'd been thinking of kissing Daphne often while they'd been apart, and he'd been powerless to do anything but allow her what had to be one of the most unforeseen moments of his life.

She was always doing the unexpected, and he couldn't deny that he found such unpredictability to be one of the things he enjoyed most about her. She was enchantingly unique, and although they truly had not known each other long, he was determined to convince her they were well-suited and, as such, should make every attempt to become better known to each other.

He was beginning to hope, given how she had kissed him, that the convincing might not be as difficult as he'd been imagining. Yes, she seemed to enjoy her status of independent woman, but he didn't want to take her independence away from her. Instead, he wanted to —

"Difficult question, was it?" Eunice asked, interrupting his thoughts, and then causing him to give a bit of a start because she'd somehow managed to sidle right up next to him without him realizing it.

"Not exactly difficult, but I don't believe now is the moment to discuss it. Daphne is expected at her publishing house soon, which means we need to get on our way."

Daphne consulted the small watch pinned to the sleeve of her gown. "I'm not expected for over an hour at my publishing house. That means I have plenty of time to have a word, or three, with my brothers. It will not serve the situation well if I leave them with time on their hands to plan." She turned to Herman. "They've always been protective of me but have never had an opportunity to turn that protectiveness against another gentleman because I've never had a gentleman call on me before."

Herman frowned. "What about that Thomas fellow?"

She waved that off. "He doesn't count because he never formally called on me.

And besides, he's friends with Jack." Daphne's brows drew together. "With that said, though, Jack was unaware that Thomas tried to convince my mother to have me institutionalized. There's every hope that he'll now have a talk with Thomas in the not-too-distant future, at which point I can also hope he'll discourage Thomas from pursuing my sister."

"Thomas is pursuing your sister?"

"Apparently. I told Lydia in no uncertain terms that she was to avoid the man. Lydia's contrary at times, so I probably shouldn't have been so forceful. She's likely to encourage Thomas out of spite, so it'll be up to Jack to get that disturbing situation in hand."

"I don't believe you're going to have to seek your brothers out," Cooper suddenly said, gesturing down the hallway. "They seem to be waiting for you by the front door."

"Why does that not surprise me?" Daphne muttered before she took the arm Herman offered her. Together, they strode down the hallway, stopping in front of where Jack, Arthur, Frank, and Burton were waiting by the door, their overcoats already on, as well as their hats.

Jack drew out his pocket watch. "You're

cutting it somewhat close, Daphne. You said your meeting with your publisher is at noon, and it's already eleven. Men, I'm sure you realize, don't care to be kept waiting."

"Women don't care to be kept waiting either, Jack," she returned.

"What does that have to do with anything?"

"Well, nothing. I was just making an observation because far too often men don't take into consideration that a woman's time is just as important as a man's. With that said, though, none of you are coming with me."

"We most certainly *are* coming with you," Burton countered. "You're undoubtedly going to be facing an unpleasant and, need I add, daunting situation, and you'll need our support."

Arthur, Jack, and Frank nodded in clear agreement to that, earning a shake of the head from Daphne in return.

"You're not coming. I'm already taking Eunice, Herman, and Cooper. I assure you, I don't need additional support."

Jack frowned. "Who, pray tell, is Eunice?"

Eunice stepped around Herman, earning a widening of the eyes from Jack, a gaping mouth from Arthur, and a touch of a jump from Frank. She glided up to Daphne's

420

brothers and extended her hand. "Eunice Holbrooke, owner of Holbrooke boarding-house and partner to Daphne at the Bleecker Street Inquiry Agency."

Introductions were remarkably swift, and Herman couldn't help but grin when Daphne's brothers moved closer to the door, as if they found Eunice rather unsettling, which, in all honesty, she was.

"We should get going," Jack said firmly, opening the front door.

"You're not coming with me," Daphne reiterated.

Jack's gaze darted to Herman. "I'm not sure I understand why Mr. Henderson gets to accompany you and your own family does not."

"He's a well-respected published author. I thought he'd come in handy because he's been in the publishing world for years."

"Then what about Agent Clifton and Mrs. Holbrooke?" Arthur pressed.

"They're going because the Bleecker Street Inquiry Agency is still involved with Herman's case. Someone could very well have followed Herman to Boston. That means we can't let our guard down, so Eunice and Cooper will be accompanying him on the way, during, and then after my meeting with my publisher."

Daphne's father stepped forward. "You can't travel about the city in the company of two gentlemen who are strangers to me."

"Herman's a household name, and Cooper's a Pinkerton agent. There's really nothing more you need to know about them."

Burton crossed his arms over his chest and took to staring at his daughter. A full minute ticked away until Daphne threw up her hands. "Fine. But none of you are going into my meeting with me. You'll wait in the lobby."

"Does Herman have to wait in the lobby?" Frank asked.

"No, because again, he might be useful. He also doesn't annoy me the way the rest of you do."

Herman grinned, earning a grimace from Jack, who moved up next to his sister, took her arm, and ushered her out the front door.

Daphne looked over her shoulder. "You may join me in my carriage, Herman, as may you, Eunice, and you, Cooper."

Eunice shook her veil-covered head. "I think I'll ride with Arthur and Frank," she began, earning wide-eyed looks from Arthur and Frank in return. She gave a wave of her black-gloved hand to Jack. "I have a feeling the ride inside the carriage may get a little . . . contentious."

"I believe I'll join you, Eunice," Cooper said, trying to hide a grin as he took Eunice's arm before he nodded to Herman. "I'll be better able to keep an eye on your carriage if I'm riding behind you."

"Excellent point," Eunice said. "I believe, instead of riding inside the carriage with Daphne's brothers, I'll join the driver. That way I'll be able to keep my pistol trained on Herman's carriage at all times, as well as be able to keep a sharp eye out for any suspicious behavior."

Jack rubbed a hand over his face. "Begging your pardon, Mrs. Holbrooke, but I'm not certain I'm comfortable with the idea of you keeping your pistol trained on our carriage. What if you accidently discharge your weapon?"

"I've never accidentally discharged any weapon, and I can hit a target from hundreds of feet away, so if someone would happen to ambush you, I'll vanquish any threat before you'll even realize you're under attack."

"How reassuring," Jack muttered before he tugged Daphne toward one of two black carriages that were waiting at the foot of the sidewalk.

It didn't escape Herman's notice that after Jack helped Daphne into the carriage, he moved aside for his father to climb in, who immediately sat down next to Daphne, a pointed move if there ever was one. Swallowing a laugh, Herman settled on the seat beside Jack, who seemed to be taking up more than his fair share of space on the seat, leaving Herman pressed against the window.

"Jack . . ." Daphne warned, to which Jack merely smiled and shifted, taking up even more of the seat.

As the carriage jolted into motion, Herman found himself under the daunting gaze of Burton and Jack, something Daphne evidently realized as well because she let out a huff.

"I knew I shouldn't have allowed you to accompany us. If both of you have forgotten, I suffer from nerves at the best of times, and meeting with a publisher who is certainly put out with me has caused my nerves to suffer more than usual today. It's not helping my nervous state to watch the two of you try to intimidate Herman."

Jack rolled his eyes. "First off, your nerves don't seem all that concerning right now, which suggests you've been getting them well in hand. And second, did you ever consider that it might come in handy to have three attorneys and a judge with you, since you're obviously in breach of your contract?" Jack leaned forward. "If you've forgotten, Arthur and I specialize in contracts, while Frank specializes in criminal law and can be counted on to step in if your publisher turns nasty and threatens to sue you."

Daphne bit her lip. "I suppose you do have a point about your expertise with contracts, although I'm not certain how much help you'll be at this point. I am, after all, in breach of my contract and fully expect my publisher to part ways with me."

Jack nodded to Burton. "Father is a well-respected judge in Boston. He carries considerable influence. You could use that as leverage to keep writing for them, if that's something you want to do."

"I'm not resorting to threats, Jack. They either want my books or they don't. It's as simple as that. If they feel Montague Moreland books will no longer sell because they're written by — oh, the horror — a woman, they'll discontinue their relationship with me."

"But if that's not the case, you're going to need someone to help you negotiate a new contract because you're in breach of your current contract. That makes it null and void. And before you argue with me" — Jack turned to Herman — "you have an attorney look over your contracts, don't you?"

"I do." He caught Daphne's eye. "I never sign a contract without input from my attorney, something I recommend you begin doing. And before you think I'm just saying that to encourage your father and brother to discontinue glaring at me, I recommend attorneys to all the writers I know."

"I never said I'm opposed to attorneys. I just never considered having my brothers or father look over my contracts because, well, that would mean disclosing my true identity to them."

"That's why they have a thing called client-attorney privilege," Jack said. "Even with our being related, I'm, by law, not allowed to tell any of your secrets."

Daphne blinked. "Would that mean that if you, Arthur, and Frank became my attorneys that you'd then not be able to tell Mother anything I may get up to?"

"No, but nice try."

"That's too bad." She readjusted her spectacles. "I suppose it does make sense to include all of you from this point forward. With that said, though, I'm not certain I'll need any legal advice because, again, I'm definitely in danger of parting ways with my publishing house."

"Do you have any books still under contract with them?" Jack asked.

"Just one. They've already paid me an advance for that book. I've been wondering if they'll ask for that money back because I breached the contract."

Jack exchanged a glance with Burton before he settled back against the seat. "Excellent."

"How can you call that excellent? I just said they may want their advance money back from me."

"It's excellent because if they're foolish enough to part ways with you, it'll allow me to negotiate a new and, need I add, more lucrative contract for you with a different publishing house."

"I earn a more than respectable income from my books."

"But if you'd had me in charge of your contracts from the start, you'd be making even more money." Jack smiled. "I'm very good at what I do, dear sister."

"Which is why," Burton chimed in, "at the very least, you should let Jack accompany you into the meeting." He gave Daphne's hand a pat as the carriage began to slow down, then pulled to a stop in front of Hammerstone, Lander & Company.

Herman wasn't exactly surprised when Daphne shook her head.

"Why not?" Burton asked.

"Because women will never be taken seriously or allowed to write mysteries under their real names if we constantly tow our fathers, brothers, or husbands into meetings with us and allow them to handle everything, as if we women are incapable of understanding business. Yes, your help with my contracts might have secured me better royalty rates, but *I'm* the one who figured out how to sell my books to a publisher, and *I'm* the one who writes those books in the first place. I have to be allowed to see if I can rectify my mistake of disclosing my identity on my own." She smiled. "But if I run into any difficulty with that, I'll send Herman to fetch you."

"But we wouldn't be accompanying you into the meeting as your relatives," Jack argued. "We'd be there as your attorneys."

Daphne punched him in the arm. "No, you wouldn't be. You'll always be my brother first, Jack. If any member of the publishing board says something you take issue with, I fear the brotherly side of you will overtake the attorney side. No one except Herman, as well as Eunice because I believe her somewhat spooky appearance might come in handy, is coming with me. End of story."

CHAPTER TWENTY-TWO

Herman wasn't surprised in the least when, ten minutes later, he, Daphne, and Eunice were sitting in a conference room at one of the largest round tables he'd ever seen, without the company of Daphne's family. Daphne's father and brothers were waiting behind in the lobby, along with Cooper, and all were less than happy with that arrangement, although their rather vocal arguments about the matter hadn't swayed Daphne's decision to leave them behind.

"The members of this publishing house certainly wanted to make an intimidating statement," Eunice whispered to him, leaning closer as she nodded to the thirty men sitting around the enormous table, all of whom were staring at Daphne with frowns on their faces.

Daphne was oblivious to the frowns because she was currently rummaging through the limitless confines of her bag, pulling out her trusty notepad and a pencil, which she placed on the table before she lifted her head and nodded to Mr. Harrison Wiggler, a senior acquisitions editor, who immediately rose to his feet and sent Daphne a bob of his head.

"Miss Beekman," he began, "we're so pleased you were able to travel to Boston to speak with us."

"You say that as if I had a choice in the matter, Mr. Wiggler. I was delivered a summons, which I am now answering."

Mr. Wiggler's eyes widened behind the lenses of his spectacles. "Ah, well, yes, I suppose it was a summons, but we thank you for delivering yourself in person." He cleared his throat. "Do you understand why you're here, or would you like me to take a few moments to explain the particulars to you? Unless, of course" — he nodded to Herman — "your attorney has already explained the basics."

Daphne wrinkled her nose. "I'm here because I'm in breach of my contract, Mr. Wiggler. I assure you, there's no need for you to explain that to me, or, heaven forbid, assume I don't understand what the word *breach* means. I am a wordsmith, after all. I understand the definitions of words such as *breach, contract,* and *particulars,* if you were

430

under the impression that went over my head." She turned and sent a lovely smile to Herman. "And this isn't my attorney. He's Mr. Herman Henderson, a contemporary of mine, and an author I'm sure all of you are familiar with."

The table at large sent nods Herman's way before Mr. Wiggler directed his attention to Eunice. "And the lady in black?"

Eunice sat forward. "I'm Mrs. Eunice Holbrooke, one of the partners in the Bleecker Street Inquiry Agency." She set her large reticule on the table, opened it up, and began pulling items out at random, one of those items being a dangerous-looking pistol that she immediately placed in front of her. "Ah, here they are," she exclaimed, pulling out her calling card holder.

She plucked out a card, rose to her feet, then strolled ever so slowly around the table, the train of her black gown rustling with every stride. She handed Mr. Wiggler the card. "This is for you in case anyone at your publishing house ever needs the services of an inquiry agency. We handle all manner of cases, from theft, to character investigations, and even attempted murders." She turned and strolled back to her seat, inclining her head to Herman as he helped her resume her seat before he retook his own.

Mr. Wiggler looked over the card. "I'll certainly keep your agency in mind, Mrs. Holbrooke, if any of us here ever has need of it, but I'm a little confused about why you're here. And for heaven's sake, please put that pistol away. I hardly believe there's any need for it to remain out and so . . . conspicuous."

Eunice didn't so much as touch her pistol. "I'm here, Mr. Wiggler, because Daphne is my fellow partner at the agency, and I thought she might have need of my support. Besides that, Mr. Henderson has hired our agency to keep him alive. We take that responsibility very seriously and are not relaxing our guard as pertains to Mr. Henderson's safety, which is also why I'm here. That is also why I need to keep my pistol readily available in case an unexpected threat presents itself."

"It appears as if Eunice has taken issue with the way my meeting is being handled," Daphne whispered, leaning closer to him before she sent him a wink and then returned her attention to Mr. Wiggler, who now had sweat beading his forehead.

Swallowing a laugh, Herman couldn't help feeling that, once again, he'd landed smack-dab into the midst of a very unusual situation, one that was turning more amusing by the moment.

"I'm sure there will be no, er, threats here today," Mr. Wiggler finally said before he set aside Eunice's card and turned to Daphne. "And now, back to the business at hand, although . . . I seem to have forgotten what I was saying."

"That's perfectly understandable," Daphne returned. "I believe I last told you that Mr. Henderson is not my attorney. Nevertheless, in the spirit of full disclosure, my attorneys are waiting in the lobby for me to summon them if I feel their expertise is needed."

"Did you say attorneys, as in more than one?" asked a man by the name of Mr. George Harris, who was head of marketing, sitting forward.

"I've brought three attorneys and a judge."

"Why would you bring a judge with you?" Mr. Harris pressed.

"He's my father, the Honorable Burton Beekman. The three attorneys are my brothers, Mr. Jack Beekman, Mr. Arthur Beekman, and Mr. Frank Beekman."

"You're a member of *that* Beekman family?" Mr. Wiggler asked, pulling a handkerchief from his pocket and giving his forehead a dab.

"Indeed, but my family has nothing to do with why I'm here, which, again, is because I'm in breach of my contract, having disclosed I'm the author behind the Montague Moreland books."

"In Miss Beekman's defense," Herman said, sitting forward, "she was provoked into disclosing her identity after Mr. Charles Bonner attempted to suggest Montague Moreland was behind the attempts on my life."

Mr. Harris turned a pleasant smile on Herman. "Allow me to speak for all of us here at Hammerstone, Lander & Company, Mr. Henderson, and say we're very thankful to find you still alive and well. And if you're ever wanting to switch publishing houses, we would be honored to publish your extraordinary novels."

Daphne waved that aside. "Really, Mr. Harris, this is hardly the moment to try and steal Herman from his publishing house. So, returning to the matter at hand, which is me, if all of you have forgotten, what say we get to the meat of the matter? I've breached my contract, and . . . ?"

Given the way the clock ticked away as Mr. Wiggler merely stared at Daphne, it was becoming clear the gentleman had not been expecting Daphne to approach her situation with such a no-nonsense air.

He finally glanced around the room, nodded to a man who was nodding encouragingly back at him, then returned his attention to Daphne. "We have a few options, Miss Beekman. We had you sign that nondisclosure because we feared readers would not buy your books if they knew they were written by a woman. Publishing is, first and foremost, a business, and if we don't make money on our books, we don't stay in business."

"Which means you'd like to terminate my contract?" Daphne asked.

"Since you're in breach of it, your contract is no longer valid."

Daphne scribbled something down in her notepad. "True, and I do understand that it was null and void the moment I disclosed who I am, if you were under the mistaken belief I didn't know that. I also understand that publishing houses like to make matters official. I'm guessing there must be some paperwork you'd like me to sign before I part ways with you."

Mr. Wiggler took another swipe at his forehead. "You still owe us a book."

"Indeed I do, unless I return your advance money, which I'm perfectly happy to do. That will allow me to do whatever I please with my next book because there's nowhere in my old contract that says I can't sell it to another publishing house if I'm not under contract here."

Murmurs met Daphne's response, murmurs that had her sending Herman another discreet wink.

He settled back in the chair, hard-pressed not to laugh again because clearly Daphne was capable of holding her own, even in a room filled with businessmen who'd certainly underestimated her.

"We were thinking more along the lines of giving you a new contract with different terms for that book you owe us," Mr. Wiggler said.

Daphne's eyes narrowed. "What type of terms?"

Another mop of his forehead was Mr. Wiggler's first response to that. "A slight decrease in royalties and an agreement that you can't publish any mysteries with any other publishing house within the next five years if you were to decide to leave this house."

As Daphne returned to her notes without saying a single word, Herman looked around the room, noticing the anxiety that was lingering in more than one man's eyes.

Understanding struck in a split second.

He leaned closer to Daphne to whisper what he'd just realized in her ear, but before he could get a single word out, she lifted her head.

"How are my sales this week?"

"Excellent question, Daphne," Eunice muttered under her breath as all the men began to exchange incredibly telling glances.

Obviously, Daphne's sales had been stellar, something she had figured out on her own, proving once again that, behind her occasionally distracted air and propensity to suffer sudden swoons, lay a woman of extreme intelligence.

"They were . . . up," said Mr. Stanley Matisse, who was director of sales, or so claimed the plaque sitting in front of him.

"How up?" Daphne shot back.

"Ah, well, substantially."

A smile of clear delight lit up Daphne's face. "How extraordinary. But tell me this, Mr. Matisse, who is buying my books this week?"

Mr. Matisse consulted his notes, although Herman was sure he already knew the answer to that. "Erm . . . from what the booksellers are telling us, women seem to be purchasing the majority of your books this week."

"Excellent, and that's with my being

consistently told that no one would purchase a mystery if they knew it was written by a woman, not even fellow women."

"We might have been wrong about that," Mr. Wiggler said, shuffling his notes around on the table before he sat down and slumped in his chair.

Daphne rose to her feet. "Allow me to see if I'm understanding this correctly. You don't want to discontinue working with me, but you do want to pay me less money, even though my books are apparently selling better than ever. Do I have the gist of that right so far?"

"I don't know if I'd put it quite that way," Mr. Wiggler said.

"Then what way would you put it, sir?"

When Mr. Wiggler didn't respond, Daphne placed her hands on the table and leaned forward. "It seems we're facing a dilemma, gentlemen. According to my brother, Mr. Jack Beekman, who, if you don't know, is a contract attorney, I can return my advance, part ways with you, and not be obligated to give you that book I'm working on."

"How is that book coming along?" Mr. James Durnham, Daphne's editor, asked, smiling at Daphne.

"I've run into a slight snag with the story

line, but I've figured out the problem, and I'm sure a solution is soon to follow, Mr. Durnham."

"You always run into a snag, claim it's going to be the death of you, then deliver a story that neither I, nor your readers, can put down," Mr. Durnham said. "I have faith this latest work will turn out fine and arrive on time, if you decide to continue on with us. Speaking for myself, I've found you a joy to work with. I appreciate your dedication to your craft and also your wonderful work ethic."

"Hear, hear," Mr. Wiggler said as the rest of the gentlemen began nodding and murmuring their agreement to that.

"Thank you, Mr. Durnham," Daphne said. "I've appreciated working with you, as well. I value your suggestions after you edit my work and would truly miss you if I leave."

"Are you going to leave?" Mr. Wiggler asked.

"It depends on whether or not you agree to my conditions."

"You have conditions?"

"I do."

"And?" Mr. Wiggler pressed when Daphne returned to her notes, flipped through a few pages, then lifted her head.

"I'll want an increase in my royalty rate, as well as my advance rate, and I would suggest those increases be substantial because you'll be working with my brother on the contract. He's very protective of me and will want to make sure I get the best possible deal. He'll also reach out to other publishing houses to see what they might offer. Given my increase in sales, I'm sure all of you realize that other publishing houses would love to acquire my next book, as well as future books."

Glancing around the room again, Herman almost found himself feeling sorry for the gentlemen who'd surely underestimated Daphne and her ability to stand up for herself — almost felt sorry for them, but not quite, given that they'd just been trying to take advantage of her.

"Anything else?" Mr. Wiggler asked weakly.

"I want to write under my name, although I'll keep the Montague Moreland name. I was thinking something along the lines of 'Montague Moreland Mysteries,' and then have Daphne Beekman right underneath that on the cover."

"I don't believe that would be too much of an issue."

"I also want to do a few book signings

because I'd like to know how that feels, although I don't want to be scheduled for any author speeches because that would make me queasy." She smiled. "I don't enjoy speaking in front of people."

"You seem to be enjoying yourself right now," Mr. Wiggler muttered.

"I do, don't I?"

"Most assuredly. Are there any other conditions?"

"I'm sure there are, but I'll leave it up to my brothers, except . . ." She pulled her large bag from the floor, dropped it on the table, pulled out a spare notepad, two handkerchiefs, and a change purse before extracting the manuscript Sheldon had given her.

She held it up and smiled at Mr. James Durnham. "I'd like you to read this. It was written by a brilliant new writer, Mr. Sheldon Clarendon. I read his book in its entirety in one sitting, and I'd like your thoughts about it." She walked over to Mr. Durnham and handed him the manuscript. "You'll want to acquire this, but I should warn you that Sheldon will probably be represented by my brothers as well, so do make sure to give him a good offer."

Daphne returned to her chair, stuffed everything back into her bag, then nodded.

"I believe that's all, gentlemen. Shall I send my father and brothers in now? I'm sure they have matters they want to discuss with you."

"Right now?" Mr. Wiggler asked.

"They are here, after all."

"We might as well get this over with," Mr. Harris muttered.

"That's the spirit, gentlemen. And now, if you'll excuse me, I have other matters to attend to. I'm sure I'll be in touch. And Mr. Durnham?" She smiled at her editor. "I'll have that new book turned in on time, no need to fret . . . that is, if I am amenable to the terms of a new contract."

With that, she slipped the strap of her bag over her shoulder, took the arm Herman immediately held out to her, waited until Eunice returned her pistol to her reticule, and then walked out of the conference room with her head held high.

CHAPTER TWENTY-THREE

"I don't believe I've thanked you yet for delaying your trip back to New York in order to attend the Devonshire Ball with the family," Clara said, taking hold of Daphne's gloved hand and giving it a good squeeze.

Daphne returned the squeeze. "I know you were disappointed, Mother, that I'm not moving home after all the shenanigans I've been a part of lately. Attending the Devonshire Ball was the least I could do to make it up to you."

"You also put a great deal of effort into making amends with Lydia, and that, in and of itself, went far to banish my disappointment about you going back to your life in the big city."

Daphne shot a look to where Lydia was currently holding court, at least seven gentlemen vying for her attention. "All I did was give Lydia one of my Phillip Villard creations and promise her I'd personally see to getting her an appointment with Phillip to order a new fall wardrobe."

"An appointment I was unable to secure, given how much in demand Phillip Villard is these days."

Daphne grinned. "Here's hoping my connection with Phillip will leave me in Lydia's good graces for the foreseeable future." She shook her head. "I've never really understood why Jack calls me *brat* when clearly Lydia fits that description far better."

Clara sent a fond smile Lydia's way. "She is a temperamental creature, but I do think she has potential. She simply needs to grow up a bit more."

"At least she no longer needs to fear my reputation as a notorious woman will stifle her chances of securing an advantageous marriage."

Clara's eyes twinkled. "I'm sure Lydia is thrilled that you're now the toast of the town. Who would have thought so many ladies would rally around you, lending you their support over your unlikely occupations?"

"That is hopefully a sign of the times and a sign for things to come. It would be lovely if, in the future, the inroads ladies such as myself have made will help other women achieve their dreams."

Clara smoothed back a curl that had escaped Daphne's pins. "I am very proud of you, darling. I hope you know that."

Daphne's vision turned a little blurry. "I always thought you were disappointed in my life choices."

"Not disappointed, dear. Concerned. Choosing an unorthodox path in life is never easy. I would have preferred you live an uncomplicated life, but obviously that's not the type of life you wanted to embrace." She nodded to someone over Daphne's shoulder. "But speaking of complicated, we've yet to discuss Herman Henderson."

Daphne glanced around and found Herman deep in conversation with Jack. "There's not much to discuss, although I need to thank you for securing invitations to the ball tonight for him, Cooper, and Eunice. I'm sure all of them are enjoying the festivities."

Clara's gaze darted to where Eunice was standing still as a statue against a wall, all the guests giving her a wide berth. "I'm not sure Mrs. Devonshire appreciated my asking for an invitation for Eunice. She does seem to make people uncomfortable. I believe it's all the black she wears, and perhaps the slight menacing air that seems to waft around her."

"She cultivates that air on purpose."

"For what reason?"

"No idea. Eunice is fairly close-lipped about her personal life. She normally refuses to attend large social gatherings, but because our agency is still on Herman's case, she thought it prudent to attend this evening so that she can keep an eye on him."

"Do you really believe there's a possibility whoever wants to lay him low would have followed him to Boston?"

"Probably not, but it would hardly do the agency's reputation much good if we allowed one of our clients to come to a bad end because we let our guard down."

"I certainly don't want to see Herman Henderson come to a bad end, because it's not every day a man like that shows up at my door, seeking out my daughter."

Daphne laughed. "Since I don't have a witty response to that, nor do I believe that sparkle now residing in your eyes, which always precludes a bout of matchmaking, is going to bode well for me, I believe this is where I'm off to mingle with the guests." She consulted the small diamond watch that encircled her wrist, a watch her mother had insisted on giving her earlier. "And what fortunate timing. I believe the first dance is about to begin, and Mrs. Devonshire

446

thought it would be lovely if I took to the floor with Herman. She believes her guests will enjoy seeing two famed authors twirling around the room together. She thinks it'll be a novelty because there aren't that many women authors out there — or rather, women authors who attend balls and are escorted to those balls by the, and I quote, 'oh-so-handsome Mr. Henderson.' "

"Herman is certainly handsome."

"And on that note, I'm off to join him before you start interrogating me."

"I wasn't going to interrogate you, dear, although I am curious as to whether you and I should schedule some time to begin picking out china."

"It's far too soon for china."

Clara's gaze sharpened. "How interesting that you're not flatly denying that china shopping could be a possibility in the future."

Daphne settled for sending her mother a bit of a wink before she turned on her heel and began gliding through the crowd, nodding every now and again to the guests who were smiling and sending her looks that didn't seem to have a single trace of judgment in them.

It was nice not being looked at as an oddity by people who, in the past, had barely looked at her at all.

"Coming to claim our dance?" Herman suddenly asked, stealing up beside her and taking hold of her arm.

She smiled. "I was, and it's good timing because my mother was beginning to, well, do what mothers do."

Herman's lips curved. "Taking a page out of my grandmother's book, is she?"

"Too right she is, and I should warn you, she has you in her sights."

He grinned. "Are you actually surprised about that, given that she did witness you, well, kiss me?"

Heat immediately settled on her cheeks. "I really should have thought through that kiss a little more."

"It'll work out in the end" was all Herman said to that, a rather vague reply if there ever was one.

Before she could question him about how exactly that could possibly work out, Herman was leading her onto the ballroom floor, turning her to face him.

"Jack has already warned me to be mindful of my toes," he said.

"Of course he has, but I should have warned you about that myself." Daphne smiled. "I've never been light on my feet while dancing, even with my mother hiring

448

an entire brigade of dance instructors for me over the years. I'll beg your pardon in advance for the state of your toes, which will undoubtedly suffer during our time on the floor."

Herman pulled her closer to him as the first note of a waltz rang out. "Arthur told me you're not nearly as horrible as you believe yourself to be. And he said the best way to avoid damage is to distract you. I thought we could speak of the hero you've been trying to develop." He sent her a smile and moved smoothly into motion, guiding her effortlessly about the room.

"So?" he pressed after they reached the far side of the ballroom.

Finding herself astounded that she'd made it across the ballroom without stepping on a single one of his toes, while also feeling a very unexpected shiver of something that felt downright exhilarating when he whirled her around, she frowned. "I'm sorry, what was the question?"

"Your hero. What are your thoughts about him?"

"He's a lovely dancer," she said, even though she'd had no intention of writing a hero who could dance until just that moment.

"Interesting attribute. One I'm sure your

heroine will appreciate," Herman said, a trace of amusement in his voice as he drew her a touch closer and moved his mouth directly beside her ear. "You're doing wonderfully well, and you don't appear to be bothered by all the people gawking at us."

She stepped on his foot, stumbled, but regained her balance because Herman pulled her even closer as he steadied her. "People are gawking at us?"

"My mistake. I'm probably imagining that."

Daphne readjusted spectacles that had gone askew and looked over Herman's shoulder, finding far too many guests lined up on the edges of the ballroom floor, their gazes directed her way. She stepped on his foot again. "I don't think you're imagining the gawking."

"Perhaps pointing that out wasn't the best way to distract you. Arthur's definitely going to be disappointed with me."

"While Jack's going to gloat and spend the rest of the ball questioning you about the state of your feet."

Herman grinned. "I'm sure he will. Speaking of your brothers, I must admit that I'm very impressed with how supportive they are of you. When we first met, I got the distinct impression you were at odds with your family."

"I'm always at odds with my family because they try to boss me around. Even so, that doesn't mean that I don't love them all dearly. I especially love the new contract my brothers are working on, which will see my bank account increasing significantly if readers continue to buy my books."

"I don't think you need to worry about that. From what quite a few of the guests were saying to me earlier, they find you fascinating. A few gentlemen, though, had the nerve to question if I'd been helping you with your writing because, according to them, you write like a man."

"I trust you set them straight?"

"Indeed. I told them that you write better than most men I know. I also told them you don't write like a man, you write like a Daphne."

She stepped on his foot again, impressed when he didn't so much as wince. "Forgive me, Herman. There I go again, but your defense of me was beautifully done. I wish I had my notepad handy because that would be a marvelous thing to have one of my characters say. Unless, of course, you intend to use it in your work."

"Since I took the liberty of helping myself to your 'impatience is not a virtue' comment, it's only fair that you help yourself to what I just said."

"I believe I will," she said as the music drew to a close. "Goodness, but that didn't seem to take long at all, and it wasn't nearly as painful as dances normally are — for me, at least. I think it might have been somewhat painful for you, though. For that I will apologize again."

"There's no need to apologize," Herman said, taking her arm and leading her off the floor. "And I hate to escort you off the floor and leave you, but I've promised your sister the next dance."

"You'll enjoy that dance much more because Lydia is a lovely dancer. Do make sure to compliment her on the Villard gown she's wearing. She's very pleased about that," Daphne said. "I believe I'll take this time to repair to the retiring room."

"Because you're itching to take some notes?"

She grinned. "It's rather disconcerting how you know that, but I suppose that's because you've done the same thing a time or two."

After Herman grinned and made his way over to Lydia, Daphne walked through the crowd, stopped every few feet by guests who were interested in speaking with her about her books or her position as an inquiry agent. By the time she finally made her way from the first floor to the second, where she'd been told there was a retiring room that was never crowded, she'd almost forgotten all the words Herman had spoken that she'd wanted to write down.

Not wanting to forget everything he'd said, she headed for a small table that was placed against the hallway wall, setting her evening bag on top of it and pulling out the miniature notepad and pencil she'd not been able to leave home without. She immediately settled down to her notes, her pencil flying across the page.

"Daphne, I was hoping to have an opportunity to speak with you."

The hair on the nape of her neck immediately stood to attention.

Forcing herself to finish her notes and return her notepad to her evening bag before lifting her head, she found Mr. Thomas Sibley standing two feet away from her, the sheer size of the man making her feel as if he were standing closer to her than he actually was.

Thomas, as usual, was dressed to perfection in black formal attire, his white shirt and collar impeccably pressed, and his tie knotted in the latest style. His black hair was combed back from his face, every strand in place, and the smile he was sending her showed off the white teeth he'd always been proud of.

Frankly, Thomas Sibley was proud of everything about his appearance, his vanity one of the characteristics Daphne loathed about him the most.

"Mr. Sibley," she said, taking a step back from him.

Thomas's smile widened. "Come now, Daphne. There's no need for formality between us merely because we've been out of touch for the past few years. We've been friends forever."

"We've never been friends."

His smile dimmed. "You know that's not true. Granted, the last time we shared a personal conversation, you did seem slightly put out with me, but that was years ago. You're not still distressed that I suggested your mother have you committed to an institution for a tiny little stay, are you?"

"I'm fairly sure I was more furious than distressed, and no, that fury has not diminished over the years."

"Your inability to release your anger indicates that I was spot-on about your needing the rest and relaxation an asylum would have provided."

"And on that delusional note, I believe I'll bid you good evening."

"I'm not done speaking with you."

The hair on the nape of her neck stood to attention again. "I don't appreciate your tone, but I suppose, upon further reflection, I'm not done speaking with you either. I understand you've recently taken an interest in my sister."

His eyes glittered. "Is that jealousy I detect in your voice?"

Reminding herself that shrieking at the man like a fishmonger was probably not going to benefit her in any way, Daphne summoned up a smile. "What a vivid imagination you have, Mr. Sibley. Have you ever considered that *you* might be a good candidate for a stint in an asylum? Imagining my being jealous is not only delusional, it's also incomprehensible, something only a rational mind would understand."

Thomas edged closer. "You know full well I'm a rational man, more rational than any man you probably know. I take great pride in being able to read people, and I detect jealousy all over you, my dear Daphne. With that said, I don't believe your time away in New York has been good for you. You seem more contrary than usual, and men don't appreciate contrariness in women, although we're not opposed to inspiring a dose of jealousy every now and again. Tends to keep women in their place."

The urge to shriek at him like a fishmonger grew stronger. "And that right there is why you should thank your lucky stars that I didn't want to marry you. I've never been a woman who particularly cares to be kept wherever men believe I should be kept."

"As evidenced by your ridiculous actions of late. Publishing under a man's name was bad enough, but working as an inquiry agent? That's a bit of lunacy if I've ever heard some. No matter that you seem to believe differently, women do not have the intellect to solve crimes, something I believe was proven when you failed to uncover who wants to harm Mr. Herman Henderson, at least according to the article in the paper."

Daphne's hand clenched into a fist, and it took a great deal of effort to refrain from punching the insufferable man. "That article was penned by a man with an agenda. And while you're not wrong about Herman's case still being unsolved, I hope to rectify that as soon as I return to New York City. However, that has nothing to do with you. What does have to do with you is my sister."

Thomas's tongue darted out of his mouth

as he licked his lips, sending revulsion slithering up Daphne's spine. "Ah, the delectable Lydia. Now, there's a lady a man wouldn't be embarrassed to have on his arm."

"She won't be on your arm because you're going to leave her alone."

Thomas took another step toward Daphne, crowding her in a way he'd done often in the past. She edged backward until she ran up against the small table she'd been writing her notes on, finding herself trapped.

He licked his lips again. "I could possibly be persuaded to lose interest in Lydia. In fact, I can guarantee I'll lose interest in her the moment you agree to marry me."

"What?"

He leaned an inch closer. "I've always thought that you and I would suit well together. And even though you've been up to unappealing antics over the past few years, Bostonian society has decided you're now the darling of our city." He smiled. "Having the darling of Boston as my wife would certainly see me advancing rapidly at my law firm. As I fully intend to make partner in the next few years, I can't ignore the fact that you could be the means to achieve that status sooner."

Daphne narrowed her eyes. "Are you sure that's the reason you want to marry me? Or is it merely that you've never cared for rejection and haven't been able to reconcile yourself with the fact I rejected you all those years ago?"

"Nonsensical thinking like that lends credence to the notion you'd benefit from a stay in an asylum."

"It's not nonsensical thinking."

Thomas arched a brow. "Then explain to me why, if you'd really rejected me, you used to spend your time watching me and doing deliberate things to capture my notice? Your refusal to marry me was yet another womanly ploy on your part to truly attract my attention."

Something heavy settled in the pit of Daphne's stomach. "What things did I ever do to attract your attention?"

"You'd take off your shoes and stockings when you'd go wading in the creek with your brothers and me. And you were always twirling your hair around your finger when you'd read those books you were always reading. I saw those things for what they were, though — your way of trying out your feminine wiles on me."

"I don't think I've been wading since I was ten, and I started putting my hair up when I was fourteen, which means I would have been younger than that when you saw me twirling my hair. Believe me, I was not trying to attract your attention."

"You most certainly were, and your attempts increased the older you got. You were always acting coy around me, pretending to avoid my company — or better yet, swooning, which resulted in your being placed on a chaise in a most appealing fashion as people plied you with smelling salts or waved a fan in front of your face, causing your hair to flutter. I always knew what you were doing, though. You were whetting my appetite for you and making sure that you kept my attention on you and no one else."

The heaviness in her stomach began to turn to nausea, something she'd felt before when being this close to Thomas.

He moved so quickly she didn't have time to react, taking hold of her arm, smiling pleasantly at her all the while.

"Let . . . go . . . of me," she managed to get past a throat that had turned constricted.

"I don't think I will. It's past time you and I made things . . . right between us."

Daphne tried to scream, but it was as if she was suddenly incapable of sound as Thomas dragged her down a hallway that was devoid of people. Before she knew it, he was pulling her into a room, shutting the door with his foot, and then dragging her toward a divan that sat in front of a window.

Halfway across the room, little black dots began to obscure her vison.

She fought against the dots even as she tried to wrestle her way out of Thomas's hold, but the dots increased instead when she felt Thomas place his hand over her mouth.

"Take your hands off her."

Mere seconds after she heard Herman snarl those words, Thomas's hand was no longer covering her mouth. Given the thud she heard, and then a resounding crash, she assumed Herman had punched Thomas, but she didn't know for certain because she was slowly crumpling to the ground, Herman's strong arms catching her before she hit the floor.

CHAPTER TWENTY-FOUR

Rage threatened to consume Herman, but he couldn't allow himself to let that rage loose, not yet at least.

For now, he needed to get Daphne safely away from a threat she should never have had to face on her own, one that could have destroyed her if the man he'd seen trying to attack her had been successful.

Pulling Daphne's limp form close, Herman nodded to Cooper, who was already standing over the man Herman had punched. "Stay with him. I'll return shortly."

As Cooper withdrew a pistol from his pocket, Herman strode out of the room and into the hallway, debating which way to go, wanting to keep Daphne far away from the prying eyes of guests.

Thankfully, Eunice suddenly stepped from the stairs and into the hallway. She faltered for the briefest of seconds but then hurried forward, her attention settled on Daphne.

"What happened?"

"I don't have time to explain, but Daphne needs to go home. Immediately."

Eunice shoved up her veils, her eyes narrowing at the slight tear on the delicate neckline of Daphne's gown. She gave a jerk of her head and spun on her heel. "Follow me. We'll take the servant stairs."

In no time at all, Herman was placing Daphne on the seat of her carriage, Eunice having returned to the ball to gather Daphne's family. He opened Daphne's small evening bag, blowing out a breath when he found not a single vial of smelling salts nestled inside.

"Of course this would be the night you'd decide not to have smelling salts readily available," he muttered as the carriage door swung open, revealing Clara and Burton.

"Eunice told us Daphne fainted," Clara said, climbing into the carriage, kneeling on the hard carriage floor and taking Daphne's limp hand into her own. "And here I made light of her earlier complaint about how tightly she needed to be laced up in order for that gown to —" She stopped talking, quite as if she realized that speaking about corsets in front of him was hardly proper.

"She didn't faint because of her corset,

Mrs. Beekman," Herman said, abandoning the rules about unmentionables because he didn't have time for exceptional manners at the moment. "But I'm afraid I can't go into the details now. I have a matter of supreme importance to handle. I'll explain everything when I return to your house. It won't take me long to deal with . . . well, I'll get more into that later."

With that, he left Clara holding Daphne's hand as she searched in her own reticule with her other hand for her smelling salts. He climbed from the carriage, stopping when Burton laid a hand on his arm.

"Shall I come with you?"

Even knowing that, as Daphne's father, Burton had every right to be included in what needed to happen next, Herman knew that a father could not be expected to deal well with learning what had happened to his daughter. His reaction could very well draw attention from the guests, something that would leave Daphne's reputation in tatters.

"That wouldn't be wise. You should escort your daughter and wife home. As I mentioned, I won't be long, and then I'll explain everything."

Burton opened his mouth to argue, but before he could speak, Eunice hurried their way, Lydia holding fast to her hand.

"Has she come to?" Eunice asked.

"Not yet," Herman said.

"Lydia, get in the carriage, dear," Eunice said before she turned to Burton. "You need to get in the carriage as well, Mr. Beekman. Herman will handle the matter, as will Cooper, who is already on the case, so to speak."

"But I don't know what this matter is about," Burton said.

"And I can't tell you out here, so get in the carriage. The sooner we get back to your house, the sooner I can tell you what I think happened."

When Burton refused to move, Eunice took hold of his arm, all but shoved him into the carriage, climbed in after him, then slammed the door shut as the carriage surged into motion.

Drawing in a deep breath, Herman headed for the house again, not bothering to retrace his steps to the servants' entrance when he saw Mrs. Devonshire standing on the front steps, waving at him.

"I just heard that Miss Beekman suffered a fit of the vapors," Mrs. Devonshire began after Herman strode up the steps to join her. "May I dare hope she's already feeling better, Mr. Henderson? And dare I hope that it was nothing too troublesome that brought about that fit of the vapors?"

Herman summoned up a smile, a feat that was almost impossible to accomplish. "I'm certain Miss Beekman will be fine, Mrs. Devonshire. She remarked to me after our dance that she was feeling warm. She repaired to a retiring room, but I fear she must have been far more overheated than she realized. Thankfully, I went to check on her not long after she left the ballroom."

Mrs. Devonshire raised a hand to her throat. "How fortunate you were there for her."

"Indeed," Herman said. "But if you'll excuse me, I believe I left something in the ballroom."

"Would you care for me to have the servants help you in your search?"

"I don't believe that'll be necessary." Presenting Mrs. Devonshire with a short bow, Herman strode into the house, his progress to the second floor impeded time and again when guests pressed close to him, anxious to hear the details of Daphne's swoon.

By the time he made it to the stairs, his control over his temper was tenuous at best, that temper turning to rage once he climbed the stairs and stalked into the room where he'd found Daphne being accosted.

The man he'd punched was slouched down in a chair in a room that appeared to be a guest bedchamber, given the beautifully appointed furnishings but lack of personal items. Blood dribbled from the man's nose, something that gave Herman a great deal of satisfaction.

"He's not said a word, Herman," Cooper said, his pistol held in a steady hand that was directed at the man.

Herman stalked closer. "I hope you won't be too distressed to hear that I'm going to tear you limb from limb for having the audacity to lay so much as a finger on Miss Beekman."

The man withdrew a handkerchief from his pocket and dabbed at his nose. "You might want to reconsider that after I tell you that Daphne was more than receptive to my touch, and —"

Herman didn't hesitate to draw back, his fist connecting with the man's jaw a second later, sending the man to the ground.

"We just heard about Daphne and saw you going up the steps, Herman, but . . . *what* is going on in here?"

Shaking out his hand, Herman found Jack, followed by Arthur and Frank, striding into the room. Frank, thankfully, had the foresight to shut the door behind him.

Herman returned his attention to the man now pushing himself up to a sitting position. "You should ask him what's going on, although be warned, he's a liar."

Jack came to an abrupt halt. "Thomas?"

The man swiped his hand over a lip that was now bleeding and grimaced. "Jack. I sure am glad to see you." He gave a jerk of his head to Herman. "This lunatic just attacked me."

Herman frowned. "You know this man?"

Jack returned the frown. "This is Thomas Sibley, a friend of the family."

"Given what I just caught him trying to do, he's no friend to Daphne."

"What do you mean?" Jack turned his attention to Thomas. "What happened with Daphne? Mrs. Devonshire ran me to ground on the ballroom floor to tell me she'd fainted, then told me Herman came back into the house to retrieve something." His brows drew together. "I'm beginning to think Herman didn't return to fetch an item but instead to settle some type of matter with you."

"There's nothing to settle," Thomas said. "This man is obviously possessed of an overly active imagination. He clearly misunderstood what he walked in on, but instead of behaving rationally, he assaulted me." Thomas narrowed his eyes on Herman. "I'll expect an apology for attacking me without cause, just as I'll expect an apology for you interrupting my time with Daphne."

"If anyone has an active imagination or a proficiency with twisting truth to suit your own purposes, it's you," Herman said. "I didn't misunderstand anything." He turned to Jack. "I came to check on Daphne after I finished a dance with Lydia. I couldn't find your sister at first, and even sent a maid into the ladies' retiring room to see if she was in there. She wasn't, which is why I headed down the hallway, thinking maybe she'd gone to find a quiet place to write. I got halfway down the hall when I heard something through the door of this room. It didn't sound right, so I went to investigate. When I walked in here, I saw Thomas attempting to force himself on Daphne."

"That's not true," Thomas shot back, getting to his feet. "What you actually saw was Daphne and I enjoying an, ah, intimate reunion."

It took less than three seconds to reach Thomas again, and a mere second more for Herman's fist to connect with the man's jaw, sending him stumbling backward, although this time Thomas stayed on his feet.

"Daphne would never agree to an *intimate reunion* with you, especially since her opinion of you, Mr. Sibley, is not favorable," Herman said through teeth that were now clenched.

Thomas ignored that as he turned to Jack. "You must know this man is lying."

"But what exactly *were* you doing with Daphne?" Jack asked. "How did it come to be that the two of you were alone in the first place?"

Thomas dabbed his handkerchief over a lip that was now bleeding freely. "Your sister sought me out earlier in the night, longing to speak privately with me. She'd heard I'd been paying attention to Lydia and wanted to discuss the matter. We agreed to meet up here after the first dance was over."

"That's not true," Herman said. "Daphne came up here because she wanted to have a quiet moment to jot something down in her notepad."

Thomas rolled his eyes. "I would have hoped she'd abandoned her habit of carrying that dratted notepad around with her at all times by now. However, I suppose it's not something I need to worry about for much longer since she won't have a reason to jot things down after we're married. I fully intend to demand that she gives up her writing days."

"She won't be marrying you," Herman shot back, words Thomas once again ignored as he turned to Jack.

"Your sister and I *are* to be married. We came to that agreement once Daphne disclosed how jealous she was about the attention I've been giving Lydia. She then went on to beg my forgiveness for turning down my suit years ago." He dabbed at his lip again. "You know I've always had a soft spot in my heart for Daphne. I, of course, assured her that she still held my affections, and then we were merely sealing our renewed happiness over being reunited when that man burst in on us."

Jack frowned. "I never got the impression Daphne ever held you in any affection, Thomas. Quite the contrary. In fact, she recently reiterated her dislike for you, and believe me, she didn't mince words."

Thomas waved that aside. "Come now, Jack, surely you noticed how Daphne watched me over the years."

"I never noticed Daphne watching you," Jack said slowly.

"Of course you did."

"When, specifically, would I have noticed

her watching you?"

Thomas tilted his head before he smiled. "The night of Fourth of July, it had to be . . . maybe ten years ago or so? She made it a point to twirl her hair in what was a most provocative manner, knowing that the twirling would capture my attention."

Herman's body stilled as his thoughts whirled into overdrive. "Fourth of July . . ." he muttered under his breath. "The stray dog."

The night when Daphne had experienced a horrendous fit of the vapors, a night where something had terrified her so much that she'd lost consciousness, as well as lost almost all memory of what happened to her.

His hand clenched into a fist, but before he could move, Arthur and Frank were racing across the room, Frank grabbing hold of Jack's arm while Arthur moved to stand directly in front of Jack, blocking his way to Thomas as Jack tried to lunge forward.

"Let me go," Jack rasped.

Thomas frowned. "What is wrong with all of you?"

"That night was twelve years ago, and my sister would have only been thirteen years old. A child still," Jack bit out. "She wouldn't have been twirling her hair to attract your attention, she would have been twirling it because she had a habit of doing so when she was daydreaming up those stories of hers." Jack's eyes narrowed to mere slits. "I swear, you better not be about to tell me that you touched my sister that night."

"Don't be ridiculous."

Jack strained against the hold his brother still had on him. "Let me go."

"Hear him out," Arthur said quietly. "We need to know what happened, and we won't discover that if you render him senseless."

Herman watched as Jack drew in a deep breath, drew in another, then nodded to Frank, who didn't release him but did seem to relax his hold.

"I remember Daphne repairing to the carriage to fix her hair that night," Jack said. "I also distinctly remember her fainting, as well as all of us searching around in the dark for whatever it was that frightened her. What I don't remember is where you were when she repaired to the carriage, Thomas."

"I would hazard a guess that Thomas was with Daphne, which is exactly why she fainted," Herman said when Thomas began taking a marked interest in blood splatters on the front of his formerly pristine white shirt. "I also wouldn't hesitate to say that Thomas could very well have been trying to force his attentions on her that night, exactly like he was trying to do tonight."

"Is that what happened?" Jack demanded.

Thomas looked up. "I don't need to force my attentions on any woman. They flock to *me,* seeking *my* attention, not the other way around. Your sister, difficult as this is going to be for you to hear, is no exception. She followed me that Fourth of July night and begged me to kiss her. I am a man, after all, and we men enjoy kissing women, but before I could enjoy a kiss with your sister, she crumpled to the ground, apparently so overcome with excitement that she fainted. That put a rapid end to any thoughts of romance on my end and . . ."

The rage that had been coursing through Herman increased in that moment. He didn't bother to rein it in as his legs ate up the space that separated him from Thomas, who was still going on about Daphne, although what he was saying, Herman had no idea, giving the sound of his heart beating furiously in his ears.

Ducking his head, he rammed into Thomas, taking him to the ground. Rearing over top of him, Herman grabbed the lapels of Thomas's jacket and gave him a shake. "Daphne was an innocent child. How dare you try to cast blame on her for your repulsive behavior, but that's what men like you do, isn't it? Excuse your behavior by claiming no responsibility for your actions and instead lay blame at the feet of your victim."

Arthur suddenly had ahold of Herman's arm, pulling him away from Thomas, who rose to his feet, glaring all around before his attention settled on Cooper. "I don't appreciate you keeping that pistol trained on me. I suggest you put it away before you accidentally shoot me."

"I'm a Pinkerton. I don't accidentally shoot anything."

Thomas blinked. "A Pinkerton?"

"Indeed," Cooper said.

Thomas rubbed a hand over his face. "I wasn't expecting that, but are you intending on taking me in? I assure you that would be a waste of your time. While I won't deny that I was alone with Daphne this evening, she was willing, eager even, to be with me. And if she were to deny that, no one would believe her. Nor would any charges you may wish to press against me stick. My father wields considerable influence in the city, as do I. Besides, if I were to be taken in, word would get out about Daphne being alone with me and she'd be ruined. Granted, once she marries me, those nasty rumors would disappear, but until then, well, she would surely suffer under such . . . scrutiny regarding her morals."

"That's it," Jack snarled, wrestling out of Frank's hold, only to be grabbed by Arthur before he could reach Thomas.

Thomas arched a brow. "Do you really think a fight between us would be fair, Jack? I'm decidedly outnumbered. Five to one."

"And you think what you obviously were trying to do to Daphne was in any way fair?"

"As I said, she was more than willing."

Herman's rage increased, and it took a Herculean effort to control it, but as he drew in a deep breath, the perfect solution to deal with Thomas sprang to mind, one inspired by an unlikely event at his house party. He nodded to Jack.

"Thomas has a point. He is outnumbered, and we, unfortunately, are gentlemen, born and bred to adhere to certain rules, if you will." He began stripping one of his dress gloves from his hand. "Obviously, as gentlemen, we need to proceed with an air of civility." He strode directly in front of Thomas, smiled, then slapped Thomas across the face with his glove. "I demand satisfaction."

Thomas took a step backward. "Are you challenging me . . . to a duel?"

"Indeed." Herman looked to Cooper.

"You'll be my second?"

"It would be an honor."

Thomas rubbed a hand over his face where a red mark had already begun to form. "Duels are illegal."

"True," Herman agreed. "You'll need a second as well."

Thomas blinked before he nodded to Jack. "You can be my second."

"Are you out of your mind?" Jack demanded. "You tried to ruin my sister. The last person on earth I'd stand in for would be you."

Thomas turned to Arthur. "You can do it, then."

"He really has taken leave of his senses," Arthur said. "My answer is the same as Jack's, a resounding no."

"And don't even bother asking me," Frank said. "Although I think Herman is going to have to stand aside, because Daphne is my sister and *I* demand satisfaction for her honor."

"But since I'm the eldest brother, Arthur, you're going to have to stand aside because it should be me who meets him at dawn," Jack said.

"It'll be me," Herman said, stepping closer to Jack. "I was the one who caught him trying to dishonor Daphne, and because I intend to . . ."

"Intend to what?" Jack asked when Herman stopped talking.

"I can't say more about that, not now, but I'll be the one to meet Thomas at dawn." He caught Jack's eye. "You may arrange the particulars, and I'll need someone to find me a rapier."

"A rapier?" Thomas repeated.

"Seems a fitting weapon of choice, although I believe I'm supposed to allow you to choose the weapons, at least according to research I did on duels for a previous book. However, because duels aren't a usual event these days, I don't believe I'll allow you to choose the weapon, so rapiers it'll be."

Thomas eyed Herman up and down. "We seem to be of a size, but I warn you, I'm an expert on the fencing field."

"How delightful. So am I." Herman inclined his head. "We'll duel until first blood."

"Not death?"

"There's no guarantee with duels, Mr. Sibley, and rapiers, after all, are deadly weapons." Herman turned to Jack. "Cooper can help with arrangements. But now, if you'll excuse me, I need to get to Daphne."

He headed for the door, looking over his shoulder at Thomas, who was looking pale, as well as wary, probably because he was being stared down by all three of Daphne's brothers, as well as Cooper. "At dawn, Mr. Sibley. Don't be late."

CHAPTER TWENTY-FIVE

Readjusting the cool cloth her mother had placed on her forehead, Daphne summoned up a smile for Lydia, who'd been holding her hand when she'd finally come to and had not let go of that hand since. "I'm fine, Lydia. Truly."

"You don't look fine. You look pasty."

"Lydia, what a thing to say to your sister," Clara said, hurrying into the room with a fresh basin of water, which she promptly set down on the floor beside the fainting couch Daphne was resting on. She plucked the cloth from Daphne's forehead, plopped it into the water, then slapped it over Daphne's face, giving her a bit of a drenching in the process.

"Forgive me, Mrs. Beekman, but I'm afraid you're going to drown your poor daughter," Eunice said from her position at the end of the fainting couch.

"It's fine, Eunice. The water's actually

rather refreshing, and I much prefer water to smelling salts," Daphne said, lifting the cloth from her eyes and then squinting as the blurry face of her mother met her gaze. "And while I appreciate the fussing, Mother, I get the distinct impression you're about to suffer from your own case of the vapors. As I told Lydia, I'm fine. You should get comfortable in your favorite chair, put up your feet, and try to collect your nerves."

"You know I always fuss when I'm distressed, and that state isn't going to go away until you're able to tell us what happened to you."

"She only just came out of her swoon fifteen minutes ago, Mother," Lydia pointed out. "I wouldn't think Daphne will be up for an inquisition on your part for at least another hour."

"I think it will be best for everyone if I explain what happened now, Lydia, although if you could locate my spectacles for me, I'd appreciate that. It'll be difficult enough for me to explain what happened without wondering what type of expressions my words are garnering."

A blink of an eye later, Lydia was putting Daphne's spectacles on her, and a second after that, the room came into focus. It came as no surprise when Daphne found her

480

mother, sister, and Eunice, who'd abandoned her veils, gazing back at her with clear concern on their faces.

"Perhaps I should keep the spectacles off," she muttered right as her father stepped into the room, his hair in disarray, which spoke volumes regarding the state of *his* nerves.

Burton moved to kneel beside her, taking hold of her hand. "How are you feeling?"

"I'm much better, Father, thank you — so much so that I'm ready to tell you what happened to me, which resulted in what I have to think was one of my more spectacular swoons to date."

"Are you certain you're up for talking about it?" Burton pressed.

"Frankly, I'd prefer never to speak about it, but that would hardly be fair to any of you."

Clara sent a pointed look to Lydia. "I'm afraid, my dear, that you're going to have to repair to your room now."

Lydia raised her chin. "Absolutely not. Daphne's my sister. I want to know what happened to her."

"I'm sure you do, but you're a young lady barely out of the schoolroom. I'm quite convinced that what your sister is about to disclose is not appropriate for you to hear. You'll repair to your room, and I'll hear no

481

argument about that."

"Fine," Lydia said, leaning forward to give Daphne a kiss on the forehead before she dipped her head closer. "I'll be right outside the room if you need me."

"There will be no eavesdropping," Clara said, earning a huff from Lydia before she rose to her feet and marched out of the library.

"I'm not sure it's in Lydia's best interest to be ordered out of the room," Daphne said, struggling upright on the fainting couch before she leaned against the frame, the cloth her mother had slapped over her face sliding down to her chin. She pulled it off and caught her mother's eye. "What happened to me could, regrettably, happen to Lydia someday. She'd be better prepared if she weren't kept in the dark about such matters."

"And I'll speak with Lydia about what happened to you later, but for now, I need to concentrate on you, not on Lydia, who would certainly become distressed over what I fear you're about to disclose."

Daphne inclined her head. "In the interest of making this easier for you, Mother, I suppose it is for the best that she's not here. However, I don't believe young ladies are well served being sheltered from the realities of life. It leaves them far too naïve and vulnerable to what can happen when a young lady least expects it. Lydia needs to understand the dangers that are lurking just around the corner for her, dangers she might be better prepared to handle and react to if she's not kept in the dark because of the assumption that it's indecorous for young ladies to know what can occur at the hands of unscrupulous men."

"And, again, I'll speak to her. You may even join us if you're worried I won't be direct enough."

"I think I'll take you up on that offer," Daphne said, blowing out a breath. "And now, I suppose this is where I begin a story that I, even as a storyteller, have no desire to recount. Before I begin, though, I'm going to say that I have to thank the good Lord above for Herman, because if he'd not been at the ball tonight, I fear my reputation — not to mention my life — would now be in tatters."

"My intervention would have been timelier if I'd reached you sooner."

Daphne's attention shot to the doorway as Herman strode into the room. Her first thought was that he looked dangerous, with his tie undone, his hair decidedly messy, and his eyes glittering with what seemed to be anger. As he strode closer, the glittering softened, and by the time he reached her, concern was the only emotion left in his eyes as he knelt by the side of the fainting couch, her father having removed himself to stand beside Clara. He took her hand and gave it a squeeze.

"Nice to see you awake," he began. "Dare I trust you're all right?"

"It's nice to be awake. From what I've been told, I was out for quite some time. As for how I am, as I've stated to everyone numerous times, I'm fine. Annoyed with myself for fainting because I thought I was getting over that pesky business, but fine just the same."

"You shouldn't be annoyed over fainting, Daphne. You experienced a traumatic incident," Herman said, surprising her when he raised her fingers to his lips and gave them a kiss, one that left her feeling light-headed, or more light-headed than she'd been feeling, until she caught a glimpse of his knuckles.

"Why are your knuckles bruised?"

"They came into contact with Thomas Sibley's face numerous times."

"Did they really?"

"I'm sorry, but did Herman just say he hit Thomas Sibley?" Burton asked before Herman could do more than smile at her again.

Daphne pulled her attention away from Herman's face, quite the feat because he was regarding her warmly and she had the strangest feeling she could actually drown in his eyes, and not drown like what she'd experienced on the Hudson or how she'd felt when her mother had slapped that cold cloth over her face.

"Am I correct in thinking that Daphne has yet to disclose what happened to her?" Herman asked, drawing Daphne from her thoughts of drowning, and eyes, and Herman — well, not really because it was difficult to not think about Herman, given that he'd just saved her once again.

She cleared her throat. "I've not told them yet, but before we get into that nasty business, I need to thank you for saving me once more. You seem to make that a habit, even though I'm the one who was supposed to save you from a murderer."

Herman gave her fingers another kiss. "It's my pleasure to save you, Daphne, although I don't believe I'd mind if you'd avoid troubling situations for the foreseeable future. But as for you saving me, that's not what you were supposed to do at all. You were supposed to figure out who wanted to murder me. Cooper was then supposed to save me from being murdered."

"That's just semantics."

"It's not, and I'm not certain you're actually using the word *semantics* properly, although I might be wrong about that."

Daphne frowned as she considered the matter. "No, you might be spot-on, but I won't know for certain until I can consult my dictionary."

Eunice gave a bit of a snort. "Is this really the moment for the two of you to descend into a conversation regarding words and their proper uses?"

"There are no wrong moments to discuss words," Daphne argued. "Although I suppose we could delay that particular conversation until after we explain what happened this evening." She returned her attention to Herman. "With that said, though, did you just challenge me over the use of *semantics* as a way to decrease the level of anxiety I'm feeling over having to talk about the events of this evening?"

"Did it work?"

Her lips began to curve. "Surprisingly enough, it did."

"Good."

Once again she found herself in danger of drowning in the cool depths of Herman's eyes, even as the curious thought sprang to mind that if she continued thinking in terms of drowning in a person's eyes, she might have to consider trying her hand at a romance novel. Romance novels always seemed to have the heroine drowning in the hero's eyes. They also usually included somewhere in the pages such things as the hero becoming very dear to the heroine, and there was no question that Herman had become very dear to her. But more importantly, he didn't seem bothered by her many quirks and idiosyncrasies, which could surely act as a source of inspiration for her if she decided to change genres.

"Perhaps she's still suffering effects from her swoon," Daphne heard Clara say. "She's acting quite unlike her usual self. Her eyes seem somewhat unfocused — or perhaps dreamy would be a better way to describe them."

Daphne tore her gaze from Herman. "I fear I'm *not* quite myself just yet, but I'm sure I wasn't looking dreamy. However, that has nothing to do with the situation at hand, and all of you must be waiting on pins and needles for an explanation." She nodded to Clara. "It may be for the best if you were to take a seat. You as well, Father."

As her parents settled themselves on a settee, Daphne gave Herman's hand a squeeze.

"Will you help fill in the places I'm a little fuzzy about?"

"Of course."

Gripping his hand tightly, Daphne drew in a breath and began to speak. No one interrupted her as she told her tale, although Clara's face turned concerningly pale. Eunice pulled her pistol from her pocket and began eyeing the door, as if she were longing to go in search of Thomas herself, and Burton rose to his feet and began pacing around the room, his expression turning more and more thunderous.

"What could have possibly possessed Thomas to do such a thing?" Clara asked a mere second after Daphne finished disclosing what she knew about the evening.

Daphne was spared a response to that puzzling question when Herman sat forward on the chair he'd pulled up next to the fainting couch.

"Thomas appears to be a man who doesn't understand rejection," Herman began. "He, from what I've been able to conclude, told Daphne he was still willing to marry her. I believe that after Daphne told him rather forcefully that she wasn't going to marry him, Thomas lashed out." He shook his head. "I know men like Thomas, men who believe it's their right to treat women however they please, whether those women are receptive to their advances or not."

He took hold of Daphne's hand again. "I learned something else tonight that I'm uncertain whether you know. It seems that Thomas was what, or rather who, frightened you all those years ago on that Fourth of July night."

She stilled, taking a moment to let that settle. "I think there's always been a part of me that knew it was Thomas, but another part of me wouldn't let myself remember the details." She closed her eyes for the briefest of seconds. "The memories are still hazy, but I can remember some of it now."

"What happened on the Fourth of July years ago?" Clara asked as Burton returned to sit beside her.

Daphne closed her eyes again, queasiness settling in her stomach as she forced herself to remember. She opened her eyes. "I don't recall all the details, but I believe Thomas snuck up on me when I had returned to the carriage to fix my hair." Daphne closed her eyes again, shuddering as memories assailed her. She opened her eyes, her vision blurry due to the tears stinging her eyes. "He grabbed me from behind, then spun me around to face him." She shuddered again.

"It was dark outside, but I could see his face from the light cast in the distance from the carriage. The expression on his face terrified me. I think I might have let out a little shriek, but then he might have told me to be quiet before he began dragging me toward the forest."

Herman pulled a handkerchief from his pocket and wiped away tears that were now trailing down Daphne's cheeks. "But you fainted, or at least that's what Thomas told us, which stopped him from seeing through what he'd intended to do to you. I believe your coachman heard your shriek and alerted Jack and your brothers."

Daphne thought about that for a moment. "I distinctly remember Thomas dragging me, and I remember struggling to get free. As he was dragging me, he said something about my never mentioning anything about this to anyone. He said if I did, he'd tell everyone it was my fault. I think that's when I began struggling harder. He didn't like that so he stopped, and . . ." She bit her lip. "The last thing I really remember is his face coming closer to mine and then . . ."

"You fainted," Herman said when Daphne stopped talking.

She caught his eye. "You don't think he did anything to me after I fainted, do you?"

Herman shook his head. "Thomas is a braggart at heart, Daphne. He would have made certain to mention his prowess with women or some such nonsense if he'd done more than try to kiss you. Besides, from what I understand, Thomas was unsuccessful getting you into the forest, and a coward like Thomas would not have wanted to chance being caught out in the open by your brothers."

"You call him a coward, but I'm far more cowardly," Daphne said, shaking her head. "I panicked tonight when I found myself alone with him. I could barely get a squeak out of my mouth when he dragged me into that room, my less-than-courageous spirit once again leaving me feeling more helpless than I've ever felt in my life."

Eunice returned her pistol to her pocket before she sat down beside Daphne on the fainting couch. "Over the time I've known you, you've often claimed that you're not a courageous woman. I'm going to suggest that way of thinking ends tonight because you've proven time and again, tonight included, that you possess more than an ample amount of courage."

"But I couldn't speak because I was so afraid."

Eunice waved that aside with a flick of her

black-gloved hand. "You were taken by surprise and overpowered by a man who is almost twice your size. Being afraid doesn't mean you lack courage, though. Only a courageous person would have the strength needed to continue living a productive life after what happened to you as a child."

"Daphne used to ask God all the time to give her courage," Lydia said, stepping into the room, even though doing so was a clear indicator she'd been eavesdropping at the door. She sent Daphne a small smile. "I made it a habit to listen to your prayers at night. I was hoping you'd disclose something you'd done wrong, something I could have used to get you in trouble with Mother."

"Further proof that everyone needs to stop addressing me as the brat of the family," Daphne said, returning Lydia's smile before she sobered. "But I did pray that every night — and still do. I've never really believed God heard those prayers, or if He did, that He wanted to answer them."

"I think, given the life you've been able to lead, Daphne, that God heard you," Eunice said. "I also think He answered your prayers by giving you additional courage throughout the years whenever you were in need of it."

"Then how does that explain my frequent

swoons?"

"I'm not a theologian, nor am I an expert when it comes to matters of faith. With that said, and until you can broach this particular matter with a man of the cloth, I assume your swoons are a defense mechanism that allows you to deal with excess anxiety, the root of that anxiety being Thomas's repulsive behavior toward you."

"Even if you're right, Eunice, and God has given me courage, I don't believe I've been given enough of that courage to ever want to face Thomas again." She caught her mother's eye. "Because of that, I'm afraid I'll have to avoid visiting home often because I don't want to take the chance of running into the man."

"You'll visit home whenever you please," Burton said firmly. "I won't tolerate Thomas Sibley being responsible for my never getting to see my daughter, and you'll never need to fear he'll try to contact you again. I'll take care of him; you have my word on that. In fact, I believe I'll do that now." He glanced to Herman. "Did you leave Thomas at the Devonshire ball?"

Herman ran a hand over his face. "I would imagine he's taken his leave by now, given that I left him rather bloody. But there's no need for you to seek Thomas out tonight because I'm meeting him tomorrow . . . at dawn."

Daphne's mouth gaped open. "That almost sounds as if you challenged him to a duel."

"That's exactly what I did."

"But why?"

"I would think that's obvious. He tried to dishonor you. He needs to pay a price for that."

For a moment Daphne couldn't breathe, or think rationally for that matter, until a single thought suddenly sprang to mind, one she'd been searching for all along but that had eluded her grasp.

It was little wonder her idea to create the perfect hero from a pirate had been wrong. She'd written her story wrong from the very beginning, because heroes weren't swashbuckling pirates who went from one adventure to another, experiencing life in a haphazard fashion.

Heroes were gentlemen who didn't hesitate to defend a woman and didn't hesitate to put their lives in jeopardy over a matter of honor.

Heroes were gentlemen exactly like Herman.

Her fingers itched for her pencil and notepad so she could right the wrong she'd cre-

494

ated, but before she could gather her wits enough to ask someone to fetch them for her, Jack stomped into the library, Arthur, Frank, and Cooper behind him.

"Bad news on the dueling front, Herman" were the first words out of Jack's mouth. "Thomas's father has stepped in and put a halt to everything, saying he'll notify the police if we try to force Thomas into meeting you at dawn."

"How did Thomas's father get involved in all this?" Burton asked.

Jack emitted a grunt. "Ralph Sibley was in attendance tonight. He apparently grew concerned when Thomas was missing from the ballroom for so long and went searching for him. He was not pleased to discover his son bleeding and . . ."

"Being pinned down on the floor by Jack," Arthur finished when Jack stopped talking.

Jack shrugged. "He tried to get away as I was questioning him further about what he'd done to Daphne. Since I wasn't done questioning him, nor did I feel that Herman should be the only one to extract a pound of flesh, I wasn't willing to let Thomas slither away."

"Unfortunately, Ralph Sibley threatened to make a ruckus," Frank added, shaking his head. "We couldn't let him do that because questions would then be asked and that wouldn't go well for you, Daphne."

"Jack did punch him, though, right before Ralph hustled Thomas out of the room," Cooper said. "I was going to use my position as a Pinkerton to detain Thomas and take him in for more questioning, but Ralph put an end to that business since he's an attorney." He sighed. "Everyone seems to be an attorney here in Boston."

"Ralph ended it because Thomas didn't do anything that was actually against the law," Jack said with a roll of his eyes. "I never realized that a man could try to force his attention on an unwilling lady and not suffer *any* repercussions from it — and I'm one of those Bostonian attorneys, for crying out loud."

"That's just because you didn't specialize in criminal law, but I could have told you that," Arthur said. "Women don't have many, if any, rights when it comes to the law." He moved across the room to stand in front of Daphne, bending over to place a kiss on her forehead. "You doing all right, brat?"

Daphne smiled. "I'm fine. Relieved that none of you were injured tonight. Thomas is a large man, and he could have done damage to any of you."

Frank jostled Arthur aside, taking his place and giving Daphne a kiss on the forehead, as well. "Thomas is a coward, Daphne. He may be large, but he's not got an ounce of courage in him, because what he did to you tonight goes far in proving how lacking he is as a man."

Her fingers itched once again for her notepad, but the sensation disappeared when Jack took Frank's place, kneeling beside her. "I have something else to tell you," he said quietly. "It was Thomas all those years ago, that night when you fainted on the Fourth of July."

"I know," Daphne said. "I remember what happened now."

"Can you ever forgive me for not protecting you?"

"There's nothing to forgive," Daphne said, tears springing to her eyes again when she noticed the anguish in Jack's eyes. "You couldn't have known what Thomas wanted to do to me."

"I should have known. You were always nervous around Thomas." The anguish in Jack's eyes increased.

"He was your friend, Jack. One doesn't expect that type of behavior from a friend."

"He's no friend of mine."

Daphne glanced around the room, taking

in all the pale faces that surrounded her. She swallowed past a lump that suddenly formed in her throat. "I'm sorry about how much trouble I've caused everyone this evening. I'm also ashamed to have brought this type of humiliation onto the family."

Silence descended over the library until Herman gestured to Jack, who got up to make room for Herman to sit down beside Daphne on the fainting couch.

"There's nothing for you to be ashamed of," Herman said quietly. "This is Thomas's shame, not yours." He took hold of her hand and entwined his fingers with hers. "Because of your work with the Bleecker Street Inquiry Agency, you have seen some of the worst that men can do to women. And all of those women, if I'm not mistaken, have been led to believe that somehow the damage done to them at the hands of men is their fault. Women, I'm afraid to say, have been taught that if a man makes inappropriate advances, it's because of something they did — perhaps showing a hint of an ankle or flashing an overly bright smile. But that's not the truth, Daphne. You know it's not."

She swiped at a tear rolling down her cheek. "The rational part of me knows that. But there's another part of me that believes

I was somehow to blame, at least to a small extent."

"Thomas — and Thomas alone — was responsible for his actions," Herman said. "And while I have no idea how just yet, he will pay for what he did to you."

"I'll make certain of that," Burton said, speaking up. "It's a delicate matter, though, because we certainly can't allow Daphne's reputation to suffer." He caught Daphne's eye. "Unfair as it seems, that would happen if word got out you were alone with Thomas. But he won't get to go on his merry way. If nothing else, I'll make it impossible for him to achieve those promotions he longs for at his firm. I'll also take steps to assure he won't be on the guest lists for any Bostonian society affairs."

"Hardly seems like much of a punishment," Clara said with a sniff. "I still believe Thomas deserves to meet Herman at dawn." She sent Herman a small smile. "I have a feeling you handle yourself well with a pistol."

"It was going to be rapiers," Herman said.

Clara's eyes widened. "You're proficient with a rapier?"

"I can hold my own," he said before he turned back to Daphne. "You must be exhausted. May I dare hope you'll allow me to convince you to repair to your room for the night? It's been a troubling evening, and I'm sure you could use some sleep."

"I am exhausted," she admitted, "but I don't believe I'll be able to sleep just yet."

Herman considered her for a long moment before he got up from the couch, moved to one of the many bookshelves that lined the library, perused the spines, then plucked out a book. As he retook his seat, he said, "How about if I read to you? This book just happens to be a riveting read, one that should distract you from any troubling thoughts that linger in your mind."

She glanced at the title of the book and smiled. "It's one of yours."

"Indeed. Why else do you think I said it was a riveting read? But before I begin, allow me to say that I'm delighted to discover one of my books here."

"All of your books are here. I send them to my father whenever they release because he's a Herman Henderson admirer."

Herman shot a look to Burton. "You enjoy my work?"

A smile flickered over Burton's face. "Well, yes, but I didn't want to fawn over you. That might have been awkward."

"We're admirers of your work as well, and after tonight's events, that admiration has

500

now grown to include being impressed with you as a gentleman," Jack said as Arthur and Frank nodded. "I'm sure I speak for all of us when I say that your care of our Daphne tonight was extraordinary, and that none of us will ever forget what you did for her or be able to thank you enough."

Herman cleared his throat. "I'm certainly no hero, because I'm sure all of you would have done the same if you'd happened upon such a troubling situation. But how about we put all talk of tonight's troubling events aside? I'm more than happy to have all of you listen as I read."

As Herman opened his book, Daphne settled back against the fainting couch, the sound of his voice as he read out loud going far to settle nerves that were still a little ragged.

The thought sprang to mind when he finished chapter one and began chapter two that he fit in well with her family. Her brothers had stopped giving him the evil eye, her father had been suitably impressed that he'd challenged Thomas to a duel, and Clara and Lydia were watching Herman closely as he read — when they weren't watching her, of course.

That she felt more connected to him than she'd ever felt connected to a person in her life, even though she hadn't known him long, should have concerned her.

Oddly enough, it didn't, but that was something she'd need to contemplate further at a later date. For now, she was content to listen to Herman read, finding a sense of peace through the sound of his voice — a sense of peace she'd not truly felt in years.

CHAPTER TWENTY-SIX

"Why did you need to speak with Burton privately before we left Boston?" Cooper asked as he waited with Herman to collect their luggage from Grand Central Depot. "Did it have to do with how Thomas slithered out of the city late last night, probably because he was worried we'd find a way to circumvent his father's threats and hold that duel after all?"

Herman took the large trunk that had Daphne's name stamped on it from a porter and set it aside, turning to take yet another one of Daphne's trunks, finding himself grateful that it wasn't winter, like Phillip Villard had mentioned, because they'd then have had to hire a brigade of carriages to get all of Daphne's trunks home. "Burton and I did speak about Thomas. Neither of us is surprised he disappeared from town, a circumstance I know disappointed Burton after he slipped out of the house last night to have a word, or at least that's what he claimed he only wanted to have, with Thomas and his father."

"It seems Burton is following through on his word to make Thomas persona non grata within Boston society."

"Burton's unquestionably using his influence to make certain Thomas is not included in society events, and I can't blame him for that. He wants to ascertain other young ladies don't suffer Thomas's repulsive attention, although there's no saying he won't land on his feet in another city and begin stalking the fair ladies there." Herman accepted another trunk from the porter that was so heavy he stumbled backward. "What could Daphne possibly have in here?"

"She mentioned something about borrowing a few of her mother's romance novels."

"By the weight of this trunk, I'm thinking she must have taken half the library."

"I wouldn't be surprised, given how fond Daphne is of books, but returning to your conversation with Burton. Was there anything else of note the two of you spoke about?"

"Why do I get the distinct impression you're fishing for a specific answer?"

"Because I can't help but wonder if the

conversation traveled into personal territory."

"It might have."

"And?"

"And nothing. It's not something I can discuss with anyone other than Burton until after I broach the matter with Daphne."

"You're not going to tell me? I thought we were friends."

"You told me you wouldn't be my friend until after you solved my case."

"I did tell you that, didn't I?" Cooper asked. "I suppose now that we're back in the city, I'll have to speed up solving your case so you can tell me your secrets."

"Why would you want to know my secrets?"

Cooper hefted one of Eunice's trunks onto a cart. "Your secrets, if I'm not mistaken, concern Daphne. Daphne's a friend of mine. As such, she may seek my counsel at some point regarding you. I'll be better equipped to lend her that counsel if I know what you're intending with her."

"Which is very commendable of you, but I'm not telling you what I spoke with Burton about."

"Did you ask his permission to marry Daphne?"

Herman arched a brow. "You're very

relentless, but no, and we're going to leave the conversation at that."

"I'm a Pinkerton. I can't leave a conversation when there are so many unanswered questions."

"That's unfortunate, because until I speak with Daphne, I don't have any answers for you."

Grumbling under his breath, Cooper tossed the last piece of luggage onto the cart, then walked with a porter toward where Daphne and Eunice had secured them transportation for the ride home.

Striding after Cooper, Herman slowed to a stop when he caught sight of Daphne. She had her ever-handy notepad out, scribbling in it as Eunice directed the porter to put the luggage into a separate carriage.

That there was simply something about Daphne that fascinated him was no longer in any question. She was unique and intriguing, and he couldn't help but feel oddly thankful that someone had decided to kill him, because if they'd not made that decision, he would have never met her.

She took that moment to abandon her notepad and lift her head, sending him a smile, which had Herman striding into motion again.

That Daphne might have lost that smile if

he'd not been there to intervene with Thomas sent a sliver of rage running through him, as well as a vow to make certain she was never placed in such a terrifying situation again.

"You're looking very fierce all of a sudden," Daphne said when he stopped beside her. "Is something the matter?"

"Nothing that a duel wouldn't have solved."

She took hold of his arm. "You're going to have to let that nastiness with Thomas go. He's left Boston, and his father certainly isn't divulging his whereabouts. But if it makes you feel better, I get a great deal of satisfaction knowing his transgressions were brought to light and that you and my brothers drove him out of town."

"It's not enough."

"But it'll suffice." She gave his arm a pat. "What say we get on our way? I know you have writing to catch up on, and I, well, I have your case to solve."

"What if we put my writing and my case on hold, if just for this afternoon? I'd prefer to spend the day simply enjoying your company."

Pink immediately tinged Daphne's cheeks. "I suppose it wouldn't hurt to take an

afternoon off, because that sounds delightful."

"It does indeed," Eunice said, stepping up
to join them. "And no need to fret that Herman's case will suffer. I'll get right to work
on it once I reach the boardinghouse. Hopefully Ann will have uncovered some unsavory gossip concerning our list of suspects
in the meantime."

"I wouldn't mind hearing what Ann might
have uncovered," Cooper said, helping
Eunice into the carriage after Herman got
Daphne settled.

"I'm sure you wouldn't," Eunice said, lifting up the layers of veils concealing her face
and revealing a grin. "Shall we head to the
boardinghouse first, then?"

"If it wouldn't be too much trouble,"
Daphne began, "I'd appreciate stopping off
at Herman's house first because Sheldon is
staying there. I'd like to tell him as soon as
possible about the news regarding my editor wanting to acquire his book. I well
remember how anxious I was before I got a
contract." She smiled. "I know if I go to the
boardinghouse first, I'll get distracted with
catching everyone up on what happened in
Boston."

"How long do you think it'll take to tell
Sheldon the good news?" Cooper asked as

Herman instructed the driver to take them to his house and the carriage rumbled into motion.

"I wouldn't think it would take more than an hour," Daphne said. "But there's no need for you and Eunice to wait for us."

"There most certainly is, considering I'm in charge of keeping Herman alive," Cooper shot back.

"True, but since no one had any advance notice that you and Herman were returning to the city today, I doubt anyone's going to be able to plan an attack in the next hour."

Herman sat forward. "Daphne has a point. Go to the boardinghouse, Cooper. As you know, I'm always armed, and I'm perfectly capable of defending myself for an hour. I hate to see you delay your reunion with Ann simply because Daphne and I want to share some good news with my cousin."

"You'll only be an hour, and then you'll come to the boardinghouse?" Cooper pressed.

As Herman nodded, talk turned to the suspects in his case, although there wasn't much to talk about, given that there'd been no new attacks on his life lately. Before he knew it, the carriage was pulling to a stop in front of his house. After helping Daphne out, and after assuring Cooper once again that they'd meet him at the boardinghouse within the hour, he took hold of Daphne's arm.

"I've been wanting to ask you something, Daphne, but I wanted to wait until we were alone because it could be a sensitive topic," he said as they walked to his front steps. "Why did you bring an entire trunk filled with your mother's romance novels back to New York with you?"

She smiled. "That's not a question I was expecting you to ask, but speaking of questions, I have one to ask you, as well. What did you mean when you told Cooper you need to talk to me before you can answer his questions? I didn't catch the rest because Eunice needed help procuring a carriage."

"You were eavesdropping on my conversation with Cooper?"

"I'm a writer. You're a writer. Does that question even need to be asked?"

He grinned. "An excellent point. And to answer your question, there are many things I need to talk to you about, one of those being the reason behind the romance novels."

Her nose wrinkled. "I was hoping there was something a little more . . . . substantial you wanted to talk to me about other than romance novels."

"Oh, there is, but now I'm curious about the romance novels because it seems to me you're trying to avoid the issue." He caught her eye. "As a writer, you must know that once my curiosity is roused, I'll be hard-pressed to talk to you about anything else until my curiosity is satisfied in regard to the romance novels."

"Is it odd that I actually understand that type of reasoning?" she asked, her eyes twinkling. "And because I well understand that you'll be hard-pressed to concentrate on anything else but romance novels until I explain, I'll tell you. I brought them back with me to read because I've had an idea that might help me improve my story, but" — she quickly added — "they're for research purposes only, in case you were about to ask that next."

"I wasn't, but now I have a few more things to add to that list of matters I want to discuss with you."

Walking with her up the steps and trying to conceal a grin over the look of exasperation she'd settled on him, Herman paused in front of the door, his grin fading when that door remained staunchly closed. "That's odd. I'd have thought Perkins heard the carriage. He prides himself on always knowing when I'm arriving."

"Did you send a telegram letting him know you were returning from Boston today?"

"No."

"Then I'm sure he's merely counting the silverware or attending to his other duties, unless . . ." Her voice trailed off. "You don't think something concerning happened while you were gone, do you?"

Herman thought about that for a brief second before he shrugged the idea aside. "We're probably being paranoid." With that, he stepped forward and turned the doorknob, frowning when he discovered that the door was locked. "Or maybe we're not being paranoid."

Daphne pulled a pin from her hair. "Lucky for us, Gabriella showed me the basics of picking a lock. It shouldn't take me more than" — she winced — "an hour or two to get into your house."

He laughed before he nodded to a potted plant on the porch. "No need to try your hand at picking the lock. I keep a spare key hidden under that."

"You're a mystery writer, Herman. Surely you know that keys shouldn't be hidden in such a conspicuous place. You're lucky you haven't been murdered in your bed by now." She tapped a finger against her chin. "I have to wonder, though, if whoever was sneaking around your secret passageways knew about your spare key. That would have made it remarkably easy to access your house."

"A valid point, and know that I'll find a better place to stash the key. But for now, how about you stay out here while I go investigate, just in case there *is* something concerning afoot?"

"You're clearly forgetting that I'm an inquiry agent, so I won't be dithering on the porch." She fumbled with her bag, dropping a book, two handkerchiefs, a few pencils, and a spare pair of spectacles to the ground before she pulled out the derringer she'd once leveled on poor Andrew. "I'm ready."

"Forgive me for asking this, but do you actually know how to shoot a pistol?"

"I've learned how to fire a pistol, so yes, although my aim isn't great. Cooper suggested that if I'm threatened, I should get as close to that threat as possible to at least have a chance of hitting them." She slung the strap of her bag over her shoulder and nodded. "Lead the way."

"I'm not sure learning you need to be close to a target is a great vote of confidence."

"True, but if I miss, I'm sure the surprise

of being shot at will at least slow a culprit down."

"An interesting theory," Herman said before he retrieved the house key and slid it into the lock a moment later. "You'll at least need to follow me, and whatever you do, don't shoot poor Perkins if it turns out he merely locked the door because he *has* been in the silver room."

"I'm not going to shoot your butler. That would certainly give Charles Bonner additional fodder to share with the press about me."

Feeling the most peculiar urge to laugh, Herman unlocked the door and moved silently into the entranceway. He stopped a moment later to take a look around, Daphne barreling into him before she stumbled backward.

"Good heavens, Herman, have a care," she whispered. "I could have shot you. These derringers are known to be temperamental, and I fear I shoved it right into your back."

He held out his hand. "I think it's for the best if you let me handle the weapon."

"But you have a pistol of your own on your person. I'll just tuck mine away."

"Or you can just give it to me, and I'll see after it until the nerves I'm now feeling from having you jab a pistol in my back dissipate."

She blew out a breath. "An excellent point, and one I have nothing of worth to argue against since I really could have just shot you."

Taking the pistol from her, he tucked it into his pocket, then took her hand and headed down the hallway, trepidation settling over him when he saw not a single member of his staff.

"Where is everyone?" Daphne whispered.

"I have no idea." He tightened his grip on her hand and headed for the library, hoping that Sheldon would be there and that there was a perfectly reasonable explanation for why his house was devoid of staff. He reached the library door, which was not fully closed, and gave it a push.

His gaze immediately settled on Sheldon, who was tied to a chair, blood dripping from a gash on his head, and who had what appeared to be a handkerchief stuffed in his mouth. Sheldon's eyes widened when he caught sight of Herman and he began trying to speak, his words too muffled to make out.

Releasing Daphne's hand, Herman strode to his cousin's side, snatching up a letter opener from his desk, which he immediately used to cut Sheldon's bonds.

Daphne joined him a second later, fumbling with the handkerchief before she pulled it away from Sheldon's face, earning a sigh of relief from Sheldon in the process.

"Thank the good Lord the two of you are here, but it's not safe."

"Clearly," Herman said, giving the rope a final slash. "What happened?"

"I was ambushed. But they're still here."

"Who's still here?" Daphne whispered.

"No idea. They're wearing pillowcases over their heads, with small slits cut out for the eyes."

Daphne frowned. "Not professionals, then."

Herman strode to his desk, pulled out a drawer, opened a secret compartment, and withdrew a pistol. He handed it to Sheldon, then returned Daphne's pistol to her, even though doing so could be a recipe for disaster. He withdrew his own pistol from his pocket.

"Where are they?" he asked Sheldon.

"In the passageways. But Herman, there's more. They have your grandmother."

Chapter Twenty-Seven

Daphne kept a tight grip on the derringer as she followed Herman down a narrow passageway, Sheldon bringing up the rear.

Who was holding Mildred at the moment, or why they'd decided to take her with them, was anyone's guess, but the fact that two people had broken into a house that was manned with a full staff . . .

She stopped walking, Sheldon stumbling into her before he regained his balance, steadied her as well, and released a snort. "Have a care, Daphne. It's close quarters as it is."

"Forgive me, Sheldon. I've just had a thought."

"What thought?"

"It's a curious thought, but I'm fairly confident I'm right about my conclusion."

"You do realize that's not really an answer, don't you?" Sheldon whispered.

"Too right it's not, but I'm still puzzling

the matter out."

"Could you puzzle and walk at the same time?" Herman asked, turning around, which caused the light from the candle he was holding to cast shadows on the wall. "If you've forgotten, someone has taken my grandmother."

"Which is concerning, but Sheldon said the people who absconded with her disappeared into the passageways, so we know she's probably still in the house. We'll be better equipped to rescue her if we know whom we're dealing with." She closed her eyes for the briefest of seconds, then opened them as pieces of the puzzle fell into place. "Yes, I do believe I've figured this out. And even though I was adamant about this with Charles, in this particular instance, it *is* the butler. We're looking for Perkins."

Herman's brows drew together. "How do you figure that?"

"Because there's no staff in your house. Sheldon hasn't said a word about any staff suffering the same fate he did. That means someone gave the entire staff the day off. It had to have been Perkins, unless your housekeeper is the one who is responsible for staffing."

"No, that job falls to Perkins."

"Well, there you have it. It's Perkins, and

honestly, you have no idea how much that annoys me because Charles *was* right. The butler *has* done it."

"We don't know for certain it's Perkins."

"It is, although I have no idea who the second person might be, unless it *is* your housekeeper and they're colluding together."

"I can't see my housekeeper, who attends church services three times a week, assists at several missions in the city, and has to be at least seventy, participating in any shady shenanigans."

Daphne's nose wrinkled. "She's probably not a viable suspect, then."

"Agreed, but Perkins being a suspect doesn't make any sense. He knows Sheldon is staying at the house. It's not as if he could have told Sheldon to take the day off."

"But I did leave the house today," Sheldon said. "In fact, I'd planned on being away all day. I needed to go to the bookshop to pick up an order of research books, and then I was going to visit with my parents afterward and stay at their house for dinner. Unfortunately, I stopped at a bakery to enjoy a cup of coffee and spilled that coffee down the front of my shirt. I returned here to change."

"Perfectly understandable," Daphne said.

"But after you returned here, what happened?"

"I went upstairs to change, and then I went into the library to drop off those books I picked up."

"Was anyone in the house when you returned home?"

"Well, come to think of it, I didn't see anyone."

"Was the front door locked?" Daphne asked.

"No."

"Hmm," Daphne said. "Then what happened?"

"I'm not exactly sure. I heard something behind me, but then . . . nothing. I woke up tied to that chair, with Mildred slapping me across the face to get me to come to." He frowned. "I distinctly remember telling her to stop it, but then she slapped me again — and who knows why she did that because I was conscious. Then two people burst through the bookcase, wearing those pillowcases on their heads."

"They burst through the bookcase?" Daphne asked. "That must have been quite the sight. Seems like a daunting feat."

"They didn't burst through all the books. There's a passageway located behind the Shakespeare section. They were clutching pistols, and after they caught sight of Mildred, they grabbed hold of her and pulled her through the bookcase, shutting the concealed door after them."

"What did they look like?"

"Two frightening people with pillowcases over their heads."

Daphne resisted a snort. "I'm sure they were frightening, Sheldon, because who wouldn't find people with pillowcases over their heads somewhat disturbing. However, you're a writer and you can do better. What do you remember about them?"

Sheldon's brow furrowed. "One was rather taller than the other."

"That's it?"

"If you've forgotten, I was knocked unconscious. I came to when a seventy-year-old woman slapped me. Can you honestly claim to be surprised that my wits are a bit scattered after all that?"

"I suppose not, but your description is hardly helpful. At least we know one of them is Perkins."

"You *think* one of them is Perkins," Herman said.

"It's Perkins. As your butler, Perkins knows what's readily at hand that could be used to hide their faces. Unless your house is run differently, I assume your linens are kept in a locked closet and he would have a key. Sheldon's unexpected return also explains the front door being locked when we arrived. He wouldn't want to be taken unaware again while he's up to whatever it is he's up to."

Sheldon blinked. "That's some amazing deductive reasoning on your part, Daphne, and does explain why your books are so captivating."

"Thank you, Sheldon." Daphne smiled. "That's very nice of you to say. I have to admit that my time at the Bleecker Street Inquiry Agency has allowed me to hone my deductive reasoning abilities and —"

She stopped talking when Herman cleared his throat.

"Sorry," she muttered. "This is probably not the time for talk of my deductive reasoning abilities."

"Which are, as Sheldon said, impressive, but we really should see if we can locate my grandmother and, better yet, discover exactly what Perkins and his accomplice are doing."

She blinked. "You believe me about Perkins?"

"You've presented a compelling argument. All that's left to do is find out if you're right," Herman said before he began making his way silently down the passageway again.

Daphne hurried behind him, tugging on the back of his shirt. "Where are we heading?"

"The dungeon."

"The what?"

"It's not a real dungeon. My mother simply named it that because the walls are stone and it's located deep underneath the house. It's where my parents stored many of the artifacts they procured on their adventures. Some of those artifacts are somewhat disturbing, like the ball-and-chain they found at a prison in England." He smiled. "There's also an elaborate coffin stored there. I believe they found that in Spain. Mother thought it would make a wonderful container for planted flowers, but the reaction from guests who came to visit wasn't favorable, so into the dungeon the coffin went."

"I bet that coffin was quite the conversation starter, though."

"A lady swooned after she got her first glimpse of it, which exactly explains why it was banished to the dungeon," Herman said, reaching a fork in the passageway and turning right. "You can only access the dungeon through the passageways, but mind your step. We'll be heading down a steep staircase soon. The dungeon seems a likely place to start, but if my grandmother is not there, we'll begin searching the other floors."

"I could write an entire series of mysteries set just in this house," Daphne said.

"I took a bit of liberty with some of the details of this house in my own book," Sheldon whispered as they reached the staircase and began creeping down it.

"So there's actually a dumbwaiter that has hidden doors you can only access if you're in the dumbwaiter, something you included in chapter seven of your book, I believe?" Daphne asked.

"You had time to read my book? And better yet, remembered details about it?"

"I did, and I've got some wonderful news to share if we get out of this alive."

Herman stopped walking and looked over his shoulder, the candlelight allowing Daphne to see what appeared to be a trace of amusement in his eyes. "Daphne, Sheldon, this is not the time to become distracted with talk of books."

"I bet you would become distracted if we were talking about one of your books," Sheldon grumbled as Herman sent Daphne a grin.

They crept downward a good fifty steps before Herman stopped. "I'll enter the dungeon first. You two hang back until I can assess the situation. If I run into trouble, you can then rush to my aid, hopefully taking the people holding my grandmother by surprise."

"Excellent thinking, Herman," Daphne said, taking the candle from him as he moved to what looked to be a solid wall at the bottom of the stairs, one that had a cleverly disguised door built into it.

She held her breath as Herman opened the door and eased through it, leaving her and Sheldon behind.

"Herman," Daphne heard Mildred exclaim. "Thank goodness you're here. As you can see, I've landed myself in a pickle."

"You can come in," Herman called. "It's just my grandmother. The pillowcase-wearing culprits aren't here."

Daphne hurried into the room, Sheldon dogging her steps, which was why he plowed straight into her when she came to an abrupt halt after she spotted Mildred sitting in a chair, a ball-and-chain attached to her foot.

"Bet that ball-and-chain won't be long for this house," Sheldon muttered after he helped her regain her balance from his almost knocking her off her feet.

"Do you happen to know where the key for this lock is, Grandmother?" Herman asked.

"They took it with them."

"That's going to be a problem."

Daphne plucked a hairpin from her hair and stepped closer to Mildred. "If there's no key available, we can hope the scant skills I've developed with picking locks is enough to where I can get that off you, Mrs. Henderson."

"I think you can abandon the Mrs. Henderson business, dear. You may call me Mildred."

Daphne knelt on the floor. "Might that sentiment change if I can't get this unlocked?"

"Will it motivate you if I say yes?"

"Couldn't hurt."

Bending to the task at hand, Daphne inserted the pin into the lock, wiggling it to the left, then to the right. She then wiggled it up, then down, and grimaced when nothing happened. "This may be trickier than I imagined. In all honesty, I've only been able to pick one lock and that might have only been because Gabriella talked me through it. Perhaps while I attempt to get you free, you should tell us what happened. Also, if everyone would stop watching me, I may find success sooner. The staring is making my fingers turn into thumbs."

Mildred's lips twitched the slightest bit. "I suppose I'll begin my story by stating that I stopped by here earlier because I wanted to inquire from Perkins or Sheldon if they'd heard when Herman was returning because I have news to share."

"What news might that be? Herman asked.

Mildred waved his question aside. "I'll get to that after we find ourselves out of this sticky situation. Obviously, I was unable to get my question answered about your return, dear, because I was snatched up by two odd-looking criminals wearing pillowcases over their heads." She tapped a finger against her chin. "Curiously enough, one of the culprits sounded familiar to me, even though it was clear he was taking pains to disguise his voice."

"It was Perkins," Daphne said.

Mildred's eyes widened. "Perkins? Good heavens, but you know, now that I think about it, it did sound like Perkins."

"What of the other man? What can you tell us about him?" Daphne asked, frowning when the hairpin she'd been using broke. She tossed it aside and plucked another one from her hair.

"I don't think it was a man, because the second person was wearing a gown, and a rather nice gown at that, suggesting the person is not of the servant class."

Daphne stopped working on the lock and arched a brow at Sheldon. "You didn't notice that one of the people who attacked you was a woman?"

Sheldon winced. "The dress might have been a good clue about that."

"I would think so," Daphne said before she turned back to Mildred. "Why did they leave you in the dungeon?"

"Because they believe I told them where to find what they're searching for." A flicker of smugness flashed through Mildred's eyes. "They're currently in the attic and could be up there for hours. And not that I want to make you nervous, but if you could speed up picking that lock, we could make our escape from the house and summon the authorities."

"I'm going as fast as I can," Daphne said before she looked at Herman. "But someone should go and summon the authorities."

"A wonderful suggestion. I think you should be the one to fetch the authorities, and Sheldon should go with you in case you run into the culprits in the passageways."

"Nice try, but of all of us here, I'm the only one who is an inquiry agent. I'm staying. You should go."

Herman's brows drew together. "While it's true you are an inquiry agent, I assure you I'm more proficient with a pistol."

"Then Sheldon can go on his own."

"And I'd be more than happy to do that," Sheldon began, "if it turns out you can't get Mildred unlocked within the next five minutes. We'll be safer if we retain the advantage of being three against two."

"There's four of us in the dungeon," Mildred pointed out.

"True, but you're shackled at the moment, so you're not really much use."

Mildred's nose wrinkled. "I believe I've just been insulted."

Daphne gave her an unexpected pat on the knee. "I'm sure Sheldon didn't mean it that way, but if you'd like to feel more useful, you could tell us what Perkins and his accomplice are searching for."

"I was hoping I wouldn't have to disclose that."

"I think that's a hope you're not going to be able to realize," Daphne said, "so disclose away."

Mildred blew out a breath as Daphne returned to the lock. "Oh, very well. They're searching for a map, or rather, the copy of a map my son left before he departed for his last adventure."

Herman pulled up a chair shaped like a clamshell next to his grandmother and sat down. "I've never heard anything about any map."

"That's because I've never mentioned it to you." Mildred leaned forward and took hold of Herman's hand. "It's a copy of a specific map — the map your parents took with them on their last trip. Your father acquired it from an antiquities dealer and was quite thrilled to have found it, even though he knew there was a strong possibility the map wasn't authentic."

Herman stilled. "Do not tell me that you're about to say my father found a map to El Dorado."

"I'm afraid that's exactly where that map was supposed to lead, just as I'm afraid I have to tell you that your parents and grandfather were off on a quest to see if they could find that ridiculous city when they died." Mildred shook her head. "I told them it was a futile mission, but your father thought it would be the adventure of a lifetime, as did your mother."

"But why were you left with a copy of the map?" Daphne asked.

"I was opposed to them taking the trip. Evan wanted to leave me with a way to find them if they didn't return within six months. Unfortunately, they didn't make it past Florida."

Daphne stopped fiddling with the lock. "How horrible."

"Indeed." Mildred sent Herman a fond smile. "However, Herman and I recently had a long overdue talk about the matter, and I think any lingering regret I was holding over not being able to talk them out of it has gone."

Daphne gave the pin a twist and released a bit of a grunt when it broke. "This lock-picking business is far trickier than I imagined." She caught Mildred's eye. "How certain are you that Perkins might need hours to find that map in the attic?"

"Very certain, because I didn't actually hide that map in the attic."

Sheldon sat forward on the coffin he was sitting on. "You lied to them?"

"I did. I thought it would buy me time to figure out how to escape."

"Which was very clever of you," Daphne said before she plucked yet another hairpin out of her hair. "I am beyond curious, though, regarding how anyone knew about that map in the first place."

Herman frowned. "I suppose Perkins might have heard stories about it from his family members. He is, after all, a relative of Mr. Conkling, my father's butler, who perished with my parents when their ship went down."

"How long has Perkins worked for you?"

"About five years or so. He joined my staff when my former butler retired after suffering a broken leg when he came down to this very room to store an ugly vase that —" Herman sent his grandmother a wince.

"So that's what happened to that puce-colored vase I got you," Mildred said, shaking her head. "You could have told me you didn't care for it."

"And hurt your feelings in the process? I think not." Herman gestured to the coffin Sheldon was sitting on. "It's in there, along with a few other puce-colored items."

Mildred's gaze lingered on the coffin for a moment before she frowned. "Should I take that to mean you don't particularly care for puce?"

"It's never really appealed to me."

"Duly noted."

Daphne sat back on her heels when she broke yet another hairpin. She tossed it over her shoulder before she withdrew another one from her hair, causing her hair to straggle in front of her face, obscuring her vison. She pushed it aside. "You don't think there's a chance your former butler was pushed down those stairs by Perkins, who would then be able to present himself as the perfect candidate for your next butler, do you?"

"An interesting theory," Herman began, "and one I'm hoping you're wrong about. With that said, though, Perkins wasn't a perfect candidate, nor has he been an exceptional butler. He's surly with the staff and doesn't seem particularly enthusiastic about his duties in the first place, although he did come with stellar recommendations."

"Did you follow up on those stellar recommendations?"

"Well, no, because he also had that connection to my father's butler. I felt it only fair to hire the man since his relative had perished while in service to my father."

Daphne stuck the new hairpin into the lock and gave it a jiggle, which did absolutely nothing. "But why would Perkins wait all these years before trying to find that map? Or if he's been searching for it all this time, why escalate his attempts now?"

When Herman simply shrugged, Daphne returned to the lock, her thoughts whirling. "You were considering setting your current novel in El Dorado, or at least sending your characters there as a plot point. When did you decide to do that?"

Herman looked to Sheldon. "What was it, three, maybe four months ago?"

"That sounds about right." Sheldon tilted his head. "We'd been combing through Sarah's journals to come up with a setting for Herman's new book, and there was a small note written off to the side in one of those journals that had El Dorado circled. We then reread all the journals to see if we could find more details about that place, but other than a mention here or there, Sarah didn't elaborate on the lost city of gold. It was somewhat curious because she always followed up those little notes left in margins with pages and pages of research, but in the case of El Dorado, there was nothing."

"I stashed Sarah's last three journals away," Mildred admitted, wincing as she looked Herman's way. "I didn't want to take the chance that you'd read them someday and decide to finish your parents' quest for them."

"That explains why we couldn't find any more mentions," Sheldon said. "But we still have so many questions left unanswered, such as . . ."

As Sheldon continued speaking, Daphne's mind began to wander, sifting through everything that had happened, everything they knew, and everything they didn't. Taking a second to wiggle the hairpin in the lock a way she'd not wiggled it before, she stilled when a piece of the puzzle suddenly snapped into place.

Abandoning the lock, she rose to her feet, pacing around the dungeon as she thought through how the remaining pieces might fit together. She came to an abrupt stop when an interesting idea sprang to mind. "I think I know who Perkins's accomplice is."

"Who?" Sheldon asked.

"Not anyone I suspected until just now," she said, heading for the coffin and taking a seat beside Sheldon. "Before I disclose my theory, though, allow me to say that I'm sorry."

"Sorry for what?"

"You just said that you spent a lot of time searching through Sarah's journals, as well as discussing the matter of El Dorado often with Herman. Perkins clearly overheard some of those conversations, but he would have needed a way to get closer to you, or rather, have someone no one would ever suspect get closer to you in order to find out if there was anything else you'd discovered. I'm sorry because I think the lady you seem to hold in great affection, Miss Martha Mulvey, may only have been spending time with you as a way to gain access to Sarah's journal and what Herman's parents knew about El Dorado."

"Surely not," Sheldon said right before there was a slight squeaking sound, and then two people with pillowcases over their heads stepped into the dungeon, the smaller of the two leveling a pistol on Daphne after pulling the pillowcase from her head, revealing herself to be none other than Martha Mulvey.

"I never actually liked you, Daphne, and now I finally understand why." Martha gave a wave of her pistol. "You're much too clever for your own good. But I'm afraid that cleverness has finally caught up with you because with our identities now exposed, there's really no choice but for us to silence all of you — permanently."

CHAPTER TWENTY-EIGHT

Herman reached for his pistol, pulling it out of his waistband as Sheldon did the same, while Daphne merely got off the coffin and returned to the lock she'd not been able to pick.

"I don't particularly care for that option, Martha, the one about being permanently silenced. If you've neglected to notice, you're decidedly outnumbered. Yes, you and Perkins are armed, but so is everyone else in the room, save Mildred. That means a few of us could very well get shot, and it's fairly easy to believe that the two of you will be shot for certain."

"I'm not Perkins," said the man still wearing the pillowcase over his head, his voice muffled.

Martha gave a roll of her eyes. "I think that ship has sailed, cousin."

"Ah," Daphne said, abandoning the lock again as she rose to her feet. "The two of you are related. Things are beginning to make sense."

"I don't really care if things make sense to you," Martha snapped.

Daphne tilted her head. "Would you care if I told you that once everything makes complete sense to me, I'll tell you where the map is?"

"How do you know the location of the map?"

"I only recently figured that out. I also think Mildred stashed important journals written by Herman's mother with that map, which may prove invaluable to you. From what I understand, Sarah was known to take extensive notes." She nodded to Mildred. "However, if I'm wrong about where you hid everything, dare I hope you'll be agreeable to divulging that secret?"

"If it'll get us out of this sticky situation alive, certainly," Mildred said.

"I suppose it wouldn't hurt to answer a few questions," Perkins said, finally removing the pillowcase from his head, although he immediately began looking everywhere except at Herman.

Martha settled a scowl on Perkins, which he ignored, before she shrugged and turned her scowl on Daphne. "What do you want to know?"

"How did you learn about the map?"

"The map to El Dorado has been family lore for years," Martha said. "My great-uncle, Clyde Conkling, was butler to Herman's father. He always joined the family for Sunday dinner, and he spoke often about the trip he was going to take. He apparently only mentioned El Dorado one time, though, when he'd had a bit too much of Great-grandmother's homemade wine. When questioned about the matter after he sobered up, he wouldn't say another word.

"But when he'd been deep in his cups, he'd mentioned a map, one that Herman's father purchased from a reputable antiquities dealer. He also mentioned that Herman's father had a copy of the map made, saying he'd done so for safety reasons. The family then concluded, after Uncle Clyde wouldn't speak of the matter, that he'd obviously been telling some rather large fibs — until the ship he was sailing on went down and he lost his life."

"That's when I began thinking there really was a map, or at least a copy of the map, which I assumed Herman's father left behind for safekeeping," Perkins said. "And then, about five years ago, after I lost my position as under-butler at another house, I decided it was time to devote some attention to looking for that map because . . ."

"If you found it, you wouldn't have to live your life in a position you don't particularly care for, given that the person who discovers El Dorado would become wealthy in the extreme?" Daphne finished for him when Perkins stopped talking.

"Herman's parents evidently believed there was a chance the map was real or else they'd never have gone off to look for El Dorado," Perkins said.

"They were adventurers," Daphne countered. "Frankly, there was every possibility they knew they'd never discover that missing city but were unable to resist the lure of a good adventure."

"Be that as it may," Perkins countered right back, "the map alone can fetch a handsome price, and there are many adventurers out there who'll not balk at paying that price. If nothing else, my family deserves to reap some sort of benefit from the El Dorado situation. After all, my great-uncle lost his life in service to the Henderson family."

"I paid Clyde's next of kin a handsome amount after I attended the service for him," Mildred said, her eyes flashing. "And not that this has anything to do with that, but I would appreciate it if you, Perkins, would get this heavy shackle off my leg. I trust you still have the key?"

Perkins frowned. "I do, but I'll wait until I have the map in my hand before I give it to you. That might give you an added incentive to disclose the location of the map if Daphne's wrong about where it's hidden." He turned from Mildred back to Daphne again. "As I was saying, I applied for the position of butler, and I was pleased I was offered the job."

"Seems a little too convenient that a butler position just happened to open up after you lost your position at that other house."

The tightening of Perkins's jaw suggested he'd been responsible for the former butler's unfortunate tumble down the stairs, but he didn't admit his guilt. Instead, he moved to the clamshell chair Herman had abandoned and sat down. "Unfortunately, I discovered after I began working for Herman that he seemed oblivious to the copy of a map Uncle Clyde had suggested existed. He never spoke of the map, nor did a map to El Dorado ever show up in any of his books. I took it upon myself to begin exploring the secret passageways whenever I was able and was almost never caught doing that until recently, when I happened to stumble behind the wall of Herman's bedchamber when I was searching about. He heard me, and I was reluctant to search the passageways again, even though I'd begun to hope he might be close to learning about the map because I overheard him speaking with Sheldon about El Dorado."

"That talk between Herman and Sheldon is why Perkins sent me a letter seeking my assistance," Martha added. "Perkins and I share a close cousinly relationship, and we'd often discussed Uncle Clyde and his last adventure. Perkins told me that Mildred was determined to see Herman married to Finetta Shoenburger, which is why I decided to see if I could get close to her. I thought the stars were lined up exactly right when I learned her grandmother was seeking a paid companion." Martha rolled her eyes. "I soon realized that the stars weren't lined up properly at all because Finetta and Herman barely spoke to each other and certainly not about anything of consequence." She nodded to Sheldon. "That's when I set my sights on Sheldon."

"How fortunate for me," Sheldon muttered.

Martha smoothed a strand of hair back into place. "I didn't want to toy with your affections, darling, but you were an easy mark. I'm fully aware that I'm an attractive lady who knows how to use my feminine allure, and you were only too keen to spend time in my company — well, until recently, that is."

Sheldon inclined his head. "My keenness to spend time with you was waning because you seemed to be constantly seeking out my company, inserting yourself into conversations I was holding with other people, and always wanting to be at my side, even when I told you I needed to work."

"You can't honestly be surprised about that now that you've heard the reason behind my interest. Spending an inordinate amount of time in your company was the only way to find out what you knew about the map."

"But why try to kill Herman?" Daphne asked, looking to Perkins. "I must say you had me fooled, because I honestly believed your vehement denial when I questioned you about having murderous intentions toward him."

Perkins's brows drew together. "I never had murderous intentions toward Herman."

"It wasn't you and Martha who drilled holes in his boat or sabotaged the tips of the fencing rapiers?"

"That wasn't me," Perkins said.

Daphne turned to Martha, earning a

shrug in return. "I see no reason to deny any of that."

"But why would you want to kill Herman?"

"I never wanted to kill him."

"You just admitted you drilled holes in his rowboat."

"True, but . . . Herman wasn't the target that day, dear Daphne. You were."

"Why would you want to kill me?"

"I was convinced you had your eye on replacing Sheldon as Herman's assistant. That would have deprived me of the access Sheldon had to those journals."

"But you could have killed Herman as well."

"Sheldon told me Herman's a strong swimmer. I wasn't worried he'd drown." Martha released a grunt. "Who knew he'd be such a good swimmer that he'd also be able to save you, even when you were making it a habit to wear bustles that are completely ridiculous in size."

Daphne caught Herman's eye. "It's amazing how many people have tried to kill me since I've become involved with the inquiry business. Nevertheless" — she returned her attention to Martha — "am I wrong in concluding that you were beginning to panic that your plan to find the map wasn't going to succeed? Panic, from what I've seen in other cases, is a great motivator for murder, although murder is really not something you should have contemplated. Not that I want to point out the obvious, but it *is* one of the Ten Commandments. Taking a life simply because of the lure of undiscovered riches is unconscionable and has me wondering if you, as well as Perkins, might benefit from speaking with a man of the cloth. Reverend Patrick Danford of St. Luke's Chapel is a lovely person, and you might really benefit from seeking his counsel, and —"

"I don't need a lecture about murder, nor will I be seeking out the counsel of any reverend," Martha said, earning a grimace from Daphne in return.

"I disagree. I believe you need both. You just admitted you wanted to kill me. And even though you claim you weren't trying to kill Herman, you did tamper with the rapiers, which could have very easily seen him dead."

"He should have been wearing protective gear, which would have only resulted with damage to that gear — not to him."

"Then why tamper with the rapiers to begin with?"

"I needed to shift attention to his writer friends." Martha took a step closer to

Daphne, which had Herman taking a step closer to Daphne as well. "After learning the coachman was really a Pinkerton, I was concerned, and after I realized it wasn't a foregone conclusion that everyone believed Irwin was responsible for all the accidents that had taken place, I worried that attention could swing my way. Pinkertons are known to be relentless interrogators, and I needed to divert notice away from me. Herman's writer friends seemed like the most likely people to attract a Pinkerton's attention, what with all the jealousy and backstabbing they seem so keen to embrace."

Daphne turned to Herman. "Martin Corrigan *was* the one who was supposed to be paired against you."

"Until Jay took his place, and then Jay gave you the rapier."

"It was quite unexpected how that whole situation unraveled," Martha said. "I wouldn't have thought Charles Bonner had it in him to figure out Daphne's true identity, and I certainly wasn't expecting Daphne to admit she was an inquiry agent. Nevertheless, it worked to my advantage because the house party was disbanded, and we eventually were able to return here."

Daphne nodded. "I imagine you found it a great advantage to your plan when Herman and Cooper decided to travel to Boston. With them out of town, you were given an opportunity to search the house without interruption."

"We knew our time was limited," Martha said. "Cooper, as well as other Pinkertons, were now on Herman's case, so it was now or never." She shot a look to Sheldon. "Unfortunately, we weren't expecting Sheldon to return home today. It would have been difficult to explain what I was doing on the second floor of the house, which is why we waited until he moved to the library before we rendered him senseless."

Daphne sent Herman a bit of a wink. "I told you *rendered senseless* is a wonderful way to describe when someone is knocked unconscious. I bet you're thankful you decided to keep the changes I made to your manuscript now."

He was hard-pressed not to laugh or kiss her right there in the midst of what was clearly an escalating situation, one that was brimming with danger.

Before he could act on either of those urges, though, Daphne returned her attention to Martha. "I believe that answers all the questions I have. However, I do have to say that I'm amazed your actions have gone undetected for so long. Nicholas and Gabriella Quinn, two fellow inquiry agents, have often stated that in order for a plan to be successful, it has to be kept as simple as possible. The lengths the two of you went to in order to locate a map were convoluted to say the least."

"Convoluted or not, here we are," Martha said. "And you did say that if I answered your questions, you'd give me the map."

"True, I did say that." Daphne gave a wave of her hand toward the coffin Sheldon was sitting on. "I believe what you're searching for is in there."

As Martha rushed for the coffin, having to wait for Sheldon to climb off it, Mildred settled a curious eye on Daphne. "How did you figure that out?"

"You've been glancing at the coffin on and off ever since the topic of the map was broached. Herman mentioned that his mother tried to turn a coffin into a planter earlier, which means there had to have been some adjustments made to that coffin so that the roots of the plants wouldn't rot from too much watering." She smiled. "I learned that from the book on poisonous plants you thought I was reading so I could poison Herman. There's a chapter about plant care at the back of the book."

Mildred blinked, but before she could say

anything more, Martha was pulling out a false bottom from the coffin, brandishing a map a second later. She then pulled out Sarah's journals, sticking them in the pillowcase she'd used as a disguise before putting the map in there as well. She sent Perkins a nod, and they began backing out of the room.

"You forgot to unlock me," Mildred said.

"I'm afraid it won't be possible for us to unlock you," Martha said, grabbing hold of Perkins's arm as he took a step toward Mildred. "We need time to get away, and keeping you shackled should aid with that. I'm also going to lock all of you in here after we leave. I'm sure someone will find you in the not-too-distant but hopefully distant-enough future."

With that, she dashed out of the room, Perkins backing out of it after her. A second after that, the door shut, followed by the distinctive sound of a lock clicking into place.

CHAPTER TWENTY-NINE

"Dare I hope someone on your staff besides Perkins knows how to access the dungeon or, better yet, will realize we're down here?" Daphne asked, kneeling beside Mildred to give the lock another try, although she was beginning to believe picking locks was not going to be her forte.

Herman shot a look to Sheldon. "This could be a problem because I don't think anyone on staff knows how to access the dungeon, although I did give Cooper a tour of the house before we went off to Boston."

"Then let us hope that Cooper realizes you've disappeared. But instead of waiting for that, I could start banging on the walls with one of those odd-looking spears," Sheldon said, gesturing to a few spears leaning against the wall.

Daphne shook her head. "Absolutely not. Those look like they're important artifacts. It would be historically irresponsible to bang them against a wall. I say we listen for people moving around upstairs and then shoot off one of our pistols. That'll bring people running to investigate."

"As well as having all of us rendered deaf," Mildred said. "Pistols are incredibly loud, my dear Daphne, something you might want to take into consideration before you decide to fire one off in here."

"I thought you weren't going to use my given name if I couldn't get you unlocked."

"I'm feeling magnanimous at the moment."

Daphne winced. "Is there a specific reason for that? I would think, given our current circumstances, that you'd be feeling some effects from your nerves."

"I've decided that I've allowed my nerves to rule my life for far too long. I'm now trusting God to help me keep my nerves in check, which seems to be going incredibly well for me, and is certainly something I should have handed off to Him years ago." Mildred turned to Herman. "I'm also feeling magnanimous in general these days because I took your advice and spoke with James, or rather, Dr. Gibbons."

"What did you say to him?"

"I apologized and told him that it had been wrong of me to abuse our long-standing friendship simply because I was in a foul temper." Her lips quirked into a grin. "He assured me that he's put my ill-temper behind him and is willing to pick up our friendship where we left off. With that said, though, he no longer wants to be my physician because he fears he may have coddled me too much in the past due to the fondness he feels for me."

"Fondness of the romantic type?" Daphne asked.

"I'm afraid your talent for puzzling out mysteries has failed you in this regard, dear, because we're simply friends."

"I bet you're relieved about that," Daphne said, grinning at Herman, her grin fading when someone began jiggling the lock on the other side of the dungeon door.

A mere thirty seconds later, the door opened and Gabriella Quinn rushed into the room. Her gaze immediately settled on Daphne.

"Thank goodness you're all right," Gabriella said, striding forward and pulling Daphne to her feet before giving her a hug. "Cooper and Eunice became worried when you and Herman didn't return within an hour, and so we came to check on you." Gabriella released Daphne and eyed the ball-and-chain attached to Mildred's ankle, then smiled and nodded to all the broken pins littering the floor. "I take it your lock-picking skills haven't improved?"

"I think I'll stick to writing," Daphne said before she introduced Mildred, Herman, and Sheldon to Gabriella, who immediately set to work on the lock that was keeping Mildred chained to the chair.

Fifteen seconds later, Mildred was free, and everyone was moving out of the dungeon.

"How did you know where to find us?" Daphne asked as they began climbing the narrow staircase.

"Bit of lucky timing," Gabriella said. "Eunice, Cooper, Nicholas, Ann, and I had just arrived here when the front door burst open and a lady and gentleman rushed through it. Cooper didn't hesitate to jump out of the carriage, with Nicholas right behind him, because any time rushing out of a house is involved, it normally suggests something suspicious is at hand. Perkins and Martha, or at least I think that's what Cooper called them, tried to flee, but it didn't take long to capture them, and it really didn't take Cooper long to get Perkins to tell us where you were, not when he disarmed Perkins in about a second and was threatening the man with his own pistol.

Cooper gave me a rough idea of where to find the dungeon, and here I am."

Stepping with Gabriella into the main hallway of Herman's home a few minutes later, Daphne followed Herman, who was holding Mildred's hand, out of the house, where they found Nicholas, Gabriella's husband, along with Eunice, sitting on the front porch. The map and Sarah's journals sat on the step beside them.

"Where are Cooper and Ann?" Daphne asked.

"No need to worry about them," Nicholas said, getting to his feet and walking directly for Daphne. "After Perkins disclosed all, including Martha's attempts to murder you and Herman Henderson, they decided to take them straight to the nearest jail, where I'm sure Cooper will see them arrested and put behind bars, at least for now." He pulled Daphne into a hug, giving her a good squeeze. "Nice to see you survived a stint in a dungeon without suffering another swoon."

She grinned. "You'll be pleased to learn I've only swooned a few times since you and Gabriella have been gone — once when I was set upon by wolfhounds, and again when I stabbed Herman with a rapier."

"You stabbed a client?"

She gave an airy wave of her hand. "Completely unintentional. Allow me to introduce you to Herman."

Taking a second to perform introductions, and then another few minutes to catch Nicholas, Gabriella, and Eunice up on what else had happened, Daphne finished with, "So it appears we can now close Herman's case and call it a success, since he's still alive."

"A feather in our caps for certain," Eunice said, lifting up her veils before settling a smile on Daphne. "I'll place it alongside the other feather in our cap that we received just yesterday, when I was told the moment I walked into the boardinghouse that Irwin Rosenwald has been caught."

"How?" Daphne asked.

"The foolish man actually tried to kidnap Finetta, believing that if she was discovered alone with him, she'd have to marry him and thus give him access to that lovely fortune of hers."

"Why do men believe it's their right to force women into such situations?" Daphne asked. "Do they not realize that they're hardly setting themselves up for a happy future by trying to marry women who will certainly never feel anything but loathing toward them?"

Eunice frowned. "I don't think that particular type of gentleman actually has the ability to think past his own wants, Daphne, allowing their manly egos to get in the way of rational thought. However, in Finetta's case, Mr. Andrew Ware rushed to her rescue. Irwin was then arrested for attempted kidnapping, and from what Ann told me, Andrew and Finetta are even now planning their wedding. Her grandmother, who'd apparently been reluctant to accept Mr. Ware as a suitor for her granddaughter, is now giving her full blessing to the union."

"How delightful for Andrew," Herman said, exchanging a smile with Daphne before she blinked.

"Good heavens, we have delightful news for Sheldon as well." She motioned Sheldon over, her smile turning into a grin after she told him the good news about his book.

She rummaged around in her bag and pulled out Jack's calling card, handing it to a very delighted yet slightly stunned-looking Sheldon. "My brothers are expecting you to contact them so that they can make certain you are getting the best contract possible."

"And to think I loathed the sight of you at first," Sheldon said, surprising Daphne when he pulled her into a hug and gave her a hefty squeeze.

"You can't be blamed for that, Sheldon," Daphne said after he released her. "I *was* posing as Herman's secretary, and you had to take that as a threat to your position. However, I have a feeling Herman is going to be in need of a new assistant soon because I'm convinced you're going to be a very successful and in-demand author."

"Maybe you and Herman could work together on your books," Sheldon suggested. "You're both wonderful with research, and it might be that Herman doesn't even need to hire on a new assistant."

"That's a marvelous suggestion," Eunice said before she turned a smile on Herman. "And speaking of you and Daphne, may I dare hope that you have more news to disclose to us . . . news of a personal nature?" Her smile widened. "Cooper mentioned that you were planning on speaking to Daphne about a talk you had with Daphne's father."

Daphne's breath got caught in her throat as Herman rubbed a hand over his face and shot Eunice an exasperated look.

"For a Pinkerton, Cooper is not nearly as close-mouthed as he should be," Herman said.

Eunice winced. "Good heavens, you haven't spoken with Daphne yet, have you?"

She gave an airy wave of her black-gloved hand. "Just forget I mentioned anything. And on that note, shall we repair to the agency to discuss the particulars of this case and write up a report?"

Herman shook his head. "I think that'll have to wait, at least for Daphne. I certainly can't expect her to wait to hear what I talked about with her father, not since you've brought the matter into conversation, Eunice."

"That was not well done of me."

"No, but in your defense, I would have spoken with her already if we hadn't just had our lives threatened and found ourselves locked in a dungeon." He turned to Daphne and offered her his arm. "I believe this is where you and I take ourselves off for a long — and need I add — private walk."

Taking Herman's arm, Daphne willed knees that were turning just a touch wobbly to cooperate, because she'd never learn the particulars of what Herman had evidently talked about with her father if she found herself unable to move.

"There's a lovely little park just up ahead. Shall we go there?" Herman asked.

Knowing she wouldn't be opposed to speaking with him in the seediest part of the city at this point, what with how her imagination was now going full tilt, Daphne managed a smile, earning a smile from Herman in return.

Together, they headed down the sidewalk, Herman telling her little tidbits about his neighborhood as they walked, almost as if he were trying his hardest to provide her with a distraction so she wouldn't burst with questions once they reached their destination. Before she knew it, he was sitting down beside her on a park bench, taking hold of her hand.

For a long moment, he simply looked at her before giving her hand a squeeze. "I have to apologize for Cooper telling Eunice that I spoke with your father. I should have realized he would notice, given he is a Pinkerton."

"I'm an inquiry agent and I didn't overhear a thing between you and my father, nor did I even know you went off to speak with him."

"That's because I chose to request an audience with him after you went to pack your trunks with your mother, Eunice, and Lydia."

"Ah, so you wanted to ascertain your conversation with my father was uninterrupted."

"Indeed, but I, obviously, forgot about Cooper. However, with that said, what I need to tell you first is that I didn't speak to your father to get his blessing to marry you."

Daphne felt her shoulders droop ever so slightly. "Oh."

"That probably didn't come out as I intended."

"I should hope not, but what *did* you intend?"

"Certainly not to disappoint you or allow you to assume that I wouldn't *want* to ask your father for his blessing to marry you."

"Oh," she said again, having no idea what Herman was trying to say.

"For a lady who has an impressive vocabulary, 'Oh' seems a somewhat unusual word choice."

"Perhaps if you were to simply spit out exactly what you talked to my father about instead of telling me what you didn't talk about, I'd be better equipped to know which words to choose in response."

He winced. "For a wordsmith as well, I seem to be making a muddle of this."

"I'm not going to argue with that."

His lips curved. "I would expect nothing less, but to move this forward before I completely ruin the moment, what I spoke to your father about was this — I wanted

560

his permission to court you, permission he gave me."

Daphne's pulse began galloping through her veins. "You want to . . . court me?"

He leaned closer. "You're an extraordinary lady, Daphne. Intelligent, compassionate, and a better writer than I'll ever be."

"I won't agree with that nonsense. You're a remarkable writer."

"I wasn't stating an opinion, Daphne, but a fact."

"Oh."

He smiled. "There you go again, using your impressive vocabulary. But, to continue, you deserve to be courted — deserve to have me squire you about the city in an open carriage and take you out for moonlight strolls, with a chaperone, of course. I imagine either Gabriella or Eunice could be persuaded to step into that role. You also deserve the opportunity to get to know my grandmother, and she deserves the opportunity to get to know the real Daphne. You also need to get to know me, know how I take my coffee, which is black, as I need to get to know you, although I do know you take your coffee with a dollop of milk and a single cube of sugar. We need to spend time learning everything about each other, which is why I asked your father to court you instead of marry you. I would be doing you a disservice to take away what I hope will be a time you'll remember fondly after we've been married fifty years."

"You want to be married to me for fifty years?"

"How did I know you'd pick up on that? But yes, although I won't ask you to marry me until you've had a chance to get to know me better and know if you'll be able to love me."

She suddenly found it very difficult to breathe. "Love you?"

His eyes turned warm. "Indeed. Because, you see, I knew from the moment I caught my first sight of you that you were a lady that I could fall in love with — knew there was a possibility of love from that first glimpse of you standing in the hallway of the agency, wielding a pressed-paper sword."

She smiled. "Oh, I like that bit about the possibility of love from a first glimpse."

"Will you still like it as much if I tell you I stole it from Cooper?"

"Of course, especially if you'll allow me to use it in my latest book." Her smile widened. "That line is exactly what I need to help me write the book I intend to write."

"You're more than welcome to steal that

line from me, but if we could steer the conversation back to the courting business?"

She blinked. "Good heavens, forgive me, Herman. I've allowed myself to become completely distracted." Heat settled on her cheeks. "I would like for you to court me, and . . ." She drew in a deep breath, but then found the next words escaping her lips even though she'd never imagined herself having the courage to say such a thing to a gentleman. "I believe I experienced that possibility of falling in love with you — not at first sight, mind you, because you scared me half to death — but after you told me you returned Wolf and Hound because they'd tried to eat me. That was one of the sweetest gestures anyone has ever made for me."

"If that was one of the sweetest gestures you've ever received, you should prepare yourself for what will come while we're courting — and for many years to come."

"Oh . . ." was all Daphne had at her disposal to say again, but before she could get her mind into working order, Herman leaned even closer, his breath tickling her face most deliciously.

"You're certain you're agreeable to my courting you?"

"If you're certain you want to court me."

"I've never been more certain about anything in my life." He leaned closer still and claimed her lips with his own, leaving her without a shadow of a doubt that kissing Herman was going to be something she was going to enjoy for many, many years to come.

EPILOGUE

Two months later

"Honestly, Daphne, I don't believe you need to throw the medicine ball quite so forcefully. You almost knocked me over."

Daphne swiped a muddy hand over a forehead that was perspiring and grinned at Lydia, who was splattered with mud and looking rather disgruntled as she tried to find her balance after actually catching the ball Daphne had just tossed her way. "The point of this particular physical exertion activity is to help you build strength in your arms, as well as teach you how to maintain your balance if something is thrown at you."

"I realize that," Lydia shot back. "But I've only been participating in these exertion lessons for a week. You've been doing them for months. And while I realize that you're only trying to make certain I'll build up enough strength to where I can defend myself if some gentleman, heaven forbid, ever tries to take unwanted liberties, you're being a touch zealous about the matter. If you've forgotten, I've only recently returned from Paris, where Mother and I spent our time meandering around the city and enjoying far too many pastries."

"Which I would think would motivate you to really put your heart into the activities this morning. You have an appointment with Phillip Villard tomorrow. I'm sure you don't want him to have to stuff you into the gowns he already has made for you."

It was difficult to resist a laugh when Lydia blinked once before immediately throwing the ball to Ann, who grinned and threw it back to Lydia, earning a scowl from Lydia in return. A fierce throwing battle soon commenced, giving Daphne an opportunity to step away to speak with Cooper, who was watching Ann from a few feet away.

In the two months since Herman had begun courting her, much had happened.

Mildred was back to being friends with Dr. Gibbons, who'd been trying his hand at matchmaking, if Daphne wasn't mistaken. The good doctor was making a habit of showing up with one gentleman or another to escort Mildred to tea or shopping. Mildred seemed to adore the attention, even though Herman groaned every time a new gentleman entered the scene and began squiring Mildred about. Mildred, however, wasn't settling her affections on any particular gentleman, claiming she was having far too much fun to want to settle down with anyone for the foreseeable future, something Daphne knew Herman found to be a relief.

Andrew Ware and Finetta were now married, Daphne having attended that event with Herman, wearing one of Phillip's gorgeous creations. She'd balked at wearing an enormous bustle, though, convincing Phillip that a smaller bustle would assure she didn't suffer any unforeseen accidents, which would most assuredly not show off his creation in the best of light.

Phillip and Elsy were still enjoying each other's company, but no formal announcement had been made just yet. Daphne had a sneaking suspicion an announcement would be made soon, though, given the way the two made a habit of gazing soulfully into each other's eyes anytime Phillip accompanied Elsy as she drove the inquiry agency carriage out and about in the city — although they did refrain from the soulful gazing while Elsy was driving since she was still a little questionable with the reins.

Cooper and Ann had everyone guessing

when they'd officially begin courting. Cooper kept saying it was only a matter of time, whereas Ann kept saying their lack of official status was a direct result of the two of them being so busy. Cooper had recently gotten promoted to senior Pinkerton agent, whereas the society matrons to whom Ann was a paid companion were now returning from Paris, which had Ann busier than ever. She refused to give up the companion positions because of the information she gleaned by attending so many society events, even though she'd started taking a more active role within the agency, especially out in the field.

As for Daphne and Herman, they spent time every day together, Herman making good on his promise to court her to the best of his abilities — and what abilities those had turned out to be.

If he wasn't bringing her flowers or chocolates, he was driving her around the city, stopping at one café after another, where they'd drink cups of coffee, eat delicious meals, and discuss whatever writing they'd gotten done that day.

When they weren't writing or traveling about the city, they enjoyed wandering through libraries and bookshops, Daphne loving nothing more than when Herman would crack open a book and read to her out loud. She would never grow tired of hearing his voice or of the way he brought a story to life.

"Were you just lecturing your sister about her performance with the medicine ball?" Cooper asked, drawing her from her thoughts. "Because, if I need remind you, you used to be the biggest complainer out of all the ladies at the agency."

"True, but that's before I realized you were on to something and that it truly will benefit us all if we're more physically fit."

"Too right it will, although I'm sorry you came to that realization because of what happened between you and Thomas."

"Thomas and his reprehensible behavior were certainly not anything I'd care to relive again. Nevertheless, I was recently speaking with Reverend Patrick Danford, and —"

"Why were you speaking with him?" Cooper interrupted. "I haven't missed something about an upcoming wedding, have I?"

It was impossible to resist a snort. "What with how nosy you are, I doubt you would miss something like that."

"What's Herman waiting for? He clearly adores you."

Daphne's cheeks grew warm. "He does

seem to dote on me, and Eunice, being her usual blunt self, did ask him just last week what he was waiting for."

"And?"

"He told her that he couldn't very well distract me with personal matters when I was under such a daunting deadline, and that such matters would need to wait until after I wrote the end on my latest book."

"And?"

"I promptly returned to my attic after hearing that and wrote almost nonstop, except for when I went out for my afternoon jaunts with Herman. I finished my book last night and have now given that book to Herman to read. I'm hoping he'll get through it in the next week or so. I'd like to hear his thoughts about it before I turn it over to my editor."

Cooper rolled his eyes. "You gave him that book so he'd know you were finished with it, and hence, would also know you can now be distracted with personal matters."

"Well, quite, but don't tell him that. Remember, you're my friend, and friends keep confidences."

"Herman's my friend now too."

Daphne blinked. "Does that mean you're keeping his confidences?"

"Well, no, because Herman doesn't seem

to enjoy sharing confidences with me often, but that could be because he's under a daunting deadline himself. But speaking of Herman, he's walking out of the house." Cooper craned his neck. "Oh, never mind. He stopped to speak with Sheldon, who seems to be spending an inordinate amount of time lately here when we're holding our exertion lessons."

"He's a little smitten with Lydia. I'm beginning to think she might be a bit smitten with him as well, because even though she's keen to learn how to defend herself, she's never been keen to get up at the break of dawn. She's not balked at doing that since Sheldon started showing up."

"Romance does seem to be in the air. But since Herman is currently occupied, your romance with him can wait until after you finish the last exercise, which I'm sure you know is the rope station."

Daphne groaned. "I really don't want Herman to be around when I embarrass myself yet again by plummeting to the ground. Yes, I'm getting better, but I've yet to make it to the top."

"Daphne," Herman suddenly called, striding away from Sheldon, who immediately went to assist Lydia with the medicine ball she'd dropped.

Herman stopped by her side, her heart doing a bit of a lurch when she noticed he was carrying her manuscript. He gave her a kiss on the forehead and smiled. "I finished your book."

She blinked. "I only gave it to you yesterday."

"Which should be telling."

She turned to Cooper. "I'm really going to have to beg off the last activity. I simply can't wait another second to hear what he thought. I certainly can't take the time needed to climb that rope."

Cooper shot a look to Lydia, then returned his attention to Daphne. "It's hardly setting a good example for your baby sister if you abandon an activity everyone knows you don't enjoy. I mean, Lydia may decide to mimic your example and decide that since she doesn't enjoy getting up early, she should abandon these lessons that could very well keep her safe."

"Are you honestly using my baby sister as a source of guilt?"

"Is it working?"

"Of course it's working," Daphne grumbled before she spun on her heel and stalked toward the rope, pretending she didn't hear Cooper's laughter trailing after her.

"The sooner you get up the rope, the

572

sooner you'll get to hear what Herman thought about your book," he called.

As an incentive, that was actually quite brilliant and had Daphne taking the rope in her hands. A second later, she was climbing, keeping her thoughts on the task at hand, but becoming distracted when she began to think about how the agency was in the process of offering exertion lessons to any woman who wanted to take them, and how these lessons would also teach women how to escape from unexpected attacks that came at the hands of gentlemen who weren't true gentlemen but cowards like Thomas.

It still galled her that Thomas hadn't suffered any real repercussions from trying to force himself on her. He had, however, been sent off to take a grand tour of Europe in the company of a relative who, rumor had it, was a curmudgeon who was also in debt to Thomas's father and had agreed to keep Thomas in line, no matter what.

It wasn't much as far as punishments went, but at least he was out of the country, not that she was worried he'd ever get near her again. Herman would made certain of that.

Frankly, after her talk with Reverend Danford, which had come about because he'd wanted to make sure she knew, if she was ever going to get around to getting married, that he'd need at least a month's notice to reserve St. Luke's Chapel for her, she was beginning to think that what happened to her with Thomas might turn out to be a blessing in disguise.

Offering women lessons in defense was just the first step Daphne had taken to address the problem of women being abused by men. At Reverend Danford's suggestion, she'd begun speaking of the matter at suffrage meetings. Her goal with that was to allow women to realize that it was not acceptable for men to behave so poorly, and better yet, to realize that it was not the woman's fault for being abused.

In the process of telling her story to other women, she'd come to a rather unexpected realization — that being the notion that God had never ignored her prayers for courage and that He'd continued to answer them to this day. It had taken more courage than she knew she possessed to get up in front of a room filled with women and speak about a topic that was considered unseemly, but she had.

Given the number of ladies who'd approached her afterward with their own stories of abuse, it was clear it was a subject that couldn't be ignored any longer. She could only hope that more women would speak up, and that someday they'd have a way to seek justice for the abuse so many of them had experienced.

"Would you look at that, she made it."

Shaking herself from her thoughts, Daphne almost let go of the rope when she realized she *had* made it to the very top of the rope, something she'd never been able to do before. Looking down, she grinned at everyone now assembled underneath the tree.

Eunice was grinning back at her, as were Elsy and Ann. Gabriella and Nicholas were clapping their hands, and Winston and Precious were wagging their tails, although that might have been because of the clapping. Herman was simply smiling at her, watching her closely, no doubt worried she might fall.

Not wanting him to worry, she eased her way down the rope, sending Cooper a nod as she shook out arms that now felt rather weak and peeled off the gloves that had protected her hands from the rope. "I'll be taking myself off to speak with Herman about my book now, if it's all the same to you."

Grabbing Herman's hand as Cooper's laughter drifted through the yard, she tugged him into the boardinghouse, not stopping until they reached the parlor. Herman waited until she took a seat on the divan before he sat down beside her, leaned forward, and kissed her.

It took a great deal of effort to pull away from him.

"You don't want to continue kissing me?" he asked, a trace of amusement in his voice.

"Of course I do, but I would think you'd take the supreme effort it just took me to discontinue our kiss as a compliment."

"I'm not certain why I would take it as that."

"You should because obviously, I value your opinion as a writer so much that I'm willing to stop an activity I adore so that I can hear your thoughts about my book."

He smiled as he pulled her manuscript onto his lap. "It's brilliant."

She smiled as well. "Brilliant is an excellent word."

"Indeed, but I couldn't help noticing that the hero seems familiar."

"Does he?" she asked, her smile turning into a grin.

"He does. I especially enjoyed the part where he saved the heroine when their boat sank."

"Did you notice I included the bustle?"

"Phillip will be thrilled with that."

"I also put in the bit about the possibility of love after first sight."

"I noticed that, as well."

"Did you notice anything else?"

He leaned closer to her. "I noticed that you ended the book by having the hero ask to court the heroine. That might be a problem."

For the first time in what seemed like forever, Daphne felt a distinct need for her smelling salts. "A . . . problem?"

Herman took hold of her hand and lifted it to his lips, placing a kiss on the palm of it. "Yes, but it's not a problem that will be difficult to rectify."

"How will I go about doing that?"

In the blink of an eye, he was kneeling on one knee, holding her hand as he caught her gaze. "I believe the only way to rectify the problem will be to draw from real-life experience."

Her throat went dry. "Oh."

"Yes, oh." He slipped his other hand into his pocket, withdrawing a blue box that could only have come from Tiffany & Company. "Two months ago, I told you that I knew the moment I saw you that there was a distinct possibility I could fall in love with you. Now I realize that wasn't exactly true.

I believe I *did* fall in love with you that day, and my love has only intensified over the time we've spent together."

"Oh . . . my."

"Nice to see you're adding words to your sentences, but with that said . . ." He opened up the small box, revealing a beautiful diamond ring set in platinum, two emeralds nestled on either side of the diamond.

"Goodness" was all Daphne was capable of saying, earning another smile from Herman.

"Perhaps I should move on quickly before you lose all ability with words."

He caught her gaze again. "Miss Daphne Beekman, you took me by complete surprise when you charged into my life — and by charged, I mean that literally. You're an adventure in and of itself, and I want to spend every day for the rest of my life enjoying the adventure that's simply you. I would be the happiest man alive if you'd promise to share your adventures with me from this point forward and agree to marry me."

She blinked as tears blinded her before she gave a nod, unable to get a single word out of her mouth.

"I'll take that as a yes," he said, slipping the ring on her finger and then gathering her close, pressing his lips against hers in a kiss that left her head spinning, but in a marvelous way instead of the way that normally left her swooning.

Far too soon, he pulled away and smiled. "Now then, not that I wouldn't love to continue kissing you, but I believe you have an epilogue to write. One where your hero delivers a most romantic proposal and your heroine truly makes him the happiest man alive by accepting his proposal and agreeing to marry him within a month."

"A . . . month?"

"If that would be acceptable to your heroine."

"I don't think she'll have a problem with that," Daphne whispered as Herman wiped away a single tear that had escaped her eye.

"Wonderful. Do know that we'll get back to kissing soon, but for now, go write. You know you're itching to get to Almira."

Wondering how she'd gotten so fortunate as to find a gentleman like Herman, the perfect hero for her, Daphne gave him one last kiss and rose from the divan, anxious to write an epilogue she knew was going to make her story the best one she'd ever written — one that still had mystery in it but included a large dollop of romance, as well.

That dollop was only possible because

she'd had the courage to convince Mr. Herman Henderson to hire her — an unlikely inquiry agent if there ever was one. She never imagined that the courage she always felt she lacked, but that God had certainly granted her, would be responsible for bringing her the love of her life — a good man she was going to be able to call her own forever.

ABOUT THE AUTHOR

Named one of the funniest voices in inspirational romance by *Booklist,* **Jen Turano** is a *USA Today* bestselling author, known for penning quirky historical romances set in the Gilded Age. Her books have earned *Publishers Weekly* and *Booklist* starred reviews, top picks from *Romantic Times,* and praise from *Library Journal.* She's been a finalist twice for the RT Reviewers' Choice Awards and had two of her books listed in the top 100 romances of the past decade from *Booklist.* She and her family live outside of Denver, Colorado. Readers can find her on Facebook, Instagram, Twitter, and at jenturano.com.